Road to Endor

ROAD TO ENDOR

A NOVEL BY

ESTHER BARSTOW HAMMAND

★

ILLUSTRATED BY E. M. SIMON

THE BOOK LEAGUE OF AMERICA
NEW YORK

*Behold, there is a woman who hath
a familiar spirit at Endor.*

I. Samuel 28. 7.

Author's Note

This book is fiction. Although I have delved into many old records and used all reasonable care to dig up whatever historical facts are available, the research has been hampered by unusual difficulties. It is, of course, a matter of common knowledge that the Devil stole the Church Book from the Reverend Samuel Parris, Minister of Salem Village; and though it was afterwards mysteriously returned, the horrid scent of brimstone still lurks in its crumbling pages. I myself have discovered now and again a mutilated page or an erasure or a dim and smudgy fingerprint which might without much question be traced to the Father of Lies. In the face of such difficulties this story has been written, and the indulgence of the reader is craved for whatever flaws, omissions or inaccuracies there may be.

E. B. H.

Des Moines, Iowa
May, 1940

Contents

BOOK FOUR: *BARBADOS. 1673 to 1680*

BOOK FIVE: *BOSTON TOWN. 1680 to 1689*

BOOK SIX: *SALEM VILLAGE. 1689 to 1691*

BOOK SEVEN: *ENDOR. 1692*

Book One

Old London Town   1653 to 1665

1

Islington

If there were dreams to sell
What would you buy?
Some cost a passing bell
Some a light sigh.
—THOMAS BEDDOES

LONDON, 1653

*A*NNE PARRIS, moaning on the bearing stool, cried out in pain and fright as the guns in the Tower of London thundered. There was a hubbub of shouts and a blare of martial music in the streets, and Westminster Tom and the bells of Old St. Paul's and all the other church bells big and little rang out the glad tidings: Oliver Cromwell had declared himself Protector of England, Ireland, and Scotland. The Puritan faith was established throughout the realm.

Another cry, importunate and shrill, brought the midwife running from the window just in time.

" 'Tis a lusty man-child, Mistress Parris; born just as the guns were boomin' out the news. 'Tis a portent, mistress. There be great things ahead for the babe, you mark my words! The master will be proud as Punch, as well he may!"

Anne Parris sighed; "Mayhap it means troublous days in store for the laddie, God preserve him."

She turned on her pillow and looked at her newborn son, and forgot her misgivings. For suddenly she knew that God had at last given her the child of her dreams, the child of her prayers.

John and Thomas, her older sons, she loved; but they were like their merchant father, sturdy and blunt, true to their Anglo-Saxon ancestry. There had been two fair-haired little daughters, who lay in St. Stephen's churchyard. But this baby with his thick dark curls

3

and fine features was her own. Small as he was, he showed the Norman blood that was Anne's proud heritage.

Thomas Parris, Anne's husband, wanted to name the baby Oliver in honor of the Great Protector, but Anne said with a sweet firmness that settled the matter:

"His name is Samuel because I have asked him of the Lord."

It seemed to Thomas a strange thing for a woman to say of her fifth child, but he had long ago stopped trying to understand his wife.

"Have it your own way, Anne," he said, and tiptoed out of the room with the baffled look which every son of Adam wears when he thinks of the strange ways of women.

*   *   *

LONDON, 1660

Afterward, when he thought about it, it always seemed to young Samuel Parris that his life began with the letter from Uncle John Parris in faraway Barbados.

To six-year-old Samuel, Uncle John and the Magic Island on which he lived, and from which now and then he sent letters and queer gifts to his English relatives, were the nearest approach to a fairy tale that his Puritan childhood ever knew, and Samuel ran to call his brothers.

"John! Thomas!" he shouted. "Come quick! It's a letter from Uncle John!"

When he came back with the two big boys at his heels, his father was standing before the fireplace with the open letter in his hand.

"'Tis no good news, lads," he said. "Your uncle is laid low with the fever."

He cleared his throat and read slowly and gravely, while John on one side and young Thomas on the other looked over his shoulders, and his wife watched him and looked so sad and troubled that it frightened Samuel.

Suddenly she sat up very straight and spoke sharply.

"It's too late for you to go to him, Thomas. He's dead! I know he's dead. 'Twould do no good to go—after he's dead. He came to me, Thomas, last night—in my dream. Not as he used to look, but old and thin and white—like a corpse. It seemed as if he was trying to say something, but I couldn't hear. I woke up all shaking—" She put her hands over her face and sobbed.

Samuel went and put his arm around her neck and whispered: "Don't cry, mother."

But she only held Samuel so tight that it hurt him, and cried more than ever, out loud, so that she woke up little brother Martin and set him crying too. Samuel had hardly ever heard his mother cry out loud. It frightened him so much that he tiptoed upstairs and comforted little Martin and helped him dress and gave him his new woolly lamb to play with. He didn't like Martin very well, but he knew it would worry Mother if she heard Martin crying, and he wanted to do something for Mother.

When he came back downstairs the boys had gone out again, but his mother and father were still talking about the letter. Uncle John's letters were infrequent and out of the ordinary enough so that they were a nine days' topic of conversation in the Parris household. But somehow Samuel knew that this particular letter was different and much more important than any of the others. Thomas read it aloud to Anne; and then Anne took it and read it over to herself; and then she read it again to Thomas, with Samuel leaning against her chair and reading with her (though the writing was so funny and shaky that he couldn't make much out of it). And at last Thomas said in a deep, sad voice:

"Our last letter from John!"

And Anne said in a voice that sounded like praying:

"Thomas, I tell you I knew—before ever I saw the letter. Last night in my dream I saw John's specter beside my bed. It's too late for you to go to him, Thomas. He is past the need of you or anyone."

*   *   *

Of the events which followed the death of his uncle John Parris, which were to mean so much to Samuel's future, the boy comprehended little. It seemed that Uncle John had left his plantation in Barbados to his brother Thomas, Samuel's father, and that his father must go and take care of it. This much was clear. It was also clear enough to Samuel that his father wanted to go and to go at once.

But the thing that young Samuel could not understand was

that his mother did not want to go and did not want his father to go. For the first time in his life, Samuel found himself doubting his mother's wisdom and siding with his father, for the boy was excited by the picture of the Magic Island of Barbados.

Samuel's big brothers, at home from Eton on a holiday, were also of different minds. John, the oldest son, had his heart set on being a Puritan minister and affirmed that there was plenty to do right here in England without gadding off to the Indies.

"And what would I do in Barbados," he demanded, "a hotbed of Anglicans and Quakers with never a Puritan congregation in the whole island? There's plenty of the Lord's work to be done right here in my own country."

Young Thomas poked his brother in the ribs, and winked.

"Come, come, now, brother, that will do to tell. But I'm betting it's an apple-cheeked lass named Deborah, with lips ripe for kisses, that's keeping you in England. As for me, I'll bet I could find me a brown wench who'd be mighty sweet under the Southern Cross."

"Shame on you, Thomas!" his brother reproved him. "What would Mother say if she knew you were even thinking of such things? And you'd best curb that foul tongue of yours or you'll get a caning at school and another from Father! I'll not tattle, but if you ever speak of Deborah that way again, I'll thrash you myself."

As for Thomas Parris, the grief he felt at the death of the brother whom he had not seen for years was real, but it was almost forgotten in the adventure of going to Barbados. The business of being a London merchant during the turbulent twenty years just past had been a hard grind. The sudden change brought about by the Restoration of the monarchy under Charles II gave rise to even more uncertainty and anxiety for the future. Thomas Parris was forty, healthy and vigorous. He had lived the decent, sober-minded life of a middle-class Puritan; had been a faithful husband and good provider for his family. But under it all he had his full share of the venture-loving Englishman of his time. And although he would not admit the thought even to his own consciousness, but disguised it as duty and necessity, the call of the racing seas and the sunny unknown isle beyond them set his pulses pounding.

Small Samuel felt the conflict, though he could not understand it. For the first time in his memory, his mother lost her poise and seemed unreasonable. Before the children she was still her well-controlled self, but when she and Thomas were alone there were long talks in the privacy of their bedchamber—talks which Samuel, being intensely interested and personally concerned, made it his business to hear—the empty fireplace in the room above making a good listening post.

"It means the end of our life together, Thomas," Anne said. "The end of our marriage, the end of our family. You must not go, love, you must not. I can't bear it."

"Nonsense, Anne! You talk as if I were deserting you. Suppose you were a soldier's wife, or a sailor's. Men must go when their work demands it. John relied on me to take care of the estate he has built up. He made me his executor and the manager of his wife's property. He left valuable legacies to all our sons. His estate must have care; you can't leave all that to a steward. He would feather his own nest and let things go to wrack and ruin."

"Are the estates, then, worth more than your wife and sons? If we were in need, it would be different. But we have enough, Thomas. Your business provides us with all we need. We are comfortable and happy—and we are together. I am only a woman, Thomas. I have borne your sons, I have mothered them; but they need their father."

"Now, Anne, you know you can train them much better than I. You have a rare way with youngsters and the boys all love and honor you. That's a woman's mission. Besides that, John and Thomas are well grown and able to take care of themselves."

"John might," Anne said. "He is seventeen and a steadyheaded lad and firm-set in his Puritan faith and feels sure of his call to the ministry. But Thomas has a wanton strain in him. And he's just the age when he thinks himself a man and doesn't want to be tied to his mother's apron strings. He needs his father, Thomas. I'm worried about him."

Thomas laughed. "You worry about too many things, my love. Tom's swagger is just a part of growing up. He's going over fool's hill but he'll be all right, my dear. He's too much like his father to get into trouble, even if he does sow a few wild oats. Don't worry about the boys. They'll come out all right."

Anne came over and put her hands on her husband's shoulders, and her dark eyes searched his face.

"And what about me, Thomas? Am I so little to you that you can kiss me good-bye without a regret and put twelve hundred leagues of the dreadful deep between us?" There was a thrill in her voice that Samuel had never heard; it did not sound like his mother speaking. "Look at me, Thomas, my husband! I am still young and, though it be shame to me to say it, still beautiful. And I am your wife, Thomas. I love you! I want you! Will you leave me alone—all the days—all the nights?"

"Well, then, come you with me, Anne. 'Tis a wife's duty to go to the earth's end with her man, not his to stay by the fireside."

Samuel almost fell down the chimney in his terror at this. Would his father take his mother away to the island and leave him at home with Martin and the nurse? Oh, dreadful, dreadful! He wouldn't be left behind—he would kick and scream and fight and make them take him too—he would kill his father and have mother all to himself—

His mother was speaking again.

"And take little Martin into that hot climate to die of fever, if he were lucky enough to live out the three months on shipboard! Samuel is hardy, he might stand it; but Martin, never. And leave John and Thomas alone, a prey to atheists and papists and libertines and harlots? Or would you take them too, and end their schooling and their prospects to set them driving Negurs in a canebrake?"

Thomas lost patience. "Enough of this dissension, Anne! My mind is made up. Everything is arranged. I have a good man to take over the business and I have given my word. I have engaged passage aboard the *Hephzibah*, which will sail as soon as her cargo can be stowed aboard. If you want to come, well and good; if not, I will make provision for you to keep the house here or do whatever your fancy pleases." His tone softened and Samuel heard them kissing each other. "Mayhap I shall be back home in six months, with all the wealth of the Indies to lay in your lap. And while I am gone you may live anywhere you like. I'll buy you a home in West London, if you say so, with lawns and a fountain and a fine, broad staircase—"

Anne laughed bitterly. "And what would I do with all that, my dear, and I neither wife nor widow? I know where I will live. In the little thatched cottage in Islington, that Grandmother left me. I know every stone in the fireplace and every squeak in the floor. I think it is the loveliest home in England—for a widow."

Anne's lips shut in a firm and bitter line. In the interval before Thomas sailed, she never referred to the matter again.

Samuel was torn between his wish to go adventuring and his joy at the prospect of having his mother almost all to himself. He was bursting with questions, but as his only knowledge of the plans had been come by in a way he was sure his mother would not approve, he dared not betray himself.

* * *

There was plenty of excitement in getting Thomas started on his long trip. Of course, nobody knew when the *Hephzibah* would be ready to sail—it depended on how long it took to get a suitable cargo, and when the tide and the weather and the wind were right for sailing and the river pilot sober enough to take them down the Thames, and a lot of other things like that. But when the time was near, the boys came home for a week-end holiday, and the cook got a big dinner with all the things Father liked best, and Anne invited Deborah to come to dinner but wouldn't invite young Tom's girl because she was a forward hussy. Of course, Tom was sulky about that and finally went off and ate dinner at his girl's house and stayed till after dark. But then they found that the *Hephzibah* had sprung a new leak so they didn't get started until Wednesday, and there was nobody but Anne and Samuel at Wapping Old Stairs to see Father off on his long voyage.

Samuel could never forget the picture: The Pool of London River just below the old bridge. The crowds, pushing and jostling, shouting and joking, watching the big sailing ship preparing for departure. The Old Stairs, their crooked and uneven steps slimy with moss and rubbish; the roustabouts carrying cargo; the cripples and fools and puny child beggars, which were a part of every London crowd, stretching out palsied hands and whining:

"Pity, fer the lova Gawd! 'Arf a penny, pretty lady, fer the sweet Jesus' sake!"

And worst of all, the gallows beside the Old Stairs, where pirates were hanged; and the dreadful face underwater, distorted and grimacing in the ripples, of a young rogue who had died on the "watery tree" and by the stern old law must lie until two high tides had come and gone, as a warning to adventurous youths who might be tempted to become freebooters.

The great ship *Hephzibah* rode at anchor in midstream. For days the varied cargo had been carried out in rowboats, hoisted over the sides and stowed below. Now at last it was sailing day and passengers and personal luggage were the last to go aboard. The stairs were astir at daybreak, making ready to start when the tide was right.

Thomas Parris, having seen his belongings safely stowed away, returned to shore for a last farewell to Anne and Samuel. Samuel felt big with responsibility when his father kissed him and gave him the parting admonition:

"Always take care of Mother, my son. I leave her in your care, remember!"

Then he turned to Anne, and holding her in his arms pressed long kisses on her lips. Then came the boatman's cry, "H'all aboard!" Father ran down the crooked steps. Mother stood stiff and still, like a soldier. Father at the ship's rail waved his hat. Mother fluttered her handkerchief, then suddenly lifted Samuel in her slim arms as high as she could and cried:

"Wave, son, wave! Wave gaily—gaily! We shall never see Father again!"

*   *   *

The days following Thomas's sailing were full of work for Anne and full of adventure for Samuel. The country life was novel and exciting. The little house itself; the room under the eaves, which was to be his own and which Mother said had been her father's when he was a boy; the low sloping thatched roof and small swinging window, and just outside, a little tom-titmouse making his cell in a hollow tree; the neat bed built into the corner, with its mattress of rushes; the tiny shelf of books against the wall, with the pewter candlestick beside them; the autumn scents drifting up from the garden; the sleepy sound of slow-moving boughs and leaves making a gentle singing or whistling noise; and the soft thud of falling apples and pears—all these made for him a kind of fairyland.

But stranger than all else was the marvelous, mysterious stillness. The first few nights he could not sleep for listening and wondering at the soft strange new sounds, so different from the clatter of carts over cobblestones and the boisterous songs and shouting of constant passers-by. He was lonely and frightened at first, but Anne let him take his setter, Protector, to bed with him, and told him the little rustling sounds were made by angels' wings, and taught him a little prayer to say if anything frightened him:

> Four corners to my bed,
> Four angels round my head,
> One to watch and one to pray,
> And two to bear my soul away.

Old Emma, the housekeeper, and Daffy Joe, the gardener, had been in Anne's family all their lives and welcomed Anne and her boys with tears of joy.

"It do be so good, Mis' Anne, to have childer under the roof once more. It do be a mercy if we doant spoil the dears wi' too mych dallyin' an' fond cockerin'."

But it was little Martin who got most of the cockering. The sweet country air, the fresh milk and new-laid eggs which Anne had so counted on to build up Martin's failing strength, seemed powerless. Day by day the child grew thinner and weaker. Dr. Kenelm Digby drove out from the city and diagnosed the child's ailment in four-syllabled Latin words; he prescribed his famous Sympathetical Powders, wonderfully concocted by a secret formula, half science and half magic, and drove back to London leaving his patient whiter and weaker than before. Old Emma tried all the balms and bitter draughts which her grandmother had taught her. She mixed them with time-honored spells, but the child still drooped.

Samuel wandered aimlessly about by himself or in company with Daffy Joe, feeling lonesome and jealous, for he saw less and less of Anne, who was always busy and anxious. One day she even passed right by him just as if he wasn't there at all. Something inside of him hurt so he couldn't bear it, and he caught at her dress. She paused and looked at him then.

"Oh, Samuel, ask God to make little Martin well again. Pray hard, and maybe God will answer."

Samuel watched her as she hurried up the stairs. She hadn't

even kissed him, or called him "dear child." All she cared about was little Martin. The thing inside of him felt as if it would burst. "If I prayed perhaps Martin would get well," he thought. But he didn't pray.

The next morning when Samuel came down to breakfast, he was told that Jesus had come during the night for little Martin and had taken him to heaven where he would never be sick or suffering any more. And Martin's body was taken back to the city to lie beside his sisters in the churchyard of St. Stephen's.

Anne took Samuel in her arms and rocked and cuddled him and told him he was all she had in the world to love. Suddenly the loneliness and jealousy were all gone and Samuel was happier than he had ever been in his life. Father was gone, and Martin was gone, and at last he had Mother all to himself. He felt sure that God had forgiven him or he wouldn't feel so happy; and he resolved to be a very good boy to show God how thankful he was.

Soon after Martin's death Anne received her first letter from Thomas. By great good luck the *Hephzibah*, stopping at Madeira, had met a vessel bound for England. It was a cheery letter, full of messages and references to the boys, but it tore Anne's wound open anew. The seas were so wide and so cruel. Her husband was still outward bound, sailing farther and farther away from her. He knew nothing of her sorrow over Martin's death. Anne felt an unreasonable resentment against him for not knowing, and for being happy and cheerful. Letters at such long intervals were worse than no letters at all.

Six months later Susanna Parris, John's widow, came back to England. Her ship had been becalmed for a week and had a broken mast which delayed them unduly, but Susanna was happy to be back. She came straight to Anne's cottage, bringing letters and gifts for Anne and the boys. She had a tiny marmoset with a white face for Samuel and a parrot that talked for Martin.

Anne stood looking at the silly bird, her face frozen, her hands clenched. Suddenly she snatched the luckless popinjay from its perch, wrung its neck and flung it across the room; then dropped to the floor in a dead faint.

Samuel was dreadfully frightened. Old Emma and Aunt Susanna picked his mother up and carried her to bed and applied such restoratives as were at hand. After what seemed an endless time to Samuel, Anne began to moan softly and turned her head on the pillow. And Samuel, who had thought she was dead, ran up to his room under the eaves and cried until he fell asleep.

It was there Aunt Susanna found him after Anne had been given a sleeping draught and the household had quieted down. As soon as he awakened, she coaxed him to come downstairs and eat some supper, assuring him that his mother would be all right in the morning. But ever after that Samuel hated the marmoset because it made him remember that day. Later he traded him to a traveling peddler for a tin trumpet.

Samuel loved Aunt Susanna and wanted her to stay with them always in the little thatched cottage. She was plump and jolly. Best of all, she could tell the most marvelous stories about the Magic Island where his father had gone.

It seemed like fairyland, with its green hills and white stone castles and coconut palms, with monkeys running up and down their fuzzy trunks, and oranges picked from your own trees and little shining fishes that could fly.

Some of the tales were frightening—about black folks creeping through the darkness and sometimes a white man being found dead with a cane knife in his throat. There were tales of hauntings and of a tomb where the coffins wouldn't stay put but moved about of themselves. There were tales of bewitchments: of old Negur women with wrinkled skins and fingers like claws, who brewed strange potions which would kill and leave no trace.

Samuel was fascinated by the stories. They were even more exciting than the *Book of Martyrs*, for martyrs were just like other people until they were killed. But witches were magic—black magic.

"Hast ever seen a witch, Aunt Sue, with a peaked hat and a broomstick?" The boy's eyes were deep wells of excitement.

Susanna laughed comfortably. "Well, I dunno's I ever seen a story book witch, but I s'pose I've seen black ones aplenty in Barbados. Negurs be as full o' devilments as the Gadarene swine. When John—your uncle John Parris, you know, Sammy—took me to Little England to live, I didn't know where to turn, there was so many charms and bugwords. I was scared first off but, law, you get 'customed to anything."

Anne interrupted. "Susanna, I'm surprised at you! 'Charms and bugwords' indeed! Surely you know that such things are only other names for witchcraft—the most dreadful of all crimes, for it is in truth the worship of Satan. The Bible says: 'Thou shalt not suffer a witch to live.' Yet you speak of it as lightly as if it were only a juggler's trick."

"So 'tis, more'n half of it! Though every now an' then the Old Boy shows his cloven foot."

Samuel interrupted: "Oh, mother, let Aunt Sue tell the story. You mustn't interrupt when other people are talking. Go on, Aunt Sue. Tell about the duppies down under."

"Well," Susanna continued her story, "most of the magic didn't seem to harm white folks much—'twas black magic, likely. Our plantation there, the one your father has now, got its name, Cotton Hall, from a great tree that the Negurs think is sacred. The silk-cotton tree, we call it, but the blacks call it the ceiba or the worship tree."

"Ho!" Samuel sniggered. "Worshiping a tree!"

"You wouldn't laugh, Sammy, if you could see the tree. More'n a hundred feet high an' a spread of mebbe half again its tallness, an' a trunk twenty feet through. And the spurs shoot out aboveground like buttresses, and end in strong, twisted roots that strike deep into the earth; and dark passages windin' down atween 'em. The black folks say that duppies or spirits dwell down under, an' they be 'fraid for their lives to touch that tree."

She turned to Anne and spoke in a different tone: "John Parris loved that tree, Anne. I told him he worshiped it like the black folks did. When he lay adyin' he says to me: 'Susanna, lay me under the silk-cotton tree. Promise!' And so I did. There warn't any proper graveyard. All the parish churches was Church of England and John wouldn't go nigh 'em, alive or dead. So we was betwixt the cotton tree on one side and the Quaker buryin' place on t'other. John had no quarrel with the Quakers. He leased 'em a piece of our plantation for a meetinghouse and burying ground; but he didn't want to be found sleepin' with 'em when the last trump sounds.

"So, as I say, we laid him under the big ceiba—and after that the Negurs called it a 'worship tree' and seemed to think the ghost of the dead was harborin' in the branches. At night they'd come an' leave little messes of rice or chicken (or rum if they could get it) to pay the Old'un, and cut marks on the bark in the shape of circles or crosses; or maybe we'd hear 'em beatin' stuns together 'an singin' soft-like in their heathen tongue. The offerin's was allus gone next mornin'—but whether the duppies or the Old'un got 'em, I dunno—there's allus mice an' little lizards runnin' up an' down the trees that mebbe took 'em.

"It don't do no good to try to talk black folks out o' their heathen ways. They won't say nothin'—jest stand an' roll their eyes at you and shake their woolly heads, pretendin' they don't know what you're sayin'. But they're fearful of duppies an' ghosts that lurk in the great dark holes betwixt the ceiba roots an' come out after nightfall. You can't see 'em—but a dog howls—or a jalousie drops—or a spider web trails across your face—or you feel a hot wave of air as you pass the place where a ghost has slept. But nobody can't see 'em: nobody but old Quaco, who was born with a caul and ain't feared of ghosts. Seems like the Indies is an awful place for spooks an' witchlore. With all them black heathen raisin' the devil it's bound to be."

Samuel's eyes were popping and his small body quivered. Anne shook her head at Susanna.

"The lad won't sleep tonight if you fill him up with wonder tales, Susanna. Suppose you tell him about those little monkeys in the hills, that steal your fruit."

"All right, younkin. Just one story about the monkeys, then off you go to bed. I want to talk to your mother."

Samuel pouted. "I want Mother to put me to bed."

Susanna pointed her finger at him. "Where I come from, only babies get put to bed. I thought you was a big boy."

"I am so!" Samuel boasted. "I know how to undo all the buttons and lacings. Only Mother likes to come, don't you, mother?" He slid his arm around Anne's neck. "But you don't need to tonight, because I want to show Aunt Sue how big I am."

Anne looked after him as he climbed the stairs.

"He is all I have left, Susanna. I want to keep him with me as long as I can. The school is atop Highgate Hill and the road through the hollow way is miry with clay and the hill is steep. I don't plan to send him until he outgrows my teaching. My father gave me a good education in the common branches and a fair knowledge of some of the higher learning. And there are good textbooks to rely on. The lad is so alert and eager in his studies that it is a joy to watch the workings of his mind. We are so alike in our ways of thinking that we understand each other almost without speech.

"The older boys are so different—so like their father." Her sigh was eloquent.

Susanna looked at her shrewdly. "Don't you cosset him too much, Anne, or you'll spoil him. Any man-creature gets high an' mighty if he ain't took down now an' then."

"That is easy to say, Susanna. You never had a child. You can't know what a mother's love is."

"Maybe," said Susanna.

Anne's culture and breeding and mental balance kept her from the fanatical extremes of the lower-class Puritans. She loved music and rejoiced in the example set by Cromwell, who, being a music lover himself, had always encouraged it. But she loved beauty, and deplored the devastations of which Cromwell's soldiers had been guilty in the name of religion. By temperament and training, Samuel shared his mother's feeling; and between the two there was an unusual concord and sympathy.

"You must study very hard, Samuel, so that someday you may be a minister of God. And you will not be like some ministers, who go into their pulpits as men go into their shops. For you were dedicated to the Lord before you were born, like Samuel in the Scripture, to minister unto the Lord. Your name, Samuel, means Asked of God; and I promised God that when you were old enough, you should be lent to the Lord. Over and over I pray for you as Hannah prayed for her son; 'The Lord maketh poor, and maketh rich: he bringeth low, and lifteth up. . . . He will keep the feet of his saints, and the wicked shall be silent in darkness; for by strength shall no man prevail. The adversaries of the Lord shall be broken to pieces; out of heaven shall be thunder upon them: the Lord shall judge the ends of the earth . . . and exalt the horn of his anointed.'

"Always, whatever happens, you must remember this prayer."

Having taken upon herself the task of a tutor, Anne devoted herself to study and preparation. She ordered the best textbooks of the period: Latin, English, and mathematics. She even dipped into the new ideas of science, and read tales of travelers. Once, in a reckless moment, she ordered from Moxon's a pair of globes, celestial and terrestrial, which cost her three pounds ten and gave her a guilty joy whenever she looked at them.

But it was not to be all work and no play. Anne's youth had been spent in a country parsonage and after years of living in London it was a joy to get her feet once more on the ground or to feel the exhilaration of a brisk canter across the fields or along inviting country lanes.

With Samuel's enthusiastic approval, she bought two riding ponies: a glossy dappled bay for herself, which Samuel promptly christened Dapplesheen; a shaggy black Shetland with white stockings for Samuel, which he called Silverheels.

When the work and the study were over, the two of them roamed the countryside, on foot or on their ponies, with Protector as bodyguard, either exploring the neighborhood or talking to the countryfolk and retelling the old legends of the hills.

When the warm days came, Susanna Parris settled herself in comfortable lodgings at Hampstead and told everybody she was back home to stay.

"Back in dear old Lunnon Town for the rest o' my days. Twenty years in the Indies is enough. I told John Parris I'd follow him to the ends of the earth and I did, but now I'm back in the Lord's own land."

But when the autumn winds stripped the trees bare and brown she grew homesick. "This climate's nothing like it used to be," she complained. "Must be the good Lord don't like the goin's-on at Whitehall—an' from all I hear 'tis enough to make the heavens weep! But be that as it may, I can't stay here and freeze to the bone. I'm goin' back an' marry Jonathan Abbott. He asked me just a month to a day after John's funeral, but I told him I wouldn't have him—I was goin' back home."

"But that was a long time ago," Anne protested. "Suppose you go back and find him married to someone else?"

Susanna chuckled. "No fear of that, my dear. Jonathan's the faithful kind. He's lived single all his life. John was allus at him to get married, an' he'd say, 'How can I, John, when you've got the only woman I want?' He came down to Bridgetown an' saw me aboard the ship, an' the last words he said was, 'Don't stay too long, Susanna, remember I'll be waitin'.' An' he will, bless his heart! He's the faithful kind!

"Whyn't you pack up and come with me, Anne? Better for you. Better for Thomas. 'Tain't good for a man to be alone—specially out there in the Indies. The heat's hard on 'em. Need a wife to keep 'em steady. I've lived there twenty years and I know. You ain't doin' right by Tom, Anne. He needs you an' wants you, but he's too proud to beg—for what's his by rights."

But Anne Parris shook her head. Thomas had made his choice between her and his plantation. That choice must stand.

So Susanna went back to Barbados alone and Anne and Samuel lived their quiet lives in the little cottage at Islington. Letters passed between Anne and her husband; letters which required five or six months to bring an answer. At first Thomas referred frequently to a visit home, but the affairs of the plantation required much care and attention, and it seemed that there was always a reason why it was impossible for him to leave until a little later. Spring passed into summer and summer into autumn; then another winter, making travel difficult and dangerous. When summer came Thomas complained of a crop failure and the great expense of a new sugar mill—and later of a fever which laid him by the heels for forty days—the news of which did not reach Anne until five months afterward.

It was the inevitable future which Anne had foreseen from the beginning. She was neither surprised nor disappointed. She had known it would be like this: the parting with Thomas had been a parting forever.

After a while she ceased even to dream about him.

2

Black Bartholomew's Day

And though we differed now and then
'bout outward things, and outward men,
Our inward men, and constant frame
of spirit still were near the same.
—SAMUEL BUTLER, *Hudibras.*

ON BLACK BARTHOLOMEW'S DAY, the dissenting clergymen had to conform or give up their pulpits under the Act of Uniformity.

Young John Parris, in his last year at Emmanuel College, was home for the holidays, his face stern and drawn with anxiety. It was current talk at the universities, he said, that King Charles was a papist at heart and was only waiting a chance to put things back where they were in Bloody Mary's time.

"Oh, he's a sly one, mother! His tongue is as cloven as the devil's foot! And there are plenty of the Anglican clergy who have the mark of the Beast in their foreheads too."

Samuel left off his favorite game of tracing voyages on his globe, and settled himself on a hassock beside his mother's chair. Were they going to be martyrs after all? he wondered. Now that he was nine he liked to hear John talk about the exciting things that were going to happen.

John went on. "The nation is full of plotters, working to set every man's hand against his neighbor and so weaken the Puritan influence. Who knows now what a Puritan is? There are nearly a score of sects, from Presbyterians and Independents to all sorts of queer lack-wits with queerer names: Anti-Scripturists (what do you suppose they are?) Skeptics (a fine name for a religious body!), Quakers and Shakers and Lord knows what, all lumped together under the name of Dissenters or Nonconformists— names that do not stand for any faith but only for negation. If the salt has lost its savor, wherewith shall it be salted?"

"But, John," Anne protested, "must we not observe tolerance if we would expect tolerance? Doubtless many of the Anglicans are sincere, even though they are wrong. God has not yet revealed the truth to them."

"Oh, mother, you don't understand! It is as Mr. Baxter says: 'Some opinions are tolerable and others are intolerable!' There must be no compromise with false doctrine. It must be utterly destroyed. We will have none of their popish practices!"

Anne sighed. "I am no match for you in argument, my son, but I like it not—this bickering and bitterness in the name of Him who bade us love our enemies."

John frowned impatiently. "You talk like a Quaker! They are always prating of love, and saying Peace, peace; when there is no peace. Did not the Lord Jesus say, 'I came not to send peace, but a sword'? This is no time for shilly-shallying. We stand at Armageddon to battle for the Lord."

When John said Armageddon it made Samuel think of Mr.

Hugh Peter. Mr. Peter had stood at Armageddon—that was why he had to have his head cut off when the king came home.

Samuel remembered one day when Mr. Peter had come to see his father, and the stories he had told about his sweet New England, where the woods were full of bears and wolves and wildcats and heathen savages who were the devil's spawn and had set up their last stronghold in the wilderness.

Now genial Mr. Peter was dead—a martyr—his head stuck up on a pole at Westminster and his body hewn in pieces, like Agag's in the Scripture, and the quarters carted off to different parts of the kingdom as a warning.

Samuel felt sorry for Mr. Peter because he had to go to heaven instead of going back to his sweet New England as he wanted to do. Salem-in-the-Wilderness was not so grand but it was much more exciting. Samuel thrilled as he remembered Mr. Peter's parting words. He had laid his hand on the boy's head as he spoke them.

"I have dreamed of going back, but the good Lord hath ordained otherwise," he said. "But this little lad may live to see the New Canaan far across the sea; and to stand in a pulpit where he may proclaim the Word of the Lord without fear or favor."

A change in John's tone brought Samuel back to the present. John was saying:

"I had a pulpit promised in Newton six months ago, you know —a small place but good people and a unanimous call. Now a Conformist is listed for the place. It is the same with the rest of the class, unless they conform to the new Book of Common Prayer which the Conference brought out. Nobody has seen that yet—it is being delayed on purpose, we think, to bring more pressure to bear on the Puritans.

"Some of the men will conform—but I won't. Some are taking up law or physics and abandoning the ministry—but I won't do that either. I pledged myself to preach Christ, and I will do it if I have to be persecuted from place to place and preach in a field or a barn!"

Samuel put in an excited question. "Why don't you go to New England, John? If Mr. Peter had stayed there he wouldn't have had to be a martyr."

John's lips set in a stern line. "I'll not turn tail! I'll not desert England in her hour of need. I'll see the thing through right here."

Samuel's eyes grew big with excitement. For the first time in his young life he admired his brother. John was a hero, and he might be a martyr. He didn't want John to be killed or hurt—but it would be wonderful to have a martyr in the family!

"What does Deborah say?" Anne asked.

The harshness left John's face. "Debby, bless her, is the salt of the earth! She says 'Whither thou goest I will go, John, if I have to live on acorn soup and sleep in the hay.'" He hesitated and flushed.

"There is one thing I must tell you, mother. 'Tis the only thing that worries me—much. Last Christmas when I got the promise of the church at Newton, they preferred a married minister, and the living included a neat little parsonage; and it seemed so sure and all that Debby and I were married. We didn't want to tell anybody until I finished school. And now—well, before snow flies you're like to be a grandmother, and I've no prospects for a decent living."

He dropped on his knees, his face in his mother's lap, and his big shoulders shook. Anne stroked his rough curls and spoke softly.

"The Child Jesus was born in a manger, my son. The servant is not greater than his Lord."

Samuel went back to his globe and his voyaging. John wasn't going to be a martyr, after all. He wasn't even going to be a hero. Anybody could marry a chunk of a girl like Debby and have a baby!

* * *

The Puritans who had been unceremoniously ousted from the parish churches met where they could. In country parishes like Islington services were often held in private homes, or under great trees in the summer. Throughout the country there were many of the "Gospel oaks." Under these very trees the first Christian missionaries of St. Augustine may have preached, taking over with the age-old wisdom of the Catholic Church the holy trees of the druidical worship and converting them to the new faith.

One Sabbath a terrific storm came up during the service, and the little congregation huddled together for hours under the lashing boughs. It was nearly dark when they started homeward. Every dip in the road was a muddy torrent; on every slope the ponies slipped and slid, picking and choosing a foothold, and lifting their feet straight up out of the miry holes their hoofs had made. It was quite dark when they came to the hollow way, and ahead of them a coach and four completely blocked the way. As they came closer they made out through the murky darkness a horseman alongside; then shouts and angry oaths and pistol shots.

"Merciful heaven, it is a robbery," Anne gasped.

A man lay writhing in the mud, apparently done to death. Another was stretching his arms high while the robber searched him, then struck him over the head with his pistol and left him where he fell.

"What shall we do?" Anne moaned. "To turn back is impossible. The ponies are spent; they could never climb that slippery hill."

And then the bandit (there seemed to be only one) came toward the two terrified witnesses, stepping lightly and swiftly through the mire.

Samuel cut his pony with the whip, driving the little beast in front of his mother's mare. His voice was shrill with terror, but he spoke up boldly.

"You shan't touch Mother," he yelped. "I'll kill you!"

The bandit caught the pony's rein as he spoke to Anne. There was laughter in his voice.

"You have a gallant defender, fair lady. I would not *dare* lay hands on you, even if such were my wish. But I assure you, madame, you are quite safe. Your youth and beauty, which even this dim light reveals, are your passport. I only ask of you, as a token of our meeting, the ring which gleams upon your finger."

Anne snatched off the diamond and handed it over.

"And now," the rascal said, "with your permission—"

He took her pony's rein and led her past the coach, carefully circling the corpse and the other man, writhing in his death agony.

"Good night, my lady fair!" he said, and pressed his lips to her hand. Then slapped the ponies across their rumps to speed them homeward.

At daybreak the mired coach and four was found in the road, with two dead gentlemen beside it. But Anne was too terrified to tell what she knew about the robbery, and bade Samuel and the servants never to mention it.

"It wouldn't help the poor dead gentlemen," she justified herself, "and that dreadful man might take revenge on us. After all, he was merciful in sparing our lives, and we owe him something for that."

But more robberies followed. Now and again a coach or a lonely rider met the bandit. The stories were much the same: a dashing highway man, always alone, who dealt quick death to those who resisted, but caught the fancy of the times by his debonair manner and mock gallantry. Even Anne Parris, frightened and angered by the attack, wove a little secret romance around the adventure and wondered to herself whether his compliments were all mockery, or if in very truth her beauty charmed him. It had been a long time since a gentleman had kissed her hand.

Some time later Samuel came home in great excitement.

"I saw the robber again, mother," he cried, "and I spied on him and found out where he lives—in a little cottage in the Devil's Lane, just a half mile or so off the hollow way."

Anne gasped. "Why, child, you must be mistaken. There surely are no robbers in Holloway, and 'twas so dark that night you wouldn't know him from Adam if you *did* see him."

"I'm *not* mistaken, mother. I saw this man coming along the lane and I ducked behind the hedge and watched him, and he walked just like the robber, so light and springy, like dancing— and the quick way he turned his head, like a bird. He's the very robber! And his name is Mr. Duval."

Anne turned white.

"Samuel," she said earnestly, "you can't be *sure*—it was too dark—and if it were the man, he's a most dangerous murderer. If he thought you knew, he would kill you. You are surely wrong about it, and you must never, never say such a thing again about our neighbor. Promise me!"

Samuel looked at her disgustedly.

"All right, mother. If you're afraid, I won't tell on him. Prob'ly nobody else would believe me either, if *you* don't. But I don't see why it couldn't be. A robber has to live *somewhere*, doesn't he? And down in that dark old Devil's Lane is just the right kind of a place."

When the hollow way was not too muddy, Anne and Samuel liked to walk to Highgate.

At the top of the hill on one side of the road was Cromwell House, built by the Great Protector for his daughter Bridget and her husband, General Ireton. Now the big house was gloomy and deserted, its lawn grown up to weeds.

On the other side of the road was the modest cottage of Andrew Marvell, poet and statesman, who in a time when it was said that every man had his price had the honor to live simply and honestly. During a good part of the time this house, too, was lonely, left in the hands of a caretaker. The lovely garden was untended but no less charming for the neglect.

There was one of Marvell's verses that Anne Parris said must have been written about this very garden; a verse which she liked so well that she made a plaintive little air to fit the words:

> I have a garden of my own,
> But so with roses overgrown
> And lilies, that you would it guess
> To be a little wilderness.

One summer afternoon as Anne and Samuel were in the cottage singing it together, they heard a loud whinny just outside the gate.

Samuel ran to the door and called to his mother: "There's a gentleman on horseback at the gate."

Visitors were rare in the Islington retreat, and Anne rose from the spinet and went to the door just as the gentleman dismounted and came up the path, hat in hand.

"Madam, I crave your pardon for disturbing you. I intended only to eavesdrop for a moment and then pass on, but my mount gave such a hearty greeting to the little mare in your stableyard that he betrayed me. The truth is that I did not suppose anyone liked my rhymes well enough to make songs of them; and I was so immensely flattered that I had to stop and listen."

Samuel felt all excited, for this was a real gentleman, with a hearty, pleasant-sounding voice and a strong-set body, clad in good London-made clothes which he wore with an air. He had a roundish English face and cherry cheeks and the merriest hazel eyes which seemed to see everything at once without looking at anything. His hair was beautiful, with the color and gloss of ripe chestnuts; not cropped in the Roundhead fashion, but worn in long, loosely-curled lovelocks which fell on his shoulders.

Anne's cheeks wore a pretty flush: "It must be, then, that you are our neighbor, Mr. Marvell." She smiled. "Though if I had not thought that you were somewhere across the Channel I should never have ventured to sing your lovely verses. The tune is not worthy of them."

"On the contrary, I thought it very sweet," the poet replied. "May I ask who is the composer?"

Samuel gave a chortle of delight. "Why, it was only Mother. She just made it up."

So then the three of them began to laugh together like old friends, and Anne invited Mr. Marvell to come in.

"I will if you'll figure out a bass for me so that I can sing my own song," he said. "I've never sung one of my own songs."

Samuel clapped his hands: "Oh, that will be fun! Please do, mother!"

He stayed so long that Anne said: "Now you must share our supper."

"Of course, I will. I was just hoping you'd ask me, because my Mary isn't expecting me, and likely won't have any supper ready."

After that Marvell was a welcome visitor at the cottage whenever he chose to stop. His easy manner and ready wit made him at home anywhere, and he found the companionship of both mother and son very interesting. He advised Anne as to the boy's lessons, and told Samuel old student yarns of Oxford: about boat racing and cricket and countless escapades. He had been at Eton for a time as tutor to Cromwell's ward, Will Dutton, in the house of John Oxenbridge.

"Will was a lovable lad," he said. "In truth, I loved him so well I couldn't see his faults, and every now and then I had to have Mr. Oxenbridge examine him, that he might detect if there were any lightness in the coin which I should be bound to make good. If he passed Oxenbridge, I knew he was pure gold, for Oxenbridge was strict. He never let his heart run away with his head, as I am prone to do.

"Yet he was a good companion," Marvell went on, "and full of stories of his travels, for, as he used to say, he had tumbled about the world in uncertain times. It was his stories of the Bermudas which inspired my 'Boat Song.' Can you make up a tune for that, Mistress Parris, so I'll have an excuse to come again?"

Anne laughed and blushed and said, "I'll surely try."

To change the subject, she asked, "Do you know anything about the island of Barbados, where my husband's plantation is?"

Samuel ran to get his globe, so that they could find the island.

"Now, that's a strange thing," Marvell said. "The last letter I had from Oxenbridge, he said he was planning to go to Barbados to preach. It isn't such a big world after all, is it?"

Then he talked of his work with Mr. Milton in the diplomatic service, and told them about the new book Mr. Milton was writing.

"The greatest book of all," he said. "Not a political tract this time but a wonderful poem called *Paradise Lost*—an epic of heaven and hell."

Samuel, who had little interest in poets, asked if he knew any stories about the king; Marvell chuckled and said he did, but most of them wouldn't do to tell in present company. Marvell leaned back in his chair and sighed. It seemed to Anne that he looked very tired and discouraged—as if the struggle was against hopeless odds.

"Ah, 'tis a rotten court," he went on, "and a Parliament to suit it! And an awful pity, for Charles is a man of parts. But he lives for his own pleasure and devil take England. Strange, too! He spent his whole youth striving for the kingship, and now that it's won it bores him. He comes to the council chamber only when he must, and instead of listening to the affairs of state (which the Lord knows are dry enough sometimes) he fondles his dogs and scribbles frivolous notes which he passes to one or another of the council—for all the world like a lazy boy in school.

> I'll have a council shall sit always still,
> And give me a license to do what I will!

"But come, Mistress Anne, let's have a song and forget the cares of state. The Scottish one that the laddie likes."

And with Anne at the spinet, he sang with a broad Scottish burr:

> Says Tweed to Till—
> "What gars ye rin sae still?"

Says Till to Tweed—
"Though ye rin wi' speed
And I rin slaw,
For ae man that ye droon
I droon twa."

"And now Ben Jonson's pledge to Celia, 'Drink to Me Only
With Thine Eyes,' and then good night."

But he was not always in a mood for talking.

"I like your house, Mistress Anne," he told her once, "because
it's the only place I know where I can do just as I please and
have no responsibilities. Now, when I'm at home by my own
hearth I have to provide the firewood and see that the chimney
doesn't smoke. My Mary does me better than I deserve, but
she has one fault: she thinks the master of a house should do
something to merit the honor.

"Mary is an ardent Puritan herself and has respect for my
public career (she has only a vague idea as to what I do, but she
thinks it's exceedingly important and never disturbs me at my
writing) but she thinks I spend far too much time in the garden
scribbling trumpery rhymes. I overheard her telling a visitor
one day that my study was 'the master's closet where he writes
sense; but when he writes poetry he sits below in the garden!'"

It often happened that just when the little thatched cottage
would begin to look for his coming, Marvell would be gone for
months at a time, busy on some political mission to the North
of England or perhaps across the Channel.

Anne Parris dared not admit to herself how much she missed
him. Islington seemed suddenly lonely: a pretty stretch of country, but only milkmaids and dairy cattle for company.

There were no near neighbors of her own class and Anne was
in no mood to seek new friends. Her two elder sons she saw
only at long intervals; their minds were full of their own affairs
and offered her no real companionship.

More and more her interest and love centered in the child
Samuel. They were alike in their tastes, in their love, in their
jealousy. The lad's keen mind was a constant joy and pride to his
mother; his adoration was balm to her lonely heart; his growing

beauty a delight to her eyes. That such a relationship was unwholesome or unwise never came into her mind.

And Samuel was utterly and completely happy. He loved his mother with all the passionate devotion of his intense young soul. When he was little and they all lived in London, family life, which had made it necessary for him to share her with his father and brothers, had been a torture, devastating him with a tempest of jealousy, a mad, childish terror of losing his beloved; and since his tantrums were punished by his mother's frown and banishment from her presence, he learned almost in his babyhood to repress his ugly impulses; to thrust them down into some dark dungeon of his consciousness where only God and the devil could see them.

Now at last he knew with a deep understanding that he need fear no rival. It was rather a bore when John or Thomas came home for visits. But he didn't mind it so much as he used to. Since his mother had told him about the prophet Samuel, he knew with a deep understanding that he need fear no rival. Even when his brothers came home for their brief visits he felt no fear.

The simple living at the cottage required little of its mistress, for Old Emma was capable and willing. The little household was astir at daybreak, ready for the long English day. Anne's quiet tastes and Puritan principles alike forbade all extravagances of dress or manner of living. She wore a simple russet gown and cape, its fashion never changing; and Samuel had only a short tunic with long knitted trunk hose for winter, and but shoes and bare brown legs in summer.

While Samuel studied, his dark head bent low over a table by the window, or in the evening stretched full length before the hearth, reading by firelight, his mother sat knitting or sewing or spinning, ready to answer questions or to argue knotty problems or, it might be, silent for hours at a time.

In studying with her son, Anne was learning as much as he. And through Andrew Marvell both of them had widened their view of the world. Anne felt very proud when Mr. Marvell approved her choice of books. He also suggested others, lately come from the press, setting out some of the new wonders of science.

"The world is changing fast these days," he said, "and we must keep abreast of it."

Mr. Marvell (who certainly ought to know) thought that Samuel had a very fine mind, unusually mature for a lad of his age. "Work him hard and keep him up to his best," he advised; "never let him get the idea that he knows it all; and try to broaden his contacts; he needs other lads, the give and take of games and sports and a good fight now and then to muss him up and keep him humble."

But Anne only laughed at that. "I don't want him mussed up or made over, Mr. Andrew Marvell, and I love his boyish pride and self-confidence, and with all due respect to you, sir, I think a mother knows more about bringing up her own child than a bachelor, even if he is a Member of Parliament."

But Marvell persisted: "He ought to be in school."

Anne tossed her head: "Not till he is older. He shan't go to a common school among yokels' sons nor be bred up with mechanics. Nor will I have him whipped by some sorry pedagogue! Time enough for school when he outgrows my teaching."

But each new term found her deferring the change. As the Conformists grew stronger there were religious restrictions, and entrance requirements which demanded certain statements of faith hateful to Puritans. Even the schoolboys going along the road jeered at Samuel:

"Highflier! Hot Gospeler! You can't go to *our* school!"

And when he didn't wear oak apples on the King's Birthday, they chased him and flogged him with nettles and chanted:

> The 29th of May is Oak Apple Day,
> If you don't wear an apple,
> You can't come and play.

It was easy for Anne to persuade herself that the boy was better off at home, even if he lacked in classical learning.

* * *

It was after an unusually long absence that Marvell returned one blustery March evening in the spring of 1665. He had been for two years secretary to Lord Carlisle, the ambassador to Russia, Sweden, and Denmark, and the thatched cottage had not heard from him during his absence, and knew nothing of his return till his old rum-te-tum-tum with his riding whip resounded on the door.

Samuel shouted, "It's Mr. Marvell," and rushed to let him in, and Anne helped him take off his cloak and fixed him a hot toddy and called Daffy Joe to put some more logs on the fire. But after the first excited minutes, it seemed as if he had never been away. He sat down in his old place on the settle, lighted his pipe with a coal, and in his old, informal way made himself quite at home.

He was in one of his quiet moods, and listened with interest to Samuel's eager chronicle of all that had happened since he went away; asking a question now and then, watching the boy with a curious, speculative air that puzzled Anne. It had been almost two years since he had seen Samuel, and during that time the lad had grown surprisingly. He was now eleven years old, tall for his age and strong, with a clean-limbed, supple body, eager brown eyes, a clear, dark skin, and a rippling mass of black hair, cropped in his neck, after the fashion of the time. To his mother he seemed the most beautiful and perfect thing that the Lord God ever made; a model which a painter might desire for the Boy Christ in the temple. Yet in Marvell's intent regard she was quick to sense some lack: not exactly disfavor, but rather a reserve of commendation; and though she indignantly thrust from her the unwelcome thought, it disturbed her.

But Marvell gave her no clue as to what was in his mind until several weeks later. Then he came in the afternoon of a day which gave the first early promise of spring, and asked Anne to ride to town with him. She smilingly gave assent and Samuel sprang to his feet.

"I'll get the ponies," he cried. "I can saddle Silverheels myself now, Mr. Marvell, and I want to go too."

Marvell laughed and shook his head. "Not this time, lad. Today I'm taking your mother." Then, as Samuel's face darkened, "Next time I'll take you, young fellow, and leave Mother to pout at home."

Anne was surprised and a little embarrassed, but as she had already agreed to go she made no objection, and the two set out together. Marvell chatted of this and that for a mile or more, then suddenly brought his horse to a stop and faced her.

"I left the lad at home because I wanted to talk to you alone," he said abruptly, "but I hardly know how to begin."

Anne's heart began to pound and she felt her face flush. There could be only one thing to say which he would approach in that manner, and with a woman's inconsistency she dreaded and yet wanted to hear it. There could be only one answer, of course. She was the wife of Thomas Parris, and above reproach.

Marvell was not looking at her. He spoke gravely. "It's about the boy, Anne." (He has never called me Anne before, she thought.) "He's growing up. You don't see the change, being with him every day, but to me it is very clear. I hate to say it, my dear, but for the lad's good it must be said. He's with you too much. It's making him a milksop. He needs a man's hand; and he needs the companionship of his own kind. It's going to hurt you, I know, Anne, but you ought to send him to school—away from you—to an academy. He's a great boy, Anne, a boy to be proud of, but you must give him a chance to be a man."

Anne could not speak for the throbbing in her throat and Marvell blundered on: "I met my friend Charles Morton today. He was a fellow at Oxford when I was tutoring there—a very brilliant scholar. He was turned out, of course, because of his liberal views, and started an academy in his home at St. Ives. But this morning he told me that he has recently moved to Newington Green, only a mile or so northeast of here. His school would be the finest place in the world for Samuel; and it is so near that he could come home frequently for week-ends. I spoke to Morton about the lad and he was interested at once and said he would be glad to have him as a pupil."

Still Anne did not speak, and Marvell stopped abruptly and looked at her. She was white with anger, her face so drawn that she looked ten years older.

"So! It is all arranged! Nothing left for me to do but to thank you two gentlemen for your capable handling of the matter! I tell you, Andrew Marvell, you don't know what you are talking about. I will not let him go! It would kill me. What do you know of a mother's love? You are only a man—and a bachelor."

The words were like a sob.

To Marvell, whose intentions had been the best in the world, Anne's unexpected outbreak was like a slap in the face. His temper caught flame from hers and he met anger with anger, sarcasm with sarcasm.

"Well said, lady, you are right! I, a mere man, had thought a mother's love was above selfishness; that it had in it a touch of the divine. In that I have erred, I humbly ask your pardon." His voice softened. "There was a mother once, long ago, who rebuked her son when she found him in the temple, questioning the doctors; and her son replied: 'Wist ye not that I must be about my Father's business?' No doubt she would have been happier if she had kept him at home."

Anne caught her breath. "I might forgive your impertinence and interference with my affairs," she cried, "but I will not listen to blasphemy!"

She whirled her mare and with a sharp cut of the whip galloped back down the road they had come. Marvell watched her until she turned in at the cottage gate. The cynical twist left his lips.

"Poor little woman!" he sighed. "Poor, lonely little woman!" Then in quite a different tone: "Confound that husband of hers, anyway! Why doesn't he stay at home where he belongs?"

Anne lay late in bed the next morning. Her head ached and her whole body was tense with quivering nerves. Little by little, through five lonely years, she had built up an ideal of devotion to Samuel. Her refusal to go to Barbados with her husband was a sacrifice for her children. Her lonely life; her isolation at Islington; her withdrawal from her friends—all these had been for the sake of Samuel. She could see in her dreams the great future of her son; see him standing in the pulpit; hear the deep tones of his voice as he proclaimed the Word of God; feel the emotion of the congregation under conviction, kneeling and crying aloud in agony, "God be merciful to me, a sinner!"

But most clearly of all, she could see the love in the great preacher's eyes, and feel the strength of his young arms enfolding her, and the tenderness of his voice whispering: "It was your love and training, mother dear! I owe it all to you."

It was this dream that lay in ruins; brought low by the cruelty of Marvell's angry words which still echoed in her mind: "Selfish —making him a milksop—give him a chance to be a man—"

"Oh, he is cruel. And it isn't true!" she insisted to herself. "I'm not selfish. Why, I've given up everything for Samuel! I've never thought of myself at all!"

She lay with her face to the wall, refusing the breakfast that Old Emma urged her to eat. She even refused to see Samuel. She wanted only to be alone with her misery.

It was about noon when Emma pushed the door open gently, and seeing through the crack that her mistress was awake, bustled in, carrying a small, flat basket, woven of reeds.

"It were Mr. Marvell's gardener as brung it, Mis' Anne, but if ye arsk me, it's a quare nosegay fer a gentlemen to send a lidy. To my notion, a bunch of early crocuses an' winde-flowers, all ringed round wi' fern an' tied wi' ribands, 'ud be more proper-like, an' much easier come by. Where he found all this stuff, I dunno."

Anne passed a slender hand over her throbbing forehead.

"Oh, Emma! Why did you disturb me? Set that basket down and go away!" Then as Emma scuttled through the door, "Was there any letter?"

"No, mom! No letter nor message nor nothin' but this bunch o' weeds. 'Fer Mistress Parris,' the gardener sez, 'from the marster!'" She backed out of the room and closed the door.

Anne snuggled her face in the pillow and lay still for quite five minutes. Then she stole softly out of bed and went to the table where the basket stood. It was, as Emma had said, "a quare nosegay." On a bed of bark covered with lichens lay evergreen sprays of rosemary and arbor vitae; and upon these, woven together and bound with ivy, a cluster of red columbine, the buds scarcely open, and a single sprig of hawthorn blooms—a poet's apology.

It was chilly in the room and Anne crept back under the quilts; but she set the basket on the floor by the bedside, and lay close to the edge of the bed, deciphering the message of her "quare nosegay." Anne's Latin was none too good and her French was sketchy, but no well-brought-up woman of her time was without some knowledge of the language of flowers.

There was rosemary for remembrance and constancy; and arbor vitae denoting unchanging friendship. Anne curled her lips sneeringly at the suggestion. But at sight of the humble lichens, pleading dejection and loneliness, she softened; and smiled at the quivering red columbines, anxious and trembling; and the tiny bit of hawthorn, daring to hope; all bound round with the clinging tendrils of ivy, striving to please.

She reached down and gently touched the quivering columbine. The ivy curled a pale-green tendril around her finger and clung there. Anne tore it away and pressing her hands to her hot cheeks, cried softly, silently, finding comfort in the tears.

For a full week Anne struggled; a struggle which left her pale and stricken, but once more mistress of herself. She had received no further word from Marvell. Several times she had seen him riding by, and once he had called a greeting to Samuel, playing with his dog in the garden path, but he did not so much as glance at the house. He had offered his apology. It was for her to make the next move.

On the eighth day she sent Samuel to bed early, and sat late at her writing table, composing her letter:

Forgive me, Dear Friend, Your wordes were hard to beare, but they were needful to bring down my pride. I have spent houres of agonie on my knees, and at last the Lord in His Mercy hath shown mee the waye, that I should walke in itt—hath prest to my lips the bitter draught that I must drinke. I have been so lonelye all these yeres. I am a wife but I have no husband. I have mothered six and shall bee left desolat. John my firstborne, since hee left College, has been a wandring preacher and is now in charge of a lyttel meeting-house at Ugboro on the other side of England. Yong Thomas is prenticed to a stricte Master in West London and I have not seen him these manye moons. Martin my baby, sleeps with his two little sisters at St. Stephens. Samuel is all I have left in the world and of him I have made an idol. I did not meen too, God knows. When he lay att my brest, I gave him to God's service. I have kept that ideal befor him all ways. I have trained him as best I could for that High Calling. But in my very zeal I forgott hee was not Mine. For the Lord whose name is Jealous is a Jealous God. His Will bee done. Like Hannah of olde, I am readye to saye—as longe as the childe liveth hee shall bee lente to the Lord.

Doubtless it was the Lord's Hand that brought Mr. Morton to Newenton Green. I pray you too forgive my hastie wordes and as soone as may bee—beefore my courage ebbs—take mee to see him.

ANNE PARRIS.

She sprinkled the letter with sand to dry the ink; folded the paper and sealed it with wax, and carefully addressed it, as though loath to let it go.

Early in the morning she sent Daffy Joe to deliver it to the

Marvell cottage . . . but by that time Marvell was again on his way to Kingston-on-Hull, far in the North of England, and the letter lay unopened on his writing table. The shy red columbine withered and died; the hawthorn trees strewed their white petals over hill and hollow; the roses once more overran the garden wilderness; but the master of the cottage did not return.

3

The Trail of the Blazing Star

A Blazing Star,
Threatens the World with Famine, Plague and War;
To Princes, Death; to Kingdoms, many Crosses;
To all Estates, inevitable Losses;
To Herdsmen, Rot; to Ploughmen, hapless Seasons;
To Saylors, Storms; to Cities, civil Treasons.

—SHAKESPEARE

I T WAS Samuel who saw it first. He had snuffed out his candle and stopped at the window a minute before he got into bed. The nights were very dark in Islington and the stars stood out brilliantly against the blackness. When he was a tiny boy he had thought they were peepholes with the glory of heaven shining through. But he was older now and knew better—they were only stars.

He shivered in the cold room and was turning away—and then he saw it! Eerie and far away in the eastern sky it gleamed and glowed—not twinkling brightly like the other stars but with a faint dull and languid color.

He forgot he was cold and ran to the stairway.

"Mother!" he called. "Mother, come here! There's a new star in the sky!"

That was early in the winter. As the season advanced, each night the star drew nearer, with a motion heavy, solemn, and slow. Each night it glowed a deeper red; each night it hung lower, lower, lower over the city, leaving a ghastly lurid trail in its wake.

And the mother and son in the thatched cottage were not the only ones who watched its approach with foreboding. For centuries the legend had been passed down from father to son. Such a star, not held in its course in proper fashion but wandering through the heavens by some uncanny law of its own, always presaged disaster.

True, there were men of science at the universities who claimed that these comets were part of the same orderly system as the other stars and the friendly sun and moon, that they obeyed the same laws and were no more dangerous. But who could believe such a theory in the face of the testimony of those now living who knew of their own knowledge, or by tales told them by their own grandsires, of Blazing Stars they themselves had seen in their youth, and the dire calamities that followed their fiery trails?

"What does it mean, mother?" Samuel asked.

Anne could only shake her head. "I don't know, son, but I fear—I fear! It must presage some dreadful happening!"

"'Tis no proper star, one can see that, mother. It's red and glowering—like a goblin's eye! I've knelt by the window and prayed every night, but it keeps coming closer. Some night it's going to strike the earth! Oh, mother, why doesn't God stop it?"

"I don't know, son. Perhaps it is a judgment for the sins at Whitehall Palace." Anne's throat was tight with fear. She remembered only too well the harrowing tales that haunted her childhood.

"But, mother, it would kill us too! We can't help what the king does. It wouldn't be fair to burn us up because the court is wicked!"

Anne could only repeat: "I don't know. We can only pray—and trust God."

In January the Black Death broke out in the parishes of St. Giles and St. James. In one month's time it had slain hundreds. The message of the star was made clear; and by its very motion it seemed to foretell the heaviness of God's judgment—slow and terrible and frightful—as was the plague!

In every church prayers for the sick were read; and each secret meeting of dissenters, after their own fashion, cried to Almighty God for forgiveness and mercy. And the Lord heard their prayers, and stayed His hand for a time, that the people might repent and live. But the revels at Whitehall went on; the robbery of the poor continued; the persecution of the saints became more bitter with each new act of Parliament.

Yet for the space of a hundred days God withheld His hand.

Later, when spring had come: the fields of Islington were drifts of strawberry blossoms and the slough in the hollow way was gay with buttercups. Anne and Samuel on their ponies had ridden as far as Parliament Hill and turned at its crest to look down over the city. The pall of smoke, which was becoming a part of the London winter scene because of the growing use of sea coal, had been blown away by the sweet spring winds. The sun had driven back the marsh mists, leaving a shining city in the valley of the Thames. Above the gables and peaked roofs rose a host of old towers and belfries and crosses and slender spires gilded by the dawn. Even the gray walls of Julius Caesar borrowed glory from the morning sun.

The lofty gates, which were locked and barred at night, now stood wide, and from their point of vantage Anne counted four of them: Aldgate, Bishopsgate, Moorgate, Aldersgate; while Samuel insisted he could make out a fifth farther to the west, Cripplegate.

In the center of the picture was Old St. Paul's, partially restored after its violation by Cromwell's troops, who had stabled their horses in its sacred nave and melted its leaden roof into bullets for the Irish campaign. Far to the east lay the Tower, part fortress, part prison, haunted by ghosts of the past. To the westward stood Westminster (beautiful without its towers) and Whitehall the infamous. To the south, under the great bridge, through the crowded pool and the marshes, was old Father Thames.

It was a lovely scene: the beauty of the picturesque variety of architecture, the fanciful charm of sunlight on old roofs and walls. Yet to Anne it brought sadness and dread; for with the first warm days the sickness had broken out again, and under many of these roofs people were sick and dying. Many a door of mansion house or hovel bore the crimson token:

LORD HAVE MERCY ON US

Even from this distance the bells could be heard, tolling, tolling; large bells and small, one encroaching on another, clashing indecently without respect for one another's sorrow.

They brought to Anne's mind some old verses, dating back to that other year of plague more than seventy years before. She could hear her grandsire's doleful voice as he intoned the fateful words:

> Swords may not fight with fate;
> Earth still holds ope her gate;
> Come! Come! the bells do cry;
> I am sick, I must die—
>   Lord, have mercy on us.

Her throat tightened as she thought of young Thomas, serving his apprenticeship in a West End shop where the sickness was at its worst. The brightness of the morning seemed cruel and garish.

She shivered. Perhaps the sickness might even spread to Islington. John, safe in his little country parish, had written; "We hear many reports about the spread of the sickness. If you are in danger, come to us for a time. Our cottage is small and poor, and Deborah is expecting another child, but we'll share the little we have with you and Sam."

But Anne could not bear to think of joining the pitiful crowd of refugees.

"Let us go, son," she said, "the wind is chill."

All along the road back they met people on foot, on horseback, in wains or drags, for there was talk that the Lord Mayor would refuse to issue health certificates, without which no one would be permitted to enter another city or village. Under the terror of being penned in the plague-stricken area, panic seized the populace, and they rushed away with such of their possessions as they could carry, abandoning the rest.

On this May morning the migration was only just beginning. Before another week passed, the people were coming in hordes. Unwelcome from the first, they soon became a menace to the villages of the Northern Heights. The Islington farmers and tradesmen guarded the road at the Angel Tavern and drove the crowds back with pitchforks, axes, clubs, or whatever weapons were at hand; whereupon the swarms settled in the open fields and woods and made shift as best they might. There was little food to be had even for those with money, and there were many who had none. They had no choice but to forage for what they could find, stealing cattle, sheep, poultry, garden truck; cutting the trees for firewood and shelters. Every morning Anne sent Daffy Joe with big baskets filled with provisions and medicines of Old Emma's brewing, for the refugees brought sickness with them, the dread Black Death stalked beside them, and their privations bred all sorts of minor ills.

The first week in June young Thomas came home. His master was dead of the plague; two others of the family were sick. The shop and the living rooms above it were shut up with the crimson sign on both front door and rear: the sign of the cross and above it the fateful *Lord Have Mercy on Us,* and a guard set at each door to enforce the quarantine and give such service as was needed in bringing supplies. There were eight people in the house, shut up to die, as young Thomas said, though five of them were still in health. It was more than the boy could bear, and so he had broken quarantine. Climbing through an attic window on a dark and rainy night, he had run over the neighboring roofs and down an unguarded stair; along crooked, narrow, evil-smelling streets, lighted only by the feeble gleam of lanterns, set out before the houses to light the traveler's way.

Once outside the city, the roads had been black under the cloudy sky, and slimy underfoot, making hard going, so that young Thomas more than once stumbled and fell, or lost his sense of direction and pushed on aimlessly through the murk praying for dawn. It was noon when he had reached the cottage at Islington, drenched and drabbled and shivering with chill and fright. He had burrowed his head in his mother's lap and had sobbed with relief at being home again, as he told the story of his escape.

Now Anne comforted him and got him into dry clothes borrowed from Daffy Joe, and gave him a hot drink and a good dinner. Motherlike, she gave no thought to her own safety, though she sent Samuel to the barn on pretext of helping Joe weave a new hamper to take ᵗhe place of one that had broken; and at suppertime set the boys at opposite ends of the long table. It was all she could do, except to pray.

Each night for many nights she had read the ninety-first Psalm at evening prayers. Tonight, as usual, Samuel brought her the

Great Bible out of its carved oaken box; and her voice was serene and steady as she read the Holy Word:

He that dwelleth in the secret place of the most High shall abide under the shadow of the Almighty.

I will say of the Lord, He is my refuge and my fortress; my God; in him will I trust.

Surely he shall deliver thee from the snare of the fowler, and from the noisome pestilence.

He shall cover thee with his feathers, and under his wings shalt thou trust: his truth shall be thy shield and buckler.

Thou shalt not be afraid for the terror by night; nor for the arrow that flieth by day;

Nor for the pestilence that walketh in darkness; nor for the destruction that wasteth at noonday.

A thousand shall fall at thy side, and ten thousand at thy right hand; but it shall not come nigh thee.

Only with thine eyes shalt thou behold and see the reward of the wicked.

Because thou hast made the Lord, which is my refuge, even the most High, thy habitation;

There shall no evil befall thee, neither shall any plague come nigh thy dwelling.

For he shall give his angels charge over thee, to keep thee in all thy ways. . . .

She closed the book with reverent touch and gave it back to Samuel. Carefully the boy placed it in its box, which he closed and locked and returned to its place of honor on the high shelf. It had been only during the last few months that the lad had grown tall and strong enough to be trusted with this duty of the head of the house, and he was very proud of the trust. When the simple ceremony was over, the little group knelt and together repeated the Lord's Prayer before they separated for the night.

Samuel had seen and heard enough of the terror of the plague so that he was frightened by Thomas's home-coming. He needed no word of caution from Anne to keep him as far away from his brother as the little house would permit. But his mother's calm faith was reassuring. God had given His promise of protection. Samuel said the comforting words over and over as he lay in his narrow bed and listened to the rain dripping from the thatch:

There shall no evil befall thee, neither shall any plague
come nigh thy dwelling. . . .
A thousand shall fall at thy side, and ten thousand at thy right
hand; but it shall not come nigh thee. Only with thine
eyes shalt thou behold and see the reward of the wicked.

Over and over he whispered the words, over and over, as a kind
of abracadabra, until he fell into a deep and untroubled sleep.

He was wakened at the first gray streak of dawn by terrible
screams. Samuel sprang up, but almost as soon as his frightened
feet had struck the floor his mother was at his door, her face
white and frozen, like a marble statue. Samuel had never seen
her look so, nor speak so, in all his life. She told him what had
happened; what he must do. The specter of the Black Death had
trailed young Thomas. He must dress quickly, pack all his things
into a hamper and go to the barn to sleep with Daffy Joe until
young Thomas should get well. He must make haste—before the
doctor should come and shut up the house. He must be brave and
help them all; and he must help his mother by obeying her commands like a good soldier. And above all he must pray without
ceasing and with faith that the merciful God would hear and
answer his prayer and heal and protect them all.

Samuel ran to her with arms outstretched: "Mother! Mother!
You must come too!"

She slammed the door shut between them, and he heard her
sob as she ran down the stairs:

"Do as I tell you, son!"

Held speechless and terrified by the strength of his mother's
will, Samuel obeyed.

There was little that the physician could do except to set the
guards and mark the doors. Samuel watched with fascinated
horror while the officer did his duty, painting on front door and
back the hideous red crosses, and above them the words:

LORD HAVE MERCY ON US

Old Emma elected to stay by her mistress.

"If it's written in the Book o' Judgment that my time is come,
belike I'll not change it by runnin' to the barn," she said. "Here
I be an' here I stay!"

Samuel, crouching in the hayloft, tried to pray, but his throat was so tight that no words would come. He couldn't even think of a proper prayer. Over and over in his dull mind the same words echoed: "O God, O God, O God." But the words didn't mean anything: God didn't answer.

By and by the words didn't even echo back to him—they went out of his mouth and on and on and on endlessly. Far off in the western sky the Blazing Star glowered at him, mocking and threatening. He turned over in the hay so that he couldn't see it, but he could feel it following him—coming closer and closer with its ghastly glare.

Now he heard Thomas screaming again, and bargaining with God.

"O God, have mercy on me! I've sinned but I'm sorry for't. I'm scared to die. I've undone a maid, but I'll make her an honest woman if You'll heal me: I swear I will! Don't let me burn in hell! O merciful Jesus, save me! O Mother, ask God to forgive me! He will if you ask Him. Tell Him I'll be a good boy."

Then Anne's voice, gentle and soothing, praying for Thomas and comforting him. Samuel couldn't hear her words, but he knew she was asking God to forgive Thomas his sin and heal him of the sickness.

So for three dreadful days Thomas battled for his life. On the night of the third, the death cart took him.

Anne watched the cart go down the road. Then she turned: "I'm the next, Emma," she said.

"Oh, no! Miss' Anne! God forbid."

Anne stripped off her bodice and lifted her right arm. Underneath it was the telltale blue swelling.

"It's been there since yesterday, Emma. But I didn't want to tell you till Thomas was gone!" She staggered back to the bed and fell in a dead faint. The next night she, too, was carried off.

Old Emma's time had not come. She remained alone in the cottage, which by the law of quarantine must be kept closed and guarded for a month. And Samuel and Daffy Joe remained in the barn, also under quarantine, but isolated.

Strangely enough, there were no other deaths in Islington. The bodies were taken to the burial pit at Finsbury, farther south.

Samuel could not believe it when they told him his mother was dead. God had promised and His promise could not fail. And when at last he learned the ghastly facts, he raved like one possessed. Faithful Old Emma was shut away from him, and Daffy Joe's poor wits could find no comforting thing to say. The rector of St. Mary's held his handkerchief over his face and let his haste get the better of his dignity when it was necessary for him to pass the cottage. Anne's solicitor sent generous provision for the needs of the household; wrote to Thomas and John and sent word to Emma that as soon as the month of quarantine was up, he would make whatever temporary arrangements seemed best, pending instructions from Thomas.

But there was nothing to meet the need of the heartbroken boy of twelve, whose temporal and spiritual world had crashed into ruins. Life without his mother was unthinkable, unbearable; he could not live without her; he must find her; must follow her into the Beyond. He flung himself out of the hayloft, but got only a few painful bruises; he ran to stand beneath the great oak at the gate during a terrific thunderstorm, disregarding Emma's shouted admonition:

"Beware the oak, it draws the stroke!"

He shook his boyish fist at the angry sky and shrieked all the blasphemies he knew into the lashing boughs above his head, daring God to strike him dead. The guard, huddled against the door for shelter, and Old Emma, helpless at the window, held their breath in shocked terror—but nothing happened. The storm ceased as suddenly as it had begun, and Samuel made his way to the barn, a forlorn and bedraggled figure, and lay all night in his wet clothes without taking any harm.

He had not shed a tear since Anne's death; he slept little and suffered with dreadful nightmares; he ate next to nothing, and angrily repulsed Daffy Joe's well-meant attempts at consolation. Daffy Joe's opinion, freely confided to Emma through the kitchen window, that "the lad is gone clean daft" was not far wrong.

It was about two weeks after Anne's death when Samuel, having tossed on his bed of hay until midnight, rose stealthily and crept past Joe's sprawling body, down the ladder from the loft and out into the stableyard where the ponies spent the soft June nights. Running quickly to Silverheels, he slipped a caressing arm around her neck; and with the other hand over her nostrils, gently hushed her soft whinny of greeting and led her to the stable door, where he quickly saddled and bridled her and, letting down the bars quietly, led her out the roadway behind the barn; mounted and picked a silent way across the fields to the east until he came to the Essex Road. Having thus safely eluded pursuit, he put the pony at a gallop down the road toward town.

At last he had thought of a way to die that would be sure and sudden. The Black Death did not dally with its victims—and the Black Death was stalking the London streets.

Of that night ride of terror, Samuel had no clear memory afterward. Where he went and what he saw was only another form of nightmare, scarcely more vivid than the dreams which had haunted the preceding nights. There was only the memory of riding endlessly through dark and crooked streets which all looked alike; between houses big and little with crimson crosses on their doors; of Silverheels, snorting and shying to avoid an occasional dead body; of wails of terror and torment; and of the death carts and their drivers clanging their bells and calling: "Bring out your dead! Bring out your dead!" and most vivid of all, of a gaunt man with a black beard, like a Hebrew prophet, a man clad only in a breechcloth and striding through the streets carrying a blazing brazier on his head and crying: "Yet a few days, and London shall be destroyed! Yet a few days! Yet a few days!"

And as a final climax to the phantasmagoria of horror, there was the Great Pit, surrounded by flaring torches. To Samuel's fevered brain it looked like the mouth of hell, and then—as a horrid stench almost suffocated him—he knew what it was: the place where they had taken his mother! With a maniac screech, he dug his heels into his pony's flanks and would have driven straight into it—but Silverheels balked and whirled, and urged by a shout and a blow from a workman, took the bit in her teeth and bolted for home like a mad thing.

Book Two

Newington Green   1665 to 1671

4

Andrew Marvell

Remembrance wakes with all her train,
Swells at my breast and turns the past to pain.
—OLIVER GOLDSMITH

IT WAS midnight and Andrew Marvell was riding home to the cottage on Highgate Hill. Since noon he had been busy with conferences and consultations regarding matters pending in the House of Commons. It was a troubled time. War was imminent. Demands for money were constant. The plague was raging. Yet none of these things brought respite from the constant persecution which nagged the Nonconformist group.

Andrew Marvell was weary and let the big bay go his own gait. Leaving the walled city behind, they headed north along St. John's Road through Finsbury. Away from the city's lanterns the moon shone bright and the unpaved road was soft underfoot. Roses and honeysuckles bloomed in the dooryards. But the sickness was bad in Finsbury and many windows which should have been dark and still with the peace of midnight glowed with candlelight revealing sickroom scenes of pain and terror. Mingled with the breath of roses was a stench of filth and carrion, borne on the soft June wind from the burial pit half a mile to the east.

The horse shied away from a dark heap at the roadside, and quickened his pace to a gallop. As they neared the Angel Tavern, the distressing smells were left behind.

The door of the tavern stood wide and threw its hospitable light to greet the traveler. But before they reached the friendly doorway, a pony and rider galloped wildly up from the east and turned into the Upper Road leading north through Islington. Marvell had only a glimpse and could not be sure of the rider, but from the rear the black pony with the snowy fetlocks was unmistakable.

"Silverheels and Sam, or I'm a Dutchman!" Marvell exclaimed. "I'll wager Anne Parris knows nothing of this!"

He spurred his horse and the long legs of the big bay soon overtook the runaway. Marvell leaned from his saddle and brought the pony to a halt.

"Well, well, young sir, and what's the hurry?" he greeted.

Samuel let the reins slide out of his hands and slowly turned his blank face to Marvell.

Marvell looked at him a minute in shocked silence, then he asked gently, "What has happened, my dear boy?" Samuel made no response. "Samuel! What is wrong?"

Samuel stared at him stupidly and spoke three words: "Mother! She's dead!"

And after a question or two, Marvell took the pony's rein, and riding slowly, brought the boy to the cottage on Highgate Hill.

As the pony stopped in the garden path, Samuel slid from her back and dropped down in the soft grass, passive and limp. Marvell was met at the door by Mary, his housekeeper, who had heard their approach. He spoke in a low tone.

" 'Tis the Parris lad from down Islington way," he said, and in a few words told what little he knew of the situation. "There may be a risk in taking him in; how much, I don't know. If you want to go—"

Mary looked at him, hurt and indignant. "By the looks o' yon laddie, belike ye'll need help wi' him, I'm thinking."

Marvell patted her shoulder. "Forgive me, Mary. Fetch me some clean clothes for the lad, and some warm water and vinegar."

He bathed Samuel from head to foot as he lay on the grass and helped him into the garments Mary brought, then put him to bed on a pallet in his own room. Mary brought a steaming bowl, fragrant with a rare old liquor.

" 'Tis the last wee drop of the bishop's Christmas gift," she whispered reverently as she handed it to Marvell. "I've been a-hoarding of it for time o' need."

Samuel, exhausted and unresisting, drank the potion, and sinking back on the pillow was soon deep in sleep. Marvell, who had been watching beside him, began to make ready for bed.

Mary beckoned from the doorway and whispered, "There's a motley of letters waiting."

"They must wait until the morning, Mary," Marvell replied wearily.

But Mary insisted, producing one from her apron pocket. "But this one mebbe ye'll want tonight. The witling that chores for the lad's mother brought it the day after you went north. It seems like a special providence now that the poor lady is dead."

Andrew Marvell read Anne Parris's letter as he sat alone by the flickering rushlight. His eyes were wet when he had finished, and he stood with bowed head looking down at Anne Parris's son.

"I'll do my best for the lad, Anne dear," he murmured. "May God help me!"

He put out the light.

In spite of his late hours, Marvell was astir early the next morning. Matters of state had to wait while he gave his first attention to Samuel's affairs. First he made a trip to the mayor, asking permission to harbor Samuel until the month of quarantine was up. Then he went to Anne's solicitor, to whom he presented her letter as showing her desire for her son's future. The lawyer was only too glad to relieve himself of responsibility by giving Marvell temporary custody of the boy until his father could be heard from. He went next to the tailor for a new outfit of clothes and stopped at the Parris cottage to acquaint the nearly distracted Emma and Joe of Samuel's whereabouts. Finally he went back to Highgate Hill and dispatched letters to Thomas Parris in Barbados and to Brother John at Ugborough. Now he sat quietly at Samuel's bedside, not knowing what to expect when the boy's returning consciousness would bring back that night of terror.

At last the sleeper stirred, and as his heavy lids unclosed, Marvell saw with relief that his eyes were clear and sane, though haunted by pain and grief. They were no longer the eyes of an eager child; and in their new maturity and sadness, they were so like the eyes of his dead mother that Marvell caught his breath.

In the days that followed, Marvell turned back the pages of his career. The man of the world, the diplomat, the sharp-tongued railleur and satirist, returned again to the ministry of his youth; became once more the healer of sick souls. But the simple faith of

Samuel's childhood could never be restored. God's pledge of protection had been broken; and the reward of the wicked had destroyed saint and sinner alike.

Trained in all the subtleties and quibbles of theology and political diplomacy, Marvell was nonplused by the straightforward questionings of this child of twelve. He was driven back to the perplexing alternative: had God deliberately broken His Word? or was the plague (the scourge in the devil's hands) too strong for Him? Nothing could change the boy's view.

"God promised. And my mother trusted Him. And He let her die! Why, she wasn't even buried! O Mother, my beautiful darling mother to die like that! There isn't any God; there can't be, or such dreadful things wouldn't happen. Oh, I wish I could die too!

"I know why Thomas died," Samuel said gravely, "and Thomas knew. He had done wickedness and sinned against God. He cried and prayed so loud that we could hear him out in the garden. But God turned away His ear and wouldn't hear his prayer. Thomas had undone a maid. Exactly what does it mean to undo a maid, Mr. Marvell?"

Andrew Marvell gave a perfectly Puritan answer. "God grant you may never know, my boy!" he said piously.

Samuel was hurt and perplexed by Marvell's evasion. He flushed and said no more.

Little by little Marvell learned of Samuel's attempts to end his life; and whether by the strength of Marvell's persuasions or because the impulse of self-destruction had worn itself out, Samuel talked reasonably and agreed with Marvell that he could never hope to find his mother by that path. For the gates of the Heavenly City where his mother had gone would be shut fast against a self-murderer. The only way to find his mother was to follow the path her feet had trod, so that someday they might be reunited in eternity. But even that blessed sense of security faded to a forlorn hope. In the end, there was only The Word to rely on; and The Word had failed him in time of need.

"Mr. Marvell," he asked earnestly, "do you think I am going to die soon? I have cursed God and the Bible says, 'Curse God, and die.' I thought God would strike me down with His thunderbolt. I wanted Him to. But He didn't and I didn't die. Why didn't I?"

"You precious little idiot!" Marvell cried. "Do you think the Lord God Almighty is going to hold it against you because you were out of your mind with grief? If you cursed *me*, would I lay a finger on you, do you think? And is not God greater than man? If you want to quote from Job, listen to this: 'Surely God will not hear vanity, neither will the Almighty regard it. . . . He looketh upon men, and if any say, I have sinned . . . he will deliver his soul from going into the pit, and his life shall see the light.' And hear the words of the Psalmist: 'If Thou, Lord, shouldest mark iniquities, O Lord, who shall stand? But there is forgiveness with thee, that thou mayest be feared.' "

"It seems very mixed up," Samuel said wonderingly "It's all God's Word, but sometimes it says one way, and sometimes another. I don't think I'll get it straight. I've tried and tried, but it's no use!"

Marvell laid a caressing hand on the boy's shoulder.

"Don't try any more, laddie. No man by searching can find out God. Somehow, in His infinite wisdom, God has made sorrow and pain and death a part of His great plan, just as much as joy and life and health. We don't either of us know why."

He put his arm around the tense young body.

"I think I must tell you something, Sam. It happened when I was only a few years older than you are, and it still hurts to speak of it. I had a wonderful father, Sam. And I loved him—perhaps as much as you love your mother. He was drowned one day in the turbulent Humber River—because a girl who was our guest insisted on going home in the midst of a tempest. The boatman tried to dissuade her and my father tried, but she insisted. So, because he felt himself bound in honor and conscience not to desert her, they prevailed on the boatmen to hazard it and started across the racing stream. They never made the shore, and somewhere in the depths of the river or the sea their bones will lie till the seas give up their dead."

Marvell walked to a rack by the door and brought back a gold-headed cane. "This was my father's. He carried it with him always. As the boat shoved off, he threw it to a friend on the shore and shouted above the storm: 'Ho, for heaven! Tell Andrew to remember his father!'

"That was the way he met Death.

"I was bitter and resentful too, Sam. I hated that foolish girl who had taken my father's life. I hated God for allowing it. Then, after a while, the girl's mother sent for me. She talked to me and told me of her love for her only daughter, who was so much her idol that she could hardly bear her out of her sight. That was why the girl had risked her life and lost it rather than alarm her mother. 'You and I are together in our grief, Andrew,' she said to me, 'and you shall be to me as my own son. I will provide means for your education; and when my earthly life is done, all that I have shall be yours.'

"That was the way she met Sorrow."

Samuel listened in silence, his solemn dark eyes searching Marvell's face. In his mind he saw the picture: the raging river, the capsized boat, and above the roar of the storm the Voice of Very God: "When thou passest through the waters, I will be with thee; and through the rivers, they shall not overflow thee." The Lord strong and mighty, not lifting His finger—while the overturned craft swirled seaward. But he said nothing.

Andrew Marvell thanked God, thinking that his eloquence had prevailed!

"Well, my lad, I must go north again soon."

They had just finished dinner and were in the garden, Marvell with his pipe and Samuel stretched full length on the grass, watching the cloud ships sailing overhead.

Samuel sat straight up. His sensitive lips were trembling.

"What are you going to do—about me—Mr. Marvell?"

He stood up and faced his friend, his hands clenched at his sides. (Like a prisoner awaiting sentence, poor little beggar Marvell thought.)

It was mid-July, four weeks since Mr. Marvell had brought him to the cottage on Highgate Hill. He had known he could not stay here always, of course, but he had tried not to think about it.

"Have you heard from my father?" he asked, trying to keep his voice steady.

"No, and can't hope to for some time. Probably my letter has not had time to reach him yet. But in the meantime Mr. Muggleton, your father's lawyer, and I must do what seems best."

"I had a letter from John," Samuel said slowly. "He and Debby are going to have another baby, and Debby can't have the trouble of me this summer. John needn't worry; I don't want to go to live with him, anyway."

"No," Marvell agreed, "that wouldn't do. Suppose we go over to see Mr. Morton at Newington Green tomorrow. He hasn't really got his academy started yet, but I think he would take you for the summer at least, until we hear from your father. Let's start early, before the sun is hot.

"You will like Mr. Morton. He has had plenty of trouble, but you'd never think it to see him. It takes a brave man to lose everything and still keep his courage and his temper and his faith in God and men, but Morton's done it.

"His Puritan views lost him an honored fellowship at Oxford, and he went back to his little rectory in Cornwall; and then along came the Act of 1662 and ejected him from that; so he went back to teaching. Then there was trouble about some property in London, which brought him here; and Mr. Milton and I and some other friends urged him to set up an academy (which, after all, I believe is the work the good Lord designed him for)."

Next morning they rode to Newington Green. It was hard for Samuel to be mopish with his pony between his knees. He had not had the heart to ride much since he came to Highgate, and Silverheels pranced and capered and took all his attention. The ride to Newington Green was not half long enough.

Mr. Morton came out to welcome them, running down the steps like a boy. He was a big man, ruddy of face and sturdy of body. He wore an old homespun suit and his hands were grimy.

"Never try to rejuvenate an old house." He laughed. "I never knew there could be so much dirt anywhere, nor so many things out of fix. The windows won't open and the doors won't shut; the chimneys are stopped with martins' nests and the cellars are alive with rats.

"Come in! You're just in time for breakfast. Andrew, you know Mistress Morton. And this is Samuel Parris, my dear."

Samuel thought Mrs. Morton was the saddest looking person he had ever seen. She was tall and dark, with a sallow complexion and a woebegone droop to the corners of her mouth.

Her face is all north and south and not a bit east and west, like **Mr. Morton's**, he thought. She sat almost silent during the meal, while Morton and Marvell talked and Samuel listened. But Mrs. Morton didn't seem to be listening nor even eating much, just playing with her food as if she was too tired to put it in her mouth.

While they ate Morton told more of the history of the mansion house.

"It's beautiful!" Marvell said, looking around. "Well worth the trouble it takes, I'd say. It must be very old."

"Yes, it dates back to the Wars of the Roses. Remember the story, Samuel? Two centuries ago, when the White and the Red were united under Henry VII. Richard III lost the battle on Bosworth Field and left his crown hanging on a hawthorn bush, and Henry Tudor found it and put it on his own head; while his army rallied round him and sang the Te Deum.

"That's where my ill-famed ancestor came in: Bishop Morton, you know, afterwards cardinal, who devised the tax known as Morton's Fork to extort money from rich and poor alike. If they lived handsomely, they could afford to pay; if frugally, their thrift must have laid something by. One prong or the other got 'em all.

"The bishop built this house and lived here—which gave it its name, Bishop's Place (and may account for the evil odor in the basement).

"The place is well suited to our needs," Morton went on, "roomy and comfortable, well located and easy of access, yet secluded and circumspect enough to afford a measure of protection from the bishop's informers. It has been abused and neglected but it's not beyond repair, and the fact that it has been vacant for some years may be to our advantage. With the aid of yourself and some other good friends, Andrew, I hope soon to have the old place fit for its new vocation."

"Didn't Henry VIII use this house at one time?" asked Marvell.

"Yes, it became the residence of Lord Percy, and while the Merry Monarch dallied with more than one alluring beauty of the court when he was supposed to be following the hounds over the Royal Chase, which lay northerly from Kingsland to Enfield, Lord Percy made love to Henry's Queen, Anne Boleyn.

"Now, nearing the end of its second century, the house has settled down to a respectable old age; and like many another old reprobate, has set itself to guard the morals of the rising generation."

When breakfast was over, Morton called a servant boy: "Zeke, this is Master Samuel Parris, who may be one of our students. Show him the stables and the grounds and what we hope will be the tennis courts and cricket fields if we ever get the place in order—and put our best foot foremost so that he will want to come."

Zeke pulled his carroty foretop and grinned. In an undertone he said to Samuel, "The master do be the beatenest I ever seen. He's allus talkin' foolish like that, but they do say he's smart as they come, when he wants to be."

Having thus disposed of Samuel, Morton settled down for a talk with his friend Marvell, of whom he had seen far too little of late. He was enthusiastic about his academy and grateful for the backing of his London friends. He was full of plans. He intended to have the best equipment available, especially in the line of the sciences. Physics and chemistry were just emerging from the realm of magic. The new Copernican astronomy was still the subject of much hot and abusive argument, and judicial astrology was approved by many intelligent men. Geography had not yet divorced itself from the highly colored tales of travelers. The Royal Society established by Charles II in the interests of science was three years old, but it was already rousing hot discussions in both scientific and religious circles.

"I aim to place the emphasis on the practicalities," Morton said. "To try in my small way to counteract what some of us feel is the overclassical influence of Oxford. After all, we live in the seventeenth century, and all the learning in the world didn't end with Greece and Rome."

Morton was angling for the support of the greatest scientists in London when he installed a laboratory equipped with such rarities as an air pump, a thermometer, a telescope, and all sorts of mathematical instruments; while with the other hand he held out to the youngsters themselves the attractions of a fine garden, a bowling green, a fishpond, and the unheard-of and alluring suggestion of democratical government among them, each man being allowed to propose laws and punishments and vote by ballot.

This first summer, while the house and grounds were being put in order, there were only a few pupils, most of them day scholars or lads from the universities who came for coaching in special subjects.

"I'm glad it happens so," Morton told Marvell. " 'Twill give me time to prepare Samuel for the routine of the school year. Poor laddie! I've a notion he needs mothering and fathering more than schooling for the present."

Marvell disagreed. "He needs discipline and training more than anything. He's had too much mothering already."

Morton laughed. "Hear the old bachelor! What's he know about younkins? Don't worry, Andrew. Whatever he needs we'll try to give him.

"I think I shall put him to room with Timothy Drew. They're about of an age, though Drew is a little fellow, and friendly and talkative.

"I'm not trying the dormitory plan, for the present at least. With all this house we might as well spread out. But the boys have their meals at a commons table, which gives Mistress Morton and me a quiet interval." He smiled. "We shall need a place of refuge when the house fills up. Boys can make more noise at table than a pack of hounds. I don't mind it, but it's hard on my wife. She's had a lot to bear these last few years."

The sun was in the west as they rode home.

"Tomorrow we must have you measured for your uniform," Marvell said. "Mr. Morton will attend to getting the books and other things you need."

Samuel nodded. He could not bear to think of leaving Marvell, but the prospect of going away to school was exciting. It seemed to add inches to his stature: to put him in a class with his brothers who had been to Eton.

For the first time since his mother died he began to plan for his future. Life ran on before him like the road.

He put Silverheels to the gallop and called back to Marvell: "I'll race you to Highgate!"

And Marvell shouted like a boy as he gave chase.

Early in August, Samuel and Andrew Marvell went again along the road to Morton's Academy. But this time they drove in a small horse cart, for Samuel had a traveling box full of the new clothes his friend had bought him; a new school uniform, some warm bed coverings, and a heavy greatcoat for the winter.

As they rounded a bend in the dusty road Samuel saw over the hedges that lined the road the ivied house that was to be his home. He felt that curious emptiness in his middle that he had when he first visited Morton's, a mingled feeling of dread and happy expectancy. Zeke, who had shown Samuel around before, met the pair at the gate and helped unload the cart, carrying the small trunk to Samuel's room.

Marvell went to talk with Morton while Zeke helped Samuel unpack. But Marvell did not have much time for dallying, for he had to be back to his cottage before sundown to make ready for his own departure. Early the next morning he was going back to Hull for a stay of several months.

After about an hour's time Zeke brought the cart back from the stables.

Marvell said good-bye cheerfully.

"I shan't be away for long," he told Samuel. His voice was well under control, but his eyes were misty. "I will try to write you as often as time permits. I know Mr. Morton will be as kind as a father to you, for we are close friends and see things in much the same way. Work hard in whatever tasks you do, whether they be at your studies or on the sporting fields. I am proud of you, Samuel, and I love you for yourself and because you are your mother's son. She was a wonderful woman, my boy, and she had great hopes and plans for you. Never do anything that would make her ashamed."

Marvell swung up into the cart with easy grace, and turning the horse toward the road drove away at a smart pace, the dust flying behind him.

That evening at supper Samuel felt even more lonely than before, more because the hall was full of boys who knew each other than because he missed the known companionship of Andrew Marvell. He sat next to his roommate, Timothy Drew, whom he had not seen before. He was a genial little fellow, whose constant patter bored Samuel more than it entertained him. But it was difficult to be moody to the tune of Timothy's comments about everything and everybody.

After the meal was over, Mistress Morton came over and spoke to him very kindly.

"I know how difficult it sometimes is," she said, "when a lad is new to a place. I have known many scholars, and there have been none of them who wasn't a bit queasy at leaving home. If anything might be troubling you now or later it would make me very glad indeed to know that you would come to me and talk about it, just as you would talk to your own mother."

Samuel swallowed hard. He tried to think of something else to say to this stranger with the sad, tired eyes, who wanted him to make believe she was his mother. But he couldn't think. By and by he managed, "Thank you, ma'am, there ain't anything."

Little by little Samuel learned to hide his fear and grief and loneliness; to build within himself a sanctuary where he might hide from reality. But the new shelter was in no way the same as the lovely house of dreams in which he had dwelt as a child in Islington, and which had failed him utterly when the storms beat upon it. It was a grim castle with a moat and drawbridge, into which his frightened child heart might retreat and hide itself from the sorrowful past and the difficult and dangerous future. The towers and battlements looked brave enough, but the place was garrisoned by a lonely child, crying for the lost security of his mother's arms.

Anne Parris, intent on bringing up her son in the nurture and admonition of the Lord, had forgotten to prepare him for the all-important contacts of everyday living. He had never learned the give-and-take of normal childhood, nor the tact and friendliness which come to the ordinary schoolboy as a natural result of rubbing elbows with his fellows in work and play.

As Mr. Morton had said, the emphasis in his academy would be on the practical side of life and learning. Samuel never suspected his interests would lie much on these lines. But he was fascinated by the observatory high up in the tower. Here Mr. Morton kept the large telescope which on bright nights enabled one to see the most extraordinary markings and convolutions on the face of the moon.

Once Mr. Morton let him stay up until late in the evening to see the planet Saturn and her fiery rings. Samuel was so terrified by this sight of the awful strength and power of the Lord that he had feverish nightmares in which he dreamt he was being roasted over a huge spit and thousands of cackling fire-devils were laughing at him. He awoke the next morning with a painful remembrance of the plague. In the months since his mother died, her memory had become sweet and cool like her hands, but the dream had brought back the stark terror of the days he had tried so hard to forget.

Although neither shy nor timid, Samuel was reticent and ill at ease among his new associates, sensitive and resentful of laughter and teasing; and as a defense assumed an aloof manner which made him a target for all sorts of minor persecutions.

Charles Morton, busy with many and varied problems of his own, had little time to devote to any one pupil; but when Samuel complained to him, he rebuked the older boys to Samuel's entire satisfaction. But this only led to further hazing of a sly and secret kind and made the new boy more unpopular than ever, for Samuel had committed the unpardonable sin of the schoolboy's code, and wherever he went he was given the cold shoulder and insulted with the rhyme:

> Tell-tale-tit, your tongue shall be slit;
> Every dog in the town shall have a little bit.

At this stage an ignorant lout of a stableboy came to the rescue. It was one day when Samuel, harried and bullied beyond endurance, had run to cover in the big barn to escape his tormentors, that Zeke found him hiding in the hay, shaking with fright and sobbing his lonely heart out.

"Why, ee damn snivelin' little dolt ee, whyn't ee stand up to 'em an' put up yer fists? Ye'll ne'er be a man an' ee run like a started hare! Dammy, doant ee ken whut fists be for? Come ee here till I show ee how to lam 'em good! Ee's big enough to lick 'em an ee got ee guts, but ee'll ne'er get nowheres actin' like a damn Quaker. Come here, dammy, an' put 'em up!"

The words were harsh but the tone was kindly, and Samuel, at the end of his tether, thankfully accepted an offer of aid or encouragement. And Zeke was as good as his word. He not only gave lessons in the manly art, but he put heart into his young pupil and made it his business to see that there was something like fair play. He cursed the boys roundly for "a pack o' craven whelps, a whole crew pickin' on a little feller," and arranged a series of bouts in which Samuel was matched against a boy of somewhere near his own size and weight. Best of all, he taught Samuel not to whine when he was licked. All this, of course, went on without Mr. Morton's knowledge.

Samuel worked hard all winter. He learned fast, and more than once did Mr. Morton speak to him in front of the whole class and tell him that his studies were progressing very favorably indeed. Andrew Marvell wrote Samuel two letters that winter. The first came from Hull soon after the autumn term began. It was quite short, but the little contact it offered with the world in which Marvell moved was welcome in Samuel's tediously busy school days. He wrote Samuel again, this time from York. The letter was a little more newsy than the first, but it said nothing of the mission he was performing, which, Samuel thought, must be of high importance and secrecy.

Samuel was beginning his second half year at Morton's when he received a letter from his father:

Dear son, The news of oure sad bereavements has lately come to mee by letters from Mr. Muggleton, as also from Mr. A. Marvell, Mr. Chas. Morton & your bro. John, asking my approval of their plans for youre scooling with Mr. Morton with view to the ministrye. The beggarly poore estate of your Bro. John makes me thinke one preacher in our family might be aplenty, as he writes me that he can scarce find food and roofe for his owne let alone an other, i.e. yourself. It might seem more to the point you should follow my calling than your Bros. This lonelie life is hard on a man an I feel my yrs all 45 of em and tis a sorry blow to mee that Young Tom is gone That I had counted on to come to my aid next Sumer when his prentice time were up an hee fitted to take over the accountin and parte of the worke of the plantation.

Hee were ever a steddy lad with a keen head for Trade but Hee is gone & John is set for Preachin tho hee starve att it & youre Mother & her Friends bee of the same mind for you.

Yett it has ever been yr Mother's plan for You & her last Wish & Charge to Mee. Shee wrote mee when Young Tom came home and she feared hee might bring the Sickness. She Dreampt she saw you Wandering alone in Thicke Darknesse & shoud it bee that God took Her Shee Charged mee to send you to Mr. Morton.

Soe this I am in dutie bound to doe att least for the time. The more that I woud't know what in Gods World to doe with a Younkin of 12 in a Sugar Plant.

If there's Preacher Stuff in You nows the time to Prove Yourself by Giving a Good Account in youre Studies & Deportment.

Your Lovin Father,

Thos. Parris.

Mr. M. advises Mee that for a yeare your Worke will be Practicalities like figuring Shorthand Arithmeticks &c which will be Goode in Anny Calling. T. P.

There was also a letter of sympathy from Aunt Susanna Parris (now Abbott) beginning: "You poor Lonesome Littel Lammie how I wish your Olde Aunty could take you in her armes and wipe youre Teares Away."

Coming as it did after Samuel had lived six months in a boys' school; had grown to the proud height of five feet one; had been addressed as Parris and come to regard himself as almost grown up, the letter seemed an affront to his manly dignity and left him shamefaced and humiliated. Breaking the rule that all letters should pass through Morton's hands, Samuel tore the missive into bits and burned it on the hearth. Yet there were times when the nights were still lonesome and he felt vaguely comforted by thinking of Aunt Susanna.

But he had no desire now to go to Barbados. His relationship with his father had never been a close one, and the years that Thomas had been in the Indies with only the contact of infrequent letters made him seem almost a stranger. The childish wish to share his father's travels had faded as his ideals had been shaped by his mother and by his own naturally quiet tastes.

He liked and respected Morton. He had formed some schoolboy attachments with a few of his mates, and had developed an eager interest in the larger world of ideas which was opening for him.

The winter was unusually severe that year, and Samuel was grateful for the heavy woolen coat Mr. Marvell had insisted on buying for him, although Samuel felt sure he would never use it. The small brooks and the shallow lake at the foot of the hill froze solid, and many was the afternoon that Samuel spent there skating with Drew, or with John Crooks and Sidney Delavan,

Drew's two old cronies who had become good friends with Samuel.

Crooks and Delavan were a comical pair, for they were of uneven height, Crooks being an easy foot above Delavan. They were inseparable, and usually were at the bottom of any disturbance and prank which befell at the academy. Their imaginations were bottomless, and they could think up more devilry than a whole cargo of West Indian monkeys.

Early one April night Samuel tossed and turned on his bed unable to sleep. He leaned over and whispered to Timothy Drew, who also seemed to be awake:

"I say, Drew! Look at that moon! 'Tis as bright as a new-minted penny and the grass gleams like silver. Here's no night to be pounding our pallets when the pixies are about. You can well see their fairy rings in the close-cropped grass."

"You want to be wandering this evening and catch a good caning from the master, who'd be sure to hear you sneaking down the creaking stairs. He's just been giving Crooks a proper wigging and I'll wager he's not asleep."

"What's Crooks been up to?" Samuel asked.

"Oh, he felt the spring in his blood and was out driving in the cart with Mistress Morton's niece who's visiting. They didn't get back till well after the supper bell. Mr. Morton was fair angry with him, even though he do be a favorite of his."

There was an almost inaudible creak outside the door, when suddenly it opened and two shadowy forms slipped in.

"Well, for the luvva—" Drew began, but a hand was clapped quickly over his mouth.

"Be still, you fools! This night has ears and the wood is alive with the little folk!"

"Delavan and Crooks!" whispered Samuel. "What in the Name are you up to, roaming about like this?"

"We have a plan," said Crooks, coming over and sitting on Samuel's bed, "and it's this—"

"Oh, Lord, you and your plans," said Samuel in mock anger, "you'll get a body into trouble quicker than you'll eat a cherry tart. Well, what is it?"

"You recollect that slimy fat vicar at St. Joseph's as comes complaining of us raiding his apple orchard? Well, I was talking to Zeke this afternoon as he was rolling down the bowling greens and he said as how he heard his father cussing out the vicar for all he was worth for the seducing of young Mary Cooper who's been as moonstruck as this April night ever since the spring freshets began—"

"The good Lord only knows why he should be playing the moralist," interrupted Sidney Delavan, "what with a son like Zeke and himself playing after the lasses as wait at the alehouse tables."

"I'm telling this tale, if you please," said Crooks impatiently. "Now, we went over to the village this afternoon and managed to sneak a large speaking trumpet from Gortson the tinsmith. We hauled it over the top of Stamford Hill which overlooks the old vicar's parsonage.

"Our plan is to slip over there tonight—'tis only a few minutes' walk—and then we could shout scandals at the old boy and tell the whole village of his lechery. He'd sure think it was the Word of God tumbling down from the heavens to punish him for his sins!"

Samuel was a bit uneasy. "If Morton catches us it's sure to mean a caning!"

"I thought you wanted to go on a lark, and now your knees are shaking!" Drew gibed. "Come along. Let's put on our darkest clothes so nobody can see us in the night."

So the four boys sneaked down the creaking stairs and out into the night without a soul hearing them; and went streaking it across the wet fields to Stamford Hill.

They found the trumpet still hidden behind a copse on the hillside and they lugged it out and propped it up on some stones. The moon was settling slowly behind the hills. Soon it would be dark with only the bright stars for light.

The village lay sleeping below them. There was hardly a sound in the air, save for the soft throb of the crickets and the chuckling of the distant valley stream.

Sidney Delavan said it was his idea, so he was to go first. He put the mouthpiece to his lips and took a deep breath.

"HEAR, ALL YE GOOD TOWNSPEOPLE! HORRIBLE SCANDAL!" He added a few growls and grunts to attract more attention. "LISTEN TO THE TALE OF POOR TOM COOPER'S DAUGHTER! UNDONE OF HER VIRTUE

AND VIRGINITY BY THE WILLOWS OF YON
STREAM!"

The trumpet magnified the boy's voice to a startling degree
and his mouthings volleyed back and forth from the sleepy house-
tops. Crooks then took the trumpet and told in a voice even
louder of the shameful act of the vicar who had so disgraced his
God-given profession, and took from a poor witless lass her most
precious and defenseless of possessions. His glib tongue went into
many dramatic and imaginary details to make his story colorful.

By this time they noticed lights appearing in windows and
doors here and there and people running and shouting.

"Hurry up and let me speak in the tube," cried Drew. "Before
you know it all the village will be up and about to see what's to
do!" Crooks gave him the trumpet and Drew puffed out his
chest and boomed:

"LECHER! ADULTERER! RAKE! THIS IS THE
VOICE OF DE-S-T-R-UUUUUCTION!" But on the last
word his voice gave way to a shrill shriek, which so tickled the
ribs of the others that they were convulsed with laughter and
rolled on the grass.

"We had best make for the academy before we get took," said
Crooks in alarm.

"Yes," replied Samuel, who was beginning to worry, "we have
done our duty by Mary Cooper—the pretty lass. We will be lost
if we linger much longer."

They hid the trumpet where they found it, and ran for the
academy as fast as their legs would carry them. The moon had
gone down behind the hills now, and with their dark clothes the
boys could scarcely be distinguished from shadows. They could
still hear the muffled shouts and cries from the village. They
whispered among themselves wondering if anyone at the academy
could have heard them. Suddenly a light flickered in Mr. Morton's room. Frightened, the boys hid behind the shrubbery that
bordered the house. Timothy Drew and Samuel were crouching
behind a small cedar close to the entrance, when suddenly the
door opened and out strode Mr. Morton in his nightgown and
cap. He looked down in the direction of the village, craning his
neck this way and that. Samuel was terrified lest he and Timothy
should be seen. They crouched as low as possible. Mr. Morton

turned to go back into the house, when a branch snapped under Timothy's foot.

Morton stopped with his hand on the latch and looked around. Then he opened the door and went in. Samuel thought he heard a chuckle as the master closed the door behind him; but he wasn't sure. The boys waited for what seemed hours before they dared venture in. The door was locked and barred, so they spent the night in the hayloft and bribed Zeke not to tell tales.

5

The Witch of Edmonton

By what art may the thing called Familiar be purchased?
—THE WITCH OF EDMONTON

ALTHOUGH Samuel liked and was anxious for the companionship of others, there were times when he preferred to be by himself. He liked to walk alone in the woods, perhaps taking notes on the birds and small animals he saw. He was often seen of a bright afternoon walking down across the fields toward the woods. His life at Islington had fostered that love of the outdoors which is the heritage of all good Englishmen.

One morning he had been exploring a tangle of weeds in search for a ground thrush's nest and had stumbled over an ancient sundial. He forgot the nest and patiently cleared away the weeds and scraped the moss to discover its carven motto:

AMENDE . TODAY . AND . SLACK . NOT
DETHE . COMETH . AND . WARNETH . NOT
TYME . PASSETH . AND SPEKETH . NOT

(Who had set the dial, Samuel wondered, and who had phrased the motto? Was it perhaps the archbishop who thus spoke down the centuries in solemn tone, and had the unfortunate Lord Percy watched the moving shadow on the dial measuring the brief life span of himself and his beloved Anne Boleyn?)

There was the fascinating maze directly below Samuel's window, where flirtatious lords and ladies of an earlier day had pleasured themselves, now overgrown in an impenetrable thicket of inter-woven branches where rabbits scuttled. There was the fishpool farther down, its sedgy borders overhung with willows, where kingfishers watched for their prey and darning needles poised on wings gleaming opalescent in the sun.

For stormy days Samuel enjoyed the fascination of the old mansion itself, which held a romantic charm for him. Morton, seeing his interest, encouraged him to explore the place and dis-cover whatever he could of its secrets. The house was built in the form of a hollow square, a court in the center, and with small doors opening from one room into another—for no one knew when the king's men or personal enemies might come! The walls were darkened and discolored by two centuries of dust and smoke, but some parts of the wainscoting still showed the rich gilt of better days and were ornamented with paintings, dim and uncer-tain in detail, done by some long-forgotten artist's hand.

The design of the place, with its maze of doors and passages, suggested mystery and intrigue. There was a fearsome thrill in prying open a closet door which might reveal who knew what dark story of days long gone.

Samuel spent hours searching for a secret stairway or a hidden chamber—accessories without which no ancient mansion could be quite complete. He told Timothy Drew of his looking for a room which might be carefully concealed behind the patined oak paneling of the old library. Although not much given to idle and romantic thoughts such as this, Drew was much intrigued by Samuel's story and together they decided to see what they could find.

One afternoon when no one was in the library, they carefully locked the big door and began a systematic search of the room. They tried to push and pull and slide every possible knob or noggen they could see, but of no avail. The walls and bookcases were as solid as they looked. They had spent well over an hour doing this and were about to give up, when Timothy uttered a muffled cry.

"Oh, Lord love us! Parris, look at that!" The whole section

of bookcases on the side of the fireplace slowly yawned open before them. Samuel was so excited that his hand shook as he took the pewter candlestick from the mantlepiece and lit it. He held it high above his head and they peered into the dark room from which came that dank smell of a place shut up for many years. The dim light showed them all of the small chamber, which was only about five feet square and lined on three sides with bookshelves. In the middle was a small table and chair.

"We had best come back later, perhaps at night when all is quiet to explore this chamber," said Samuel, "for someone is likely to come down here, and we're lucky enough as 'tis no one has come yet."

They swung the heavy door back carefully, remembering where the secret switch was.

They could hardly wait until night came. Supper seemed to drag endlessly in the large dining hall, and Samuel and Drew were listless and uninterested in the talk of their friends. But the evening preparation hour for classes the next day was a nightmare of years. Samuel could not for the life of him concentrate on his book, but spent the whole time staring at the pages unseeing or passing notes to Drew across the way. When the time for retiring finally came the boys were all but exhausted from sheer nervousness. They tossed and turned on their pallets waiting for the time when it would be safe to creep down the noisy stairs and the long gallery which led to the library. The moon was high in the heavens and the old house long since quiet with sleep when Samuel and Timothy softly opened the library door. For a few minutes neither of them could remember where the secret switch was, but they found it at last, and again the huge door opened. They lit the candle and went inside. Timothy put the candle down on the rough wooden table that was in the middle of the floor and began to look at the queer shapes and sizes of the books on the walls. But Samuel was more interested in the large folio volume which was lying on the table beside the candle. It was bound in vellum, Samuel saw, and dingy with dust and dampness. In the flickering light he could just barely read the title which was stamped on the back:

THE WITCH OF EDMONTON

"We'd best be getting back, Samuel," said Timothy, his teeth chattering from the damp chill of the chamber, "or we'll both come down with the fever."

Samuel was fascinated by the large book before him. So he blew off the dust and dirt and carefully tucked it under his arm. He could wait until tomorrow to look at his find.

The following day after his midday meal he took the book out of his traveling box and settled himself comfortably by the window in his room. He opened the heavy cover and was at once spellbound by the title page and what it betokened of the old book's contents.

Witches were common enough and Samuel had heard and read tales of enchantment and the evil eye. But he had never before seen or read a drama, for the playhouse and all that pertained to it was utterly evil. To a lad bred to the dull prosiness of Puritan tracts and sermons, the story of the Witch of Edmonton was engrossing beyond anything he had ever experienced.

He read the book hungrily from Prologue to Epilogue, stage directions and all. He did not know that he had happened on a masterpiece of dramatic art. He had never heard of any of the divers well-esteemed poets who had so vividly brought to life for him the direful history of old Mother Sawyer. He felt no pity for the miseries of a filthy old hag whom only the devil would aid. In his mind he sat in the pit and watched each scene. He saw the first act which introduced Frank Thorney, who, like his own brother Thomas, had shamefully undone a maid, and after this first wickedness waded deeper into mischief until by the help of the Black Dog he murdered his wife. In the last act was led away to the gallows with the inevitable pious farewell:

> All help me with your prayers.—On, on; 'tis just
> That law should purge the guilt of blood and lust.

Samuel shuddered to think what might have happened to young Thomas had he lived to experience the natural consequences of his youthful sin. Perhaps, after all, the plague was merciful.

But the interest of this human drama paled beside the story of the witch, an old crone pitiably poor, buckled and bent together, shunned and hated like a sickness; beaten by old Banks

THE WITCH OF EDMONTON

A known true Story
Composed into

A TRAGI-COMEDY

By divers well-esteemed Poets;
WILLIAM ROWLEY, THOMAS DEKKER, JOHN FORD, &c.

Acted by the Princes Servants,
often at the Cock-Pit in Drury Lane
once at Court, with singular applause.
Never printed till now.

LONDON, PRINTED BY K. COTTREL, FOR EDWARD BLACKMORE, AT THE ANGEL IN PAUL'S CHURCHYARD. 1658 for trespassing upon his land to gather a few sticks to warm her; until she declares:

> 'Tis all one
> To be a witch as to be counted one,

and seeking revenge inquires "by what art may the thing called Familiar be purchased?" In answer then comes the Black Dog, who greets her with

> Ho! have I found thee cursing?
> Now thou art mine own.

After some fearful hesitation she seals the contract with her blood and receives instruction in the devil's paternoster:

> When thou wishest ill,
> Corn, man or beast wouldst spoil or kill,
> Turn thy back against the sun,
> And mumble this short orison:
> "If thou to death or shame pursue 'em,
> Sanctibiceter nomen tuum."

The charm works; mischief and evil follow her steps; blight, murrain, and madness are visited on her enemies until at last the Black Dog deserts her with these words:

> Thou art so ripe to fall into hell, that no
> more of my kennel will so much as bark
> at him that hangs thee.

Her malign power ebbs as suddenly as it came; justice triumphs, and she is dragged off to Tyburn, shrieking and crying out in hideous despair, there to perish miserably and be damned perpetually, but not without the final admonition:

> All take heed
> How they believe the devil; at last he'll cheat you . . .
> There is no damn-ed conjuror like the devil.

Samuel shuddered with horror as he put the book away. He could almost smell the brimstone!

He dared not show the book to anyone or talk about it. He hid it away where he had found it, and each clandestine reading deepened his desire to go himself to the Cockpit in Drury Lane and see the marvels of the stage.

Morton's Academy was remarkable for its democratical government and there were few arbitrary rules. A vote had been taken in open assembly soon after the beginning of the term, on the request of a few pupils, to decide whether or no the school should be allowed to go to the playhouses, and the Puritan boys, who were largely in the majority, had stood solidly against the proposition with a unanimous Nay!

Even without this expression of opinion, Samuel knew well enough that the stage was altogether evil. *The Witch of Edmonton* gave proof of iniquity darker and more vile than ever he had dreamed, but it had a baleful fascination which lured even as it repelled. There were dark implications in this matter which teased his curiosity with suggestions of indecencies unthinkable. He approached the matter gingerly with his stableboy friend, but Zeke's customary plain speaking boggled at the question.

"'Tis a dour an' dreadful matter an' best let be," he said solemnly, "e'en the thinkin' on't. I've hearn tales telled by some as sez they've seen 'em in the churchyard at foul witch feasts an' Sabbats;—but me, I knows nowt about it but only 'tis best let be an' not e'en talked about. They's witches an' allus has been witches an' allus will be jest as they's Ol' Dowl hisself, but me, I doant want to go a-whorin' after 'em. I tell ye they's best let be!"

Samuel turned the subject to playhouses. "Have you ever seen a play, Zeke?"

But plays Zeke knew little about from the spectator's viewpoint, having never been in sufficient funds to pass the door-keepers. He had once, however, spent a thrilling evening backstage as one of the mob.

"'Twere a play called *Julia Sees Her*," he said. "Whar a big lout in a nightgown were makin' a speech an' we all cried him down an' yelled as how we'd have the will an' presently he give up an' read it out to us—how it sez he'd give each one of us seventy-five drachmas—but all we got in the end was tuppence, pox take him."

Even to Zeke, Samuel dared not mention the play nor his possession of it, but he ventured another question: "Did you ever hear of the Witch of Edmonton? Was there really a witch lived there?"

"Aye!" Zeke did not hesitate. "Aye, that there were! Old Trot were a witch for true! My granther knowed her an' were in the crew as smelt her out.

"Granther he sez, 'Pluck a thatch off her hovel an' fire it, an' if she be a witch, she'll come a-runnin' in.'

"An' so she done! The thatch were good as a jury to prove her a witch. Old Hellcat come a-runnin' 's if Dowl had sent her in a barrel o' gunpowder. She did, by cock!"

6

London's Burning!

All things of beauty shatter'd, lost and gone;
Nothing of London whole but London Stone.
    —CROUCH, LONDINENSES LACRYMAE, 1666.

IT WAS the second of September, a lazy Lord's Day afternoon at Morton's, and in the air was the hot dry breath of summer. The grass on the green was stiff and dry, and a galloping wind from the east had blown all day, bringing with it no rain but only scurries of dust and leaves torn from the branches before their time.

A clatter of hoofs drummed on the bridge far down the Essex Road, and a shout, coming rapidly nearer and clearer,

"London's burning! London's burning!"

The boys ran out, shouting at the crier, but he only babbled, *"Arm! Arm! The French!"* as he swung around the curve and dashed up Green Lanes to the north.

Morton joined the excited group at the gate.

"Some mad fellow, most like. But we can see from the tower if there is a fire of any size."

So the whole crew rushed indoors and up the stairs to the turret from which, one hundred and thirty years before, Lord Percy had watched King Henry's Guardsmen coming to take him to London Tower.

A long line of heavy smoke and flame was sweeping westward from the neighborhood of the bridge, for perhaps a quarter mile along the river. At this distance, looking down on the city, the intervening buildings and the crest of the sharp rise along Cannon Street screened the low-lying foreshore so that it was impossible to tell what was burning, but the fire was bad and widespread. Even as they watched, fresh bursts of flame here and there showed where new fuel had been found, and the ominous rush of the smoke cloud rolling westward measured the merciless strength of the east wind.

Morton now pushed into the turret bringing his big spyglass. He stood silent for some time, training the glass this way and that, appraising the scene. When he came down from the lookout, his face was grave and he spoke sternly.

"This is no ordinary fire, boys. What it portends I have no idea. It may be, as the crier said, an attack by the French or the Dutch; it may be a papist uprising. One thing is sure. It is a terrible calamity and not a pageant or a spectacle to whet our excitement or delight our eyes. I must go at once to protect my property in the city if such a thing be possible. Until my return our rule of democratical government is suspended. No student is to leave the grounds for any purpose whatever. I ask you all to pledge your faith to obey this order; and I leave the school and Mrs. Morton in your care. Your hands on it, young gentlemen."

With only a moment's hesitation, Samuel stepped forward. Then Crooks put his hand in the master's, and one after another every boy followed.

While the others were seeing Morton off, Samuel went back to the deserted turret and trained the glass this way and that on the panorama spread out before him. He was filled with a strange eagerness as though fearful that he might lose something of the picture. As long as he could remember, he had seen London, bit by bit: Cornhill and the Royal Exchange; Lombard Street; Cheapside; Westminster; the Strand; the Bridge, with the boatmen shooting between its piers; Old St. Paul's, which after a century of Protestant neglect and profonation was still majestic.

Only once before he had seen London as a whole, on that day

which seemed so long ago, when he and his mother rode together for the last time and halted their ponies on Parliament Hill to look down over the city. But that picture seemed blurred and far away—dimmed by time.

Now the glass brought before him, clear-cut and close, this monstrous thing called London. And into this teeming city the fire came stalking like a giant wading through the streets. The flames driven by the wind and gorged by the fat warehouses along Thames side rose higher, shutting out the river with a wall of flame and smoke.

The London he looked upon was a medieval city surrounded by a wall in some places thirty-five feet high, with bastions and gates such as King Hal had ridden through as he went out to Agincourt. Now the walls were crumbling and black with age and the gates had lost their earlier glory, but they were still closed and locked at night, even though the city had outgrown its old limits and housed thousands of its population beyond them.

The houses, built of stout oak timbers, with walls of daub and wattle, stood against the crooked little streets which wobbled crazily this way and that, dodging the uneven frontage of the houses.

The second stories overhung the first and the third overhung the second, so that a prentice in his garret might kiss his sweetheart across the way. It was indeed a city built to make a general bonfire.

It was some queer prescience which kept Samuel at the window long after the others had gone: some subconscious foreboding in his sensitive mind that warned him that he would never again see the old London.

The noon bell rang, and Samuel walked slowly down from the turret to join the others in the noisy dining hall. There was plenty to talk about now, plenty of room for speculation and argument, which more than once became disagreeably personal and at times almost abusive.

Young Foster, who was suspected of having an aunt by marriage who had been baptized a papist, and Delavan, whose name had a suspiciously French sound, were taunted almost beyond endurance as being under suspicion of treasonable sympathies.

Wild tales of threats against the king or the government were recalled, and a host of prophecies by Quakers, astrologers, and self-styled seers were recounted as having predicted the destruction of London as retribution for its wickedness.

As the hours wore on and no word came from Morton, the restlessness increased and it was strongly urged that more than likely the master had met with trouble and his scholars should go to his aid. Their promise did not contemplate so long an absence. Suppose Morton had met with accident or foul play and did not return at all.

As dusk turned to dark the excitement grew. The darkness brought the fire into high relief against the southern sky. Even from the first-floor windows the glow illuminated the whole heavens. The night was clear and a bright moon rose, but the firelight was brighter still, and now and then, when a tall steeple caught fire, leaping flames could be seen. No boy could be expected to go to bed like a nursling when London was burning. Even Mrs. Morton, whose calm faith in her husband's wisdom seldom faltered, became nervous and perturbed, and when an excited young orator sprang up and shouted:

"Are we, like Nero, to sit here and fiddle while London burns?" Mrs. Morton cried distractedly:

"Oh, go! Go! Find your master and bring him home!"

They needed no second bidding. With the moon to light their way, they legged it for London, all talking at once.

As they neared the city, the road was crowded with people who like themselves had been attracted by the flames or by reports of the fire: curious people seeking excitement; workmen seeking the employment which an emergency creates; anxious people with friends or relatives in the burning district; and a riffraff of loafers and petty thieves seeking whatever their vulture claws could snatch. And even now, though the fire was still confined to Thames side, refugees were beginning to come. No one as yet realized the extent of the disaster, and the evacuation had not yet become a flight, but the homeless who had friends outside the city to whom they might go for shelter were on their way, carrying whatever they had been able to save, in bundles, wheelbarrows, or carts.

The boys' eager questions brought little information. Tomorrow and the rest of their lives the Londoners would recount their tale of adventure. Tonight they were like cattle driven before the storm: dumb, inarticulate, grunting and groaning as they struggled under their loads.

Above the wall, the towers and church spires, their stone faces blanched a ghastly white, reflected the fire in an intense light, each steeple standing like a white lamp and flashing back its signal of dismay. London, which only yesterday had been the throbbing heart of the great English nation, had become a city of despair.

Inside Bishopsgate the crowd became thicker each minute, and in the background, down the hill and as far west as the eye could see, was fire.

Crooks suddenly took command.

"Hey, fellows, come on!" he yelled. "We can pull down houses as well as any! Come on!"

He went galloping down the street to the nearest church, with little Delavan close behind him. They darted in at the open door and in a minute were back again with one of the long fire hooks. In another minute they had the hook over the cornice of a burning house.

The other boys caught hold and, swinging their bodies to keep time to a sailors' chantey, threw their combined weight to pull the house down. The frail wattle and daub construction offered little resistance and a few minutes' work brought the front wall down with a crash. The other walls came too, and soon the rickety house was a smoking pile of brick and clay.

Samuel and Drew found buckets and carried water from a cistern to keep the fire from spreading.

But another house was blazing, and as the roof fell the burning thatch was scattered by the wind, setting fire to two or three more.

Now flames were climbing Gracechurch Street; they had licked up everything south of Cannon Street, which topped the steep ascent rising from the Bridge, and their heat was already driving the merchants out of Lombard Street, where only a few hours before many had placed their goods for safekeeping.

Until now, to Samuel, the fire had been only a spectacle; but in Lombard Street was his father's old shop, and just around the corner, in a little crooked lane, the house where he was born, and the churchyard where his baby sisters and little Martin lay. With a sudden cry that was less a shout than a sob, Samuel rushed crazily down Lombard Street, pushing people right and left, ducking and diving between them, jumping over bundles and barrows, to reach and save before it was too late the little spot of London that had been his own.

But his father's shop was dark and deserted. The clerks and the prentices had already removed what they could and abandoned the rest to the oncoming flames. As Samuel paused before the door, which in the hasty flight had been left open, the bell tower of old St. Stephen's broke into flames. The shop door, swinging in the wind, filled the boy with desolation and panic. His London was doomed. In his excitement he had cut and run from his schoolmates. He was alone in the city of flaming death.

What happened after that was only a recollection, confused and blurred, of an eternity of wandering up and down crooked, cobbled, crowded streets filled with struggling, cursing, weeping humanity with carts, barrows, stretchers, and cots, all bearing their burden of calamity, like scenes in a nightmare.

And as in a nightmare, the boy was powerless to leave. The fire gripped and held him in a horrid enchantment. It seemed that there was nothing in all the world but fire and smoke and terror and suffering. There was no peaceful countryside; no shining sun; no cooling shade—only a hot hell of flame in which the damned must wander eternally.

There was a stretcher on which a woman in labor moaned and writhed in her torment; there was a man, old and blind, feeling his way along the walls, not knowing whether he was going toward the fire or away from it; there were flights of pigeons driven from their cots in the church towers, yet refusing to leave, circling about till the flames scorched their wings and they came fluttering down to be trampled under the feet of the fleeing mob; there was a plump pig lying roasted where the fire had caught him; there were, it seemed to Samuel, thousands of people, all loaded with goods, struggling along with no plan or aim except to flee from the pursuing flames.

A fine gentleman rode up shouting, "Make way, folks. Make way!" He was shouting at my lord mayor above the din.

"The king commands you spare no houses. Pull 'em down before the fire every way. The duke bids me tell you if you want more soldiers you shall have 'em. Take the long fire hooks out of the churches where they are stored, and pull down houses!"

And my lord mayor with a handkercher about his neck, cried like a fainting woman:

"Lord, what can I do? I am spent; people will not obey me. I have been pulling down houses but the fire comes on faster than we can do it."

"D'ye need more soldiers?"

The mayor waved his arms and wailed:

"No! They can do nothing. I've been up all night. Oh, I'm spent, I'm spent. I must go home."

People kept thrusting bundles or babies or boxes into Samuel's arms, begging his help and promising shillings or pounds or the good God's blessing as reward. Sometimes they remembered to pay him when their destination was reached. His pockets were soon jingling with small coins.

Pickpockets systematically filched purses up one street and down another; and ruffians bargained to carry goods and then ran off with them. Householders ran about shouting, "Forty pounds for a cart! Any money for a cart!" and in the end gave the carter a shilling and a curse.

There was a gallant fine gentleman on a great black horse, who liked to fight fires for the excitement of it. The crowd hailed him joyfully:

"Lord Craven! Lord Craven! God love 'im! 'E's fought so many fires 'is 'orse neighs an' snorts an' like to kick the stable down when the fire bells ring!"

Samuel saw an old woman scuttling along with her apron full of downy white chickens, when she was set upon and mauled by a crowd who mistook the little fluffy chicks for fireballs.

There was a report that four thousand Frenchmen and papists were about the city in arms, at which new terror the citizens forgot the fire and the inhabitants of a whole street would run in a great tumult one way, upon the rumor that the French were marching at the other end of it.

Almost more frightful than the fire itself was the roar of its burning like the noise of a whirlwind, and the crash of houses as they tumbled, tumbled, tumbled, from one end of the town to the other. Over all was the ever-thickening cloud of yellow smoke.

But most thrilling of all to Samuel Parris was the half hour when he had held the king's horse while his royal Majesty stood up to his ankles in water under the lee of a tottering wall near Cripplegate, fighting the flames with his own kingly hands—a king whom the courtiers at Whitehall had never seen.

Samuel did not recognize him when he rode up, his gorgeous velvet costume dripping with mud and dirt; his hot face smutty with fire dust and smeared with sweat. But he was still alert and tireless—a man in his own right, a king of the olden time, leading his army into battle.

He sprang from the saddle at Samuel's very side: "Canst hold a horse, my lad?" At the boy's eager assent, he threw him the bridle.

When the fire had given ground before the royal assault and the citizens had taken heart and were passing the buckets in a steady line, the king swung into the saddle again and, from a pouch hung on his shoulder, with his own hand scattered golden guineas among the fire fighters.

Perhaps it was because Samuel was so close beside him, perhaps it was the boy's ardent eyes: with his own hand he pressed the coin into Samuel's grubby palm!

"My charger's thanks and mine!" he laughed. He wheeled his horse and rode away—and Samuel's heart beat high with pride and loyalty for England and his king. He thrust the coin into the inside pocket of his jacket and buttoned it close.

"I'll keep it always," he vowed. "As long as I live!"

He pushed eastward toward Moorgate, away from the flames which still pursued. He had seen enough of fire and his eyes burned with smoke. He elbowed through the crowd, intent only on getting through the gate into the open fields beyond the wall.

He had lost count of time. Night and day were little different under the firelit sky. He squinted upward through the smoke. Was that the sun or the moon glowering red in the western sky? His smarting eyes could not be sure.

He had been in the city since Sunday night; snatching food and sleep when and where he could, kept going by the excitement, held in thrall by the terror. Now he was on his way out with no thought in his dulled brain except the goal of safety beyond London Wall.

He ducked into a little crooked lane that he remembered. It would put him ahead of the crowd in the main thoroughfare. A little wooden gate caught his attention—a little swinging gate with a narrow footpath leading back from the street. As he was hurrying by, a girl came running down the path and caught his arm.

"Come help me!" she cried above the roar of the fire. "My mother is sick and helpless—we must save her."

She almost dragged him with her up the path into a tiny crooked garden tucked behind the houses. At the left an open door led into a shadowy room, lighted only by the glow of the copper sky.

The girl darted into the little room, still holding Samuel's hand. A tiny gray-haired woman lay on a couch, fully dressed even to her coat and bonnet, ready to go as soon as God should provide the way. She smiled up at him: "Elizabeth said God would send help, and so He did!"

"Can we carry her, think you?" the girl panted. "Oh, we can! We must!"

"Of course, we can carry her. I'll show you." He quickly wove his hands and hers together and bending down showed the little woman how to put her arms around their necks and sit in the "queen's chair."

"Here we go! Grip tight on my wrists, Elizabeth, and keep close to me in the crowd. Keep your mouth shut and hold your breath if the smoke gets thick."

Even a tiny woman is heavy to carry and the press of people in the streets made the going hard and slow. Every now and then they had to stop and set the mother down on a low wall or a wide window ledge while they got their breath and coaxed the blood back into their benumbed wrists.

In a few words Elizabeth told how her father, who was old and feeble, had gone to seek help and how she had stood in the doorway waiting and praying for him to return with aid. All of a sudden she had felt an answer to her prayer and had run down the path.

"And you were the answer!" she said, her eyes bright with tears. "It was a miracle!"

Samuel rather fancied himself as a miracle, but he said:

"Pooh! I was only taking a short cut to Moorgate."

"That is where we must go," Elizabeth said. "When Father left we agreed that if any way of rescue offered, we would go there, and Father would come too."

Moorgate was almost impassable. People were crowding into

the city as well as out, and all burdened with goods. Among them were so many carts and drags and wheelbarrows and cows and horses that it took long waiting before they could push through. When at last they came into the fair wide spaces of Lower Moorfields, they found the fields blackened with fire dust and dotted with pitiful heaps of salvage—the ill-considered litter of treasures and trash which the frightened townspeople carried with them when forced to forsake their homes.

Beside the forlorn heaps, dirty and disheveled men, women, and children kept guard over their possessions. Rich and poor, cultured and ignorant, virtuous and vile huddled together, eying each other suspiciously, like stray dogs guarding their bones. The well-to-do who had never missed a good meal and the poor who seldom had a full one lay down together in misery and woke to bitter remembrance.

But there was safety beyond the Great Wall, and though the fire still burned bright inside Cripplegate and another blaze reddened the sky above Fleet Street and the Temple, the overhanging pall of smoke had dulled from red to gray, and there was darkness over the city which had known no night for four glaring days.

After the heat of the city, the evening breeze was cool with the first chill of autumn. The little old lady lay on the grass wrapped in her cloak and with only her bonnet for pillow, while Samuel on one side and Elizabeth on the other snuggled close to keep her warm, as the dark came softly down over Moorfields.

A peddler boy came by with his singsong cry.

"Here, boy," Samuel called, "let's see your wares."

The lad held up a sample. "Thick fresh beef 'twixt two slabs o' bread. Sixpence apiece, sir."

Samuel licked his lips. "Give me three."

Elizabeth said, "If only we could get some milk for Mother."

The boy spoke quickly.

"We've a cow. If you'll go with me I'll sell you milk—as soon as my sandwiches are gone. I'm Daniel Hawley. I live in St. Giles Cripplegate only a few squares away."

He was back in almost no time with his sandwiches sold. As they walked westward, he looked at Samuel's uniform.

"You're in a school?"

"Morton's Academy at Newington Green."

"You don't say!" The voice was almost reverent. "I've heard tell o' Morton's. I'm going there someday."

Samuel glanced sidewise at the boy under the flare of a lantern. A common-looking boy with a sharp nose and chin and a big mole near his mouth.

" 'Tis a school for gentlemen's sons," Samuel said.

Daniel nodded. "That's why I want to go. Wait a minute and I'll fetch your milk." He ducked into a shabby little tallow chandler's shop and came back with a Toby jug brimming with milk. Then as Samuel turned away he ran after him to ask his name. Samuel told him.

"What does your father do?" Daniel asked.

Samuel flourished a bit. "My father has a great plantation in Barbados with blackamoors for slaves. And he has a mammoth great warehouse in Thames side."

Daniel shrugged. "What he may have in the Indies, I dunno —but whatever were in Thames side is gone up in smoke. I wouldn't give you a crooked sixpence for the whole cargo."

Then, seeing the downcast look on Samuel's face, he changed his tone.

"I'll fetch you more milk in the morning for the sick lady, if you want. But bring the jug back. It must be awful to have your things all burnt up. God stopped the fire before it got to us. Last year the plague was all about us, but my father closed up his shop and we shut ourselves in upstairs and prayed—and we were spared."

Samuel turned away abruptly and tramped back to Moorfields with his jug of milk. God had spared that woman in the tallow chandler's shop and robbed him of his precious mother!

Soon after daybreak, Elizabeth's father found his family. Tears streamed down his haggard face as he hugged first one and then the other and then both at once, while all three laughed and cried together.

Then Elizabeth drew Samuel into the circle to be praised and thanked and wept over. He had not thought much about his part in the rescue. He had helped where help was needed just as he had many times in those dreadful days of fire. But when he heard the story from Elizabeth's lips, he felt at least two inches taller. He wished the boys at Morton's could hear—the older boys who were always snubbing and belittling him!

But all he said was "Pooh! I just happened to come along in time."

Elizabeth insisted solemnly: "It didn't just happen, dear boy! God sent you when I prayed!"

Mrs. Morton was anxious and worried, for Samuel was one of the last to return to the academy.

Three of the older boys had sought out Morton and spent the days with him, fighting to save his property. But in spite of their combined efforts, his losses were heavy. However, his pupils had come back with a new love and respect for their master. They had seen him facing danger and disaster, and coming through the ordeal without complaint or bitterness.

On Saturday afternoon Samuel went back to the camp at Moorfields. But he searched in vain for Elizabeth and her family.

Now that it was too late, he realized that he knew nothing about the girl except her baptismal name, and that her father was dressed in a shabby coat of the kind worn by Puritan ministers. He went back through the desolated streets, clambering over debris and skirting spots still smoking hot; but the little gate was gone and the whole neighborhood lay in such a tangled mass of wreckage that he had no idea where the shabby houses with the narrow path between them had been.

The girl had gone out of his life as suddenly as she had come into it and there was no way to follow or find her. But his heart still quickened as her words came back to him: "You were the answer!"

She was older than he by several years—she must be—yet it was he who had led and she who had followed, never questioning his strength or his judgment. In the first stern test of manhood he had been master of the situation.

The stories of the boys' experiences were many and vivid, with every lad his own hero and his own chronicler. Samuel did his share of boasting. His tale of his service to the king was greeted with jeering laughter, until he produced his new-minted guinea as evidence. After this, he felt that he had gained standing among his mates.

But of the rescue of Elizabeth and her mother he said no word, though he knew well enough that such an acquaintance with a girl would do more to establish his equality with the older fellows than anything else. Especially as several lads had told of more or less amorous or adventurous encounters. But even for such coveted prestige he could not tell the story. He would never see Elizabeth again, he mourned, but he would cherish her memory as long as he lived.

The idea intrigued his imagination and he pictured himself as living the lonely life of a bachelor, yet remaining always loyal to his beloved Elizabeth. He thought of Andrew Marvell, who had never married, and wondered sentimentally if he, too, had loved and lost a sweetheart.

Words which Marvell had spoken in those dreadful days at Highgate Hill after Anne's passing came into his mind. "I, too, loved your mother, my lad, and I miss her sore." The boy's own experience gave the words new meaning. Did Mr. Marvell mean—that?

For the first time in his life he thought of his mother as a flesh and blood woman. The idea shocked and fascinated him. Mr. Marvell and his mother—his mother and Mr. Marvell—and in the far-off Magic Island, his father. He heard Aunt Susanna saying, "Better come along with me, Anne. A man needs a wife to keep him steady." Was it a warning? Was there somewhere a hidden romance?

Then, too, there was that morning when his mother came galloping home alone and went straight to her room without answering his curious questions about Mr. Marvell. Had they quarreled? He resolved that next time he spent Sunday with Andrew Marvell he would draw him out on these matters; but when the time came he found no words to suit his purpose and his questions remained unasked. Instead, he coaxed Marvell to tell him the story of the underground passage between his cottage and Cromwell House across the road, and the use it was put to in the troubled days of the Commonwealth. In the excitement of exploring the cobwebby caverns of the moldy cellar with its bricked-up door Samuel forgot the secret romances of his elders.

7

Dream and Dew

There is a lady sweet and kind,
Has never face so pleased my mind,
I did but see her passing by,
And yet I love her till I die.

Her gesture, motion, and her smiles,
Her wit, her voice, my heart beguiles,
Beguiles my heart, I know not why,
And yet I love her till I die.

—BARNABE GOOGE.

SAMUEL lay flat on his back on a bench by the postern gate, holding a Greek Grammar above his head while he rhythmically conjugated the verbs in the next day's lesson. Once in a while, by way of emphasis, he swung a leg up and down or sidewise in time to the rhythm.

A whistle at the gate brought him to his feet. A laughing brown face peered at him through the wicket.

"Hello! Daniel Hawley, I do declare!" Samuel smiled as he went toward the gate.

"Sh! Not so much noise! I have a letter here for you, which by rights I ought to deliver to the master first. But it may be a love letter for aught I know—"

Samuel felt his face growing red. He reached over the gate and grabbed the letter, and almost tore it as he ripped off the envelope.

Deare Samuel. Wee are going awaye—to Southampton where we have friends, if haply Mother can beare soe much travaile. She's been extreme ill but is mending, and verie cheerly at hopes of a roofe an bed again. Wee are not destitute as some, Thank God. A littel monye an goodes wch Father buryed are saved.

I'm sendin a littel token of oure love an gratitude. 'Twere my

Grandsire's—Stephen Pern—a goode man who ne'er set his hand to aught but Truth.

God keepe you all waies in his care.

Elizabeth Wray.

The token was a modest seal ring of silver bearing the monogram: S.P. It was too large for Samuel's little finger. He slipped it on his middle finger and held it out for Daniel's admiration.

"Where did you get this?" he asked, his voice shaky with excitement. "Did she bring it herself?"

Daniel grinned again.

"Naw. The old man fetched it to the shop. He said to put it in Mr. Morton's hands—to give to you. But, thinks I, where's the good o' that? If it's yours, it's yours, ain't it? So why go 'round Robin Hood's barn?"

"Why, indeed!" echoed Samuel. He swaggered a little. "It's my letter, and no concern of the master's. Not that there's any secret about it, of course."

Daniel agreed. "That's it exactly. And as Mr. Morton's nothing to me and you be sort of a friend, I'm glad to favor you—even though he'd have give me a sixpence, likely. Course by rights I should've given it to him, he being the master, and I wantin' to keep in his good graces, since I figure on bein' his scholar—"

Samuel's hand went into his pocket. He fished out thruppence for Hawley, who sniffed at it in disdain and tried to bite it between his teeth. Samuel turned and read his letter again, ignoring the tallow chandler's son who went off down the road, whistling and clinking the coins together in his pocket.

There was a sly flattery in Daniel's suggestion of an affaire de cœur and, though Samuel had wit enough to know that it was nothing more than boyish teasing, he was not at all displeased. The letter (which, of course, must not get into Mr. Morton's hands) added a touch of intrigue. He hid the missive carefully in his traveling box—tucked between the pages of *The Witch of Edmonton*.

He wrote several letters in answer but none of them seemed to be just right, and he did not have a chance to send them anyway. Before the fire there were the Duke of York's postriders who carried mail between the great cities; but now all such service was upset and the posthouse burned; and he did not know anybody who would be going to Southampton or whom he could trust with a letter. Someday, he thought, he would go and look up Elizabeth for himself.

As the months went by the memory of Elizabeth faded, as the memory of his mother had faded, and its unreality gave it new beauty and charm. So that each passing month and year made his Elizabeth more beautiful, more lovable, more perfect. No longer did he picture her face as he had seen it: drawn with worry and weariness; streaked with fire dust and sweat as she struggled along the crowded streets under her mother's weight. In the magic mirror of memory it merged and blended with another picture: the angel in the chancel window in St. Mary Islington: fair and calm and radiant with a halo of golden hair.

But for the most part he was too busy for daydreams—Mr. Morton knew boys well enough to see to that. The days were full of activities and the evenings had to be spent in study if one was to be ready for the morrow's recitation. He had a double incentive for work. He wanted to distinguish himself by his scholarship; but more than that he did not want to fail in his studies and be forced to leave the academy and become a prentice in his father's business.

Timothy Drew laughed at him. "You haven't much to worry about, Parris. If I had a rich father and a sugar plantation ready to drop in my lap I'd not work myself into a lather. I know a lad whose uncle went to the Indies, and from the stories he tells, a planter lives like a sultan or somebody like that—slaves at his beck and call and nothing to do but sit around in his shirt and sip brandy and rum—and an ebony Venus to lie with whenever he crooks his finger. Even when they go hunting, the way he tells it, they have a black boy to carry the guns and some more to tote chairs and hammocks. Lord, what a life!"

Drew's picture of soft living in the tropics awakened no response in Parris. Owning a sugar plantation might be well enough —though his father's letters had not been too alluring—but between him and such a life there stretched bleak and uninviting the years of prenticeship. He knew something about prentices and there was no romance and no glory about them.

The spring term brought Daniel Hawley, the tallow chandler's son—but his social station had undergone a change. In the sudden increased demand which came after the fire, the shops which had been spared reaped a harvest, and the elder Hawley had now enough capital to leave the chandler's trade and set up as a butcher—a much more profitable business.

Young Daniel had good money in his pockets and good clothes on his back. But Parris was not too well pleased when he found that Daniel was to room with him and Drew. However, the academy was filling up (there were forty students now) and there was plenty of room for three in the big bedchamber. The new boy was bright and teachable and of such a friendly and easygoing temper that Parris soon began to like him in spite of himself.

He soon found that Hawley was a match for any of them in intellect and wit. And after lessons were done and the boys were gathered around the hearth, he would regale them with such tales as they had never heard.

"He's an awful liar," Parris said to Drew, "but you can't catch him at it. Part of what he says is true and part is whopping big lies—you know that, but to save your life you can't tell which from t'other."

"Maybe it doesn't matter," Drew said, "so long as 'tis a first-rate tale. I get so excited when he's telling it that I swallow it whole, and afterwards I think likely 'twas all made up. But the funny thing about it is, I don't care."

8

The Maypole

It was a pleasant sight to see
A little village company
Drawn out upon the first of May
To have their annual holyday:
The pole hung round with garlands gay,
The young one's footing it away;
The aged cheering their old souls
With recollections and their bowls,
Or, on the mirth and dancing failing,
Then ofttimes told old tales re-taleing.

—HONE.

THE SPRING before Samuel was fifteen, there was to be a Maypole at Tottenham, only two miles north of Newington Green; and Samuel was wild to go, though he well knew it was a sin. During the Reign of the Saints, the old Maypoles had been cut down. The new generation growing up had never seen one and the oldsters had lost much of their zest for such frolics. The Restoration brought back the May-day festivities in London, for by royal order a pole so large that it had to be made in two sections at the royal shipyards was taken by barge up the Thames and hoisted into place in the Strand by seamen with navy block and tackle. But this was as much by way of being a declaration of independence as for love of sport. The Tottenham pole, however, was a return of the old village spirit; a community affair of processional and folk dancing, a revival of the old customs of England.

There had been hot discussions of the matter at the academy, for among the students there were both Puritans and Anglicans as well as several lighter-minded Cavaliers who did not take their religion too seriously. Even among the Puritan faction there was a difference of opinion, some stanchly holding that the only procedure was to follow the Scripture admonition to touch not the evil thing, avoid it, pass not by it, turn from it and pass away; while Hawley and Drew argued that, as preachers to be, they should view the evil in order that they might be better fitted to understand and cope with it.

Samuel was strongly inclined to the latter view: he had never seen a Maypole and therefore had only hearsay evidence against it. How could he someday preach earnestly and eloquently against an abomination which he had never seen; or warn the lambs of his future flock against temptations which he had never felt? But the stricter opinion prevailed, Morton having thrown the weight of his counsel that way, and the vote of the school was to give no countenance to the garish affair under penalty of a good caning for any rebel who broke the law.

The minority did not accept this ruling gracefully; and Samuel soon learned of the plan Crooks and Delavan were ringleaders of, to break the rule. They didn't seem very anxious to have Samuel come along with them this time, but he soon won his way by writing two themes for Crooks and an oration for Delavan, and doing the further service of stealing a rope ladder from the stables by means of which they could climb down from the first-story windows.

Delavan insisted that Samuel should wear a green serge suit of his. "We don't want to go in our uniforms and get reported, and you can't have any fun in those sad Puritan duds of yours," he argued. "We want no spoilsport trailing with us. When in Rome, you know."

And Samuel, who disliked being conspicuous, readily assented, feeling pleased and self-conscious in his borrowed finery.

Some of the conspirators backed out at the last for fear of future punishment, but Samuel quite agreed with Crooks and Delavan that the adventure was worth a caning. Shortly after midnight the three let themselves out of the postern gate and stealthily dodged from tree to tree along the winding path leading north to the old church and thence through the lych gate into the churchyard. Among the black spires of the evergreens, the gravestones leaned drunkenly this way and that. Above them, the bell in the tower swayed lazily in the breeze, making no sound.

There was a round golden moon just rising over the eastern

horizon, but it was pitch-black underfoot and the moonlight served only to cast long black shadows across their path.

Frogs croaked in the marshy hollows, and far off to the east somewhere in Epping Forest a fox barked. On a near-by hill a dog howled his dismal protest at the rising moon.

Nobody seemed to want to talk. Delavan essayed a jest or two but his voice sounded too loud, like shouting down a well, and Crooks whispered, "Sh-h-h!"

They struck into Seven Sisters Road, leading crookedly to the northeast, past the ancient public house with its creaking sign of the Seven Sisters and the circle of elms in front which gave the place its name—planted seven in a circle with a walnut tree in the middle. Crooks said a martyr had been burnt on the spot where the ancient walnut stood.

It was not so lonesome now. From every crossroad little groups of youths and maidens hurried toward Tottenham. They were in holiday attire and some carried baskets for gathering flowers and some wore gay kerchiefs and ribbons and streamers and garlands of blossoms. The youths carried hand axes or knives to cut boughs. Everybody was talking and laughing now, and shouting quips and snatches of song. A gay party from the hollow way came up behind in a jolting cart, singing lustily:

> "Let us be seen in Tot'nam Greene
> To dance for the honor of Holloway.
>   Since we are come hither
>   We'll spare no leather
> To dance for the honor of Holloway."

The moon lifted her bright face above the treetops to see what all the noise was about and winked slyly, as if she had seen many such a procession in the gay days of her youth, and knew well enough what these earth-children were up to.

The village green at Tottenham was thick with people crowded around a great wain, to which were harnessed all the oxen of the neighborhood (forty yoke, somebody said) every one with his coat brushed sleek and shining and his horns scraped and polished and hung with bunches of posies. At one side of the three-cornered green, where Samuel stood, the Ancient Cross looked solemnly down on the festive scene as it had looked on nobody knows how many such May Days. The cross was but a remnant now, blackened and worn by age and weather and worms. Its crossbeam had been torn off during the Reformation, so that it was now nothing but a high wooden pillar supported by four great spurs.

A creepy little shudder ran down Samuel's spine and involuntarily he shrank away from the ruin. But in the same moment he remembered that it was a papist superstition to reverence the cross and make of it an idol, when it was only a pillar of wood, having neither virtue nor power, whether for good or for ill. This being so, it did not matter at all, of course, where he stood— so he went on across the green to the other side.

From the George and Vulture Tavern, the musicians were coming now, and the morris dancers all dressed in gay costumes like Elizabethan peasants on a holiday, with feathers in their hats and ruffs around their necks and their full sleeves tied with ribbons sewn with little bells and their stockings and shoes jingling with bells likewise. Here they came as if they had stepped out of a picture book, Robin Hood and Friar Tuck and Maid Marian (with the feet of a man), Scarlet and Little John and Tom the Piper and the prancing Hobbyhorse and the Tom Fool with a cow's tail and a bladder to keep the crowd away and a big brass cowbell hung on his backside.

As everybody cheered wildly, the musicians (who to Samuel's surprise were old men) struck up with pipe and tabor (or whittle and dub, as the countryfolk would say) and led the way out of the village into the woods and up to the highest hilltop to greet the sun on the first day of May. The pipes shrilled a piercing call, and the tabors under the punishment of their single sticks rumbled their rub-a-dub-dub; but the tune that the old men played was not of earth or heaven, and the path that the youths and maidens followed by the light of the yellow moon was far longer than they knew, for it was the old forgotten path to Long Ago.

Samuel Parris, Puritan, who had come to look on and censure this frolic which his sober-minded upbringing condemned as foolish clowning, found his long limbs swinging to the rhythm of the music—music so beautiful and weird that it brought to his mind a legend he had heard somewhere that morris dancing had been taken away from the fairies.

His heart beat high with a strange excitement and there swept over him that uncanny thrill which he had known before, as if somewhere he had heard this music and followed it, long, long ago. Whither it had led he did not know, only that it would bring him to a familiar place and that wherever it led he must follow—there could be no turning back.

The hill was growing steeper and the whittle and dub were changing to a measure slow and solemn. Beside these young folks with their eager stride and smiling eyes, it seemed there marched in slow processional a dim host led by bards, Druid priests, and prophets—climbing to the hilltop for the May-day Festival of Beltane.

When the gay procession finally reached the hilltop, they saw before them a great flat stone in the center of a clearing. At the head of the stone stood the fairest maiden of the village, robed in white and decked with garlands, the Queen of the May. At the foot of the stone was a large heap of pine boughs and bark, trimmed from the tree which had been cut for the Maypole. Just as the sun rose majestically out of the east, the King of the May strode forward and thrust a blazing torch of pitch deep into the heap of boughs. The flames leaped, the music changed and quickened; the dancers leaped and frolicked around the fire.

But the huge stone lay bare and empty in the morning light. The Sun God looked down and veiled his face in mist. It had not been thus in the days of old before the Roman galleys brought the Cross to Britain! The Sun God hid his face, remembering the maidens of that older time, who had knelt trembling before the Druid priest and crimsoned the stone with their blood so that the crops and the calves and the children might grow tall and strong. So it had been in the old days, when through forgotten ages, Baal the Sun God, by the light of his countenance had kindled the Sacred Fire on the crimson stone, while the dancers leaped high in wild joy at the appearance of the source of life and light, blessing their sacrifice. The Sacred Fire meant nothing to these English: they had even forgotten what the stone was for, and the dance of Beltane, which once had brought fertility to man and beast and field, was now become a sport for mummers.

> Skip it and trip it, nimbly, nimbly,
> Tickle it, tickle it lustily,

> Strike up the tabor for the wenches favor,
> Tickle it, tickle it lustily.

The dance ended; and with much grunting and straining, the great pine tree, stripped of branches and bark, was loaded on the wain and the oxen started down the hill, the minstrels following.

Behind them the Queen of the May, robed in white, walked alone, attended at a little distance by her maids of honor carrying garlands of flowers and gay-colored streamers. Behind them came the morris dancers, and after them the crowd, pell-mell.

So they romped down the hill, boys and girls together, cutting huge branches of flowers or gathering bundles of rushes; pelting each other with blossoms; tagging and kissing; racing and chasing and screaming with laughter. A pretty lass snatched Samuel's cap and ran with it down a little ravine. But he came hotfoot after her, leaping over bushes and briers, stumbling over stones, till just as he reached for her, she stumbled and fell, and twisting like a cat to land on her side, she flung out a foot. He tripped over it and fell almost on top of her, their panting bodies close together, gasping for breath. Before he knew it he was kissing her; planting breathless ill-directed boyish smacks on her hot red cheeks, her tousled hair, her open laughing mouth, as she playfully beat him off with her fists, and shrieked for help. There was a gleeful halloo from the rear, and a pack of pursuers was upon them, with Delavan and Crooks in the lead.

"Ho, ho, ho, for our pious Roundhead!! Buss her good, Parris! Give her plenty!!"

The girl, still screaming with laughter, ran off through the underbrush as Samuel scrambled to his feet. His face was flaming but he had wit enough not to attempt an apology. He forced a laugh and brushed the fern and moss from his clothes.

"'Twas that confounded suit of yours, Delavan! 'Twas so 'customed to wenching I swear it ran off with me at sight of a tempting lass!"

The laugh was turned on Delavan, not at all to his displeasure. "I wouldn't put it past the suit!" he laughed.

The whole village came out to meet the Mayers, and when the pole was planted in the center of the Green, its top crowned with a gay bunch of ribbons, the ceremony of winding the Maypole began. The whittle and dub struck up a lively measure, and every lucky young one who could catch a streaming ribbon, joined in the dance; the lads going one way, the lasses the other, weaving in and out to form the pattern on the pole.

Samuel seized a ribbon, his nimble feet caught the rhythm, and his voice, which had lately changed from the clear treble of childhood to a more or less undependable baritone, took up the song.

> We've been a-rambling all the night,
>   And sometime of this day;
> And now returning back again,
>   We bring a garland gay.
>
> The cuckoo sings in April,
>   The cuckoo sings in May
> The cuckoo sings in June,
>   In July she flies away.
>
> Now take a Bible in your hand,
>   And read a chapter through;
> And when the Day of Judgment comes
>   The Lord will think of you.

There was plenty to eat and more than enough to drink and everybody was very gay. After the excitement was over, Samuel would repent his levity. Today he had no scruples, no conscience, no mind of his own. The spirit of youth was in him and held him spellbound. Free from the quibbles of Good and Evil, for this one day he reveled in the excitement of living with pure pagan wantonness. He had never been so happy in his life. Neither the immediate prospect of a caning nor the far-off Day of Judgment worried him at all.

The smart of the caning was soon over, and Samuel held his handsome head a bit pridefully among his mates who had tamely submitted to rules and missed a gay frolic and a rich experience. He had held a wench in his arms, he had known the thrill of the Maypole dance, that Puritan bugaboo; and he did not feel nearly so wicked as he should—only daring and debonair. Now he could rebuke Sin and know what he was talking about.

He thought of what might have happened if Crooks and Delavan had not been so close behind him. The lass had fought him off, but her mouth was ready for his kisses—hot and wet— Suppose he had held her—and nobody had seen—

But he had little time for romancing. Final examinations were only a few weeks off and everybody was studying hard. The classics and logic and science made jealous demands for every hour of the day and sent him to bed at night with a healthy weariness.

Only a few weeks now until he would graduate from his preparatory course and be ready to enter upon his divinity school lectures: his real goal.

His commencement oration was a sermon that many a pulpit orator in London might have envied; and his precious diploma bore the coveted words: *cum laude*.

Then in the brief holiday before the new term began, came a letter from his father—as thick a packet as he had ever received from Thomas Parris, who wrote only when he must and made each word count.

Samuel read the first paragraph. Then clutching the letter in his hand, he rushed upstairs, past his room and on to the little turret from which he had watched London burn, and shutting the door behind him, sat down on the dusty window seat. He spread the letter on his knee. It had been written six months before.

Deere Son,

I have now to tell you som onplesant bad newes. In a worde att end of this yere, you'll leave Mr. Morton his scool & bee put Prentice to my sometime valued Bro. Marcht. Mr. Wm. Felkin in Thames Side. Tho tis not fitte a Father giv his son whys & wherefores, yett tis my will to Quaint you with ye grounds for't.

1stly. My hevy losse by ye Greate Fire so cripled mee I'm £200 a worse man a Yere & Not Able to beare ye cost of so much Larnin.

2ndly. This yere bein onlye 2/3 crop, ye Lande wore out & somme Planters about to Quitte but I'll ne'er drown whilst I can Swim.

3rdly. Ye Shockin poore Estate of Puritan Prechers wch after all ye outlaye brings lyttel Honour & lesse Prophet.

4thly. Sartin Reeportes I like nott of Mr. M's loose Govt. of his Scollars wch has mayed his Scool a Nayword mongst Sober Minded Folkes. To leeve a Youth without Govt. is to Caste Him Off. Hee were as well Delivrd over to Satan.

5thly, & on ye other Hande. Ye Exellente Goode Future of Trade by Reeson of Greate Deemands for Goodes of All Sortes grown out of ye Fyre & ye Wealth & High Station of ye Marchts on wch

England deepends. Oure Royall Chas. Himselfe sayin ye Tradesmen bee ye Onelie Gentrey in England.

6thly. My Trustie Solicitor Mr. James Muggleton has found for you a Moste Fortunate Goode Openin in ye House of Mr. Felkin, where You'l gett Credit for Yr 3 yrs. Scoolin & Beginne as a Sr. Apprentice.

I can lay my Acct. on Mr. Felkin to give You such Stricte Watchcare & Correction as yr Years deemande, Hee bein Well Known for a Deevoute & Godlye Man & Stricte Puritan.

You'll Reeporte to Mr. Muggleton Suddenlie, who will Draw upp Yr Papers.

Yr. Affec. Fr.

THOS. PARRIS.

Iff you Proove Goode & Mannerlye You'll have ye Indulgence nott to Eat wth ye Other Servts. but to sitte att Yr. Master his Owne Table.

T. P.

Samuel read the letter through again slowly, looking for hope or comfort. He could find none. A father's word was law from which his minor child had no appeal. Even if Thomas Parris had been close at hand, there would be no shadow of turning once his word had gone out. But with twelve hundred leagues of ocean between them it was doubly hopeless.

A frenzy of helplessness seized the boy. He slumped to his knees and buried his face in his arms on the dusty window seat. After a while his tense nerves gave way and he began to sob.

There was a gentle knock on the door and Morton came in.

"I had a letter too, my son. May we weep together?"

His hand stroked the boy's shoulders. Samuel could not speak. He thrust the crumpled letter into the master's hand without a word. Then, remembering his father's disapproval of Morton's lenience, he would have snatched it back.

"Never mind, lad. Your father spoke his mind to me quite as frankly as he did to you, I'm sure. Thomas Parris is no backbiter. He says what he thinks, out and out, as is his right and his duty where your welfare is concerned."

Samuel's dark cheeks flushed angrily. "He's no right to blame you if some of the boys do things they shouldn't. 'Tis that old hypocrite lawyer, Muggleton, feeding him lies, about drunken and debauched pupils, when three fellows out of forty went to the

bullbaiting at Ball's Pond and drank too much lamb's wool. I
had no part in that, Mr. Morton, but I'm going to tell on myself
about another time.

" 'Twas that night when the crowd went out on Stamford Hill
and shouted through a speaking trumpet about the vicar of St.
Joseph's seducing Tom Cooper's moonstruck daughter. I was in
that scrape—and I lied to you, Mr. Morton—" He choked. "I'm
not sorry we did it—the old lecher deserved it—but I'm sorry
I lied to you."

"I'm glad you told me, lad. We'll both feel better about it.
Now let us read your letter."

He read silently. His firm hand tightened on Samuel's shoulder. "My son, you and I and all of us are in God's hands, and
the plans of the Almighty shall not fail. Commit thy way unto
the Lord, trust also in Him and He shall bring it to pass. But
remember, my son, it is God's Plan, not our own erring and
bewildered notions, which shall come to pass."

The master went down the turret stairs, leaving the door open
behind him. An enticing odor of pigeon pasty came from the
regions below. But Samuel sat staring at the dusty floor, his soul
full of bitterness.

So this was God's Plan: to snatch him back from his chosen
calling and put him somewhere in London as prentice to fetch
and carry and wheedle and flatter.

Bah! The very thought made him sick!

It was not fair after he had worked so hard at his studies.
More than once Mr. Morton had told him that he was a born
preacher, and Mr. Morton never praised fulsomely.

The words of Job came to him: He hath fenced up my way
that I cannot pass, and he hath set darkness in my paths.

He flung himself on his knees and challenged the Almighty:
"O God! Why? Why?"

But he had no need to ask: he knew why. Or if he didn't he
had only to recall the Scripture which Mr. Morton had read
once in chapel:

Blessed is the man that walketh not in the counsel of the ungodly,
nor standeth in the way of sinners, nor sitteth in the seat of the
scornful, but his delight is in the law of the Lord: . . . and whatsoever he doeth shall prosper. The ungodly are not so: but are like the

chaff which the wind driveth away. Therefore the ungodly shall not stand in the judgment, nor sinners in the congregation of the righteous. For the Lord knoweth the way of the righteous: but the way of the ungodly shall perish.

God's Plan would surely come to pass. But it was God's Plan that Samuel Parris should not stand in the congregation of the righteous as a minister of the Most High. God's voice had spoken!

9

Sam Parris, Prentice

Thou art in London—in that pleasant place
Where every kind of mischief's daily brewing.
—BYRON, *Don Juan.*

MR. JAMES MUGGLETON, Samuel's father's solicitor, having written the contract twice over on the single sheet of parchment before him, laid down his quill and carefully cut the two copies apart so as to leave a jagged or indented edge, thus making an Indenture. One copy he handed across the table to Mr. Wm. Felkin, party of the second part, and from the other he read slowly and clearly the provisions of the agreement.

Samuel Parris, on a bench against the wall, listened closely. The unfamiliar legal phrases puzzled him somewhat, but he got the sense of it.

"This Indenture Witnesseth: That Sam Parris—of his own voluntary will and with the consent of his father—hath put himself an apprentice to Wm. Felkin, Merchant, and shall serve his master truly and be of good moral conduct—taverns, inns and ale-houses he shall not haunt—at dice and cards he shall not play —he shall not use fornication with any woman—he shall not commit matrimony with any woman—he shall dress plainly with no laces velvets or other vanities—his shoes shall be tied in a style proper to his station—his hair shall be neatly trimmed not worn in curles nor ruffianly about his ears."

Mr. Felkin nodded his satisfaction. His new prentice passed his hand regretfully over the silky black locks which rippled over his shoulders. He had always been a Puritan; now he must literally become a "Roundhead"—that term of derision which the better class of Puritans had always resented. To have his hair cut around a bowl was the last indignity; it hurt his pride cruelly. He thought of the welded iron collar which the serfs had to wear in the olden time. But he said nothing. It would do no good.

Mr. Muggleton was reading the rest of the contract: what Mr. Felkin must do. Samuel didn't pay much attention. He knew about what a prentice might expect.

He set his hand to the parchments: "Sam Parris, 'Prentice," and took some satisfaction in his scriptlike signature which made the "Wm. Felkin, Mercht." just below it look like a schoolboy's scrawl.

"A fine clerkly hand," said Mr. Muggleton.

"Aye, 'tis well enough," admitted Mr. Felkin.

To Parris, the change from the seclusion of the surburban academy to the heart of the conglomerate, new-old city which was rising from the ruins was like being in another world. For the fire had destroyed ancient London—the London of his early childhood, which had still been the London of Shakespeare and Queen Elizabeth. The narrow, crooked streets were still pretty much the same (except here and there where a corner had been cut or a thoroughfare widened) but there were rows and rows of new houses—miles and miles of them—and the crazy wattle and daub exteriors had given place to brick, less picturesque but modern.

The graybeards croaked and saw just ahead of them the yawning gulf of a financial collapse; but the clang of hammers and chisels and mallets made constant din in their ears, for the new city was a-building.

All over London men sat together around the coffee tables dickering and bargaining. The goldsmiths were figuring ways to finance the new commerce, and the brokers were abroad in the land. Businessmen were beginning to think there might be something in this new idea of insurance against fire and shipwreck.

There was a newspaper which came out every once in a while—
sometimes two or three times a week. And on the back page a
few reckless merchants modestly suggested that they had goods
to sell. And now and then there were stories of merchants who
grew rich almost overnight and turned themselves into gentlemen
and indignantly denied that their hands had ever been soiled
by trade.

The fortunate opening to which Thomas Parris referred had
been made, it appeared, by the defalcations of the senior prentice,
who had robbed the House of Felkin of a sum approximating
thirty-two pounds six, most of which he had spent on a whore in
Whetstone Park before he was found out and hanged for it.
Mr. Felkin frequently told Samuel the sad story and admonished
him to shun loose women and keep his fingers out of the till,
and never to be in drink or to swear on pain of being immediately dismissed.

Mr. Felkin shook his bewigged head sadly. "Nowadays the
run o' prentices is just a crew of saucy boys and the chance of a
youth's proving good and towardly, as the world now goes, is a
hazardous one."

Yet he was well enough pleased with his new prentice. With
all his vulgarity, he had respect for "quality" and was quick to see
that Samuel's good looks and good manners would make him
popular with the better class of customers. As soon as the lad
learned the business, he would do well in the new venture: a
shop in the New Exchange in the Strand, well stocked with finery
to delight the ladies.

The indulgence of sitting at the master's table, which Thomas
Parris had craved for his son, proved a more or less question-
able privilege.

Mr. Felkin was a man of uncertain temper; by turns expansive
or surly, depending on the triumphs or trials which the day had
brought. The master's mood ruled the household.

His wife was a faded woman with a pasty complexion and
disappointed blue eyes. As a girl she must have had a windflower
prettiness, Samuel thought, and gossip said she brought Mr.
Felkin a handsome dower.

There was a son of nineteen who had his father's dapper sleek-
ness but seemed to lack the ambition and shrewdness that should
have gone with it; and a daughter who resembled her mother.

There was also the eldest prentice, a hatchet-faced youth in the last year of his term who was industriously courting the daughter with an obvious eye to a future partnership.

The other prentices, who ate belowstairs, resented Samuel's indulgences and regarded the civil speech and gentle manners which were native to him as an affectation and affront. Yet in spite of himself, Samuel found that he liked his new work—it was different and interesting, especially the shop at the New Exchange. In the mornings (before gentlefolk were abroad) he worked at the warehouse; in the afternoons and evenings he went to the Exchange. There was no better place in London to see the fine ladies and gentlemen of the court and fashionable society.

There was a lady who lived in Catherine Street who came often to the Exchange: a very beautiful lady with bright gold hair and red cheeks and lips like cherries. Mr. Felkin always waited on her himself to make sure that she had the best of everything. He explained that she was an important customer, and Samuel must be very careful to deliver her goods promptly and see that everything was to her liking.

She was very kind to the prentice boy, not making him wait on the steps or in the kitchen as many fine ladies did, but letting him sit in her parlor while she looked at the goods. Sometimes she was not satisfied with looking in her long mirror, but turning this way and that she would ask Parris:

"What think you? Ain't this scarf a shade too deep a blue? Don't it make my eyes look dull and pale?" Or, "Which suits my complexion best, this shawl or that?"

It was not always shawls and scarfs. Once she had him wait while she went into her bedroom (she called it a boudoir). Presently she came back without her dress to see if he thought the petticoats fitted snug enough over her rounded hips; and should they perhaps be a wee bit longer, not to show so much of her limbs?

Samuel felt his face getting red. He swallowed hard and tried to be nonchalant as he blurted out:

"I'm no dressmaker, ma'am, but I think they look beautiful—just as they be."

The lady laughed merrily and ran to him and rumpled his black curls and kissed him on both his flaming cheeks. Then she laughed some more because her kisses had left stains of rouge on his cheeks, which she had to wipe away with her perfumed handkercher.

"For what would Mr. Felkin say? Oh, dear me, what would Mr. Felkin say? But we won't tell him, will we, sweet boy? And what he don't know won't hurt him!"

Somehow Parris got out into the street but his cheeks were still burning hot. In his muddled head the words of King Solomon said themselves over and over: the strange woman which flattereth with her words—She had caught him and kissed him—a woman with the attire of an harlot, and subtle of heart. But the thing that frightened him most was not the woman. It was the vile thing within him that she had roused.

A few days later there was another errand to the lady in Catherine Street, and Mr. Felkin called Parris and gave him the order.

Parris drew back. "Please, Mr. Felkin, won't you send another boy? I'd rather not go there again."

Mr. Felkin was used to unquestioning obedience.

"I didn't ask you if you rather had or rather hadn't, did I? It's me as gives orders without anybody's rathers."

Parris hesitated. "I'm getting these laces ready for the Exchange, you know."

Mr. Felkin was impatient. "Jenkins can take care of the laces. The lady asked for you. It's about the stockings she talked to you about yesterday—the yellow silk ones."

Slowly Parris put away the laces. The lady had not talked about stockings yesterday. It was just a trick to bring him to her house again. She would try on the stockings and smooth the soft silk over her shapely legs and laugh at him as she had before. But she couldn't come it over him again like that. He knew her now. And he would be ready for her and act indifferent and man-of-the-worldly and show her he didn't care two straws for fancy women or their wanton tricks.

All the way to Catherine Street Parris was planning what he would say to her.

A little English maid with a round blank face let him in and seated him in a spindle-legged chair. Then she went away and left him. The room was stuffy with the scent of Virginia tobacco. The curtains were drawn and the only light came from tall candles. The new-fashioned French clock swung its pendulum and ticked the minutes away. The maid came back, her face as blank as before.

"Mistress Margot will see you now," she said. She led the way into the boudoir and went out, shutting the door behind her.

The golden-haired Margot was lying on a couch heaped with pillows. She rose with the swift grace of a cat and came toward him, her robe of black and gold brocade drawn close around her.

"You came, my pretty boy," she purred.

Samuel backed off, holding the box of stockings in front of him like a shield.

She pushed them away and laughed.

"Damn the stockings! You know what I want, pretty boy!"

She stretched out her arms. Her robe fell open and he saw her naked body, golden in the candlelight.

He turned and ran.

He was still panting with excitement when he reached the warehouse. He went straight to his master and held out the box.

"What's the matter?" Felkin asked. "Didn't she like the stockings?"

Samuel gulped. "She didn't want any stockings. I'll never go to her house any more, Mr. Felkin! I can't!"

Mr. Felkin's keen black eyes looked hard at Samuel. The new boy was not saucy or lazy. This was something else.

He spoke more kindly: "Why not? The lady's a good customer and she said a good word for you; said you was a mannerly boy with a pretty taste in colors."

Samuel looked miserable. "I'm sorry, sir. But I'm afraid to go there again—I'm afraid I'll break my contract."

"What contract?"

"My prentice contract, Mr. Felkin. That part about women, you know. I'm pretty green, I guess. I never had much to do with women—not fancy women. I s'pose I'll be all right when I get used to 'em—but just at first—I feel like a fool!"

Mr. Felkin interrupted: "Quit fiddling with your jacket buttons and look at me! Now out with it. What happened? Are you trying to tell me she played the whore with you?"

When his insistent quizzing had wormed the whole story out of the reluctant boy, he fell into a terrible rage, roaring and cursing at the top of his voice. But his anger was not because his new prentice had offended a customer and behaved like a silly child. Contrary to Samuel's expectations, it was the lady who bore the brunt of it.

He called her all the vile names he could think of and damned her six ways from Sunday for her ingratitude, till the boys in the outer room left their work to listen. Afterwards they badgered Samuel without mercy for his part in the affair and nicknamed him the Knave of Hearts.

"But stealin' the master's missy ain't the way to get rich," they told him.

Parris didn't mind the ragging so much. He had had an affair with a woman and he felt quite grown-up and worldly. But he was shocked that Mr. Felkin, his master and his father's valued friend, should break the Seventh Commandment, and that so flagrantly that even his prentices made a jest of it.

He would like to ask Daniel Hawley about it, if he could do it without betraying his own adventure. Daniel always had ideas about things. And there were many things about Mr. Felkin that his new prentice did not understand.

Mr. Felkin was always assuring his customers that "the seller is servant to the buyer," but when he made a shrewd trade he would chuckle and tell his clerks: "I bested him in that, but 'tis the rule of law: *caveat emptor*."

But for all Felkin's vulgarity and meanness, Samuel soon found that he knew his business thoroughly. Charles Morton had taught him many things, but it was from Felkin that he learned to adjust himself to his fellows.

"It is all one," Felkin would say. "The tradesman must be a hardy one: he must have no flesh and blood about him; no passions or resentment."

Samuel was somewhat disconcerted to find how closely this philosophy of merchandising was in line with the persuasive speech of the orator. He puzzled over it. Could it be that the sacred office of a minister was, after all, only a higher kind of salesmanship? It sounded almost blasphemous. But the busy days left scant time for philosophizing.

Samuel Parris, nearing the end of his sixteenth year, had never done a day's work in his life until he went prentice. But the working day of a prentice was from the spring of day until the fall of night. Felkin permitted no loafing. To Parris, the work was always interesting, but his fellow workers let him in for all the chaffing and jokes that the greenhorn in any trade must take. But Felkin gave him more and more responsibility and once Samuel heard him tell a customer:

"Aye, he's keen. The Parris blood will tell."

He was seldom sent on fool's errands any more, and he had learned to watch his change and keep a sharp lookout for bad money, and could no longer be fooled by the half crowns not worth sixpence, and the shillings not worth a penny, which were always put upon a raw youth by cunning tradesmen.

There was no law against passing worthless coins and some shrewd folk made a practice of carrying good money in one pocket and bad in another and proffering first the bad: paying no good money for anything if they could help it.

He was learning to write a plain brief business letter; and was fast developing a rapid running longhand more practical for trade letters than his academy script; and as soon as he learned the tradesman's lingo, his shorthand was useful.

Mr. Felkin was pushing him ahead.

"You must gain a judgment of wares of all sorts you're like to deal with; and a knowledge of their value; and keep books to show what gain is made and what loss if any.

"And you must learn to look into the goodness of goods and see the reason of things so that the boys in the warehouses can't bubble you as they did at first."

He had even been trusted once or twice to make up a sortable cargo for shipment to New England or Barbados: something of everything that may furnish the tradesmen there with parcels fit to fill their shops and invite their customers. And Mr. Felkin had looked over the assortment and found little fault, which from him was high praise.

One of these cargoes had gone to Boston in the Massachusetts Bay. Only a short while earlier Samuel had received a letter from Aunt Susanna. Her second husband, Jonathan Abbott, had died, and she had married Marvell's friend, Mr. John Oxenbridge, who was going to take her to Boston where he had been called to a pastorate. She must be there by this time.

Samuel was careful to include in his sortable cargo some things which he thought would take Aunt Susanna's eye: a piece of manua silk from Spitalfields and lace from Stony Stratford to trim it, and a warm riding-hood of English worsted camlet, made at Norwich.

He smiled at the idea. He must be sure to tell Andrew Marvell about the marriage the next time he saw him.

Daniel Hawley was sixteen and as tall as he ever would be, and his academic training had given him a general culture which put him ahead of the ordinary run of prentices. His master, Mr. Charles Tidrick, treated him more like a son than a servant, and he was soon keeping the books and bargaining with his master's customers.

The two boys were much more congenial than they had been at Morton's. Parris had lost much of his snobbishness and Hawley much of his vulgarity. Hawley had a passion for life and adventure, and a rare gift for making ordinary things extraordinary. He was a perfect companion for holiday jaunts or such sedate pleasures as the Lord's Day permitted, for anything from a cockfight to a sermon took on new zest if seen through his keen gray eyes.

Nor was he less shrewd in his judgment of practical matters. "Mr. Tidrick's a dissenter," he said, "but he don't let it get in the way of business. That's my idea too. No use losing a customer by too much argumentation."

Parris laughed. "When my father wrote that Mr. Felkin was a strict Puritan, he must have forgot that the fashion in religion has changed since he knew Mr. Felkin. He divides his trade in religion as well as in business. But I think it's a good thing. It gives us a chance to hear all the great preachers."

After the fire the Conventicle Act was almost forgotten for the time being. The zeal of the heretic was not slow to take advantage of such an opportunity and Puritanism throve with the tradesmen who were its main support. Before the ashes were cold, Nonconformists of every name were preaching, drawing morals from the fire as they had from the plague.

One Sunday Samuel heard a Puritan divine argue: "The fire could not have been occasioned by the sin of blasphemy, for in that case it would have begun at Billingsgate; nor lewdness, for then Drury Lane would have been first on fire; nor lying, for then the flames had reached the city from Westminster Hall.

No, my beloved, it was occasioned by the sin of gluttony, for it began at Pudding Lane and ended at Pie Corner."

Samuel fell into Mr. Felkin's habit of going from one place of worship to another to hear the great preachers. He quivered with excitement as he sat in the restored cathedral and listened to Bishop Ken boldly rebuking the king for his sins. But he had a guilty sense of sin in the cathedral, where the music woke in him a response which he condemned as sensuous.

The Sunday following he went to the big barnlike tabernacle near Bishopsgate, where thousands flocked to hear Thomas Vincent expound God's word. He gave Vincent the best of it, for he needed no organ or candles or images or painted glass to sway his audience—only his voice and a wave of his hand.

What was this mystical gift by which a shabby man in a rough pine pulpit could hold hundreds of men and women spellbound; nay, more than that, could change the course of their lives in one turn of the hourglass, so that they were transformed by the renewing of their minds?

Was it the power of God unto salvation? Just how was it different from Mr. Felkin's faculty for selling twice as large a bill of goods as his customer had in mind to buy?

And why did the king listen with respect to the public rebukes of "Little Black Ken" when he would not tolerate half that much from another?

There was another reason why Samuel went so frequently to the tabernacle meetings—Elizabeth. In the brief note she had written him, she had said she was going to Southampton if her mother could bear the journey. But her mother was very frail and ill. Perhaps they had not left the city. She was a Puritan and devout. If she was still in London, surely she would be somewhere in these gatherings of the faithful.

His eyes were always watching for her since he had come to the city. On the streets, in the parks, in the market places—but more than anywhere else, in the house of God.

Once he thought he saw her in Vincent's tabernacle. He caught a glimpse of a fair girlish face under a Puritan cap. He tried his best to reach the women's door before she did—knocking people right and left with never a "by-your-leave"—but he lost her— if indeed it were she. There were too many Puritan bonnets just alike.

He went to the tabernacle every Sunday for the next three months, but he never saw her again.

"Most likely it wasn't Elizabeth at all," he decided. "I've thought about her so much I'm beginning to see her in the daytime as well as in my dreams. I'm getting touched in the head. I'd best have a care or they'll send me to Bedlam."

Parliament was in session now and Mr. Marvell had lodgings in Maiden Lane. It was not far from the New Exchange and they were always planning for a Sunday together, but somehow the time never seemed to come. Now and then they met for dinner but there was never half time enough for the things Samuel wanted to say. Mr. Marvell had so many things on his mind: the scandalous doings of the court and the misuse of public funds and, worst of all, the threat of a papist succession. The old, easy comradeship in the cottage at Islington was gone.

Once in a while he spent a Sabbath afternoon at Morton's but there were always a lot of the fellows around and no chance to talk about the things that troubled him. It was hard not to have anyone at all that belonged to him. But there was nobody but his brother John; and John was settled in a little parish at Ugborough, away in the southwest part of the island, and the living was so poor that he could never come to London. Once in a long while John wrote to him and he wrote to John, but they were duty letters. Neither of them had anything to say. Samuel felt strangely alone in the world and did not know that this was only a part of growing up: that never again would the path of right and duty lie straight and plain before him.

There were things about his duties to Mr. Felkin that worried him. Going to all sorts of churches was not so bad; but it seemed to him Mr. Felkin went a bit too far in dressing so modish and frequenting plays and fencing matches and cockfights. But Mr. Felkin held it was good business to be seen among people of wealth from whom he hoped for trade.

Parris asked Daniel Hawley what he thought about it.

"He sends me to the playhouse to save his seat," Samuel told him. "The plays are dreadful wicked—but they're like being in a new world—wonderful diverting. Sometimes I can hardly bear to give up my seat when my master comes. I'd never go to such a place of myself, you know. But is it sinful, think you, to enjoy it when it's your duty?"

Daniel considered. "That's a hard question. But I'd say 'tis right to go (servants, obey your masters, you know) but view it with a critic's eye, and point a moral from it. And I'm not sure plays are as wicked as some folk think. After all, they just act out what you read in the Bible. Only when you see it it seems wickeder. But maybe that's a good thing."

This theory eased Samuel's conscience, but sometimes it was hard to remember the moral in the excitement of the play.

The New Theater was very fine. The pit was lighted by skylights, but the glass was loosely set and did not keep out the showers. The stage also was lighted by the sun; though on dark days there were lamps to illuminate the scenery and walls.

The plays began at three o'clock. The rule was first come, first seated, and sometimes Samuel had to sit from noon on to get a good place for his master. But it was never dull waiting: people talked and laughed and ogled and flirted; and there were orange girls crying their wares, and much gay banter and rough horseplay as the crowd stood up in their seats and pelted each other with the bright fruit.

One day Samuel was startled to see sitting close to the stage, the highwayman of Holloway, Claude Duval. He was buying from a pretty orange girl her whole stock of fruit, basket and all, which he handed to an older girl, while he drew the youngster down beside him.

There could be no mistake. Samuel was sure of the man. But he was dressed in the rich garb of a page of the court! After his first surprise, Samuel laughed at himself.

"Why should I think it strange to find a robber in court dress? Likely he's a white sheep among the black, at that!"

But he watched sharply, hoping Mr. Felkin would not come. Then the chatter of the pair was interrupted by a gaily dressed man with thick lips and a fat, red face. Lord Buckhurst greeted the girl with a shout:

"Ah ha! The singing maid of Coal Lane!"

He dragged her to the stage and shouted something that nobody could hear above the shouts and handclapping and the crying of the fiddles. Buckhurst brought down his hands and boomed, "Silence!" and as the din quieted he introduced the orange girl.

"Mrs. Nelly Gwynne, the Singing Maid of Coal Lane!"

Nelly lifted her head as a bird does and her voice was like a silver flute, hushing the crowd.

"Here's a health unto his Majesty, with a fa la la!" And as she finished the king and the duke came into the royal box and the applause for the song mingled with the king's welcome.

And then Nelly sang again, plaintive and sweet, an older song, "Sumer is icumen in," and all the people quieted and some wiped tears from their eyes. And the king leaned forward in his seat as if this slip of a girl had magicked him with her little song.

At the Exchange a few weeks later two ladies of the court were gossiping about the pretty orange girl who had charmed the king and the page who had quarreled with his Majesty and fled the court on a stolen horse. Soon the quarrel was no secret and neither was the fact that the runaway page and the gallant highwayman whom all the ladies were fearing yet hoping to meet were one and the same: Claude Duval. But knowing the rogue's name and catching him were not at all the same thing.

More and more, as time went on, Samuel Parris identified himself with the life of his fellow prentices. For the lure of the city streets had taken hold upon him. He was London born and for the first of his seven ages had lived close under the shadow of the Bow Bells tower, but his memory of the city was a quiet garden walled in stone, secure from the clamor and bustle that was London.

He returned to the city at the floodtide of his physical vitality; at an age when his emotions were unstable, when all sights and sounds and fancies were enhanced by the thrill of a newly aroused sex life. He was at the age of adventure and romance when life holds out its challenge and sets lads looking for new worlds.

The habitat of the prentice was the shop; the street his playground; the kitchen his only home. The hours of work were long and the only means of communication or conveyance was the prentice boy's feet. At all hours they tramped the streets, but the world has never yet succeeded in working a boy hard enough to keep him out of mischief.

The prentices were never too tired to police the streets "to protect the citizens" and to slake their thirst for adventure by pursuing suspicious characters who might be robbers, foreigners, or papists in disguise.

At every corner the city laid traps for unwary feet, but the son of Anne Parris had a measure of protection. He had no liking for strong drink and he had a holy horror of being fuddled or of making an ass of himself. And he had a personal fastidiousness which kept him from the grosser vices. Nastiness, physical or moral, repelled him. But an Anglo-Saxon love of adventure was in his veins; and in the Puritan this quality often found its outlet in a zeal for virtue, more often somebody else's. No sport was more popular than a Jesuit hunt in which they would search the taverns for some victim who could be pommeled in the cause of righteousness.

There were always the brothels on Shrove Tuesday—the last day before Lent, when the prentices confessed their sins one by one to the parish priest and were shriven. Then in a fervor of righteousness they raided the houses of ill-fame and captured the keepers, who were locked up in prison during the whole of Lent. The custom had its root far back in Catholic England. The Puritan prentice of Restoration days went unshriven, but he still descended in righteous wrath upon the workers of iniquity.

The second year that Samuel was in the city he went with a crowd of prentices to Moorfields. In a frenzy of civic zeal they raided the brothels, and drove the inmates out half-clad into the chill of a February night.

Each Puritan did his part, hunting down sinners as did Saul of Tarsus, breathing out threatenings and slaughter, searching streets and alleys, overturning ash barrels, prodding in every likely hiding place for the fleeing delinquent.

As Parris went racing down one alley: something caught his eye—a flutter of white in the corner of a basement stair—a woman of sin. His hand shot forward and he dragged out by one arm a shivering, half-starved girl of fourteen or so—one hand clutching a flimsy rag of a garment to her flat, childish breasts. Under the lanternlight her eyes stared like a rabbit's he had once drowned out of its hole. Was this his quarry? Was this the strange woman who lieth in wait at every corner?

A clatter of feet was behind him—the yelping pack. He thrust her back into the stairway and pressed a coin into her icy hand;

then rushed back, swinging his flail and yelling like an avenging fiend:

"To the left up the alley! Two fat harlots and a naked man!"

As the night wore on, some of the lads got boisterous and the guards were called out. The prentice gangs ran from them and flung stones and there was some blood spilled and some of the houses dismantled. The Duke of York, who was found mighty merry at one of them, complained that he had lost two tenants who paid him £15 a year for their licenses. Some of the prentices who were pretty drunk began to shout:

"Why do we pull down the little bawdyhouses and leave the biggest one of all at Whitehall?"

Samuel Parris, who had drunk more than he should, but was still sober enough to fear trouble, went home and to bed. And luckily, too, for four of the ringleaders were caught and hanged, drawn, and quartered at Tyburn and their heads fixed upon London Bridge.

Claude Duval, the dashing highwayman of Holloway, was caught at last. He did not make so brave an ending, after all, when the constables found him dead drunk at the Hole-in-the-Wall Tavern. He had on him three pistols and a sword, but the officers took him without a scratch and he woke up in Newgate Prison.

But for all that the ladies (God bless 'em) did not lose interest in him; and fat dowagers and fair damsels paid a guinea apiece admission to see and admire the gallant knight of the highway, and he was the hero of ballad and legend.

Samuel could not help wondering if his mother, had she lived, would have been among the silly fools who thronged the prison. He indignantly pushed away the disloyal thought, and yet—why had she been so sure?

In January of that year Duval went to his death, "dressed like a prince in silk and silver," a flower in his mouth and his plumed hat in his hand. And all along the road to Tyburn ladies wept and men saluted as he passed by.

When he was dead, Daniel Hawley turned to Samuel, and wagged his head. "Ain't folk the beatenest?" He forgot his academy training in times of excitement. "Menfolk is bad enough, but womenfolk is wuss, and ladies—Lord, Lord, they ain't got the sense of a dormouse. An' tonight he's to lay in state in the Tangier Tavern. Let's go! I'll meet you at Covent Garden Church and we'll march behind the flambeaux. You saw the beginning of his career and we might as well see the end on't. But be sure to empty your pockets before you start!"

A student held himself far above a prentice, for it had been the fashion among some of the boys at the academy to look down on the tradespeople. But Samuel was not long in learning that although one prentice did not count for much, that same prentice multiplied by thousands became a force to be reckoned with.

There were certain taverns where prentices congregated during their off hours, talking over their grievances and planning ways to better their lot. Or perhaps they played football in the crowded streets and scurried around corners and down alleys at the crash of breaking glass.

After the shutters were up and the shops closed, there was the Prentices' Coffee House, kept by a deaf widow in Islington, where the older lads were accustomed to meet and discuss their affairs and cement the spirit of unity which was the base of their influence.

The coffee was strong and black as soot, but there was good bread and cheese to go with it. In the small room clouds of tobacco smoke shaped themselves into visions of the future when the lads around the tables in their workday suits should have become the proud pillars of the mercantile world which was already beginning the program of commerce that would make Britain Mistress of the Seas.

The next week, Samuel and Mr. Marvell spent the day at Morton's. There was talk of a legacy that a man named Pennoyer had left to Harvard College to found a scholarship for worthy students. Samuel sighed. If only it had come a few years earlier, perhaps he might have stood a chance of winning. And if he had won, it might have changed his whole future. Instead of tramping the streets delivering goods, and standing behind the counter wheedling and flattering silly females into buying more than they could afford, he might be living in the wonderful new land of Massachusetts, where a Puritan minister was honored as much as the governor and the council.

His thoughts went back to that day when his father's letter

had come, ruining all his plans. The rebellion which he had felt then surged up again, and once more he questioned the decision of God in making him prentice. Was it a punishment for that silly Maypole frolic? Was the Supreme Being of the universe petty enough to ruin a whole life because of a silly boyish escapade? Morton wouldn't take such a revenge as that—nor would Marvell—nor would he. Was God less generous than man? He shook his muddled head, and came back to everyday matters. Marvell was saying, "There's going to be a meeting of the Rota Club next Tuesday and we may invite guests. Would you like to go with me, Samuel?"

Samuel brightened. "Is that the Puritan Club you talk so much about? Oh, yes, Mr. Marvell. I'd love to go!"

Now, Andrew Marvell was perhaps even more disappointed than Samuel at the latter's being forced by his father to go prentice and eventually to become a merchant. Both he and Mr. Morton knew that his real calling was in God's Word, that his destiny lay in His ministry, and not in the vulgar and worldly shops of the new London. The two men were almost certain that, if properly sponsored, Samuel had a good chance of being the recipient of this newly established grant from the Pennoyer Estate. So, unbeknown to the young prentice, they wrote his father in Barbados asking his permission and Godspeed to further Samuel's education as a preacher to God. Thomas Parris replied to them by a letter sent on the next vessel bound for England:

To Mr. Andrewe Marvel & Mr. Chas. Morton of London.

Yrs of 17 May att hande. Aboute ye Penoyr matter it seemes I have lyttel choyse butt to give concent sense yr planns bee so well layed out fer my son Sam. Ef hee hankers to bee a precher hee'd probly neer set his mind on shugar growen so as to make a goe of itt, soe I mays well mayke ye best on't & give him his freedom to doe whut may pleas him & his precher frends. Hee better be a good precher an a poore planter as it takes a goode man to make much in plantin now thet ye govt. bee aginst us planters & littel sign of better luck to come.

Folks tell mee yt in ye Mass Bay prechers bee doing well an lookd upp to as men of worth. Ef soe bee Sam may doe well fer he had all ways a nimble tung & a gift fer high-sounden wordes.

Yr Humbel Sarvt.

Thos. Parris.

(his hand & seal)

Marvell's invitation to Samuel to attend the Rota Club meeting was not only for the purpose of providing the lad with worthy relaxation from his prentice duties—there was something more important. Mr. Crisp, the trustee of the Pennoyer Estate, was to be present, and Marvell could think of no better place to have him meet Samuel, there among his peers, where he might be judged and appraised in the best of lights. Mr. Crisp could not fail to see that the young Puritan was the boy he had been searching for.

10

The Rota

*Good company and good discourse
are the very sinews of virtue.*
—IZAAK WALTON.

THE MOON was bright and the skies a clear blue the night that Andrew Marvell took Samuel to the Rota Club meeting as he had promised. The club met in New Palace Yard at one Miles's, the next house to the stairs.

Around a big oval table, where coffee was served, in a room every evening as full as it could be crammed, Milton and Marvell, and their Puritan friends, sat in endless discussion of political questions. And here Samuel Parris was presented to the blind poet-statesman whom Marvell introduced as "Mr. John Milton, the greatest Puritan of us all."

"Samuel Parris is a nephew by marriage of John Oxenbridge," Marvell said.

"Is he, indeed?" Mr. Milton was much interested. "Only a week ago I had a letter from Oxenbridge telling of his new charge in Boston in the Massachusetts Bay Colony—the little wooden church built in 1630, and the college called Harvard, which is training ministers to preach the truth without fear."

It seemed that the college was sadly in need of funds, for

Oxenbridge wrote that an agent was being sent to England to promote the cause among the faithful. Someone else in the company had received the same news from a friend at Cambridge, where the college was located, giving a sorry picture of the run-down condition of the buildings.

There was considerable discussion after this. A tall thin gentleman whom everybody seemed to respect said that the cause was most worthy and he would go down for £50. For the future of free government and free speech and free religion, he said, lay in that struggling little college in the Massachusetts Colony.

Samuel thrilled to his marrow at all he heard. His thoughts reached out across the Atlantic to that new country where men could worship as their consciences dictated with no fear of king or bishop and where a Puritan preacher spake as one having authority. The business of buying and selling, with its fawning servility, its tricks and cheats and lickspittle blandishments, seemed utterly unworthy. He hated himself and his father and the whole contemptible tribe of tradesmen.

Andrew Marvell, watching him, smiled and sighed.

"The lad is so like his mother," he mused. "Taut as a fiddle-string—and as hard to keep in tune. I would she could see him tonight: Galahad in a prentice suit with his hair cut round a bowl."

A keen-eyed gentleman came in and Marvell sprang up to greet him, introducing him to the group as "Mr. Crisp of Norfolk." Samuel roused from his abstraction as the interest centered in the newcomer. He was anxious to ask many questions but he modestly kept his tongue and spoke only when he was spoken to.

Mr. Crisp referred to a letter from Mr. Oxenbridge, and when Samuel was presented as the nephew of Mistress Oxenbridge, he asked a great many questions which Samuel answered as well as he could, though he said he didn't remember much about his Aunt Susanna except her fascinating witch stories of Barbados, and had never seen his new uncle Oxenbridge, though Mr. Marvell had talked much of him.

"I don't know much about New England or the college or any of these things," he said ruefully. "My master keeps me too busy for much reading. But it's wonderful to listen while you others talk about them. It was good of Mr. Marvell to ask me here tonight. I shall never forget it!"

Mr. Milton and Mr. Marvell joined in the talk and by and by

Mr. Morton came in, and with a smile which included all the group, asked:

"Well, Mr. Crisp, have you reached any decision yet?"

Mr. Crisp laughed. "I always sleep on a matter of importance."

"Fair enough! Fair enough!" Morton answered. "Come out to Newington Green tomorrow and see our fine telescope. It brings the stars within arm's reach. And Mistress Morton is expecting you for dinner."

When the group broke up, Mr. Crisp turned to Samuel. "Could you call me a linkboy to light me home? I'm stopping at the Swan."

Samuel promptly offered: "Pray let me serve you, sir! I've a good lantern, and I'm Cockney born."

The streets were dark and the fog was thickening. Mr. Crisp linked arms with his guide.

"I don't care much for your London coffeehouses," he said. "I'm craving some good English beer and bread and cheese, if I'm not keeping you out too late."

"Not a bit!" Samuel answered. "My master is strict, but when Mr. Marvell asks for me, Mr. Felkin is so flattered to be noticed by an M.P. he never says a word."

When they sat down at the table in a near-by tavern, Mr. Crisp broke out, "Gadzooks! I'd not live in London for a fortune! I apprehend a robber in every one of your crooked little alleys."

Samuel laughed. "We prentices roam the streets night after night," he said, "to deliver goods or light the master or a late customer. We think nothing of it—but we're prepared."

He held out his weapon: two short oaken clubs joined together by a leather thong.

" 'Tis known as a Protestant flail," he laughed, "and I'd rather have it than any pistol. Though 'twas devised to crack the heads of papists, 'twill serve as well for any other vermin."

"A flail, be it Protestant or orthodox, would give me no comfort," Mr. Crisp insisted. "I'd want a company of horse for escort! Why, on the road yesterday I heard some fellows talking that the London Tower had been robbed!" He laughed heartily. "But I didn't swallow that one! The rascals were drunk as pipers."

Samuel laughed too. "The funny thing is that it came near being true. An Irish adventurer named Tom Blood hatched the plot, and came within an ace of carrying it out. Just what happened, nobody seems to know, for there are as many stories as there are tellers: but Blood, dressed in a parson's cloak, went to the Tower with a lady (or a man in petticoats, some say) and under some pretext so far won the guard's confidence that he opened the case where the crown jewels are kept. The parson's lady fainted, and while the softhearted old keeper was ministering to her, Blood hid the crown and orb under his cassock but the scepter was too long to be covered, and the keeper saw it and howled for help. Blood took to his heels with guards after him. Blood fired and missed and there was a hand-to-hand battle for the crown, almost wrenching it apart; but more guards came and Blood was overpowered."

Samuel broke off, laughing at Mr. Crisp's bewildered face. "Don't blame me, sir. I know this story doesn't sound just right; but if you don't credit this one, I'll tell you three more, all different and all wrong, 'tis likely."

Mr. Crisp was bursting with questions. "Was the rogue hanged, drawn, and quartered; or would it be the ax? Was it treason, lese majesty?"

By this time Samuel was helpless with laughter at Mr. Crisp's astonishment. "Wait, wait! You've not heard half the tale. When they finally got Blood locked up and went and told the king, he shouted: 'Bring the rogue here straight away! I want to see the man.'

"So they brought the robber to the palace, and Blood swaggered in and met his Majesty with no sign of repentance or fear. He would tell nothing of his companions in crime, and as to himself he boasted, 'Twas a gallant attempt, though unsuccessful, for 'twas a struggle for a crown.'

"Charles relished the jest. Then Blood told of a day when he hid on the river bank watching the king at his bath, and raised his gun to shoot him, but his heart was checked by an awe of Majesty. He warned the king that he should go no more to bathe without a guard, lest some knave with less reverence for his royal person should attempt his precious life, to England's dreadful loss.

"Now there's naught that's sure about any of this, but 'tis said the king pardoned the fellow and gave him £500 a year and a job as guard—some say to guard the king's person and some say to guard the crown jewels. 'Tis a crazy tale, but only a shade worse than many we hear as to our king and court."

Samuel suddenly sobered, his boyish, laughing face growing mature and serious. "God knows what lies ahead of us, with Charles the Rake on the throne with a barren queen, and James the Papist in succession."

"For a prentice boy, you seem interested in politics." Mr. Crisp commented. "How old are you?"

"Going on eighteen." Samuel answered. "But most prentices are interested in politics—the clever ones. Our future rests on England's future, you know, sir, for a secure government is the foundation of trade. And the king is not unmindful of us; he has not forgot the help the prentices gave him in 1660.

"Every year on the second of August the king himself, in appreciation of that loyal service, spreads us a feast in Saddlers' Hall, where several of his courtiers dine with us, and there are speeches and the like. And last year his bastard son, the Duke of Grafton, acted as steward to serve a brace of bucks from the Royal Chase for dinner."

"My word, lad! Do you speak thus boldly of his Majesty's indiscretions?"

Samuel shrugged. "Everybody knows. There's no secret about his misdoings. One hears it everywhere—on the streets, in the Exchange, in the playhouses—both the king's and the duke's. 'Tis a favorite jest."

Mr. Crisp veered to a more seemly subject.

"Are you happy in your work?"

Samuel shrugged. "I've no liking for it, but I've no choice. My father is a merchant, so I must be."

"If you don't want to be a merchant, what do you want to do?" Mr. Crisp asked. "I think Mr. Morton told me you were one of his scholars for a time. Why did you leave his academy?"

Samuel looked surprised. "I want to be a minister," he said. "That is my work—the only work I care about. My mother's family were all ministers, you see. And before I was born, my mother dedicated me to the Lord's service—just as Hannah in the Scriptures dedicated her son Samuel. That is why I was named Samuel—my mother asked me of the Lord, and before my birth I was set apart for His service. My mother always told me I was to be a minister of God. She trained me for that service and told me it was the greatest work in the world." His sensitive face quivered. "But an evening like this—even Mr. Marvell doesn't know how much it means to me. It's like getting out of jail!"

Mr. Crisp smiled at him. "When I was your age 'twouldn't have been my idea of a holiday—to sit all evening with men twice my age talking about the future of the Puritan cause. Dallying with a pretty maid or caterwauling under her window was more to my taste."

"I've never had a chance at that," said Samuel, "save once in a while at Mr. Morton's when we broke rules. There was a female seminary across the Green we visited once or twice. And though I was younger than most of the fellows, I got on with them well enough for I had a fair singing voice.

"Now," he glanced at his prentice suit, "the maids I'd have wouldn't have me, and I've no taste for barmaids nor bedmakers nor the queans that hang about the Exchange."

Mr. Crisp regarded him shrewdly: two yards of clean-cut, healthy young manhood with vigor and passion in every inch of him. "Do you mean to tell me you've never dallied with a lass nor wrote verses to her nor treasured some token of remembrance—" he broke off, laughing as the guilty blood flamed in Samuel's cheeks and his hand closed over the little silver ring Elizabeth had given him. "Ha! At last we find Achilles' heel!"

His handclasp was so friendly and the laughter in his eyes so full of understanding that before Samuel knew it he was telling about Elizabeth—how she had come into his life and gone out of it and left only a memory which seemed like a dream.

"I guess that's why I don't care much about any other girl," he said. "I'm always measuring her up beside Elizabeth. Someday, if I ever have anything to offer her, I'm going to find her again. But I can't till I'm through with this dam—beg pardon, sir, this prentice contract of mine. And then I suppose I'll have to go to Barbados and drive Negurs on my father's plantation. I'd never have cheek to ask a woman I loved to go there. So it's no use thinking about her."

The bells were striking midnight as they reached the old Swan. Samuel pounded on the door to rouse the porter and held his lantern to guide Mr. Crisp up the steep steps.

"Good night, sir! Nay—nay! 'Twas a pleasure. Let me forget my servitude—for this one night!"

Mr. Crisp put his sixpence back in his pocket and lingered in the doorway as Samuel ran down the steps and vanished in the fog.

"Gadzooks, I think the lad'll do! A relative of Dean Martin of Ely on his mother's side, Marvell said. Good blood and good manners—at ease with his betters but not saucy." He chuckled. "Morton might have saved his telescope and his dinner. The lad'll do!"

Book Three

Harvard   1671 to 1673

In the Night Watches

Ten o'clock:
  Hear, Brethren, hear! Now ten the hour hand shows;
  They only rest who long for night's repose.
Eleven o'clock:
  The clock's eleven! And ye have heard it all,
  How in that hour the mighty God did call.
Twelve o'clock:
  It's midnight now! And at that hour ye know
  With lamps to meet the bridegroom we must go.
                    —COUNT ZINZENDORF.

THE MAY moon sailed high, silvering the waters of the bay and the Charles and the three coves which encircled the little peninsula of the town of Boston. Its mystic light brought out in high relief the bold headlands. There was Copp's Hill to the northeast and Fort Hill to the southeast, guarding the shore line; and yonder were the three tall cones which topped Trimountain to the west. Beacon Hill lay eastward with its outlying spurs, as did Mount Vernon towering over the Charles and Cotton Hill. Below was the harbor where ships lay at anchor with sails furled. The shadows softened the outlines of the prison and the stocks and whipping post which stood at the meeting house door, and gave a kindly dignity to the crooked little gravestones in the Old Burying Ground.

The town of Boston slept like the good Puritan town it was, as yet little more than a seashore village which straggled up its thicket-grown hillsides. Only the night watch patrolled the narrow streets, walking two by two, a youth joined with an older and more sober person, to call the hours and if after ten should they see lights, to inquire if there be warrantable cause.

In the house of the Reverend John Oxenbridge on the eastern slope of Cotton Hill, on this May night in 1671, there had been lights long after ten but the watch had made no inquiries. The Reverend John Oxenbridge was minister of the First Church, a man eminent for his godliness and zeal in the Lord's work, as the night watch well knew, and he often sat long at his escritoire, his white head bowed over his sermon or the Book of Books, while the watchman passed by with his singsong call:

"Ten o'clock . . . and all's well!"

But tonight the minister was neither writing nor reading but had sat all evening talking earnestly with his nephew, Samuel Parris, newly come from London as all Boston Town knew, to be a scholar at Harvard. The elder watchman, who had been asleep when the minister's nephew landed, paused in his round to look in at the dark head and the white under the candlelight.

"A well-favored lad," he said, nodding to himself, "smart an' not overpious. Oughta make a fust-rate preacher!"

When the weary weeks of sailing were ended for Samuel, and the good ship had come to land, it seemed that half the people in Boston were at the dock to welcome her. A ship from the port of London did not come in every day. It might bring good or evil tidings; news of king and Parliament; of wars or pestilence or fire; of birth and of death. There were sure to be letters, and a bundle of London newspapers and political pamphlets; and some broadside ballads for frivolous young folk; and perhaps a doll or two, dressed in the latest London fashion, to be exhibited for the delight of the ladies.

Samuel's feet hardly touched the dock before he saw Aunt Susanna. He would have known her anywhere in spite of her added years and white hair. Beside her stood a tall, spare man with a slight stoop to his shoulders—that would be his new uncle. A half-grown girl who somehow managed to look tomboyish even in her Puritan dress and bonnet stood between the pair—that would be the young cousin, Theodora.

There was nothing lacking in his welcome. Aunt Susanna hugged and kissed him before all the town as if he were the Prodigal Son. His new uncle smiled and blinked, shielding his weak eyes from the sun while he expressed his joy and thankfulness over the safe arrival. Theodora jumped up and down in excitement and asked, "What did you bring me from London, Cousin Sam?"

The walk home was a rapid fire of questions, all of them talking at once, asking for the latest news from England; stopping here and there to introduce the new nephew to people they met; and pointing out to him the places of interest.

They were proud of their town and proud of their bay; proud of their fine new Townhouse, with markets and shops beneath and rooms for the magistrates above, and at the east end a public library.

The First Church, of which John Oxenbridge was minister, stood just across from the Townhouse in a grassy plot known as Church Square. The stocks, pillory, and whipping post were set on wheels, and stood sometimes on the Townhouse side, sometimes on the meetinghouse side, as was most convenient. Just around the corner and a few rods up the Prison Lane, set back in a yard growing up to burdock and pigweed, was the prison— with the wild rosebush at its threshold, which the Antinomians blasphemously claimed had sprung up under the footsteps of their leader Anne Hutchinson as she entered the prison door.

After supper John Oxenbridge invited Samuel into his study and proudly exhibited his library. "Not so large as some," he said, "but most carefully chosen, and every book an old and valued friend."

As the sands ran through the hourglass, the old minister took his new nephew in hand in good earnest, that he might get the rights of the situation at the very start.

It was a vivid picture that Oxenbridge drew, his vigorous words outlining, as with broad swift strokes of the brush, the fifty years of adventure since the landing of the *Mayflower* at Plymouth Rock.

Oxenbridge made it very clear that the way of the New England Church was not the way of toleration for all sorts of religious notions. It was a definitely marked out path, and those who followed it must not stray, no matter how enticing the byways or how lovely the flowers in the woods.

"Eleven o'clock . . . and all's well!" cried the watch.

The talk became more personal. The old minister told the story of his own experiences.

He talked of Andrew Marvell and the life at Eton, years before the shipwreck of all Nonconformists had sent him swimming away to Surinam, when Marvell had lived in his house and tutored Cromwell's ward, Will Dutton. The first Mistress Oxenbridge was living then, a most brilliant and pious woman. They had had four children, of whom only his daughter Bathsheba was left him—and she was leagues and leagues away, married to a man of great estate in Jamaica.

Samuel had tried to comfort him: "You have your daughter Theodora."

Oxenbridge nodded. "Yes; Theodora—gift of God. The only fruit of my second union. Her mother died in childbed just a year after our marriage. Theodora is a sweet child—but a female. It was not the Divine Will to grant me an heir."

Even after all the years, his voice faltered as he told of the loss of his only son. "My Daniel," he said, "a young man of rare accomplishments as a Christian, a physician, and a scholar. He died young and unmarried, thus cutting off the Oxenbridge name; 'twas a sorry blow, but I had been overproud to boast of our descent from Adam Oxenbridge of Rye, who was one of the barons who bore the canopy at the coronation of Richard III."

The old man bowed his head. "God hath given, and the same hand hath taken away, as He hath pleased." He straightened his shoulders. " 'Tis good to have a youth under my rooftree once again, even though he be not flesh of my flesh."

The night watch was making the rounds again, calling: "Twelve o'clock . . . and all's well!"

The old minister lifted the hourglass, through which the last grains of sand were slipping.

"Tis the end of the day, nephew; the dawn of a tomorrow. It is allegorical. My day is at its close; yours is just beginning."

His pale eyes, weakened by the glare of tropic sun, blinked at Samuel. He rose and held out his hand.

"Good night, nephew. The Lord bless thee and keep thee in all thy ways! Good night—and good morrow!"

When Samuel Parris went to bed in the little west chamber his body was weary and he laid himself down stretching like a cat on the clean wide bed which Aunt Susanna had made ready for him. What luxury after the cramped bunk which had served him during the nine weeks' sea voyage! But he could not settle down to sleep. His bed still rocked and rolled with the giddy motion of the ship. And the unbroken hush of the sleeping town kept him awake. He lay listening—listening. If only he could hear again the clatter of shod hoofs on cobblestones or the creaking and flapping of mast and sail or the splash of waves—if he could hear anything at all—he might sleep.

Perhaps he was too happy to sleep. He gave himself up to the enjoyment of physical comfort and relaxation. How smooth and clean the sheets and how sweet and resilient the full-stuffed mattress of shredded corn husks on which he lay! But there was the greater happiness of fulfilled desire; for he was in Boston in the Colony of Massachusetts Bay, in the new land of hope and promise with the way miraculously opened to that High Calling to which he had been set apart while he lay in his mother's womb.

Samuel rose from his bed and knelt at the open window, looking out at the moonlit mountain. Near by and a little to his right rose Cotton Hill, and far off to the west, sloping down to the waters of the Charles, was Mount Vernon. Between these two points high above his window lay the conelike steep of Beacon Hill, topped by a ship's mast seventy feet tall, with an iron crane from which hung a barrel of tar. Two hundred feet above sea level the beacon hung, ready at the touch of a torch to send its warning of danger throughout the countryside.

Somewhere to the west across the Charles was Harvard College, which had opened its doors to him, Samuel Parris—"in recognition of his unusual talent and promise."

The cry of the night watch came faint but clear: "Two o'clock—and all's well!"

Samuel leaned out the window. An aromatic perfume assailed his nostrils, pungent and alluring: the blossoms of the locust tree which Aunt Susanna had shown him in the afternoon. There were no such trees in England. He reached out to pluck one of the drooping racemes of creamy flowers. A thorn, needle sharp, pricked his hand. The moon was low in the west and the beacon on the hill cast its ghostly shadow—a slender shaft with an outstretched arm—it looked like a monstrous gallows tree!

The scratch on his hand smarted.

The moonlight showed a drop of blood.

12

Commencement

But lest this Olive plant in time should wither,
And so its fruit and glory end togither,
The prudent Husband-Men are pleased to spare
No work or paines, no labour, cost or care,
A Nursery to plant, with tender sprigs,
Young shoots and sprouts, small branches, slips and twigs;
Whence timely may arise a good supply
In room of sage and aged ones that dye.
          —In the Almanac for 1648, By SAMUEL DANFORTH,
               the January stanza on the College.

IT WAS Commencement Day in Cambridge Town, 1671. The Great Hall of the Old College was packed with people come from all the towns and country around for the performances. Every bench was filled. People were standing at the rear of the room and along the sides and in the passage, shutting out what little air might come in through the doors and windows.

Many of the auditors had harnessed horses or oxen in the early summer dawn and driven miles through the woods to reach the college in time. They had brought hampers woven of reeds or willows, packed with food for the picnic dinner and supper; and after the exercises they would drive home through the twilight, urging their teams as night drew down and the wail of a wildcat or the howl of a wolf pack on the ridge threatened them with the dangers of frontier darkness.

Samuel Parris sat in the middle of a long hard plank, squeezed in between his cousin Theodora and her chum, plump Hannah Hull, the mintmaster's daughter. The two girls had quarreled over which should sit next to "Cousin Sam" till Susanna good-naturedly moved over.

"There now, ye can both sit next him if ye behave like little ladies, but if there's any more squabblin' I'll turn ye over my knee before the whole assembly."

Samuel felt like a fool, with two half-grown chits trying to get his attention by sly nudges and giggles, or by leaning across him to whisper to each other. He looked enviously at his uncle, sitting in quiet dignity among the ministers on the roomy platform. Someday his own place would be up there among the Anointed, with no silly females to distract him. He mopped his flushed forehead and tried to listen to the president's Latin oration, and the Bachelors' Disputations by two of the commencers, Samuel Sewall and Peter Thacher II, the latter being the son of the minister of the seceding South Church.

The two girls carried on a spirited argument in dumb-show as to the relative merits of the speakers: Hannah rolling her eyes in admiration of young Sewall and Theodora shaking her head vigorously, preferring Thacher's eloquence much more. Between them Samuel lost his dignity and the point of both prelections. He bent his head and whispered:

"Be quiet, or I'll knock your empty noddles together!" At which the silly minxes giggled more than ever.

Increase Mather, minister of the North Church of Boston, made the closing prayer, his great voice pouring sonorous phrases out the open windows and up through the listening branches of the elms, straight to the attending ear of the Almighty.

Urian Oakes, pastor of the Cambridge Church, lifted his hands in benediction.

The reverent silence broke into a clamor of sound and the hungry crowd swarmed out of the college hall and scattered over the yard. The men gathered in groups talking of the performances, the crops, the weather, the news. The women worked swiftly, spreading the bountiful dinner which their hampers disclosed. The young folks chattered and laughed and flirted.

Even the grim old graveyard came to life, for the great flat stones which covered the graves made fine seats and in the bright midsummer afternoon even the seventeenth century forgot its fear of ghosts. Heads were bent close together as Harvard scholars scraped the moss away from Latin inscriptions and translated them for admiring damsels. Between the weeping-willow branches and the whitewashed palings pledges and tokens were slyly exchanged; and the dead under the stones were forgotten as youth looked forward to love and life stretching endlessly before them.

A girl with saucy red lips and curls as black as Samuel's own, caught his hand.

"Tell your fortune?"

Samuel laughed. "Go ahead! What does the future hold?"

The girl studied his palm. "You are going to wed a tall, dark damsel."

"You're wrong. She's blue-eyed and fair as an English rose!" Samuel gibed, pulling his hand away.

She reached for it again, studying the palm, her black brows puckered. "Oh, yes! I see the one you mean. But she will play you false and wed a rich old gentleman."

Samuel bent his head, half laughing, half anxious. "Where do you see that? Show me!"

She touched his palm with a brown finger. "This is the heart line—all crisscrossed and broken. See? That means disappointment in love."

"It's nonsense. And anyway, telling fortunes is a sin. I'll have no more to do with it!"

He strode across the yard angrily. The wench was lying, using sleighty tricks to win his attention to herself—dark damsel, indeed! Who'd think to find a light-o'-love in Harvard Yard?

Yet the line in his palm was all crisscrossed and broken. It was true, just as she had said.

He thought of Elizabeth and of his sending another letter to Southampton when he knew he was leaving England. But it had brought him no reply. He had wanted to go and search for her, but the days were crowded full with the preparations for his long voyage and it was a forlorn quest at best. If his letters had reached her, she would have answered. It had been five years —she might be anywhere by now. Someday perhaps, Samuel told himself, they would meet again as they had at first, by a miracle. He was not troubled by the dour predictions of that fortunetelling minx—'twas only a trick of coquetry.

Uncle Oxenbridge was waiting to present his nephew to President Chauncy, who greeted him warmly and beckoned to one of the commencers.

"Come here, Sir Sewall! This young Englishman is our first Pennoyer scholar, Samuel Parris of London, newly come to dwell with his uncle, our beloved Mr. Oxenbridge. See that you use him well and give him all the help and advice he may need."

Then, turning smilingly to Parris: "You couldn't be in better hands, my son. Sewall and Thacher, whom you have heard disputing so ably, are to remain at the college as "sirs," or Bachelors in Residence, while they study for their Master's degrees, so you will see much of them."

Sewall, with the punctiliousness that was to distinguish him throughout his life, showed and explained everything to the new student.

"The college may look shabby to you after Oxford and Cambridge," he apologized. "There has never been enough money to pay running expenses and the president's salary, to say nothing of repairs, but the Class of '71 is the 29th class to complete the Bachelor of Arts course, and many have taken their Master's degree. So we have reason to be proud, even if we be poor."

"Oxford and Cambridge are closed to Puritans now," Samuel replied. "My brother John was in the last class to graduate, and had to content himself with a very poor parish at a starvation stipend."

Yet the new student was a little depressed by the bleak shabbiness of this "New Cambridge" toward which the hopes of the Rota pointed. It was not old according to English standards, having been built a mere thirty-odd years ago; but the necessities of that early period gave scant time for proper seasoning of timbers. And, too, masonwork and hardware came high. The builders were proud of their job and described it as very fair and comely within and without. Its plan was that of an open quadrangle: a main building with two wings, like a thick, square letter E lying on its back, its straight line fronting south, its wings extending north across the Yard. The clapboards were weathered and warped by time, and some of the cedar shingles were loose so that the rains beat in, leaving telltale stains on the plastered walls and ceilings. But there were plenty of swinging, diamond-paned windows and four great chimney stacks with fireplaces on both first and second stories. A turret of four stories, with a bell and a weathervane, gave a view as far as eye could reach across the countryside: Back Bay and the winding valley of the Charles; the Fresh Pond Marshes and the Connecticut Path.

Parris would have lingered in the turret, charmed by the view, but Sir Sewall mopped his hot face and panted, "We had best see about your chamber and study. 'Tis first come first served.

The West Middle Chamber over the kitchen is warmest, if you
can get in there."

After a look around, Parris chose the East Middle Chamber
and was lucky in getting the southernmost study with a wall
against the chimney-back. A quarter's rent was one-and-sixpence
(only thruppence more than the one Sewall favored) and the little
window beside his table looked toward the east—toward Boston
and the England he had left.

"Coming, Parris?" Sewall said to him. "We've time for a
look at the library before we go downstairs. You are lucky to
have chambers right next door. We're proud of our library.
John Harvard's original bequest of two hundred and thirty volumes has been almost doubled by various donations."

There was a snug comfort in this upper room which the big
bare hall beneath it lacked: a friendly atmosphere which well-
worn books and settles and a wide fireplace always bring to the
student and booklover. Samuel Parris, as he browsed among the
bookshelves looking for old friends, already began to feel at
home.

But Sewall was hurrying him. "You haven't seen the kitchen
yet. That's the most important room in the house. 'Tis one of
the sights of Cambridge: a whole side taken up by the fireplace,
with a brick oven for baking cut in the chimney stack; and more
iron pots than ever you see, and fifty-two pewter platters."

But it was too late, for as they came down the stairs the sound
of shouts and laughter called them out into the yard, where the
beating of a drum announced the Commencement sports. The
students and visitors began to take sides for the games and contests.

The chief interest centered in the wrestling. The college favorite was John Wise, a youth of nineteen who had just finished
his sophomore year. His big-boned body was still lean and boyish,
but his muscles were hard and strong from the necessity of labor.

Sewall spoke well of young John, but Parris thought he looked
like a common fellow who would have done better had he stuck
to his plowing and left the pulpit to his betters. Yet he could not
help admiring the strength of the man and the easy way he carried his big body with a natural grace unusual in a commoner.

Someone called, "Come, Sewall, you're to judge the wrestling."

"Coming," Sewall answered calmly. He paused to greet a
small chubby young man with a plump pink face.

"Well, well! Nicholas Noyes! Glad to see you. Thought you were in the Connecticut wilds."

"So I was! So I was! But I wanted to come back for the performances and see my old friends again. Haddam's a long ways from anywhere, but it's a living and a man can't quarrel with his bread and butter."

Sewall introduced Parris. "Meet Samuel Parris from London: our first Pennoyer scholar. This is the minister from Haddam, Connecticut, Mr. Nicholas Noyes of the class of 1667."

Noyes smiled broadly and put out his hand.

"From London! Lord help ye, what brought ye here? I'd rather go to London 'an to heaven this blessed minute! And to think you were there—and come away!" He shook his head in comical bewilderment.

Samuel laughed. "In London they think the future of liberty is in yonder building. I was crazy with joy when I knew I could come."

Noyes sobered. "Lord bless ye! Of course, you were. And we bid you welcome. But tell me, what's a Pennoyer scholar? We've never had 'em in Haddam." He laughed heartily at his own wit.

The wrestling was beginning. John Wise, the college champion, was challenged by a man three times his age: a farmer from Salem Village named Giles Corey. He was a giant in build, perhaps two inches taller than Wise. When his name was called, he unwound his long legs and stood up grinning.

"Wal, boy, ketch aholt!"

Wise, with the pride of his nineteen years in every movement, caught "aholt" confidently. But the first tackle proved it would not be easy winning. They swayed back and forth in a wary embrace, each watching for an opening. The crowd surged closer, breathing hard.

Wise knew that Corey was stronger, but he was also older. But Corey also knew his handicap and forced the battle. He pressed too hard; Wise, lithe and supple, twisted like a cat and Corey struck the turf with Wise on top.

Sewall, tense with excitement, cried, "Down!" John Wise had won.

Wise offered good-naturedly, "Later, I'll show you the hold

I used, Goodman Corey. But not now. There's a graduate from Maine waiting to show how good he is."

The man from Maine was George Burroughs, a graduate of the year before, small and swarthy and nimble as a squirrel. The two men faced each other in the small grassy ring made by the interested and expectant spectators. Wise crouched low, his arms bent out in front of him anticipating the slightest move on Burroughs's part. But Burroughs was standing upright, his legs apart and crooked a little at the knees. Suddenly they came together, and before any of the crowd could see what happened, Wise was laid out flat on the ground panting, Burroughs standing near-by with a queer smile on his lips.

"He hardly touched me, it seemed," Wise said afterward, "when the most dreadful pain shot through my hip—I thought 'twas broken—but in a few minutes 'twas all right again. What was it you did, Mr. Burroughs?"

They had come in from the college yard and were sitting in Sewall's chambers enjoying the Commencement Day refreshment of wine and plum cake.

Burroughs drew a tight-lipped grin. "If I told you all I know, you'd know as much as I do," he said unpleasantly. "My power is not in beef and brawn, like some folks: 'tis of the soul. It is a gift, an art—my talent, if you please, to use at will. So much I'll tell you. But the secret of it . . . cannot be told. It must be sought in darkness and in pain by each one for himself and if he be so happy as to find it, it must be his, and guarded as his life!"

Samuel fidgeted in his chair with a curious uneasiness in his middle as Burroughs spoke. He was almost hypnotized by the little man's steely eyes, which seemed to strike forth fire and sparks while he talked, but when he stopped they suddenly dulled to ashes. Samuel felt for a moment as though he had been removed completely from his body, and had seen strange and terrifying things of which he had no remembrance.

Nobody said anything. They sat staring at the little black man from Maine. Noyes was the first to recover. He burst out:

> Upon what meat doth this our Caesar feed
> That he hath grown so great?

Somebody laughed nervously. Giles Corey leaned forward, his eyes bulging.

"Ye ain't ben tamperin' wi' none o' them Injun powwows, has ye, Mr. Burrus? Ye sound fer all the world like them medicine men."

Burroughs did not answer. Perhaps he did not hear; perhaps he was only sullen. Sewall rose from his chair. His voice was as slow and calm as usual.

" 'Tis nearing sundown and some of us have some ways to go. Mr. Noyes, will you lead us in a word of prayer before we part?" He looked at them gravely in turn: Noyes and Wise and Parris and Burroughs and Corey. "I wonder if the good Lord will ever bring us six together again—before we meet in front of His judgment throne."

Burroughs swayed to his feet drunkenly: "Under the locust tree on the highest hill!" he said.

His eyes were staring as in a trance.

13

That Man Wise

> *Brethren, ye have been called unto liberty, therefore . . . Hold your hold, Brethren! . . . Pull up well upon the oars . . . daylight and good piloting will secure all.*
>
> —JOHN WISE.

JOHN WISE, the big wrestler, lived in Roxbury, and during Samuel's first summer in New England, Wise spent much of his time in Boston. There was not much money in the Wise home, and John had found that there were more ways to earn money in Boston than in Roxbury. (He was the fifth of thirteen children, so he wasn't needed at home.)

Dr. Sam Alcock, whose father had brought the elder Wise to Massachusetts as his indentured servant, wanted young John to study physic with him, but John had set his heart on being a preacher. His pastor, Mr. Eliot, had put that idea into his head so early that there was no getting rid of it.

Almost the first thing John remembered was going to the minister's house to learn his catechism. Mr. Eliot always told him that he must study very hard, so that someday he could be a minister of God Most High—which was the greatest calling in the world.

Once when Mr. Eliot came to John's home and found the boy bent over the table trying to do his sums Mr. Eliot pointed to the figures and then to the Bible in a case against the wall:

"Young sir, here is earth upon the table and heaven on the shelf; let not earth by any means thrust heaven out of your mind!"

So when Dr. Sam Alcock wanted John to study physic with him, John remembered Mr. Eliot's words, and was afraid a doctor's career might be putting heaven on the shelf. Perhaps he shared the common feeling that the practice of physic was more than half sorcery and not good for a man's soul. But he was thankful to turn an honest penny washing vials and making powders by the laborious mortar and pestle method and running errands all over the town. For to the young country boy, the little capital held the thrill of a great world; and through it he glimpsed the land and life beyond the wide Atlantic.

Wise had made friendly advances to the new theological scholar from London, and had asked many pertinent questions about political and religious conditions in England, some of which Parris could answer and some of which he couldn't. But Parris had not encouraged any intimacy. He felt that at the beginning of his career it was most important to choose his friends with care and not to be seen too much with his inferiors. Wise had taken the hint with good grace and had not pursued him. He had smilingly gone his way, apparently free from either the servility or the swagger characteristic of his social class.

Parris had never seen anyone quite like Wise. His clothes were plain but of good quality and carelessly worn. He carried his powerful body without awkwardness and without pride. His thick blond hair was cut short and always a little awry. The rugged strength of his features was saved from sternness by a humorous twinkle in his blue eyes and a half-smiling friendliness about his generous mouth. If Parris had seen him on the streets of London he would have taken him for the son of a country squire rather than a servant.

That was one of the puzzling things about this new colony. It was so hard to rank a man by his dress. And as for the women —a laborer's daughter might bedeck herself in silks and fur-belows—even flaunting her bedizenments in the face of the judge when she was haled into court and fined for it.

Suppose such a thing should happen in an English court! But Parris was too thoroughly English to suppose any such thing! These Massachusetts settlers were as English as London itself. Yet a generation or two in the New World broke down centuries of precedent.

When the vacation was over, it seemed that even the college, which in earlier days had been the esteemed privilege of gentle-men's sons, was filling up with butchers and bakers ambitious to be ministers.

It was this harebrained talk of liberty, equality, democracy— this idiot's dream which had enticed humble fellows in England to join the mad rush to America, where the poorest might find riches and the butcher's son had only to take off his blue apron and wipe his bloody hands to be a gentleman! So they came flocking like crows to a cornfield, landing on New England shores with nothing but the shirt on their backs; even selling themselves as indentured servants for a term of years to pay their passage money. Like that fellow Wise, for example. His father had sold himself into slavery and had been lucky enough to be given his freedom when his master died. Now here was his son in college, seeming to think that a strong voice and a nimble wit in using words would transform him into a parson and set him atop of the heap in the affairs of the colony. That was carrying the thing a little too far!

As for proper servants, the very word was becoming an affront, so that one had to suggest tactfully that a neighbor should come as "help" in order to get anyone at all. Oxenbridge had brought his slaves with him: fat black Mary and a young Congo boy from Barbados; and some of the people had Indian slaves, who were forever slipping down the forest trails to the tepees of their tribes. But only the wealthy had servants in the real English sense.

Still the common people were dissatisfied and clamoring for a voice in the government and a suffrage based on property qualifications alone, without the requirement of church membership. To the saints, it seemed a strange demand in a colony which had been founded with the avowed intent to set up a New Jerusalem.

*   *   *

The college year began in mid-August, and Parris was comfortably settled in the big northeast chamber which he shared with three other students. Windows to the north, east, and west provided ample light; and two big double beds were furnished with linens and coverlets brought by their users. Four little studies opening off the large room provided privacy and a place for personal belongings.

Aunt Susanna had made him a new cornhusk mattress and a goose-feather pillow which she told him was "stuffed with her own feathers," and Theodora had worked three weeks in the heat making green cushions for his two stools and a "carpet" to cover the big oaken chest which had been his mother's and served the double purpose of chest and seat. He was very cozy in his own little cedar-ceiled study. He thought 'twould be more free from vermin than the plastered ones, and besides this practical reason, there was a pleasant woodsy odor about it and the further advantage that the ceiling wouldn't fall about his ears as some of the plaster threatened to do.

Mr. Morton sent him a box of books carefully chosen and Andrew Marvell had tucked in a copy of *Paradise Lost*, which had on its flyleaf Mr. Milton's autograph (legible despite his blindness). Mr. Felkin surprised and delighted him with a hat of fine beaver with a brim six inches wide, and a student's cloak of broadcloth. Thomas Parris had remembered him with a kind and fatherly letter, which was addressed to Samuel in care of his uncle John Oxenbridge. It had arrived but a few weeks before, well past due, for it had been on board the unlucky vessel *Hawthorne* which was dashed on the rocks of the cape on its voyage from Barbados. Only two sailors were saved, and luckily one of them had Thomas Parris's commission to carry a letter to his son.

My deere Son,   (it read)

Letters lately come from yr friends Mr. Chas. Morton & Hon. Andrew Marvell advise mee yt. you bee in a fayre way to receeve the Skolership offerd by Mr. Penoyer his estate, it bein in a summe sufficient to provyde you a livin durin yr colledge yrs. You bein a miner they ask mee to consent to their planns for you an eksecute a releese of my rights to yr ernnins as my miner son.

Itt seams ye Lord dont meen me to have anny aide or supporte from my sonnes, John bein a poore precher not abel too keepe him selfe an Thos. bein dead an nowe you beein set for prechin all so. I muste go it aloan with no yung armes to leen on in my deklining yrs. save for hired help & Negurs. Well, if soe it be I must bow to itt & make no complaynt. I hear by give you yr freedom from yr debt to mee yr Father. Likely ye wount be wuth much as a shugar planter as bein a Precher genly spiles a lad fer usefulle labor.

Hear you will find ten guineas for to find yourself in whut bks & cloes bee most neadful. Mayke it goe as fur as twill & take care you waste nuthin on foolereys.

God be wi ye
Yr loven Father
Thos. Parris.

At the commons table he had the satisfaction of being seated well above the salt. The rank thus established was written in a large German text, in a handsome style, and hung on the buttery wall. This ranking was no empty honor, since it involved the choice of the best chambers and first helpings at table.

The college was much smaller than Parris had expected. However, education was fairly universal, for in every little hamlet there was a free school where the children of the humblest were taught to write and cipher, and most important of all, to read God's Word. The printing press was placing the Book of Books in the homes of the common people.

It was a beautiful and reverent ideal. But even in this first half century there had sprung up schisms and heresies which threatened both the religious and political life of the colony.

Even the children, thumbing over their Bibles, found forbidden meanings in the sacred pages.

Under the stimulus of the college and the pulpit, Samuel Parris responded with excitement to the drama and poetry of this new land in which he was to have his part and lot. And if, now and again, the dream of adventure and ambition and power blurred his spiritual vision so that the things of this world loomed large and the things of the spirit dwindled—what then? Can mortal man speak as God's vicegerent, and still walk humbly?

There were those, even within the sacred walls of the college, who dared to speak against the government. Not in open disputation, of course, that would not have been permitted, but in little groups around the fire of an evening, or in the college yard. John Wise seemed to be a leader in this radical group, Parris noticed.

At mealtimes he kept the lower end of the long table alert and eager, and frequently drew a burst of laughter by his wit and sarcasm. Parris could not hear what he said, but he quizzed his fag, little John Emerson, and so got a fairly good idea of the gist of it. 'Twas not to be wondered at that this son of a serving-man should set himself up to know more than his betters. Because he had a giant yeoman's body and could throw any man in the village, he seemed to believe that he could instruct the clergy and magistrates how the colony should be run; setting up a clamor for democracy, and protesting that with a population of twenty-five thousand adult males only eleven hundred had the right to vote. What of it, if only the eleven hundred could qualify?

The doors of the churches stood wide open to all who would come before the meeting and make public their accounts of the regenerating work of grace by which they could claim divine election. Let the redeemed of the Lord say so! Let the unregenerates hold their peace or go back where they came from!

14

Susanna Calls to Mind

*It would be no unprofitable thing for
you to pass over the several streets and
call to mind who lived here so many
years ago.*

Susanna oxenbridge had lived in Boston only two years,
but she knew more about her neighbors than many an older
resident.

"I never did see much in books, like John does," she told her
nephew. "It's humans I admire at. Your uncle John can set
with his nose in a book day in an' day out, an' if 'twarnt for me,
he'd never know half o' what goes on. That's what overmuch
schoolin' does to a body! Thank God, I can't read a word o'
Latin or Greek or Hebrew, but I can tell what folks is up to
as well as the next one. An' let me tell you there be more goin'
on hereabouts than's bein' spoke of.

"You're startin' in to learn to be a preacher, Sammy, an' John
can tell you all about Zion-in-the-Wilderness an' the Holy Commonwealth; but when all's said, you'll find out as Boston Town
ain't any New Jerusalem by a long ways. I've lived with all
kinds o' folks an' neighbored with 'em all; even to papists an'
Negurs an' Quakers, an' they be more akin 'n ye'd think, once ye
get down under their skins. If you want to know the Lord's
plans for His Zion, ask your uncle John, but if you want to
know about anybody in Boston, ask your old auntie Sue."

So it was through Susanna's eyes that Samuel first saw his
neighbors. On the north was Governor Bellingham's mansion,
built of native stone quarried out of the hillside on which it stood
and surrounded by well-tended grounds. Beyond that was another
of the old mansions, which John Hull, the mintmaster, had
bought from the heirs of Mr. John Cotton.

The house was just as in John Cotton's time; a big bare place set high on the slope of Cotton Hill and dreadful bleak in winter. It was one of the oldest in Boston.

Around the corner to the north Old John Endicott had lived when he was governor. At his house the trials of witches and Quakers had been held. Some said the place was haunted and there were queer noises at night and sometimes lights, so that it stood empty most of the time. There Mistress Ann Hibbens was proved for a witch about fifteen years ago and was the first body to hang on the new gallows after it was moved from the neck to a more convenient location on the Common.

Mistress Hibbens was sister to Governor Bellingham, but that didn't save her. Though the minister, John Norton, said she got the halter for having more wit than her neighbors.

"Are there any witches here now?" Samuel asked, his boyish abhorrence of the *Witch of Edmonton* flashing across his memory.

"Well, there ain't been much talk of 'em here in Boston sence I come. But back in the woods where the Injuns go runnin' round stark naked in all kinds o' weather, there be witch dancin' an' ghost dancin' an' powwowin' an' Lord knows what! I'm scared to death of them red Injuns. Negurs is bad enough, but they will work, an' they be good-natured if ye don't mistreat 'em. But these wild Injuns with eyes like hard black beads an' never a word but just to grunt 'UGH! UGH!' an' pint their fingers at what they want; Lord save me from 'em!

"'Tis said the first settlers would all have been murdered if the good Lord han't prepared the way fer His own by sendin' a pestilence to kill off most o' the redskins. And then Captain Mason attacked the Pequot village and burned it an' killed eighteen hunderd of the varmints in one big bonfire. That kinda took the fight out of 'em fer a spell till the colonists could get a start, praise God!

"Good Pastor Eliot's gone amongst 'em an' taught, an' translated the Bible into their outlandish lingo, tryin' to make Christians out of 'em—which looks to me like makin' silk purses outa sows' ears. An' as fer sendin' Injuns to Harvard to make preachers out of 'em, I'd as lief set a wolf tendin' sheep!"

Samuel interrupted. "Those I've seen in Boston don't look so fierce."

"No," Susanna conceded. "They're peaceable enough when they come into town. The squaws bring baskets wove from reeds and birchbark to sell or trade for trinkets; and the men make canoes. Some they sell an' some they make a right good livin' with, takin' folks to the neighborin' towns. 'Tis the easiest and swiftest way to travel, with no roads. That's what hampers the colony more 'n anything. 'Tis so hard to get from place to place, what with the hills and forests and swamps and all these little rivers runnin' down betwixt the hills.

"But in spite of all, Boston's a thrivin' town—the best in all the colonies. We've most everything a town needs. Harbor room an' churches and a fine new Townhouse and the best springs o' water anywhere. There's a new almshouse an' two buryin' places an' a Latin school jest round the corner with Mr. Ezekiel Cheever for master. Mr. Mather thinks so high of it that he sends his son Cotton there, though he's well able to hire a tutor."

Samuel laughed. "I know. The other day I met a little lad trudging up the road with his schoolbooks. Some bigger boys had been deviling him, and his face was streaked with tears and dust. He stopped and looked up into my face.

" 'I d-don't know y-you,' he said. He was so little and so cocky, with his dirty face and big brown eyes, it was comical.

" 'I don't know you, either,' I told him.

"He seemed astonished. 'Everybody kn-knows me! I-I am C-Cotton M-M-Mather! M-my f-father is the g-g-greatest m-m-minister in the world. I-I'm g-going t-t-to b-be a m-m-minister t-t-too.'

"The more in earnest he got the more he stammered. I couldn't help laughing at him—the idea of being a minister with that stammering tongue! It must be a heavy cross to his father to have a stammering son. But he's a bumptious little beggar." Samuel laughed. "Feels as big as anybody!"

Susanna wagged her head. "There's no accountin' fer the ways o' Providence. But mebbe the Lord thinks Increase Mather needs humblin'. I kinda think so myself. The Cottons an' the Mathers be smart an' able preachers, all of 'em. But sometimes they mind me a little bit of Moses when he struck the rock in the wilderness, 'stead of speakin' to it like the Lord told him.

" 'Hear now, ye rebels,' sez he, 'must we bring ye water outa this rock?' Seems like some folks think 'twould be pretty hard on the Lord ef He had to worry along without their help.

"As for that poor stammerin' child—he'll never be a preacher.

An' his little brother Nathaniel's a poor sickly mite as will never live to grow up. Looks as though Mr. Mather is bein' brought low in his pride."

Susanna heaved a sigh of satisfaction.

"Mr. Mather married Mr. John Cotton's daughter Maria, an' they lived here on Cotton Hill in her father's house when John and I come here. Little Cotton was born here and named for his granther. He was a pretty little lad an' friendly and curious as a setter puppy. He'd come arunnin' in all times o' day teasin' me fer comfits, an' Theodora'd make him ask over an' over, plaguing him because he couldn't say the word.

"A year or so back, they sold the place to Mr. Hull an' moved to the North End—to be near Mr. Mather's meetin'house was the reason they give, but I surmise 'twas more that he craved to live in the more elegant an' prosperous part of town."

President Chauncy had some misgivings about Samuel's preparatory course. "I fear your master Morton hath been led away by the new philosophical ideas to a length that hath made him neglectful of the classics," he commented; "and to neglect such a foundation because of an extreme admiration for the so-called New Science is to set up Newton and Halley and Descartes above St. Paul, and the *Philosophical Transactions* on a par with the revelation of the Scriptures."

So Parris put in the vacation in the study of Latin and Greek and Hebrew under the able tutoring of John Oxenbridge. The heat oppressed him. He had heard many reports of the cold New England winters, but he was unprepared for the hot summer days. On the contrary, John Oxenbridge welcomed the warmth like a salamander. To his mind, there were only three months of really comfortable weather in Boston. His energy and enthusiasm never flagged. At Oxford he had the name of being a hard master and impatient with a dull or careless pupil. But for his new nephew he had only commendation.

"He's a knowing lad," he told Susanna. "Strange that a merchant's son should be so ingenious a scholar."

"He comes by that on the distaff side," Susanna replied. "The Parrises was quick and able and an old London house. They was all merchants, back to the first Roger de Paris who came from France as a trader nigh four hundred year ago when Edward I was king. But we all knew Tom married above him when he got Anne Martin. Her father was a country clergyman with four daughters; and Anne had no dower, but she had beauty and breeding. Tom had money enough and coveted to wed a lady of quality. 'Twas a good match for 'em both.

"The first Martin came over with the Bastard in 1066 and conquered Kemys in Pembrokeshire, which give him a barony. And the Martins all the way down have been gentlemen; and many of 'em scholars, though they had little wealth. As for Anne, she was a saint and a lady.

"Trouble is, Sammy takes after both sides—and they mix like oil an' water. He is like poor St. Paul: he delights in the law of God after the inward man, but he sees another law in his members, warrin' against the law of his mind. Sammy warn't ever cut out to be a saint like his mother—but he can't be a comfortable sinner like Tom. I fear me life is goin' to be hard on the lad."

"My dear Susanna! What an expression! 'Comfortable sinner,' indeed! I hope you do not mean to justify Thomas Parris!"

"I ain't justifyin' an' I ain't condemnin', neither one. I leave that to the Lord an' His ministers," she retorted with spirit. "But I hold Tom Parris in high esteem, an' I be proud to count him my chiefest friend."

Oxenbridge returned to his interrupted sermon. Life had taught him not to argue with a woman.

So through the long summer days Samuel "reviewed the tongues." But his English love of the out-of-doors somehow found him time to adventure in town and country, making him at home in the land of his adoption.

He liked the colony and was charmed with its quaint mingling of rural beauty and commercial activity. Boston, small as it was, reminded him of a miniature London. Its crooked and narrow streets, with little courts and byways, charmed Samuel, and especially the foot passages ducking in and out, with now and then, even in this early day, a smuggler's passage leading underground from the water front by a secret way. There were crowded, peaked-roofed buildings huddled about the dock, pervaded by the smell of fish. The shops and taverns had familiar London names and swinging signs such as: The King's Arms; Blue Anchor; Rose and Crown; and Cromwell's Head. There was the Townhouse with its shops and walk for the merchants after the fashion of the Royal Exchange (even to the grasshoppers on its weather vanes); its balcony where proclamations were read to the people assembled in the Square. All these betokened its English origin, and made the newcomer feel very much at home.

If Samuel Parris was in a mood for neighborhood gossip, he had only to start his Aunt Susanna going. "Tell me some more about our neighbors, Aunt Sue," he would say. "From my chamber window I can see a place on the far side of Cotton Hill that looks deserted. Large grounds surrounded by a tall thorn hedge, and an old house with all the shutters closed, so shut in by cedars one can scarce see it, save from the hilltop. Doesn't anyone live there?"

"Aye, that's the Fairgrave place. Dr. Fairgrave went to England last spring and the house was shut up and left in charge of an old squaw that kep' house for him after his wife died. The squaw stayed round for a spell, but I ain't seen her fer some while —most like she got tired stayin' an' went back to her tribe. That's the way them Injuns do mostly. Lord save me from ever havin' to be beholden to 'em!"

"Strange that anyone would leave so large a place without a reliable caretaker," Parris commented.

"Oh, as to that, 'twill come to no harm. Robbery ain't common in Boston, an' nothin' could hardly get through that thorn hedge. That's what he called the place, 'Thornhedge.' Sounds kinda unfriendly-like, but 'tis a fittin' name. Timothy Fairgrave ain't a friendly person. He's lived in Boston years and years but nobody seems to know much about him. He used to be doctor of physic when he were young. Some say he was a quacksalver, but he made a comfortable fortune, 'tis said, an' then quit physicianing (which Lord knows is a hard life in a new country) and turned to chemistry, years back.

"He built this house out of native oak an' hedged it about with thorn. Way up garret in the south gable he has a secret chamber led to by a windin' stair that he calls an elaboratory where he brews curious potions which some say be marvelous potent. He had a good, faithful wife, but awful pindlin'—looked like she'd been drug through a knothole. She kept havin' young'uns one after another (that was before I come here) but they all died when they was little. Seems like his potions didn't do much good round home.

"Mercy Fairgrave was a good Christian woman and a member of our meetin'house. (The doctor was an outsider but tended regular—he liked to argue with John about the resurrection an' sech.) Mercy an' I neighbored a good bit. She'd slip out through a little break in the hedge and come an' set a spell with me. She'd bring her darnin' or sewin' an' work whilst we talked, only she didn't talk much. She was a hard-workin' woman and scrubbed an' cleaned from mornin' till night. She never had much luck gittin' help—except now and then Injuns, which to my way o' thinkin' is wuss 'n none. I suspicioned folks was feared of the place. There's been tales of queer doin's—ungodly stinks an' sech as that—an' some hints of something unholy about that elaboratory where he concocted his draughts and pills and potions."

"Witchcraft? Sorcery?" queried Parris.

"Nay, nay, my lad, be not overbrash! None put it in so many words. But mebbe delvin' into forbidden things. There be mysteries the Lord don't intend for folk to know, Sammy. Ef He did He'd reveal 'em. And it don't seem reverent nor respectable to pry into the secrets of the Almighty. But once I saw something with my own eyes.

"I was passin' the smithy and there was a lad sore wounded by runnin' a teeny splinter of iron into his eye. Dr. Alcock was there trying to get it with his tweezers, but 'twas buried so deep he couldn't reach it. Somebody run fer Dr. Fairgrave an' he come with a little piece of smooth-polished stone (it looked like) an' jest touched the point of it to the eyeball, gentle-like, an' drawed it back slow—with that splinter hangin' to it. He plucked the sliver off an' held it up for all to see, an' then he held it down close to the stone again—not touchin' but jest close to—and let go. An' as true as I live an' breathe, it flew out of his fingers an' clung to that stun! Y'r uncle John asked him to explain the mystery, but he only chuckled and laughed.

"'Gilbert shall live, till loadstones cease to draw,' says he; and went back home, still chucklin' to himself."

Samuel favored his aunt with the superior smile peculiar to college students. "A loadstone is truly a mystery, Aunt Sue, but 'tis not black magic. We had one at Morton's. Perhaps your Dr. Fairgrave is more trickster than sorcerer."

Susanna sniffed: "Whatever you want to call it, 'tis conjuration —an' best let be by Christians."

She went on with her story: "Mercy never talked of his strange ways, but I could see she was worried an' vexed. Only once she let out that he ne'er let even her inside his elaboratory, not even to tidy up. He kep' it locked up when he went out. An' once when she plucked up courage to ask him what he was up to, he said 'twas such a secret as is not fit for everyone, else they might do a great deal of hurt, spending an' employing of it to satisfy sinful lusts.

"John thinks he's been lured away by the Brethren of the Rosy Cross, who pretend to have from Arabia a book writ in letters of gold in which great secrets are revealed: how to turn base metals into gold; and to prolong life; and to know all that is passing on t'other side of the world an' suchlike mysteries. John says 'tis rumored there be others in the colony who defend the same doctrines—amongst 'em young John Winthrop, the governor of the New Haven Colony, which broke away from the Massachusetts in the early days, an' betook themselves to the wilds of Connecticut where they could be free to indulge their fanatic practices.

"Well, as I say, things went on, an' last winter poor Mercy Fairgrave was took with a consumption. She kep' askin' fer me an' I'd go set with her whenever I could, though her husband never made me any too welcome. One day she was very bad an' when I come home, the doctor let me out the kitchen door, an' says I to him: 'Mercy's time is short. She won't last the month out.' That was late February.

"He shook his head very confident. 'You be wrong there, Mistress Oxenbridge,' he says, an' pointed with his finger. 'When yon plum thicket is white wi' bloom, Mercy will die.'

"An' it come to pass just as he said. 'Twas the first o' May. I looked out the butt'ry window that mornin' an' I see the plum bushes were abloom an' I run right over. She had just passed away! Just like he said two months before. He foreknew the very day!

"He didn't appear to grieve much. Before the grass had started on poor Mercy's grave, Dr. Fairgrave sailed for England; an' so far's I know not a soul in Boston has heard from him sence. Though Cap'n Blunt, down to the tavern where the post is left when the ships come in, said there was a letter come addressed to Governor John Winthrop at New Haven, which he knew for certain was in Dr. Fairgrave's hand."

Samuel laughed. "So the captain keeps track of where letters come from, does he? Suppose a fellow got a letter from his sweetheart. I suppose all the town would know."

"More 'n likely. Though 'tain't anything to think shame of, s'posin' they did. In Lunnon a body might die and go to heaven any day in the week and nobody but the gravedigger would ever know it. Myself, I like to be took some notice of."

Though Samuel would never have admitted it, he, too, liked to be "took notice of." For as he sauntered around the town it gave him a feeling of importance when people whom he had never seen greeted him by name and asked him the latest news from London, and what he thought of politics and business, and whether he knew John Smith or Tommy Williams, who were cousins of theirs.

He felt quite at home already. As to its people and traditions, the place was more English than London itself, for "foreigners" were rare. To be sure, there were ships from many ports which dropped anchor in the harbor, but the sailors came and went like birds of passage, leaving only an occasional reminder of their presence in a dark-browed child, held up to shame as a Portugee bastard. The inhabitants were of one blood and the immemorial usages of England were their precedents of law and custom.

It had taken only a few seasons to shatter the hopes of the first settlers for an easy and bountiful living from the land. The shallow soil grudged them only scant subsistence, and to preserve their very lives they must turn from the land to the sea. The cold waters were swarming with fish, and the forests provided timber for shipbuilding. John Winthrop in Boston and Hugh Peter in Salem had built ships of some size and launched them; and the bays and fishing grounds along the coast were dotted with little boats and the shores were lined with frames to salt and dry their catch. Puritan New England ate fish to save their bodies from starvation and shipped fish to the countries of Southern Europe to save papists' consciences.

From the earliest days, Boston had "rope walks" where hemp was twisted into stays. The tall pines of the forest were dragged by ox teams to fashion masts. And to fit the shallow waters of the bays they built their ships after a new fashion; broad in the beam, shallow in the hull; lying close to the water, less liable to capsize and requiring a smaller crew, sometimes making the trip to the Indies with only five or six sailors to man them.

Into these crude crafts they loaded their products: pipe staves to be assembled into molasses casks; woodenware whittled out by hand during the long winter evenings after the chores were done; or perhaps cotton or linen cloth hand spun and hand woven by the womenfolk:—and set sail for the Islands of Bermuda or Barbados or Jamaica, where they traded their cargo for molasses to make New England rum and pieces of eight to buy English luxuries. Salem and Boston and the Rhode Island ports became the centers of trade and commerce and simple manufactures.

Thus did God manifest His favor to His poor saints in the wilderness. And thus the Puritan claimed the promise: The righteous shall flourish like the palm tree: he shall grow like a cedar in Lebanon.

15

"Stelligeri"

In the class lists the names of the dead were prefixed by asterisks. In the final summary the number of the dead was defined thus:
E vivis cesserunt stelligeri.—
They that bear the stars have passed from among the living. . . . To all of us who cared for the old catalogues, the dead men of Harvard were always stelligeri—They that bear the stars.

—BARRETT WENDELL.

*I*N FEBRUARY the beloved President Chauncy died. The cold had somewhat abated, but the snow still lay deep on the ground. From the president's house to the graveyard a broad way had been cleared, the snow heaped in a glistening wall on each side.

It was Samuel's first New England funeral. The colonists, not wishing to conform to the popish error that prayer is to be used for or over the dead, had done away with prayer and hymn and eulogy. This silent mourning seemed to invest the finality and inevitability of death with a new terror: an inexpressible melancholy, which no words could have conveyed.

Their last service having been done for the dead, the mourners turned away, still moving slowly and silently out through the graveyard gate, then hurried homeward—back to the land of the living. Parris was among the last. The gravedigger stopped to shovel the trampled snow in order to shut the gate, and with some effort forced the heavy bar into its groove. Parris fell into step with Sewall. He felt the need of companionship and speech.

"Why does he shut fast the graveyard gate?" he asked.

Sewall looked surprised. "To keep out the wolves," he answered. "That is why the graveyard is paled in. Cambridge is near the border and when the timber wolves are hungry in winter they often venture into town. If they smell a new-made grave they claw and dig at it like a dog for a buried bone."

Parris shuddered. For the first time he felt the terror of the forests, crowding so close to the new settlements. He threw an involuntary glance over his shoulder. Already he could feel the twilight hovering and a lean gray shadow stalking him. A strange fear gripped him, recalling the terrors of his childhood, when Old Emma and Daffy Joe had told him tales of werewolves and goblins and ghosts:—the deep-laid racial terror of the Unknown, haunting the forests where wild beasts and wild men lurked; where fire and flood and pestilence and hunger were only the mortal footprints of the powers of darkness, lying in wait for luckless human beings who might venture too far into the limbo of forbidden things.

He linked his arm with Sewall's and in a voice not quite steady began to talk of commonplace affairs. Yet he could not rid himself of the undercurrent of dread. He almost wished himself back in London, where the only things to fear were such commonplace matters as robbery and murder and war. Where the noise and hurly-burly, the clamor and clangor of bells, the raucous voices howling bawdy ballads, and the friendly lights of tavern doors had long ago routed the prince of the power of the air. Low on the eastern horizon, the first pale star of evening shone.

Sewall's prosaic voice brought him back from his thoughts.

"For the good of the college I trust there will be little delay in appointing a new president," he said. "President Chauncy's age and failing health have given them ample time to prepare for this contingency. In my own judgment we need look no farther than our own Cambridge parsonage to find on eminently suitable man: Mr. Urian Oakes. He is popular with the scholars and their elders, and for classical learning and elegant Latin he cannot be surpassed. His services as one of the censors of the press have safeguarded us from many loose and unorthodox books, for he regards 'an unlimited tolerance as the firstborn of all abominations.'"

The college bell, ringing for evening commons, quickened their steps, and as the students gathered around the board they talked of little but the all-absorbing question of the new president.

The eagerness of their interest was stimulated by the general understanding that this time the man chosen would be one of Harvard's own sons, trained in the way of the New England Church.

Yet months went by, and no action was taken.

The ministers of the near-by towns cheerfully, perhaps hopefully, took turns in lecturing. Oakes of Cambridge; Shepard of Charlestown; Mather of Boston; Higginson of Salem; perhaps a visiting divine from Plymouth or Ipswich or one of the Connecticut towns; and back to Oakes again.

Each lecturer had his admirers among the students, but it was always Urian Oakes they had to depend on. If the weather was bad or the rivers were flooded or the bridges were out, so that the lecturer from farther away did not come, Urian Oakes never failed them. He was close at hand, he was capable, he was willing and eager to serve. He was generally regarded as a suitable man for the office: a thorough scholar, a graduate of the class of 1650, a man in the prime of life, a Puritan of the Puritans.

But if the body of the clergy praised his strict orthodoxy, the more liberal element which was steadily growing in strength among the laymen disliked him for his pedantry and intolerance. The burning of books in the public square, for instance, gave offense to some who thought it smelled of Archbishop Laud. The controversy became acrimonious.

July came, and with it like a thunderbolt came the astonishing news.

Dr. Leonard Hoar had come from England, called as assistant pastor of the South Church of Boston—the seceding church which was not yet quite respectable. Leonard Hoar arrived—bringing with him a letter signed by thirteen dissenting clergymen in and about London, recommending Mr. Hoar for the presidency of Harvard.

And before anybody so much as heard about it, the General Court approved the appointment—with a fifty per cent increase of salary—£150 a year!

It was Edward Pelham, Governor Bellingham's scapegrace nephew, who brought the news to the college. Most of the students had gone home for the vacation, uncertain as to whether the school would reopen. Parris and John Wise and a junior from Hadley named Jonathan Russell were in the library when Pelham rushed in with his astounding announcement.

"A Hoar frost has blighted our Oakes," he cried. "I never heard of Hoar, but he has my allegiance. Anybody but Oakes—with his tiptoeing walk and his oily smirk and the way he licks his lips—like a cat that's been in the cream. Come on, you fellows! We'll celebrate at Gibson's tonight and drink the health of our new president, Lord love him!"

Pelham had the repute of being a wild fellow, but his father had been a former treasurer of the college and his social connections and gay humor made him popular. Parris was a bit flattered by the invitation and eager to hear all that Pelham knew, so he joined the party although Gibson's tavern was taboo and he had some misgivings.

Pelham was frankly jubilant as he told his story, and he had plenty to tell. He had been in Boston with his aunt Penelope, wife of Governor Bellingham.

"We were all at breakfast," he said, "when up rides Deputy Governor Leverett and must see Uncle Richard very urgent. He looked dubious at me, so, being a gentleman, I left the room. (I could hear quite well from the library and not embarrass him.) To make the matter short, he had received a letter signed by thirteen ministers in England—bigwigs, all of them—who I take it had been urged to contribute to our beloved college, recommending that Mr. Hoar be appointed president of Harvard. That word 'recommending' was a short way of saying Hoar for president or no support from England.

"Leverett and Aunt Pen talked it over in front of Uncle Richard—they always go through the motions of consulting him, you know. He is still governor in name (though his wits are so addled that everything is left with Mr. Leverett, his deputy). Then Mr. Leverett wrote a letter to Mr. Oakes, enclosing the one he had received and recommending (again) that the overseers be called together and the matter put through without delay.

"And I, being on hand and willing and capable, brought the message to Cambridge.

"Oakes didn't say a word when he read the letter, but I could tell from his face 'twas a sorry blow.

" 'Is there an answer?' says I, helpful as ever.

"He shook his head. 'No!' says he. 'Your uncle the governor knows his slightest wish will have my immediate attention. I will act at once.'

"Oh, the thing's sewed up in the bag!" finished Pelham.

Parris was somewhat puzzled. "But why are the ministers so anxious to have an American?" he asked. "Aren't we all of English blood and loyal subjects of British rule, whether at home or in the colonies?"

Wise laughed. "Wait till you've lived in the colony a little longer, Parris, and you will not ask that question. The Atlantic is wider than you think."

There were only the four of them at Gibson's that evening. The dinner was excellent: a fine, plump turkey, roasted on the spit; a Yorkshire pudding, in which Gibson's wife excelled; and some old Madeira from the Bellingham cellar, which Pelham said he hoped his aunt wouldn't miss.

"I must mind my ways," he said. "After my last slip, the pater made a new will (and kindly sent me a copy). It provides: 'If he is now Serious, Sober and Solid and followeth his study and avoid all idle and profuse company, and that the Trustees believe there is a Real Change in him for the better and not only to attain his ends thereby'—think of trying to live up to a will like that!"

It was almost closing time. Pelham rose and raised his glass, and standing around the table they drank a toast to the new president of Harvard.

"But for the turkey," Pelham said, "we have to thank young Urian Oakes. As you all know, I am a poor man, kept on a beggarly dole by my stern sire because of my well-known spendthrift tendencies. So today, when I wanted to kill the fatted calf, alas, I had no calf!

"I took my fowling piece and sallied forth, strong in the faith that the Lord would provide; and who did I see but young Urian, worthy son of a worthy sire, and little Percival Greene, picking up fruit in the marshal's orchard, and as I came to the fence, there sat a fine plump turkey.

" 'Urian,' says I, 'I'll wager you can't shoot that turkey.' Whereupon he set down his basket and took my gun and blazed away. And bless me if that turkey didn't fall down dead.

" 'Look what you've done!' says I. 'Now you are in for it!'

"Urian began whimpering and I picked up the bird and wrapped it in Percival's coat and put it in Urian's hands. 'Run like Old Splitfoot, and take it to Gibson's, he'll know what to do with it!' says I. And was I right? Eh, Gibson, was I right?"

Gibson roared: "Aye, sir! Right ye be! When turkeys rain down on my doorstoop, I doant ask ef the Lord or the deil sent 'em. I know what to do!"

The party broke up with shouts of laughter. But a few weeks later, after Parris had gone back to Boston, Gibson was haled into court for entertaining students contrary to law and had to pay a fine of forty shillings. Somehow the joke seemed to have turned sour and there was some unpleasant publicity for all concerned.

John Oxenbridge took the matter quite to heart. He reprimanded his nephew severely and required him to prepare and read at morning worship each day for a week a Logical Analysis of Proverbe 4:14-27, beginning:

> Enter not into the path of the wicked,
> and go not in the way of evil men.
> Avoid it, pass not by it, turn from
> it, and pass away.

By the time Samuel had gone through the fourteen verses, starting with the major and minor premise; developing in some two thousand words the argument, the question proposed, the indubitable theses, the affirmation and explanation, the description of the way of the wicked and the path of the just, the degrees of unrighteousness, i.e., enter not, go not, avoid, pass not by, turn from, and pass away, he certainly should have been led to ponder the path of his feet before they led him astray again.

Samuel had an open mind about the appointment of Hoar. When he went to Boston he found a letter from Mr. Morton praising Hoar in high terms as a Christian gentleman and a leader in scientific thought.

Oxenbridge, however, was not convinced. "After all," he said, "it seems hardly fitting for a man devoted to physic to head a college for ministers. But we must yield with as good grace as may be."

It added gall to his wormwood that Mr. Hoar was a kinsman of Mr. Hull of the seceding South Church and was assisting the minister, Mr. Thacher.

Samuel liked Mr. Hoar at sight. He was staying with the Hulls. Though Samuel did not want to offend his uncle by going to South Church, he managed to use Morton's letter as an introduction one day in the apple orchard. He listened with interest to Mr. Hoar's plans of the day when the college might have a large garden and orchard for students interested in planting; and also mechanical and chemical laboratories.

"In a new land like this, we need the practicalities," he said. It all sounded so much like Charles Morton that it made Samuel homesick. Suddenly the way of the New England Church seemed a very narrow way, indeed—narrow and cramping to the soul.

Hoar's words gave him a glimpse of a future college where the dreams of youth should be as high and free as the graceful, wide-spreading branches of the giant elms of Harvard Yard—reaching for the stars, but firmly rooted in the earth.

Samuel tried to suggest something of this to his uncle, but Oxenbridge shook his head and blinked sadly. "Strait is the gate and narrow is the way," he said, "and few there be that find it. A theologue has enough to do to perfect himself in the things of the spirit. And the spirit warreth against the flesh, nephew. Never forget that! 'Twas the subtlety of the Old Serpent that tempted the woman: when she saw that the tree was good for food, and pleasant to the eyes. We are but silly worms, turning this way and that, blindly searching for an easier way or a prettier pebble. We should answer such temptations with the words of Our Blessed Lord: wist ye not that I must be about my Father's business?"

16

Thanksgiving Day

The Lord who led forth Israel was with us in the waste:
Sometime in light, sometime in cloud, before us He hath paced;
Now give Him thanks, and pray to Him who holds us in his hand
To prosper us and make of this a strong and mighty land!
—ALICE WILLIAMS BROTHERTON.

"COME HERE, Sammy, and take a peek into the buttery. The good Lord has blessed us with his bounty and today we return thanks by eatin' all we can stuff. The parish has been sendin' donations all week."

Samuel Parris, home from Harvard for the Thanksgiving holiday, rose lazily from the settle where he had lain sprawled before the great fireplace, and followed Aunt Susanna.

"If there be anything I enjoy more than loafing, 'tis feasting, dear my aunt; and the commons table keeps us safe from the sin of gluttony. Breakfast: a cue of beer and a hunk of bread, sized out at the buttery hatch. Dinner: bread and beer and beef. Supper: hasty pudding with bacon and a biscuit, or on lucky days a mutton pie. If you want a piece between meals and have any money, you buy it at the buttery hatch, where they sell wines, groceries, and et ceteras. 'Tis the purpose of the buttery to remove from the scholars all temptation to frequent the marts of luxury, intemperance, and ruin!

" 'Tis that simplicity, so they tell us, 'which makes the fare cheap, and wholesome, and philosophical; and thus secures in the town a general style of living, at once economical and favorable to health and to study.' But we dare not protest. One of the students got a caning t'other day for merely telling the steward that the commons table was foretold in Scripture. The steward din't credit it and the student cited chapter and verse: Hebrews 13:8."

"Pity's sake!" Susanna gasped. "What said the Scripture?"

Samuel opened the great Bible and pointed, while his aunt read: "Jesus Christ the same yesterday, and to day and for ever."

"Why, Samuel Parris," in a shocked voice, "I think that is blas*phem*ous!"

Samuel, his eyes atwinkle, answered gravely: "Yes, dearly beloved! No doubt about it. That is why they caned him."

Susanna laughed in spite of herself. "Hush your foolishness, you young reprobate! Ef ye learn sech devilment at the college, ye better bide at home!"

She opened the buttery door. "Come here an' look at that tom turkey. Jed Garrett brung that. He shot five t'other day an' this were the biggest an' fattest, he said, so he give it to the Lord as a thank offerin'. An' there's a brace o' barnyard geese an' a coupla dozen wild pigeons an' a smoked ham an' a haunch o' venison— Will Barnes brought down a big duck an' he knows John dotes on deer meat. He said he stuck an' bled it while 'twas hot, so it's sure to be good. There's a bar'l o' cider from Elder Allen's orchard; an' a sack o' corn meal from Bob Jennings at the gristmill— though he do rightly belong to Mr. Mather's flock, bein' a North-Ender.

"And look here—a box of oranges from our own Cotton Hall plantation. Every year since I come to Boston, your father's never forgot to send oranges. They be scarce an' high to buy 'em here, and seems like they don't taste so good as our own, anyway.

"And a dozen o' bayb'ry candles from the Widow Smylie; she's too poor to buy mutton taller, so she gathers the berries along the marsh an' biles 'em down. 'Tis a trial o' patience—bilin' an' skimmin'—but when they're done they burn as good as taller ones an' some folks set store by the smell—I kinda like it myself —an' John's been good to her in her time o' trial.

"An' look, here's a sack of earth apples. Dan Biggs, the atheist, sent *them*. Drat him, he knows John won't have 'em on his table! But he din't really mean harm by sendin' 'em, he jest likes his joke."

Samuel broke in. "What's the joke, auntie? They look all right, though I never ate any, I think."

Susanna laughed self-consciously. "Ye're better off if ye don't, Sammy. They're not good Christian food, so they say. They're like the cussed mandrakes." She raised herself on tiptoe and whispered in his ear. "They rouse sinful passions and brute lusts, darlin', an' decent folks is shamed to even have 'em seen in their garden patch, for it shows they ain't what they'd oughta be."

She led the way back from the cold pantry and spread her hands before the glowing hearth-fire.

"We're havin' comp'ny to dinner, 'cause Thanksgivin' table set for three-four looks too stingy an' skimpin'. The Widow Smylie an' Deacon Applegate—he's a widower an' startin' to look round an' I hope 'twill do some good (though the widow, poor thing, ain't got much to offer), and our neighbor over the hill, Dr. Fairgrave and his new English bride.

"Did I tell ye he come home married? Sure enough! Brought back a young English gentlewoman. You will enjoy to 'quaint with her, Sammy, an' I hope you lay yourself out to please her and make her forget her homesick yearnings. She be as pretty and sweet as an English rose, an' only twenty-four, an' she's ne'er been from home in her life before and 'tis all so strange an' new, poor child. 'Tis sure December wed with May and I never yet see that prosper extreme well from the time of King David an' the Shunammite damsel down. But an old man has no sense o' fitness when he spies a comely lass. He forgets his years—an' mebbe she forgets too for the time bein' but 'twon't last—I've seen it time an' again.

"But I will say the doctor's done well by her. He's had the house all fixed up an' put in a new stun chimney an' fireplace in the big front chamber, an' a great canopy bedstead with damask curtains and a goose-feather bed and I dunno what not. He got Mistress Weston's thornback niece to help housekeep (she's good help if she'll stay) and seems planning to give her the moon if she asks for it. Mebbe she'll content herself when the homesickness is past.

"Mebbe you can kinda chirk her up. I told her I had a nephew come over from London last year, an' she looked wonderful pleased. 'Oh, 'twill be almost like a breath from home to talk to him!' she says. 'I used to live in London before the fire.' "

Samuel laughed. "If she's as charming a lady as you say, Aunt Sue, 'twon't be a trouble to talk to her. I've been homesick for England too; though I left behind few that I loved—save only my mother in Bunhill Fields." His eyes dimmed with tears at the thought of his mother, and he turned quickly away.

"I have a letter from President Hoar to deliver to Mr. Thacher," he said. "I had best take it at once. I should have stopped by on my way from the ferry, but I wanted to come straight home to you. Oh, Aunt Sue, you've made a home for me in this new land! You are the homiest person I know. In another week your charming Mistress Fairgrave will think you are her very own kin, and forget she ever lived in England!"

He kissed her on both plump cheeks, cut himself a generous hunk of plumcake, and danced out of reach before she could box his ears.

The Thanksgiving Day service began at eight in the morning and lasted until two.

Samuel Parris, in his place on the men's side of the meeting-house, craned his neck as much as good manners and reverence for God's house would permit, to see his new neighbor, Mistress Fairgrave. At the close of the service she was to go through the ordeal of relating her Christian experience as a preliminary to admission into the church fellowship. She had brought her letter of dismissal from the Puritans at Woking, but the way of the New England Church demanded in addition a personal relation. So young Mistress Fairgrave sat in the foreseat on the women's side, with Susanna Oxenbridge beside her to give her courage. All that Samuel could see was a Puritan bonnet of dove-colored stuff and a glimpse of fair hair around it.

The service at last came to an end and Pastor Oxenbridge called on Mistress Fairgrave to rise and testify of her Christian experience. She stood in her place and in response to the pastor's kindly encouragement began to speak in a low clear voice. Deacon Applegate put his hand to his ear and shouted, "Louder." Mistress Fairgrave's voice trembled a little as she began again.

Evidently she was no Anne Hutchinson, Parris thought smilingly, and to make a relation in a crowded meetinghouse was a trying ordeal for a modest young woman. Uncle John might have spared her that if he had chosen—many ministers did not require women to testify in public, but only to assure the pastor of their regeneration. But she spoke up bravely with only a slight quaver.

Again she was interrupted. Elder Allen cleared his throat and spoke with authority:

"Will the lady please to face the meeting?"

It was less a request than a command. The lady had no choice. She turned and faced the meeting. Her cheeks were very pink as for the third time she began to speak: "Brethren and Sisters—"

Samuel caught his breath: "Elizabeth!"

At that very moment Susanna Oxenbridge, without knowing why, turned to look at her nephew.

"My Lord above, what ails the lad?" she murmured. "Looks like he seen a ghost! Now what in tunket—"

Samuel sat staring, his face a mask. He heard nothing of what Elizabeth was saying. With an effort he gathered his scattered wits and tried to think. At last, after all these years, he had found Elizabeth—his Elizabeth—and his neighbor's wife.

In fancy he had often pictured their meeting, if God should bring them together again someday, as He had at first, by a miracle. That he might find her married never entered his head. He stared at her stupidly.

But suddenly he faced the need for decision, for action. In a few minutes he must meet her, speak to her, be presented to the old man who was her husband, sit at the board with the two of them and "lay himself out to make her forget her homesickness," as Aunt Sue had said.

And it was his part to plan for both of them, so that the meeting which would take her entirely by surprise should not betray either of them by unconsidered speech. He was thankful for the long closing prayer. It gave him time.

When the Amen was spoken, he was among the first in the churchyard, waiting. Oxenbridge came presently, with a little chubby-faced man with a short gray mustache and imperial, whom he introduced as Dr. Fairgrave. They stood in a little knot in the snowy churchyard, Oxenbridge blinking in the glare and shivering. He peered into the semidarkness of the meetinghouse, fretting.

"Where are those womenfolk? As long as they can gossip and gabble they feel no cold nor hunger!"

Parris seized the chance. "You two start on, uncle." He patted the stooped shoulders affectionately. "I will find Aunt Sue and hurry her along."

"Do please make haste, aunt of mine, before we all starve to death!" he called, entering the meetinghouse and sauntering down the aisle.

Susanna laughed. "Come here, you young rascal, I've been looking everywhere for you. I want you should meet Mistress Fairgrave, our new neighbor."

Samuel felt the blood rush to his temples as his eyes met those of Elizabeth. For a timeless second the two stared at each other, swept away by that indefinable spark that shines between a man and a woman who see each other for the first time as such and yet feel as though they had known each other for always. Samuel was the first to collect his wits. He smiled and held out both his hands.

"Aunt Susanna has been telling me of you," he said. "But 'tis a great surprise to find that you are an old friend." He turned to Susanna. "Elizabeth and I were 'quainted years ago, when we were youngsters, Aunt Sue, but I din't suspect that my friend Elizabeth Wray was your neighbor, Mistress Fairgrave."

Then as Susanna began asking excited questions: "Nay, nay! The tale can wait. Your guests are famishing. The menfolk have gone on ahead, and Mistress Smylie is standing at the door like patience on a monument. Do run along, darling, and let Elizabeth and me renew our acquaintance."

Susanna ambled up the aisle, muttering to herself: "So that's the way the wind sets! Little playmates! That'll do to tell, but I seen what I seen! Wonder how I come to look round jest then. Everybody else was starin' their eyes out at Elizabeth—which mebbe was just as well. Boston's a dreadful town for tittle-tattle."

She linked arms with the widow and started briskly up the lane toward home. If there were things that needed to be said, Sammy should have his chance.

But Susanna had no more than removed her cloak before the young pair came in, their cheeks glowing with the frosty air. Elizabeth went straight to her husband.

"Dr. Fairgrave, such a strange thing has happened. You remember I told you of our dreadful experience in the Great Fire, and the lad who helped carry mother to safety." She caught Samuel's hand and drew him forward. "Husband, this is he, Samuel Parris, the nephew of our good neighbors, the pastor and his wife."

Dr. Fairgrave tilted his head back and looked up at Parris.

"Well, he seems fit and able-bodied enough to be of extreme good help." In his pale-blue eyes there was the mingled admiration and envy of a little old man for a lusty young one.

Elizabeth spoke quickly. "Oh, but he was only a young lad then, not the tall Maypole he is now." She laughed up at him. "I shouldn't have known him, I think, he is so changed. But he remembered me."

"No doubt, you didn't know me when my face is clean," Samuel said, smiling. "When I went home to the academy, Mistress Morton said I looked like a blackamoor."

But Elizabeth did not laugh. "To me and my mother you looked like the angel of the Lord, sent to lead us out of burning Sodom!" She shuddered. " 'Twas a horror never to be forgot. Even yet I wake sometimes in the night and hear the roaring flames! Pray let us not talk about it."

Susanna bustled in. "Well said, my dear!" She patted Elizabeth's shoulder. "Come, folks, gather round! Dinner's all on the board."

John Oxenbridge lifted his thin white hands, and bowed his head.

"Almighty God, once more on this appointed day of Thanksgiving, we lift our hearts in gratitude to Thee . . ." (The mingled odors of game and fowl hot off the spit and journeycake baked on a shingle assailed their eager nostrils. Little Widow Smylie, who had thriftily come without breakfast, felt her mouth watering, as she caught a whiff of plum pudding boiling in a bag. "Lord send there's rum sauce with it," she breathed fervently.) ". . . preserve us through this day, protect us through the night, and at last save us for thine honor and glory evermore. Amen!"

The minister's hands, which habitually moved as if breaking the sacramental bread, took up the carving knife and tested its edge with a practiced thumb. Black Mary, her teeth gleaming, bore in a noble bowl of punch and placed it before her mistress, to be passed from hand to hand as a preface to the Thanksgiving feast.

At breakfast next morning Samuel announced that he was going to cut short his holiday and go back to the college.

"The new president thinks our customary assignments have been far too short and easy," he offered as excuse. "To master what is in the book is not enough. We must follow the thought this way and that until we have made it our own. And we must set it all down in orderly fashion in books made of blank pages and indexed so that we may have in brief a library of our own. I can see the value of it, but it takes a great deal of time. So I had best spend Saturday and Sunday making a digest of what I have read."

Oxenbridge blinked and nodded. "A very proper spirit, nephew. I admire to see that you are no timewaster. Not slothful in business, fervent in spirit, serving the Lord."

Susanna lifted a quizzical eyebrow, but held her peace.

Samuel had not seen Elizabeth after the dinner. He had hurried away to watch the holiday sports on the Common and had not returned till after the guests left. During the brief walk home from meeting, and in the interested questions which followed Elizabeth's introduction to her husband, he had learned a little of Elizabeth's experience after the fire. She and her parents had been given temporary shelter and care by the king's men. Her father had recovered the little hoard of valuables which he had buried in the cellar; and they had started for Southampton, where her mother's cousin could have sheltered them. But her mother fainted before they had gone half the distance, and they had to stop at Woking.

"We were dreadful put about," Elizabeth said, "for we knew nobody at all in the town. But it was the Lord's doing, for the Nonconformist minister there had recently been called to a better parish, and they gave Father the pulpit. 'Twas a poor congregation and they could pay only a little; but Father did tutoring, copying, or whatever came to hand. And I did needlework and gathered a few children in a dame school. Somehow we managed, by God's help." She smiled. "We didn't mind anything else, so long as Mother was spared to us."

Dr. Fairgrave took up the story. "'Twas only by the benevolous influence of my lucky star that I happened on an old classmate at Oxford, who told me my good friend Thomas Wray were living at Woking. So for old sake's sake I searched him out—and found he had a most loveliest pretty daughter, who set my heart aleaping."

He drained his punch and smacked his wet red lips. " 'Twas all in accord with the advice of Mr. Lilly, the astrologer, who cast my horoscope in London. 'Venus in the ascendant,' says he, 'which portends success in love.' "

He pinched his wife's blushing cheek. "Aye, my little honey-pot! Who says Mr. Lilly's a blind buzzard? We know better than that, don't we, little sweeting?"

It was at this point that Samuel sprang to his feet.

"Your pardon, Aunt Susanna! There's to be sports and contests on the Common, and it wants but a quarter till the hour by the window-mark. Pray let me be excused."

He did not dare look at Elizabeth.

He could not sleep that night. Huddled in his blankets he sat by his chamber window keeping silent watch over his neighbor's house. There was a faint gleam of candlelight from the parlor chamber; and from a little window high in the south gable a flickering red glimmer from what must have been a brazier, cast gnomelike shadows on the sloping, rough-timbered walls of the elaboratory. The wind moaned and lashed the ragged branches of the cedars against the clapboards. In the moonlight the zigzag branches of the thorn hedge, armed with long, curved spurs, stood rigid, like soldiers on guard. The candle snuffed out. The light in the brazier still glowed.

What was the doctor seeking, up there in the chill and gloom, while in the great canopy bed with damask curtains his young wife lay alone? Samuel checked his thoughts. He crept into bed and buried his face in the pillow. He didn't say his prayers. His soul was too bitter and rebellious to approach his Maker.

Back at the college next morning he found the place deserted except for the porter and little John Emerson, who lived on Turkey Shore, up Aggawam way, too far to go home for the holiday. He was pitifully glad to see Parris, and welcomed him with the exuberant eagerness of a spaniel puppy. He helped him out of his cloak and boots and brought his slippers and a mug of beer, paid for out of his own allowance. He was grinning with delight. But Parris ungraciously snubbed him, and stretching himself on the settle by the fire buried his nose in a book taken at random from the library shelves. It turned out to be one of John Harvard's: *Christian Warfare Against the Devil, World and Flesh*. He flung it aside angrily and stared moodily out the window.

So this was the end of his romancing! Elizabeth, his beloved, his angel of the chancel, had played him false and married another. And bitterest of all, that other was his neighbor: an old man with greedy eyes and sensuous mouth and an unsavory reputation—but rich in this world's goods.

He remembered the black-eyed girl who had read his palm on that first Commencement Day, more than a year before. The evil that she foretold had come to pass! The line in his palm was all crisscrossed and broken. He heard her teasing voice again: "See? that means disappointment in love!"

He stared at his palm as at some loathsome thing. 'Twas written there, just as the wench had said. In his own flesh was written, like the printing on a page, the thing that was going to happen to him, months before it came to pass.

A fear that was almost panic clutched at his heart. His palm was full of lines: crooked, crisscrossed, strangely and intricately patterned! Perhaps his whole life story was written there: written in an unknown tongue!

Could the black-eyed witch tell him other things? he wondered. He shuddered. He would not pry into the secrets of the Almighty! He was afraid!

In his long dreams of Elizabeth there had been little of passion; only the shy worship of an adolescent lad for his first sweetheart, the poetical romance of a boy's pure spirit as yet unawakened to the lusts of his flesh. In the sequestered life at Islington there had been no playmates, and Morton's was a masculine world, with only motherly Mrs. Morton to give sympathy and comfort. His mother had become the standard by which he measured femininity. The grubby little slaveys of the Felkin kitchen, and the blowsy barmaids of tavern and coffee house had little more attraction for him than so many animals.

The dramatic circumstances of his meeting with Elizabeth and his sudden loss of her gave personality to his romancing. Elizabeth's confidence and dependence on him had thrilled him with a sense of power and achievement. Through her eyes he saw his future self: noble, self-sacrificing, triumphing over difficulties, and above all, loved and successful. As guerdon for her faith and admiration, she became, instead of his mother, his sweetheart of romance, his ideal woman: someday, perhaps, in God's good time, his wife.

Now on a sudden the romance had ended as no romance should end. For the lady fair had wed the rich old gentleman and left the disconsolate young lover to pine! Though he would not have dared to put the matter so baldly, even in his thoughts, he felt that God had been guilty of great negligence, if nothing worse, in allowing such a thing to happen to one who had newly consecrated himself and his talents to the service of the Most High.

As to Elizabeth, he was hurt and a trifle resentful at her easy and natural acceptance of the situation. That she was more than glad to see him again there was no doubt. But she seemed quite unaware of the tragic barrier which her marriage had interposed between them, and greeted him with the warm and unreserved affection with which she might have welcomed her own young brother.

Parris, rejoicing in the pride of his nineteen years and his tall stature, felt a hurt to his dignity. To her, apparently, he told himself bitterly, he was still only a little boy grown tall. So be it, then. He would bury his sorrow, and none should guess his secret, least of all the woman he loved. He would live single all his days, and perhaps when he was dead there would be found among his sermons and tracts a packet of love letters (written but never sent) and a sequence of sonnets of rare, unearthly beauty, which would be published posthumously; and Elizabeth, then an old and white-haired woman (but still beautiful), would read them and drop a tear on his grave.

Just at this tragic moment the forsaken lover became suddenly conscious that he was uncomfortably cold and very hungry. The fire had burned low, the room was dark, and he had eaten nothing since breakfast except cold corncake and beer from the buttery hatch—there being no commons on holidays. He hastily put on his outdoor wear and betook himself to Gibson's with a wicked satisfaction in disobeying rules.

Crossing the yard he met Edward Pelham, who greeted him cordially and learning his destination, fell into step with him.

"Just where I am bound. Consider yourself my guest. This town is as empty as a haunted house, and about as cheerful."

"I thought you were in Boston with your uncle Bellingham," Parris said.

"So I was for Thanksgiving; but tonight we have the honor to be entertaining Parson Oakes and President Hoar at supper." He made a wry face. "I don't mind holding stakes at a cockfight but I'm not skilled in double-dealing. Aunt Penelope will make my excuses—she always does. 'Poor deah Edward is feeling too ill to eat and has retiahed for the night. The deah chaild hath been sadly overtaxing himself with his studies.'"

He pushed open the tavern door.

"Hey, Gibson! Set out your best. What! Venison pasty an' a sucklin' pig? Bestir yourself, fellow, for we're hungry as wolves!"

"Aye, sir! An' thirsty too, I'll be bound. An' I've the choicest of Barbados rum from Rhode Island, Mr. Pelham, sir! Will't be two, sir?"

Parris protested. "Good English ale for mine!"

But Pelham laughed. "Fie on you, Parris. Your father a Barbados planter and you disdain the drink that made the island famous? Bring it on, Gibson, bring it on! You've never tasted liquor till you've slaked your thirst with rum!"

Two hours later Parris opened the great door of the college. His knees were a trifle unsteady and he sang lustily as he climbed the stairs:

> In Scarlet towne, where I was borne,
>   There was a fair maid dwellin',
> Made every youth cry, Wel-awaye!
>   Her name was Barbara Allen.

> All in the merrye month of May,
>   When Greene buds they were swellin',
> Young Jemmy Grove on his death-bed lay,
>   For love of Barbara Allen.

John Emerson, left alone in the big dormitory, stuck up his tousled head out of his blankets. His eyes shone like a cat's in the flicker of Samuel's candle.

Samuel addressed him solemnly. "Boy, wert ever in love? No? Forsooth, 'tis a wise child!

> He that loves a rosie cheek . . .
> Kindles never dyin' fires.

Remember the words of the Simple Cobbler (your own fellow townsman an' a wise man):

> The world is full of care, much like unto a bubble:
> Women and care, and care and women, and women
>   and care and trouble.

It was midday when Parris awoke. He looked about him stupidly, recalling the night. The last he had seen of Pelham, Gibson was tucking a blanket around him on the hearth at the tavern. Parris lay alone in the big bed. He was alone in the college save for John Emerson and the porter, Christopher Cane.

Emerson, Parris knew he could count on, for since the beginning, he had fagged for him and worshiped him with the utter devotion of a shy young lad for one older and more sophisticated. It was reward enough for his devotion if Parris would give him a friendly smile or tell him wonder tales of London.

The porter was not so good a risk, and Parris began his overtures without delay.

"Did I wake you, coming in last night?" he ventured, munching his makeshift breakfast of stale bread and an orange.

Goodman Cane looked him over appraisingly.

"Wal, now't ye speak of it, I callate I did hear ye come in."

"I hope I broke no rules," Parris continued, smiling in his most winning way.

The porter considered.

"Wal, now, there be a rule on frequentin' taverns, an' a fine o' one-an'-sixpence. But once, I take it, ain't frequentin'. . . . Then there's a rule on drunkenness, an' a fine o' one-an'-sixpence. But though ye might 'a' ben a bit fuddled, I cain't in conscience say ye was foxed, fer ye clim those stairs as dignified as the president himself. There's a rule agin tumulchous noises—an' likewise a fine—but in my jedgment thet ballad ye was singin' warn't a tumulchous noise. Howsomever, President Hoar might think different, not carin' much about music. Mebbe I ain't quite reg'lar in my views, but jest atween us two, I kinda liked it. I ain't heard that chune since I were a bratlin' in old Lunnon Town—an' it minded me of home.

"Nay, my lad, I think we'll say naught about it—not this time. But there's better comp'ny to be found 'an that young hotspur ye were with last night—no matter who his father be nor ef he do head the list in rank. Ol' King Solomon give some purty sound counsel when he said: 'My son, ef sinners entice thee, consent thou not.' An' I'll warn ye o' this. Ne'er let Sir Sewall hear on't. He holds that a swig too much o' the o-be-joyful air a mortal sin!"

17

His Neighbor's Wife

> *Beware you of any man sniffing the breeze, and stretching out his arms and bursting into song, and letting on to you that he finds the rocks and trees delicious. He wants humbling. There's a lover in his bones.*
>
> —RICHARD MATTHEWS HALLET.

SPRING was stirring in her sleep. The sap was rising in the maples, and in the Fresh Pond Marshes the pussy willows flaunted soft gray catkins. The road to Boston was ankle-deep in slush and ice, making hard going for man or horse. But to the Harvard scholars the road to Boston was the way of freedom. It was the magic lure of the city anywhere, however small, for rural youth. And spring is the season of change.

The first wavering harrow of geese beat their way northward, and the east wind brought a flock of gulls and an occasional lone fish hawk, sailing high and straight and free, like a ship with sails spread. The Charles was out of its banks and the wind from the marshes bore the scent of musk from the muskrats' nests of mud and reeds. Hunters and trappers came tramping in from the woods, laden with beaver pelts which they had bought from the Indians for a string of beads. After dark, as soon as the ice went out, fishermen in flat-bottomed scows were spearing the fish which lay in the shallow water; the fire-jacks at their prows blazing and bobbing like jack-o'-lanterns, making them look as if they "had stolen the boat of Charon and gone down the Styx on a midnight expedition into the realms of Pluto."

With all nature at the burgeoning, the heart of youth will not be denied. Samuel Parris, who had buried love in the fall, felt passion quickening in the spring. The lure of the Boston Road was for him the lure of his Elizabeth.

But, like the man in the parable, he began to make excuses, not facing the issue squarely. He had neglected Uncle John and Aunt Susanna during the long months of winter, and must now make amends. He had seen a book in the public library at Boston which he needed in preparing his thesis. He must be measured for a new suit of clothes and a lighter pair of shoes to be in readiness when the warm days came. He must go to his favorite barber in Boston to have his hair trimmed in proper fashion for the curling lovelocks which he had proudly cultivated since the end of his prenticeship. He must browse in Mr. Usher's bookshop to find what new publications had come over from London. Oh, there were plenty of good reasons for going to Boston, none of which was in any way related to his neighbor's wife!

So the first Saturday on which the road was passable found him making for the colony's capital with a dozen of his mates.

The road seemed never so long and the ferry never so slow, so that the sun was high over Castle Island when they reached Boston. Near Scarlett's Wharf the whole party stopped at the King's Head for food and drink and to make themselves presentable, for their boots were caked with mud and their holiday best bespattered. Then the little group broke up, each going his own way.

Parris turned to the west, circling out of his way that he might pass near Thornhedge. But there was no one in sight. The leafless hedgerow still held its red berries, which the birds had let alone. The long, curved thorns and tangled branches looked hostile and menacing. Beyond the hedge the slender cedars pointed upward, like tall candles. In the gay spring sunshine they looked shabby and sad, their green leaves dull and rusty. They huddled so close together that the house was almost hidden. But there was a flutterng banner of wood smoke rising from the chimney top, and from the kitchen windows, set wide to welcome the fresh breeze of spring, a mingled odor of good cheer greeted the passer-by. Somewhere inside, Elizabeth was doing hr Saturday baking, preparing good things for the Sabbath dinner of an old man with puffy red cheeks and gloating eyes and a bulge at the back of his neck.

Samuel's pace slackened. Perhaps he might catch a glimpse . . . The oaken door swung open and Elizabeth stood beckoning and calling.

"You're not passing my door, are you, Samuel Parris? Follow the path to your right and I'll unbar the gate."

As she led the way to the house, she turned her head and said to him over her shoulder:

"Aunt Susanna has been looking for you all morning, but I told her I would waylay you if I could. Come right in and sit you down by the fire. You're come in pudding time. These caraway cakes are just out of the oven. Do you like them with blackberry cordial? They're the doctor's favorite refreshment."

Samuel hesitated, his thoughts turning to that secret chamber high in the south gable. He had no wish to meet again the master of the house.

"I mustn't hinder your Lord's Day preparations."

Elizabeth laughed. "My Saturday work is all done, until 'tis time for dinner. You see, I stole a march on Time this morning, by getting up two hours early. Nay, 'twas not diligence but necessity.

"Dr. Fairgrave had news last night of a two-headed calf born at Roxbury. So he must be off at daybreak to investigate the marvel and consider what it may portend to the colony. He has made a study of wonders and portents, you know, and is much sought after to expound such matters.

"He thought he could get back for dinner by midafternoon, unless the water should overflow the neck."

Parris settled himself in the chimney corner with a sigh of weary content.

All the way to town he had been trying to plan how he could meet Elizabeth in a natural and seemly manner. Now the difficulty had smoothed itself out.

With a trencher of caraway cakes and a bottle of blackberry cordial at his hand, and Elizabeth on a low stool near by with her knitting—what could be more pleasant?

"Tell me all about Harvard," Elizabeth prompted. "We hear a deal of gossip about the new president. What are the rights of it?"

"That all depends on whom you ask," Samuel said. "But since you've asked me, I'm free to say I'm strong for the new president, and I think he's had foul treatment. So far as I know, they hold two things against Mr. Hoar: first, he's an Englishman; second, he has some new and progressive ideas about how to run a college.

"Now, I don't mean to say a word against old President Chauncy. He was a fine old gentleman and I loved him and wept when he died. But just the same, he hadn't had a new idea for forty years and the college was dying at the top.

"I met Mr. Hoar one day when he first came to Boston, and he's a wonderful man—practical and modern-minded and scientific like Mr. Morton.

"And he made a wonderful speech at his inauguration. It was a quiet ceremony, of course, because old Governor Bellingham had died only three days before. But to me it seemed like an omen: the old governor and the old president were the last of the founders; the new governor and the new president were young men.

"And Mr. Hoar said something like that. That Harvard College was for him an instrument to be quickened into vital service for God and man. He would have his Alma Mater no longer confine herself to suckling nurslings with spiritual milk, and conserving the culture of the past. He would rededicate her to the true advancement of learning—in a word, he'd have her play the same dynamic part in colonial life as had Oxford and Paris in medieval Europe.

"But can he get any support for his ideas? No! The overseers feel 'twould be a grave mistake to depart from the traditions of the founders. They won't even patch the plaster or put new shingles on the roof. If the rain dripped on my father, why shouldn't it drip on me?"

Samuel stopped suddenly. "Forgive me! I didn't mean to run on like this, talking of my affairs all the time. Tell me about yourself, are you—" he caught himself up; perhaps 'twas not quite proper to ask a bride if she were happy—"are you—" He was floundering helplessly.

She smiled at him. "But I like to hear about your affairs; pray don't apologize! A woman's life is within four walls, her home is her world; a man's life is whatever he makes of it, the world is his home."

Samuel flushed with pleasure. So, she did realize that he was grown up: a man in a man's world!

A slender, copper-skinned Algonquian maid came silently across the sanded floor. She squatted on the farther side of the big fireplace and with a needle of thorn began fashioning a moccasin of deerhide. The single garment she wore was made of the same soft leather. Her straight black hair was plaited in two neat braids. Her fathomless eyes studied Parris with impersonal interest. By and by she smiled at him shyly.

Elizabeth spoke to her. "Put another log on the fire, Wy-no-nah."

Then as the girl left the room: "She is my new help, Samuel. Is she not graceful? I thought I should be afraid of Indians, but she is very gentle and quick to learn . . . but a strange creature. We can't talk much to each other yet, but we manage to make each other understand somehow—as one woman to another.

"Sometimes I have a feeling that she understands me better than I understand myself. Her eyes see everything, I think, and reveal nothing. She has been with me since the Yuletide, but I think she will leave me when the warm days come.

"There is a young brave who has been about the house lately. (I haven't told the doctor.) Someday soon he will go back to the forest . . . and she will follow him to his wigwam and squat beside his fire instead of mine. I shall miss her . . . but I shall not be sorry. She is as much a creature of the woods as a young fawn . . . she can never be happy in the town . . . away from her own people . . . far from her home . . . living among strangers. She must go with her lover."

The girl returned to her corner, watching with interest as Samuel and Elizabeth talked of many things. She understood little of English, but perhaps she understood better than they did the rising tides of spring.

Her eyes shifted from one face to the other, but they rested longest on Samuel. Now and then her white teeth showed in a half-smile. Perhaps as the Harvard scholar's eyes rested on

Elizabeth, she surprised the same ardor which her Indian warrior's eyes held for her. Perhaps all this chatter of strange-sounding words meant no more to these queer palefaces than the rustling of the forest leaves, when she stood beside her lover and felt his hand tremble as he touched her arm.

Elizabeth's nimble fingers flew back and forth, back and forth, as her needles flashed in and out, in and out, fashioning purple worsted into stockings for her husband. With his eyes, Samuel caressed her rounded cheeks, her mobile lips, her nimbus of fair hair. But his hands held only the ball of worsted, playing it out inch by inch, as his mother had taught him to do so long ago in the happy days at Islington.

He remembered one evening when Mr. Marvell had wanted to hold the ball, and had kept forgetting to play it out, so that Mother's knitting was all rough and uneven and had to be raveled out next day. And once when the yarn snapped—was it because Mr. Marvell had been thinking forbidden thoughts that he clenched his fingers so viciously? Elizabeth twitched the yarn laughingly—he was as bad as Mr. Marvell, perhaps, he thought.

The worsted snapped in Samuel's fingers.

"Oh! I'm sorry!" he said penitently. "I forgot."

But it was what he remembered that snapped the thread: words graven by God's finger on tables of stone: Thou shalt not covet thy neighbor's wife!

He could not remember afterward what they had talked about that morning—everything and nothing, it seemed. But they had been happy and friendly and gay until the last. Then—like the fool he was—he had broken the charm, and spoiled everything for them both.

"It seems so wonderful to meet you again," Elizabeth had said, "after so long, and in this strange new land. I am so very glad to find you." Her eyes looked into his. "I can never find any way to thank you for what you did for us. Mother and I must both have perished if God hadn't sent you—just in time."

She sat quiet for a minute, her face grave and thoughtful. "But God did send you—just in time," she went on. "And when I came to America, where I did not think there would be anyone at all that I had ever seen—I have found you again: so tall and strong and manly that I hardly knew you. Isn't it wonderful how God always finds a way, if only we trust him?"

Samuel did not answer, and after a moment she spoke again.

"Naturally it doesn't mean so much to you. You have your work and your family and friends. Men are adventurous and independent. But I had never been away from home before. When I thought of the leagues and leagues of sea—so rough and dreadful—between me and England and my mother and father —I felt so homesick and alone. You can't know how much it means to me to find someone from England—someone I know."

Since their first meeting Samuel had nursed the jealousy that was so ready to find a cause.

"Perhaps you cannot know what it means to me—to find some-one—and lose her." He leaned toward her. His eyes, dark with passion, held hers. "To dream at night—and wake—and dream again. To come across a thousand leagues of sea, leaving the dream behind. And then to find her—wedded to another!"

His lips twisted into a bitter smile as he mocked her words: "Isn't it wonderful how God always finds a way, if only we trust Him?"

They stood staring at each other. Elizabeth's eyes were wide with astonishment. The deep crimson rushed to her face, and ebbed again, leaving her deadly white. She could find no words.

Samuel turned and strode out the door and across the grass toward Susanna's house, not looking back.

Elizabeth watched him until he had passed through the break in the hedge and under the locust tree. The winter-blackened seedpods writhed and twisted on the branches above his head like goblins dancing in the sun. The dead leaves were thick and dank under his feet.

Elizabeth sighed. "How dreadful. And how mad. Why, I never thought of such a thing. He was just a younkin. And anyway, nobody could get in such a pother as that about me. He must be touched in the head! I wonder if that blackberry cordial might have stood a wee bit too long."

Slowly she rolled Dr. Fairgrave's purple stockings into a neat ball and tucked them into her basket. I can't knit any more now, she thought. I'm so trembly I'd drop a stitch, and it always shows if you pick it up. I'd better make some journeycake for dinner. The doctor likes it with new maple syrup.

Parris went back to the college in an unhappy mood, thoroughly out of sorts with himself and the world at large. In a flare-up of anger and jealousy, he had wanted to hurt Elizabeth as she had hurt him. But the bewilderment in her face had stilled the storm of passion as suddenly as it had risen.

The appraising look which Susanna had given him had made him feel like a foolish small boy, trying to show off by a tantrum. Susanna knew when to keep silence, as well as when to speak, and she had a way of saying nothing in a tone of severe reproof. After that first summing-up glance, she welcomed him cordially and casually, as if it were quite the natural thing to have her nephew from Harvard come storming into her kitchen by the back way which led to the break in the hedge at Dr. Fairgrave's house.

His cousin Theodora pounced upon him with her customary question: "What did you bring me, Cousin Sam?" He ungraciously handed her the sweetmeats which he had remembered to purchase at the King's Head. He made a hasty exit from the busy kitchen and the odor of boiling cod, into the peaceful atmosphere of his uncle's study. Here he knew he could escape from personalities into the calm realm of theological abstractions. Uncle John's nearsighted eyes would not notice his flushed cheeks and moodiness.

After the holiday was over and he was back in the humdrum round of Harvard life, his thoughts still lingered around Elizabeth, bringing back the memory of their hour together. From the dog-eared pages of Hebrew and Sanskrit her face looked up at him: laughing when he had broken her yarn; wistful and tender as she talked of Wy-no-nah and her lover. But more often he saw her face wounded and puzzled as he had seen it last, like that of a child who is scolded without knowing why.

Strangely enough, too, in his picturelike memory he saw what he had not noticed when he looked at her in the flesh. Beneath the laughter and tenderness of their meeting there was something of sadness and loneliness—perhaps of fear. Surely her face was thinner and whiter than when he had seen her on Thanksgiving Day. Was she unhappy? Had her marriage turned out badly? Was she working too hard, taking care of the big, rambling house with only an Indian maid to help her?

As he went over the matter in his mind, he was a little ashamed to discover that almost all their talk had been about himself and his affairs. Most of the time it had been he who talked and she who listened, with interested questions and comments—about the life at Harvard, and Morton's and his prentice days, and his plans for the future. Looking back, it seemed she had been curiously silent about her own life.

Why had she married this old man, and left her home and family to come across the seas to the New World? Why had she left her mother, ill and helpless and poor, with no one but her elderly father to care for her? Why should she marry for wealth, when wealth seemed to mean so little to her? She lived as quietly and dressed as plainly as the humblest of her neighbors. Could it be that she loved this vulgar old man? There was nothing to indicate it. She rarely spoke of him, and then in a dutiful, impersonal way, almost as if he were a stranger.

His thoughts went back to that November night when he had watched the flickering light in the gable window—the strange, distorted shadows in their goblin dance on the sloping walls of that mysterious elaboratory where the doctor sought for "such a secret as is not fit for everyone, else they might do a great deal of hurt, spending and employing it to satisfy sinful lusts." What was this dark secret, with its potentialities of evil? Suppose he found it, could this man, with his greedy eyes and sensuous mouth, be trusted with such a secret?

Might it be—the thought brought him up standing—that this old charlatan who had stolen his sweetheart was in unholy alliance with the powers of evil, and had used some mystical charm or secret philter to abet his senile love-making and satisfy his sinful lusts?

Parris had heard such matters whispered of but had never more than half believed the tales. But suppose such a thing were true, and his darling—so innocent and saintly—had been drawn against her will into this unseemly wedlock!

He remembered a song sparrow at Islington charmed by a cat, fluttering with little cries of terror—yet coming nearer and nearer! And now that the bird had been caught and caged, what further enchantments might be brewing in that secret room at the top of the winding stair?

In the glorious spring weather, Parris made frequent trips to

Boston on the Saturday holiday, but he saw little of Elizabeth. His ill-timed declaration had snapped the thread of their friendship as his fingers had snapped the yarn. He dared not approach her as a lover.

Fool that he was, he had by his own egotistical folly put her out of his reach forever. She might be sad and lonely: he could not comfort. She might be in danger (more dread because unknown): he could not help. He was too self-conscious of his guilt and folly even to talk about her to Aunt Susanna. And it suited Susanna's contrary mood to mention her neighbor only in the most casual and unsatisfactory way.

One Saturday late in April, Parris found only Theodora at home. She said her father and mother had gone to pray with a sick neighbor. Samuel had settled down to read in the study when Theodora called him.

"Come quick, Cousin Sam! Dr. Fairgrave's had a fainting fit. What'll we do?" She jumped up and down.

Elizabeth was waiting in the kitchen, looking white and scared. "He fell down the garret stairs and I can't lift him," she said.

Samuel took command. "Theo, run for Dr. Alcock. If he isn't at home, find him!"

Then he ran with Elizabeth through the break in the hedge.

Dr. Fairgrave opened his eyes as they bent over him. As Samuel started to lift him, he protested.

"Let me lay a minute, can't ye? I dropped my key. 'Tis round here somewheres."

Elizabeth picked it up from the floor—a heavy iron key, big enough to lock a prison.

" 'Tis here, doctor."

"Aye, that's it! Now, young man, lock that door at the stairhead and bring back the key." Then as Samuel started up the little winding stair: "An' waste no time looking round ye! There's naught up there 'at concerns you!"

Samuel's temper flared. He muttered as he ran up the steps, "I hope he dies and the devil flies away with him!"

But a moment later as he bent over the crumpled little figure, his voice was steady.

"Now then, doctor! Put your arms around my neck and we'll have you in bed in no time."

The doctor was heavier than he looked. It took all the young man's strength to carry him to the parlor chamber and lay him in the wide bed where Elizabeth had drawn aside the curtains and turned down the sheets.

For the first time, Dr. Fairgrave recognized Samuel.

"Well, as I live and breathe, Elizabeth! If 'tain't your Good Samaritan again! Always on hand when a lady's in distress!" He groaned. "Ease up that left leg a little, young feller! Ye've got it twisted an' it hurts like the devil."

Dr. Alcock found his patient in no serious condition. Apparently he had fainted and fallen down the stairs, but suffered no injuries except a wrenched leg and some bruises. Dr. Alcock mixed a draught for him, which Dr. Fairgrave sniffed suspiciously and refused to take.

"Sam Alcock ain't the doctor his father was," be growled.

John and Susanna arrived soon after, but Fairgrave would not see them.

"I ain't sick enough to be prayed for," he said.

Samuel had only a moment alone with Elizabeth. She followed him out on the doorstone when he left. The sun was bright overhead; the cedars sported gay green tips on their shabby winter branches. The yellow-green leaves of the locust tree were covered with silvery down.

"Please don't mind what Dr. Fairgrave said," Elizabeth apologized. "He is not unkind, really. But he can't bear the thought that he is getting old, poor gentleman. I think he feels life ebbing away from him and it makes him frantic, almost."

Her voice dropped to a whisper. "Samuel, I must ask you! When you went up to shut the door of—that room—did you see anything?"

"I didn't look," Samuel answered shortly. "But I smelled something."

"Oh, Samuel! What?"

Parris hesitated. "It smelled to me like—brimstone!"

Elizabeth's lips quivered and she locked her hands together till the kunckles stood out white.

"I ought not to tell you—he would never forgive me—but I know I can trust you never to breathe a word to anyone. He is searching, up there in that dreadful little room alone, for a great secret. I know not what 'tis, but in his sleep he talks of a stone and an elixir. I think it is some kind of medicine to make him young again."

Samuel stared at her. "But the elixir is an exploded bubble. Men have searched through the ages—and failed. There is no elixir. 'Tis but a fool's dream. Bethink you what the Scripture saith: We spend our years as a tale that is told. The days of our years are threescore years and ten; and if by reason of strength they be fourscore years, yet is their strength labor and sorrow. No good can come of going against the Scripture, nor of a research that smells of the pit. 'Tis a heresy prompted by the devil!"

"Oh, Samuel, say not so!" Elizabeth's eyes were full of tears. "He has followed the quest so long! Surely it may be true—it could be, couldn't it? There are others who believe too. Why, he has had letters from Governor Winthrop about it—encouraging letters—asking him to visit him. And surely the governor is a godly man. The doctor is always searching and searching—while the years slip away from him. Oh, sometimes I fear it is madness; but 'tis his very life! 'Give me just five more years,' he says, 'just five little years, and I will find it!'

"He is so fearful that someone will discover his secret: that is why he was so rude to you about the door. Please forgive him, Samuel, won't you?"

Samuel bent his head. "I will forgive him anything, if he is good to you." His eyes held hers. "Oh, Lizbeth! I have no right to speak—but you must know what I would say! You think a boy cannot know what love means—but I tell you that a boy is never too young to start loving, and as he grows the love grows too, until he belongs to you, body and soul. No, no! Don't stop me! It is not sin for me to give you the best that is in me—since I ask nothing in return. You will let me be your friend, will you not, Elizabeth? To watch over you—as your brother might?"

Elizabeth sighed. "Oh, 'twould be wonderful—if we could be just friends. I do need a friend."

He smiled down at her. "Then that is what we shall be: just friends."

Dr. Fairgrave was calling. Parris turned away quickly and went down the arbor path to the break in the hedge. The dry berries glowed dull red against the polished bark. The new leaves,

thin and keen-edged and shining stood a-tiptoe to keep out of the
way of the zigzag branches thrusting down at him with their
long sharp thorns.

On a sudden joyous impulse he shook his fist at the menacing
cockspurs and broke into song.

18

None Like Her, None

None like her, none.
Just now the dry-tongued laurel's pattering talk
Seemed her light foot along the garden walk,
And shook my heart to think she comes once more;
But even then I heard her close the door,
The gates of heaven are closed, and she is gone.
                    —TENNYSON, *Maud.*

THE FIRST week in July brought Samuel home for the summer vacation. Dr. Fairgrave had made his visit to
Governor Winthrop and returned filled with new zeal. He
worked long hours in the elaboratory, bending over his sooty
fire while the summer sun streamed in at the uncurtained window.
He made mysterious references to his experiments; his pale-blue
eyes shone with the fire of a zealot and the credulity of a child.
Elizabeth told Susanna that he brought home with him a small
vial of red tincture from which he dropped three precious drops
into a glass of brandy and drank each night at bedtime.

Little Widow Smylie had stayed with Elizabeth during Dr.
Fairgrave's absence and Elizabeth would gladly have kept her
longer, but she would not remain after the doctor came home.
Susanna's matchmaking had not come to anything and the little
widow was on short commons, but she wasn't going to risk her
immortal soul by stopping under the same roof with a Sadducee.

Elizabeth was busy, for the summer brought the additional
work of preserving and drying fruit, and the care of the garden.

The yard was atwinkle with oxeye daisies, self-seeded from old John Endicott's neighboring yard.

The cherries were red ripe, and Samuel's neighborly offer to help with the picking was thankfully accepted. The plums would be ready in a week, the apple trees drooped under their load, and the grape arbor shading the garden path was heavy with green clusters.

Down in the marshes by the Mill Pond the blueberry bushes still held their own, with the pride of the earliest inhabitants who will not give way to upstart immigrants. All Boston Town went berrying in season. The wild strawberries on the hills were gone, but the blackberry thickets and elderberries and wild currants tempted housewives and children into the woods which crowded close upon the towns.

The pact of friendship between Samuel and Elizabeth prospered during the long hot summer days, for Parris thought it not amiss to lend a helping hand to his neighbor, the mistress of Thornhedge. They were always busy and they were seldom alone. Theodora and her friends; or a neighbor woman or two; or a flock of children with baskets and pails, were always close at hand, whether they went blackberrying in the woods or clamming on the beach.

But there was one Lord's Day eve, when they sat by themselves on the old well curb in the early twilight and watched the dusk come down and the little lights flash out here and there at candlelighting time. And Samuel questioned Elizabeth about her marriage.

"How did it come about? And who takes care of your mother now that you are gone?"

"Oh, that was all arranged," she said. "You see, Dr. Fairgrave and Father had been classmates at Oxford, and he looked us up when he was visiting in England. He came down to visit us, all unexpectedly. Things were very bad with us, and when he stayed to dinner, we had only bread and cheese. But he was very kind to us all. He stopped at the inn for a week; and before he went back to London, he asked for my hand.

"Father told him of our poverty (which, of course, he had seen for himself) and explained that I had no dower, and besides that, was sorely needed at home, so that I was not free to wed. And Dr. Fairgrave said"—she gave a modest little laugh—" 'twas only the maid he wanted and not her dower; and as to Father and Mother, he knew just the place for them in a little cottage on the coast of Devon, with a widowed cousin of his to do for them, and an annuity as long as either of them should live. He would provide for me also, he said, with a wedding gift, and make a will giving me all his estate at his death. So Father told me of his offer.

"Oh, Samel, if you could have seen the hope and relief in Father's face and heard his poor voice tremble when he came to me and said:

" 'Daughter, I don't want to urge you. You must consult your own heart. But he is a good man and more than generous; and if you should find it in your heart to accept him, 'twould make me very happy to know that your future is provided for.'

"I knew not what to say, for I had never laid my account on marriage with anyone (being dowerless and no beauty) and I was frightened at the thought of leaving England and crossing the huge ocean.

"Dr. Fairgrave was wonderful patient. He went back to London Town and stayed a fortnight (to give me time to get 'customed to the idea, he said) and then he came back for another visit. He hired a carriage and took us all to see his cousin. It was a cozy little cottage they had, with a small chamber overlooking the beach for Mother, and a garden and orchard where Father could putter about. Mother loved it, and Father sat on the kitchen doorstone and looked up at the apple trees full of ripe fruit and wiped his poor dim eyes—his sight had failed so that he couldn't teach any more.

"I sat down beside him on the doorstone and put my arms around him—his body was so thin, poor dear!

" 'Father,' I said, 'tell Dr. Fairgrave I will go with him— whenever he is ready.' "

A whippoorwill was calling, down by the river. Faintly from the western shore came the shrill answer.

There was a question Samuel must ask: "You married him. But did you love him, Elizabeth?"

Her reply was almost a whisper: "Mother said a maid was not supposed to love a man—till they were wed. 'Twas hardly decent."

The western sky still glowed with opalescent light, but under the ancient cedars Samuel had to bend his head in order to see her face.

"And after—did you love him? I must know, Lizbeth! Do you love him now?"

"How shall I say?" There was a tremor in her voice. "He has been generous and kind and I am grateful. I am his wife, faithful and fond of him and careful of his comfort. Is not that love? And can I give him more? 'Tis not his fault that he is old, nor that his love is more than mine. I have no right to speak of it—nor you to ask!"

Parris took her hands and drew her to her feet. "I have a right to ask—because I love you! And you have answered! How old are you, Elizabeth?"

"Twenty-four—going on twenty-five."

"And how long have you been married?"

"A year come September."

He caught her by the shoulders roughly. "Yet you talk like a novice in a nunnery! You're faithful and careful of his comfort—and grateful! God in heaven, what for? Because he bought you to serve his senile needs! And you call that love! By my faith, Elizabeth, I half believe you're still a virgin!"

She caught her breath—a shudder shook her body. Her voice was a hushed cry.

"No! No! He is most fond, and beds with me each night. Shame on your naughty prying—shame, I say!" She thrust him away from her, beating clenched hands against his breast.

His long arms went around her, crushing her body against his own; his kisses burned her lips.

"I'll let you go, my sweet. I'll not hurt you. But don't prate of love till you know what love is—what love could be—for you and me."

He released her gently, steadying her as she swayed away from him. Then with one arm around her waist, he led her to her door and kissed her gently on her white forehead.

"Good night, little Elizabeth! Now you know how I love you —how my soul cries out for you. A young man's love is a burning flame. An old man's love is only ashes—of forgotten fires which will not blaze again."

It was mid-July when Samuel received a letter from his father. The writing was shaky and hard to read, quite different from his usual neat business hand, and the message was brief.

Dear Son: I have been laid by with Feaver 3 wks. & am just out o'bed an weake as water. Must have help with the planting.

Doe you come by 1st Shipp. I need you sore.

Compton good & trusty but Negurs need a Marster. You must come to itt someday & you'd best know summat about itt befoar. 13 yrs since I've seen you. Long time. Wouldn't know you, likely. God speed ye.

Thos. Parris.

Samuel read the letter. Then without a word he handed it to Aunt Susanna and went upstairs to his little west chamber. Out of the far past his mother's voice came to him as she made her protest to his father. "Would you take your sons and end their schooling and their prospects to set them driving Negurs in a canebrake?"

Now that was to be his life. That was the end of his plans and hopes and his two years of study for the ministry: Driving Negurs in a canebrake!

Lying on his bed with his arms wrapped tight around his head, he tried to think of a way out. There was none. He still lacked a year of his majority: he was as much his father's chattel as the Negroes and other livestock, he thought bitterly.

He dropped on his knees by the window and looked out upon Trimountain: Cotton Hill and Mount Vernon and the conelike steep between them where the beacon stood in the westering sun, casting its shadow—a slender shaft with an outstretched arm—like a giant gallows tree. The locust leaves outside his window whispered and sighed. The perfume of flowers was gone. Only the thorns remained, and the green pods that curled and twisted and tapped against his window in their goblin dance.

He gave little thought to his father. Thomas Parris was only a name and a far-off childish memory of a brusque, ruddy-cheeked man who came between him and his mother, and whose word was law in his household. Now, like a thunderclap, his voice had spoken again across leagues of rolling ocean to demand his son's presence and service.

During the days before he could make his arrangements and get passage for the island, he went about like a sleepwalker. He would accept no word of comfort from Elizabeth or his uncle John, he only listened in silence to the latter's homily on filial duty. But Susanna, rough-shod though she was, understood Samuel as his mother would have, and managed to talk to him one morning as he was having his breakfast alone.

"Now, Sammy darlin'," she said, "there's nobody feels worse about you leavin' Boston an' the college an' all than your old auntie. You know that. But all the same you ain't takin' it like you oughta. There's a pile o' things might befall a lad worse'n bein' ast to go help his old father when he's laid up with fever. You're most twenty year old now, an' big an' strong as they make 'em, an' you never done a jot of real hard work in your life. An' come what might in good times or lean, there's been money comin' ev'ry ship for all your needs. An' there's been aplenty times when 'twarn't easy for your dad to send it. I lived in Barbados an' I know. But good times or bad, I'll say this for Tom Parris: he took what the Lord sent an' made the best of it.

"You're like your mother, Sammy, an' she was a saint an' a lady. Your father warn't made o' quite the same clay; but he was a good man, Sammy, an' he never shirked nor whined, an' that's sayin' plenty. Now the fever's got him down, an' it'll be the good Lord's mercy if he holds out till you get there, for once tropic fever gets into a man's bones he ain't got much chance.

"But whatever comes, Sammy darlin', you've no call to think shame of your father for things he's done or ain't done. An' don't forget Aunt Sue said so an' yer old auntie *knows*.

"An' here's another thing ye'd best bear in mind. Barbados ain't New England an' it ain't Old England. Ye'll see a heap o' doin's there you don't see in Boston Town—though that ain't to say there ain't plenty done in Boston 'at ye don't see. But the tropics warms more'n a man's skin. It mellers him up clear through an' seems like it softens his backbone till he ain't got much power to resist, an' jest drifts along the easiest way.

"An' what with the heat an' the rum an' the Negurs, an' bein' lonesome an' hardly ever gettin' sight of a decent white woman, things look different to him from what they used to back home an' he forgets a lot o' Puritan ways. So, if ye see things ye don't like, don't be too brash to judge. Remember it's the Lord's business to do the judgin' an' even He don't do it till the whole account is figgered up an' balanced."

As the time of parting drew near, his disappointment at the loss of his career gave place to the more intolerable pain of losing Elizabeth. The thin disguise of friendship which had veiled their relations fell away, leaving only the stark fact of their love for each other.

In the dusk of his last evening in Boston, Samuel waited till the little light flared in the south gable at Thornhedge. Then he went through the break in the hedge and along the garden path to his neighbor's house: to his neighbor's wife, sitting on the well curb.

Elizabeth came to meet him. In the shadow of the grape arbor they stood together.

"Elizabeth," he pleaded, "I love you with all my heart and soul—and I must leave you! Will you not say you love me also? Give me this word to take with me in my exile?"

And Elizabeth, looking him full in the eyes, spoke the word: "Though it be sin and shame to say it, I will speak true. I love you—love you—love you!"

Samuel caught her to him. "Darling, darling, 'tis my last night in Boston. Down by the river where the elderberries grow and the whippoorwills are calling—do you love me enough to meet me there—to give yourself to me before I go? It may be years, love, it may be forever. Will you give me one night of love—to remember?"

She looked down, her face quivering.

"I shall be waiting there," he went on. "I shall wait until the whippoorwills stop singing and the moon goes down."

Suddenly she lifted her head. The moonlight made a nimbus of her fair hair and her eyes were shining. Again she brought to Samuel's mind the angel of the chancel.

"One night of sin," she breathed, "and shame ever after. I could not bear it—nor could you, my blessed."

"No, no!" he protested. "It would not be sin, for you are mine. When the flames came so swift and terrible, did not God send me when you prayed? 'It was a miracle,' you said. And when in this new land we met again and you were wed, I nearly died of jealousy. But now I know it was your need that drew me.

You called me and I came. You belong to me—you must come to me for this one night."

He held her close, his lips against her hair. "No one will ever know, darling. 'Twill be our secret."

She lifted her head. "God would know—and you—and I," she insisted. "We could never forget. Someday, perhaps, beloved, if God is good, you may come back to me, but now—" She broke off, sobbing, and they clung together. They could not speak.

Suddenly she wrenched herself away and sped up the garden path without looking back. The door shut fast behind her and Samuel heard the heavy bar drop into place. Under the locust tree he turned and looked back. High in the gable window a brazier flickered and flared.

At daybreak Samuel boarded ship for Little Britain.

Book Four

Barbados   1673 to 1680

19

Trade Winds

Some for the Glories of this World; and some
Sigh for the Prophet's Paradise to come;
  Ah, take the Cash, and let the Credit go,
Nor heed the rumble of a distant Drum!
                              —OMAR KHAYYAM.

A SEA VOYAGE to the West Indies was at best an unpleasant experience. To Samuel Parris, homesick, lovesick, and sick at his stomach, every day added to his feeling of ill luck and martyrdom. "Sailing straight south till the butter melts" meant that each day the water casks were warmer and staler; the biscuits were drier; the salt cod and meat less palatable. The ship's cow broke a leg in a storm and had to be killed, glutting them with fresh beef for a day or two but depriving them of milk for the rest of the voyage. A crate of poultry was washed overboard; and the corn meal and wheaten flour were musty and wormy from the dampness.

Yet these discomforts of the flesh were easier to bear than the hurt to his spirit. He had made his offering to the Lord. He had dedicated his life and his talents to the high calling of preaching Christ. But the Lord had rejected his offering. It was a sore rebuke, a dark and difficult dispensation, and the bitterness of aloes was in his mouth.

None the less, the first glad cry of "Land! Land!" set his heart pounding with excitement. Wakened at daybreak by the unusual noise and bustle aboard ship, he tumbled out of his hammock and rushed on deck, eager for his first sight of Little Britain. The drizzling rain which had lulled him to sleep had quickened to a smart shower. The long roll of the waves had quieted to a gentle rocking.

On board was hurry and confusion in preparation for unloading the cargo, which was being brought up from below and stacked about on the slippery deck in motley heaps. Salt cod from Marblehead; Bibles, bowls, and barrel staves from Boston; cannon bullets and iron hoops from Taunton; salt and soap from Salem; balm of Gilead and sassafras from Cambridge; shoes and saddles from Lynn; rowan-wood walking sticks from Roxbury (guaranteed witchproof); cradles and coffins from Charlestown—all hobnobbed together as the rain fell alike on the just and the unjust, waiting their turn to be hoisted over the sides and lowered into the smaller craft which plied back and forth from ship to mole, propelled by sinewy black arms.

The ship was entering the roadstead of lovely Carlisle Bay, upon whose blue and tranquil waters were anchored vessels of various types: men-of-war and merchantmen; fishing smacks; and a slaver from the Gold Coast, reeking with a stench like nothing else in the world; all were lying at anchor, while little boats of nameless variety darted here and there like water bugs in a pond. Nobody seemed to mind the rain or pay any heed to it. The rainy season had begun in June and would last until Christmas; meanwhile the everyday activities of living must go on. The Negro boatmen sang at their work, keeping time with their oars, their muscles rippling under gleaming black skin, as the rain made little rivulets down their naked backs. The bumboat women, naked except for a brief and scanty petticoat, crowded around the ship, bartering their wares among the sea-weary crew, balancing with careless grace in their teetering craft as they tossed oranges, bananas, and coconuts to the sailors and caught the coins in hands or open mouths. They were gay, careless, friendly, and to Samuel's disgusted astonishment, utterly unconscious of their nakedness.

The clear-up shower ceased suddenly, the clouds broke away, and the rising sun looked upon a world so bright and dazzling with beauty that Parris caught his breath in delight. His eyes took in the myriad scenes before him: the wind-ruffled water of the bay, blue as no northern water could ever be, so clear that he could see the fishes and coral rocks in the shallows; the long, slim crescent of beach with the foaming surf racing up and down its silver sands, and circling the curve of the shore line; the city of Bridgetown, with its shops and stores and warehouses, its white houses and green jalousies; its Bridge stretching from the mole back across the marshes toward the cathedral of St. Michael's where the matin bells were chiming: the whole framed and guarded by a thick grove of coconut palms at one end and the fort at the other, with the British flag fluttering up the staff as the guns barked their morning salute. Rising in the background were terrace upon terrace, the green, green hills of the sugar plantations and the wild highlands of "Scotland" with the morning mist still lingering on their summits: the entire scene vested with the unearthly glory of a tropic sunrise.

Samuel's spirits rose to meet the day. Exiled he might be, but perhaps after all it was only a part of God's plan, who chasteneth whom he loveth and scourgeth every son whom He receiveth. In the beauty of the morning he felt the comfort of God's smile.

His father's steward was waiting for him when he came ashore. He was an English indentured servant named Henry Compton, whom Thomas Parris had mentioned as being good and trusty. He had formerly held a responsible position as steward of a gentleman's estate in Essex, and owed his downfall to becoming involved in one of the many political intrigues of the time.

Samuel took an immediate liking to the man. His manner was frank and straightforward and he had none of the look of a jailbird.

Briefly, he told Samuel the news of his father's death, which had occurred two days before. The body had been prepared for burial and placed in the cool crypt of the parish church, and the funeral delayed as long as possible in the hope that the only mourner might arrive in time for the service, which now could be held that afternoon.

An hour after he landed, the sun was hidden under thick clouds again, the doleful drizzle of rain had recommenced and Parris, astride a lop-eared sure-footed little assinego, was trailing his father's steward up and down a rambling little way in the woods toward his new home at Cotton Hall plantation, fifteen miles north of Bridgetown on the leeward coast. He had been given his choice between riding the donkey or trusting himself to the uncertain fortunes of a two-wheeled ox-cart.

"Haven't you a horse on the place, my man?" he asked disgustedly.

"Yes, sir," was the answer. "There's the sugar horses, as no gentleman would care to ride, sir; an' a two-year-old colt as has never been saddle-broke; and a thoroughbred Virginia mare that the master rode—but she's due to foal in a fortnight and we can't risk her in the gutts."

"In the what?" asked Parris, puzzled.

"Gutts, sir. Gullies they be in England. Since the floods they're slick as butter an' full o' roots an' like to cave in. When the little ass-nigger comes to a slick place, he jest kinda squats an' slides, but a horse'll get panicky an' plunge an' likely break a leg, sir."

The road leading north from Bridgetown lay along the west, or leeward, shore of the island, between the terracelike foothills and the white sands of the beach. It was a rough and treacherous trail. Sometimes a mangrove swamp made the road detour inland—a muddy estuary, where the sun never penetrated the lugubrious twilight nor warmed the primeval chill. Even at midday, with Compton acting as guide and shouting back cheerful comments from time to time, Parris felt a goose flesh of terror as he peered into the gloomy jungle of interwoven boughs and roots.

"A devilish queer plant, the mangrove," Compton said. "Sprouts its seeds while they lay in the fruit, and throws down long stout snaky roots to catch ahold in the mud, an' then turn round an' grow up'ards again, put out their leaves an' make another mangrove tree, until they get in such a tangle nobody can't find head or tail, root or branch. But down under in the muddy ooze there grows the finest oysters you ever set your teeth in—only the Negurs don't like to gather 'em for fear o' snakes an' sechlike varmints."

A little farther on, a stubborn point of jutting rock crowded the path down almost to the water's edge, so that the salt spray drenched the travelers as they passed. Now and then a rude bridge of logs spanned a gully; or a stone causey, built by slave gangs who had long ago found rest, made a dry passage over a marsh.

Once they stopped to rest and drank from a spring at a place called The Hole, where a crude cross marked the landing of the first English ship, the *Orange Blossom*, whose sailors took possession of the island in the king's name and on a near-by tree carved an inscription:

JAMES K OF E AND
OF THIS ISLAND
1605

Here had once been the capital of the island, but the seat of government had long ago been moved to Bridgetown. All that remained of Holetown was a wandering little street with tumble-down houses on either side, and sleepy, ragged natives who roused themselves enough to beg for a bit before going to sleep again.

At the north end of the village the parish church stood beside the main road, on the way to Cotton Hall. The rector was watching for them, and met them at the rectory gate. He was an elderly man named Marshall, with a gentle, patient face and a weary stoop of the shoulders. With fine tact and kindliness he welcomed Thomas Parris's son and insisted that he come in and share their simple dinner and then rest himself until the hour of service. His invitation was warmly seconded by Mrs. Marshall, a little, old-fashioned English lady who made Samuel quite at home, leading him into a tiny bedchamber already provided with a bowl of water, towels, and a pitcher of sweet wine. On the bed was laid out a suit of white cotton cloth, coarse but clean.

"I'm feared it may be a wee bit short in the arms and legs, my dear," she smiled, "but 'twill be dry and clean and will maybe do till you've had a bite to eat and a nap. Then you will feel more like getting your things unpacked."

It was two hours later that Samuel followed the little minister down into the quiet crypt, and looked into his father's face for the first time since he was a child of seven. Unconsciously, he had always thought of his father as the same young, heavy-set, vigorous man he had known in his childhood. But the face in the coffin was worn and thin, with sagging cheeks and deeply fur-rowed brow. The rebellious red mop of hair was now scanty and lank and white as a Boston winter. The full-lipped, passionate mouth drooped at the corners and the pale lips sagged against toothless gums. Thomas Parris at fifty-three was an old man. Life had done with him.

Samuel had never loved his father and he felt no real grief at his loss, but as he stood beside the bier there suddenly flashed into his mind a picture out of his boyhood memories: the king's procession through London and Thomas Parris, vigorous and proud, gloriously arrayed and gallantly mounted, splendid in his black velvet coat with gold chains, riding in the King's Triumph. He turned away from the old man in the coffin and broke into uncontrollable sobs.

The rector laid a comforting hand on his shoulder. "Don't take it too hard, my lad. Your father had been ailing a long time and life was not easy for him. He was a just man, and though he was perhaps in some ways not so godly as I might have wished, he made his peace with God at the last and I administered the sacraments before he died.

"He wanted to lie in St. James's churchyard, and he gave me an inscription which he wanted on his tombstone. He said he had seen it on a stone in Greyfriars in London years ago and had always remembered it:

'This life is but a winter's day,
Some only breakfast and away,
    Others to dinner stay
    And are full fed;
The oldest man but sups
    Then goes to bed.
Large is his debt
Who lingers out the day.
    He that goes soonest
    Has the least to pay.'

'Tell my son to have it graven on my stone,' he said to me. 'It won't mean anything to Sam now—he's too young—but someday he'll make a sermon of it.'"

Samuel accepted the arrangements without protest. He hardly heard the service which the vested priest read from the Book of Common Prayer. He was weary from his long voyage and weighed down by a dreadful loneliness and depression as he stood beside the grave of his father, a group of strangers in a strange land to bear him company and the slow tropic rain soaking him to the skin.

He had supposed his father would be buried beside Uncle John Parris under the big ceiba tree at Cotton Hall. He was a little shocked at what seemed an eleventh-hour conformity—but after all it didn't matter; there was no one to know or care—only himself, alone in a strange land where he cared for nobody and nobody cared for him.

After the funeral Mrs. Marshall insisted that he stay the night. "'Twill be quieter here," she urged, "and you will sleep better the first night."

He accepted thankfully and fell asleep as soon as he touched the bed. To his surprise, he woke next morning feeling thoroughly refreshed. After an early breakfast of fresh fruit and cassava cakes, he rode on to his new home. Mr. Marshall, saying he had an errand farther up the coast, rode with him, chatting cheerfully. Samuel suspected that the errand was only a cloak for the rector's kindly wish to keep him company, and he was grateful. He was a good and friendly man, despite his conformity.

Cotton Hall dated back to the early days of the colony; a typical Great House of the fabled sugar-boom days. The new master, seeing it for the first time with the sun rising over the hills behind it, and the blue ocean splashing on its white stone steps in front, thought he had never seen so beautiful a dwelling. It was solidly built of white native coral rock, its three-foot walls and deeply recessed windows with heavy wooden shutters serving the double purpose of cool comfort and security. For in the Indies every man's house was literally his castle, built for defense against hurricane, invasion, pirate raids, insurrections, or the more-to-be-feared night attacks from the blacks of his own household. It stood on the natural terrace a few rods back from the beach and was of the type known on the island as a "downstairs house" of one story only, with a low, rambling roof and no ceiling, the heavy hewn rafters of solid mahogany being left exposed.

Its suggestively warlike appearance was softened by a wide veranda approached by a flight of broad stone steps and furnished with folding chairs and hammocks, of woven net, and a table or two. The great hall served the purpose of living and dining room, its heavy doors of hewn timbers opening hospitably to the east and west and north. But there was a grim suggestion in their iron bolts and bars. From this room the several sleeping apartments opened. A trap door in the hall led to the cellars, half underground, which were used for storerooms and stable. From here heavy doors, high enough to clear a man on horseback, opened out on the main road, which lay along the foot of the terrace, between the house and the sea. As in all West Indian houses, the kitchen, or cookhouse, was in a detached building at the rear.

In the furnishings was a record of Barbadian history. The boom days represented by costly treasures imported from the homeland, their upholstery now faded and threadbare; an immense table of solid mahogany flanked by long benches of the same wood, cut from the native forests and designed by the estate carpenter; a portrait painted by Lely in the days of Charles I, of Uncle John Parris in his youthful prime, the face wrinkled by many seasons of heat and seamed by the maws of irreverent worms; and just underneath it, a couple of cheap canvas chairs. The whole place was pervaded by the disreputably careless comfort of a lonely man, far from his womankind.

The master's bedroom, which faced the sea, contained an enormous mahogany bed, with a canopy and curtains of dingy mosquito netting. The bed was unmade, the feather ticks and pillows still bearing the imprint of the departed master's body.

The smaller bedrooms were even more untidy and draggled in appearance and showed unmistakable signs of Negro occupancy. Evidently they belonged to the plump black housekeeper, whom Compton had introduced as Candy, and her three coffee-colored pickaninnies, who at their new master's approach had quit their puppylike gambols on the veranda and followed him about, their big eyes rolling and their white teeth gleaming in shy and friendly grins, disregarding their mammy's orders to "Clar out, now, an' doan' be apesterin' young Massa Sam!"

Parris turned impatiently to Compton. "I thought the slaves lived in their own quarters," he said.

Compton's eyes shifted. "Yes, sir. The field hands do, sir. But Mr. Parris was kinda easygoin' an' give Candy the run o' the house, as ye might say. He was lonesomelike toward the last, sir, an' Candy done for him. She's been here a long time, you know, sir, an' knowed his ways an' catered to 'em, sort of."

A dark suspicion gripped Samuel. "How long?" he said.

Compton hesitated. "I don't rightly know, sir. She was here before me. Six-seven year I reckon, sir."

"And she has always lived in the house?"

Compton's face would have done credit to the king's own

butler. "That I couldn't rightly say, I'm sure, sir. . . . Would you like to see the stables, sir? And the Virginia mare?"

Parris strode across the room to where the woman was busily polishing a pewter tankard with her dirty apron.

"You and your brats are to move to the cookhouse. Get all your belongings together and be gone when I get back!"

Without waiting for a reply, he turned away. His voice was well under control.

"Very well, Compton, let's go take a look at the mare."

Lying that first night in the big bed that had been his father's, Samuel recalled what Aunt Susanna had said when his father's summons had come. This, then, was what Susanna had been preparing him for. This fat black harlot whom his father had dared to put in his sainted mother's place. Susanna had known it all these years—the oldest of the coffee-colored offspring was proof of that—and, knowing, had by her silence condoned the abomination. John Oxenbridge had known it too, and had dared to talk to him about filial duty and loyalty.

Worst of all, there came another thought. These naked little monkeys, rolling and tumbling about on the veranda, were not only begotten of his father—they were his own blood relations, his half brothers!

Before he went to bed that night he gave orders to Compton that the wench Candy and her brood be taken to Bridgetown the next morning and sold to a slave trader bound for Virginia. He made it clear that they must not remain in the island, which now had become too small to hold both them and him. But the bitterness of his knowledge could not be disposed of so easily. That would stay with him forever, he thought, eating deeper and deeper, like the vulture in the story of Prometheus, eating but not consuming.

He felt very sorry for himself.

Compton had gone so far as to venture a respectful protest.

"You're losing a right good cook, sir, and they're hard to get and come high—begging your pardon, sir. Should I buy another wench at the Bridge, sir, or will you go in yourself?"

Parris had no liking for another trip to Bridgetown.

"Haven't you anyone on the place who can cook?"

Compton scratched his head. "Can't rightly say I have, sir.

To tell the truth, we've been running shorthanded for quite some time back, sir. Times has been cruel hard. Sugar is down an' slaves is up. We need more field hands for the planting, an' I could get two-three o' them for the price of a cook, sir. But there's nobody a tall—exceptin' Tituba, that is, sir."

"Well, then, why not have Tituba? If she can get a simple meal and keep the house decently tidy, I don't ask anything more."

Compton considered. "As to that, sir, Tituba is a good house servant, trained in a Spanish gentleman's family—and she's too small and too old for field work—must be close to fifty—her husband, John Injun, is a good yard man an' gardener too. It oughta work out fine, thataway. But there's somethin' queer—I dunno, mebbe it's jest her breed. She's part Negur an' part Carib—native Injun, you know, sir. And mixed blood's the very devil, sir, if you know what I mean, sir."

Parris was curious. "What's wrong with her? What does she do? Or what doesn't she do?"

But Compton was reticent.

"I know naught about her, sir, though she's lived here a long while—longer than me. I'm told your father bought her of a Spanish gentleman, who pretty nigh beat her to death—for over-lookin' his wife, he said, sir,—but as to that, I couldn't rightly say. There's queer tales told—as may be true an' maybe ain't. I really couldn't say, sir. But all in all"—he wagged his head dubiously—"I couldn't bring myself to recommend Tituba, sir."

"You don't think she is a witch, do you, Compton? Surely my father would not have bought or harbored a witch!"

"Oh, no, sir! Not by no means, sir!" Compton was shocked. "But your father weren't one to bother much about the evil eye or mumbo-jumbo, and he gave no ear to the Spaniard's tales. He hated a Spaniard next to Ol' Dowl hisself, sir, anyway. He said that ratted Spaniard (them were his very words, sir, begging your pardon, Mr. Sam) were naught but a windy-headed witch-pricker an' drunk enough to see the devil by daylight.

"But witch or no, she'd never harm the master, sir, Tituba wouldn't. She were grateful an' faithful as a dog. An' when he were took bad an' so tormented he couldn't sleep, nobody could do for him like Tituba. He did say her simples eased him more 'n all the leech's draughts an' bloodlettings. But her an' Candy was like fire an' tow, an' Candy says—"

"Enough, Compton!" Parris cut him short. "I care naught for Negur tittle-tattle. Tell Tituba (or whatever her heathen name is) to serve my breakfast in the morning. You can trade for those field hands you need instead of buying me a cook. I can eat almost anything, after two years of college commons, and we've got to get the planting done, you know, Compton."

Weird noises from the native village kept the new master awake that night. Compton had prepared him in advance, so that he was not really frightened. It was only the Africans' way of mourning their dead master and wishing him a good journey to his future home. But the intermittent beat, beat, beat of goomba drums and the clatter of calabash rattles, with occasional blasts of a conch-shell horn, wore on his nerves. Worst of all was the endless rising and falling cadence of the keening: a woman's voice, high and shrill in the wild funeral wail or recitative, and the chorus of lament:

> Massa Tom, him dead an' done,
> Massa Tom, him dead, o-o-oh!

Compton said it would do no good to forbid them. It would only make them sullen and ugly and perhaps dangerous. It was real sorrow, he said, not pretending. They had all loved Massa Tom for his kind and good-natured ways, and they had to express their feelings Negur fashion in a 'set-up,' which was a kind of wake.

It was not till cockcrow that the revelry ended. Although Parris did not know it, Compton and the white overseers were awake and watchful throughout the night, knowing, as the new master did not, that the black man's mood might change without warning, that their happy excitement might arouse the sleeping savage in African blood.

The ringing of the estate bell woke Parris at six in the morning, but he did not rise until he heard Compton start on his trip to Bridgetown.

Candy departed joyfully, jolting along in the oxcart with her hilarious offspring, escorted by two Negroes, with Compton riding behind. Compton had told her that Massa Sam said she could ride to Bridgetown. She had no idea that she was to be shipped overseas—the fate most dreaded by a slave.

Compton returned from Bridgetown well pleased with himself. "I've made a rare good bargain," he told Parris. "I've traded Candy and her brats for a brace of likely wenches and a strappin' big buck; all Korumantis fresh from the jungle; hightempered devils but the best there is for field work, once you get 'em broke. I'll admit I took a chance on the buck—he's got a bad foot. He's an ornery devil, and raised so much hell aboard ship that they had to keep him in irons all the way over. His right ankle is raw and putrid where the chain galled it.

"If it gangrenes on him, he's as good as dead," Compton said appraisingly, "but if I can pull him through I got a bargain. A buck like that's worth thirty pounds easy. The captain practically throwed him in with the two wenches. I'll sure do my best for him. He'll make a fine breeder an' the gang needs new blood."

Parris did not think much of Compton's bargain. The big Negro lay on a bed of straw in the cart, his arms bound behind him. In deference to his bad foot, Compton had removed the ball and chain from his ankle and bound his legs together with ropes wound around his knees. He lay motionless and offered no resistance when four men picked him up and carried him into the small iron cage which served the double purpose of jail and hospital. Laying him on the sanded floor, they unbound his arms and legs and came out, locking the door. The big fellow did not stir, and Parris, watching him through the bars, thought he had fainted, until he saw that his eyes were open and alert, rolling from side to side, estimating his new situation.

The eyes came to rest on his master's face. Despite the bars between, Parris stepped back in fright. The eyes held his: desperate, vengeful, savage, with a flicker of scorn as Parris cringed. For a long minute they measured each other, and it was the white man who turned away.

The eyes next turned on Compton, but the steward's eyes were calm and cold as blue ice. This time it was the slave's eyes which faltered, and Compton, with a basin of water in one hand

and bandages in the other, coolly entered the cage and bound the black man's wound.

"Weren't you afraid of him?" Parris asked afterward. "He's the most vicious brute I ever saw. It's dangerous to have him on the place. I can't see what you wanted him for in the first place. I'd as soon have a baboon."

Compton knocked the tobacco out of his pipe. "No-o, he ain't what I'd call vicious, sir. He's mostly homesick and scared; an' he's had a pretty tough time of it comin' over; you can see that. Niggers is like horses, sir. It don't do no good to whop the liver out of 'em. It's like to make 'em bad-tempered.

"About bein' feared: I ain't much feared of a nigger if he's got good common sense—an' this boy's smart. But I don't like a fool nigger. There ain't no way o' tellin' what he'll do."

Compton was inordinately proud of the two new women. "A brace o' beauties, sir, if I do say it as picked 'em," he boasted a few days later. "You oughta see 'em since they've been scrubbed an' fed. One thing your father always said, sir, an' he was right: niggers ain't no nastier 'n other critters if you give 'em a decent chance. He give each man his little plot o' ground, an' let him build his hut an' plant his yams an' greens an' work fer himself on Sundays. You ain't rode over the place yet, sir, an' I want you should see it."

"All right, Compton, get the horses and we'll go now if you like."

It was in the cool of the evening after the day's work was done, and Parris thoroughly enjoyed the ride. The scene was so different from the England of his breeding and the Massachusetts of his adoption. It was good to ride a horse again— he had not had much chance in New England.

The plantation was larger than he had supposed. The land was split up into wide fields of cane and cotton; groves of fruit trees, guavas, oranges, lemons, and limes; corn, potatoes, plantains and cassava, and the ubiquitous yam. The plantation had a sugar mill, a boiling house, a filling room and stillhouse. There were good stables, a smith's forge, and a storehouse. The animals consisted of some oxen and a few cows, a number of assinegoes and some goats. And last of all there was the Negro village, with its frowsy-thatched huts and small gardens.

It was a rare honor to have a visit from the new young master.

Every hut overflowed with pickaninnies, dogs, cats, and now and then a goat or pig, all out to welcome the distinguished guest. The two new slaves had been assigned to separate families and were shy and reluctant. The older one hid herself under a bunk and refused to come out, and Parris ordered her let alone. He had already seen more blackamoors, big and little, than he wanted to. But Compton hurried him along to the second hut where the younger one was lodged.

"Bring Sheba out," he told the fat brown woman in the doorway, "the massa wants to see her."

Sheba came, walking erect and fearless, looking at the visitors with an air of proud indifference. In the mellow light of the sinking sun, her dark skin gleamed like satin, marred only by some darker bruises where the slave ship had left its mark; and a raw brand, newly burned in the flesh of her shoulder— the Parris brand. It made Samuel a little sick for a minute.

Compton got off his horse and stood beside the girl, turning her this way and that, stroking her smooth skin, exhibiting the beauty of her straight back and long limbs and rounded hips, precisely as if she were a filly groomed for a race.

In spite of himself, Parris felt his cheeks flush, and as he turned his eyes away he was conscious of a flicker of amused pride in the eyes of the slave. Across the wide Atlantic, across centuries of culture, across the barrier of race and color and condition, the eyes of the woman met the eyes of the man. With the grace of a tiger waking from its sleep, she stretched her arms above her head, turned her supple body with a lazy, luxuriant ease, and glancing at him once from seductive, heavy-lidded eyes, walked slowly back into her hut.

"I swan to man, but she's a bold jade," was Compton's comment as they rode away. "That there name Sheba is Korumanti, they tell me, short for Quasheba, meanin' born on Sunday. But damme if she don't think she's the queen that come to visit Solomon!"

Parris was outraged. "Impudent hussy! I ought to have her whipped!"

But Compton shrugged. "A few days sweat-out in the cane will take the nonsense out of her. 'Tain't no place for cannibal queens."

Parris spoke with some hesitation: "It seems to be the custom of the country, but it is so indecent for any human creature in a Christian land to go stark naked. Don't you think we should get them some clothes—at least for the women?"

Compton laughed. "Lor', sir, they won't wear 'em. The law says every man must have a loincloth an' every wench a petticoat. But they take 'em off an' leave 'em in the bush. They ain't born nor bred to wear clothes, and the fact is, sir, you might as well put a petticoat on a cow.

"An' no more you can't make Christians out of 'em, though our pious-minded King Charles had a law made that every master and overseer should 'tend worship reg'lar with their families (meanin' niggers!). That was some years ago, they tell me, but I ain't ever seen any planters traipsing down the road on Sundays with their families traipsing behind 'em. That law is enforced about as well as the one that says if you be caught cussin' you must pay four pound o' sugar for every cuss!"

The change from Harvard Yard to a Barbados sugar plantation left Samuel Parris in a daze. If he had died and gone to the home of the blessed or the abode of the damned, he would have felt more at home.

Barbados was indeed a far country and his contacts with it had been few. Letters from his father had been infrequent and brief. Aunt Susanna's recollections had been mostly unimportant or amusing trifles. John Oxenbridge had told tales of the tropics, but strictly from the missionary viewpoint: an unregenerate land of heat and rum and license, where Negurs and chiggers and Quakers and High Churchmen were about equally pestiferous.

By great good luck, Samuel had found in the Oxenbridge library a copy of Henry Whistler's *Journal*, written during his visit to the islands some years before. Whistler pictured a land of comfort and luxury, where the gentry lived far better than they do in England and a man could say his possessions were truly his own. It was a land where they had that liberty which England fought for so long. But the islanders abused it.

He told of an island open to all sorts, even to Spaniards and Jews; where Indians and miserable Negroes were born to perpetual slavery—they and their seed—and sold from one planter to another like sheep. An island in itself delightful and pleasant, he related, but the dunghill whereon England cast forth her rubbish: rogues and whores and suchlike people.

"A rogue in England will hardly make a cheater here," he declared. "A bawd brought over puts on a demure comportment; a whore if handsome makes a wife for some rich planter."

A pleasant and friendly island, said the book, where if a traveler came to a house to inquire the way, they would make him drink, and take it very unkindly of him if he refused.

An ingenious island, Whistler told, which tried to design windmills to grind its sugar, for the mills it used destroyed so many horses that it beggared the planters.

But none of these accounts brought to Samuel's imagination the picture of an emerald island in a bright blue sea—of nights swarming with fireflies and a purple sky bending low under the Southern Cross.

Now, for the first time in his twenty years, he was, as the saying went, his own man. Compton's experience and good sense were invaluable, but after all, Compton was a servant and the real responsibility had always been his father's. Now Thomas had laid his tired bones in the little churchyard, and by one stroke of his pen had passed his burden to younger hands:

> To my eldest son, John Parris, now in England, my property in England and Ireland; to Samuel Parris, my son, all my estate here in Barbados.

Each day brought some new problem, the final decision of which was for him, the new master. It gave him a queer feeling as he went about his domain, greeted everywhere by the smiling "Mawnin', Massa Sam," the black boys pulling their woolly foretops and the wenches ducking in a kind of curtsy. In every dark eye, behind every greeting, was the fawning subservience, the silent appraisement of the new master: this slender youth, who had come from some unknown world beyond the rim of the ocean to wear his father's shoes.

Would he be a "good massa"? Would he give them plenty of corn and yams and plantain greens, with now and then salt beef, or would he ration them so short that they must rummage the garbage heaps for old bones to boil for soup, and hunt rats in the cane thickets? For to these black folk of his he was the ultimate arbiter. They were his to do with as he pleased. Their time, their women, their children, their lives, were in his hands.

The sense of power went to his head a little. He felt like a king; like God—he hushed the blasphemy.

Samuel Parris intended to respect the Parris family tradition and not ill-treat his slaves. On his tour of the plantation he had observed the cage—now used as a hospital for Cudjo, whose lame foot was healing rapidly—and the whipping post. These, of course, were necessities. But he was pleased to notice that harsher means of discipline—the spiked collar, the thumbscrews, the pincers—were covered with rust and spiderwebs. He piously resolved they should remain so.

But he was far more concerned with the scarcity and high prices of slave labor and the uncertain and unsatisfactory supply of indentured whites. He had learned something of these problems from Oxenbridge and much more from Compton.

The Irish "Redshanks," prisoners of war taken by Cromwell in his Wars of the Lord, had died long ago or had survived, and began their freedom as broken and worn-out men. The horde of Nonconformists, four hundred and more, most of them Quakers, who had been transported by Charles II under the Conventicle Act of 1664 for ten years' servitude were almost at the end of their terms. Rebellions had proved an uncertain source of supply and the transportation of felons had been resorted to with unsatisfactory results to the planters.

All in all, the white servants were a strange lot. Some of them were decent unfortunates, victims of the injustices of the times; but many of them were ignorant, vicious, and ambitionless: waifs and estrays beached by the waves of disaster.

Barbados was gradually being transformed from a prosperous British colony into an island of black slaves, kept in hand by a small band of planters and white overseers. Every year the population of blacks was growing larger—and when Samuel arrived it was practically two to one. In the widely scattered plantations the proportion was far larger—perhaps ten to one. And if, in the yellow moonlight, shadows came and went among the rustling cane, what wonder if Samuel's knees were a bit uneasy as he made fast the wooden shutters and dropped the iron bolt across the stout door, and made sure that his firearms were ready.

"If there's any commotion, the next neighbor to it fires his musket to give the alarm," Compton had warned him one day, "and upon that the next shoots and so the next and next, till it goes through the island and they all make ready."

There were also pressing political problems. It was four months since the body of Lord Willoughby, governor of Barbados, had been conveyed on board ship for England. Willoughby had been an able and influential man in defending the rights of the little colony against the king's aggression. But what of the new governor? The Barbadians anxiously waited for news.

The export duties on intercolonial trade limited the island more and more strictly to an English market. The Navigation Acts were jeopardizing the trade with England and threatening ruin to the all-important New England trade. The four and a half per cent tax, which had been the burden of complaint in Thomas Parris's letters ever since Samuel could remember, was taking its toll on every pound of exported sugar, and now there was a growing threat of an import duty into England.

These were serious matters. They had borne down more and more heavily on Thomas Parris until the weight of them (or so Compton thought) had broken his health and sent him to his grave. But to his son, fresh from New England, where every mouthful must be wrung from the meager hillsides or battled for against the pitiless waves of the Atlantic, Barbados seemed a land flowing with milk and honey. He thought of Marvell's lines about the Bermudas—equally appropriate here:

> What should we do but sing His praise
> That led us through the watery maze
> Unto an isle so long unknown,
> And yet far kinder than our own? . . .
> He gave us this eternal Spring
> Which here enamels everything, . . .
> He hangs in shades the orange bright
> Like golden lamps in a green night,
> And does in the pomegranates close
> Jewels more rich than Ormus shows;
> He makes the figs our mouths to meet
> And throws the melons at our feet. . . .

His father and John Oxenbridge were two old men, prone to look on the darker side; their failing powers exaggerated the difficulties of any undertaking. Barbados was a new land. It needed new blood, new courage, new enthusiasm, new methods. In a word, it needed youth: youth which knew no fear and met its difficulties as Christian met Apollyon. Samuel flexed his supple young arms, already browned by the tropic sun, and filled his lungs with a deep breath of air rich with seductive tropical perfumes.

The high pulpit and the Bay Psalm Book were forgotten.

20

Tituba and Sheba

> *Moral virtues could no more be expected out of a Charaïbe than reason and good sense out of a woman.*
>
> —PÈRE LABAT.

WHATEVER Samuel Parris had been expecting, he was not prepared for Tituba. Compton had estimated her age to be close to fifty, but to Parris she looked much younger: a small, wiry person, with a slim, straight, supple body like a boy's, flat-breasted and narrow-hipped. It was a surprising contrast to the voluptuous curves of most of the black women he had seen. Her skin, the color of a Spanish olive, was of a clear, dark smoothness, somewhat like that of an East Indian. The resemblance was heightened by a turban of coarse white linen, jauntily adjusted to set off a smooth and shining mass of perfectly straight, jet-black hair, of which, as Parris afterward learned, she was inordinately proud, because it set her apart from the Negroes with their lusterless, kinky wool, just as the turban distinguished her as a house servant and socially far above the despised field hands.

Samuel's Puritan sense of propriety was immensely relieved that she was fully clothed in a white garment, neatly belted at the waist and spotlessly clean. A heavy gold earring—only one— and a talisman necklace made of red seeds spotted with black (which he later learned were jumbee beads) completed her costume.

Her face was oval, with small, straight features, neither negroid nor like the Indians he had seen in Boston. But it was her eyes that held him: eyes lacquer-black, almond-shaped under brows a little oblique—eyes of a penetrating quickness like those of some wild creature of the woods. The eyes looked at him keenly: searching him, appraising him, measuring him, and with no perceptible hesitation, approving him.

Parris felt absurdly gratified, and annoyed with himself for feeling so. Yet the thing took only as long as his "Good morning, Tituba," and her response spoken in a soft, throaty voice, as she made a curtsy:

"Mawnin', Massa Sam, breakfuss waits."

The breakfast was delicious. Tituba was acutely aware of the honor of being promoted to the Great House and had worked hard over that first meal. She had set the table on the broad veranda overlooking the sea, and heaped upon it the riches of the land—a big pewter platter laden with fruits: luscious rosy-hearted melons fresh from the vine; bananas, oranges, limes, and figs; a drink made of parched cocoa beans, flavored with cinnamon bark from his own trees and sweetened with the juice of sugar cane from his own fields; little flying fish just out of the sea, fried in coconut oil; and a Creole dish called duckanoo—a corn-meal pudding baked in a plantain leaf.

Standing behind his chair was a small, black, naked girl-child shooing flies with an orange branch.

Samuel had never eaten such a meal, so different from the heavy beef pudding and ale of his English boyhood, and the everlasting stewed pumpkin and clam broth and journeycake of everyday New England.

Tituba served him quietly, stepping lightly on bare brown feet; a pleasant contrast, indeed, to the clatter and disorderly haste of the Oxenbridge breakfasttime.

"Where did you learn to make a breakfast like this?" he questioned. She explained that she had lived many years in the family of a Spanish gentleman, and there had learned "w'ite folks' mannuhs an' behayviour": to cook, to sew, to wait upon her missie, to keep the house neat (not like that sluttish Candy, who should have lived with the pigs).

"My ol' massa ver' gran' hidalgo," she concluded proudly.

"He beat you almost to death, didn't he?" Parris prompted.

Tituba sighed and nodded her head sorrowfully, deploring the frailties of gentlemen.

"But only when he were what you call in the cup," she excused him.

Parris did not mince words. "Didn't you bewitch your mistress?" But this Tituba emphatically denied:

> By Sain' Petuh, by Sain' Paul,
> By de livin' Gawd ob all,
> Ah nevuh put 'er so!

Parris the Puritan spoke solemnly: "Tituba, are you a Christian? Do you know the meaning of an oath?"

Tituba's head lifted proudly: "Me, Tituba, I *Carib*. But I know Chrishtun swears."

Parris stopped questioning her and devoted himself to his breakfast. Tituba silently withdrew. The orange branch waved lazily over his head.

His spirits responded to the surroundings and his healthy appetite added zest to the food. The unease of the night before was forgotten. He looked out at the sea, where blue waves spilled their spray over the coral reef. He looked down at the road where a young black boy leading the bay colt to a watering trough greeted him with a wide smile and a "Mawnin', Massa Sam."

He looked upward over the green slopes where the slave gangs toiled in the cane fields: his house; his beach; his plantation; his Negroes. He felt like some Oriental potentate.

A soft breeze, heavy with tropical odors, came from the tangled garden, recalling the words of Solomon's Song:

> Awake, O north wind; and come, thou south; blow upon my garden, that the spices thereof may flow out. . . I have gathered my myrrh with my spice; I have eaten my honeycomb with my honey; I have drunk my wine with my milk: eat, O friends; drink, yea, drink abundantly, O beloved.

He forgot the spiritual imagery of the inspired words, the theological interpretation of the mystical union of Christ and His church. Here, under tropic skies, the garden had come to life. The Oriental phrasing glowed with human passion.

Only one thing was lacking—the presence of the woman he loved. His whole being cried out for Elizabeth—Elizabeth—Elizabeth!

As a lily among thorns, so is my love among the daughters. . . . Stay me with flagons, comfort me with apples: for I am sick of love. . . . For, lo, the winter is past, the rain is over and gone; the flowers appear on the earth; the time of the singing of birds is come, and the voice of the turtle is heard in our land; the fig tree putteth forth her green figs, and the vines with the tender grape give a good smell. Arise, my love, my fair one, and come away.

Impatiently he sprang up from the table and stretched his arms towards the sea—miles of it—leagues of it—between him and his beloved!

From the door of the cookhouse Tituba watched him, and smiled.

The months went by and the year drew to its close. The snow lay deep and cold on Harvard Yard, and there was the usual trouble with the ungodly ones who lugged home their Christmas trees in violation of law.

But in Barbados the cane was tall as a man, the rainy season was over and the sun's rays were keen as a hot sword blade. The hard-driving New England energy which Parris had brought with him was flagging. But his New England conscience only whipped him the harder as the task became wearier, and an ever-increasing sense of bafflement added its spur.

The longer he stayed in Barbados the more he saw of the difficulties of the planter. For the island, the beautiful, bountiful island, was being sapped by the planters' greed. They did not know that even a tropic land must rest, and the ground needed refertilization, even though nature did not lay an icy hand upon it after the harvest. When the cane was pindling and the yield poor, they repented of their sins and prayed:

Spare us, good Lord.
From all evil and mischief; from sin; from the
crafts and assaults of the devil; from thy wrath
and from everlasting damnation,
Good Lord, deliver us.

From lightning and tempest; from plague, pestilence and famine; from battle and murder, and
from sudden death,
Good Lord, deliver us.

However, this year the fields gave luscious promise of a generous yield. The cane was in its full beauty, flaunting feathery,
purple-gray plumes above its emerald leaves. And all that hard
work could do to produce a crop the young master of Cotton Hall
had done.

Compton had complained of being shorthanded, but to Parris
it seemed that they had twice as many hands as should have been
needed for the work. But the Negroes, a pox on their lazy hides,
didn't get anything done. With an overseer to every ten hands,
plying the whip and cursing, they only dawdled, keeping time
with their hoes to an everlasting singsong chant, their bodies swaying to its easy rhythm. The overseers were little better. They
hadn't enough ambition even to crack the whip as if they meant
it. Parris tried working them longer hours (against Compton's
advice) but it seemed that no more had been accomplished when
sundown came, and it made the blacks sullen.

Yet on Sundays, when the slaves worked in their own little
truck patches, they seemed alert and active enough. One night
when Compton had taken Samuel down to their village to watch
one of their feasts they danced without any sign of weariness. It
was only because of Compton's insistence that the new master had
let the dance go on.

"It is the most lascivious exhibition I ever saw," he protested.
"I will not allow it on my plantation. Look at that girl Sheba,
and the big baboon she's dancing with! Let go my arm, Compton!
I am master here and I will not permit—"

Compton forgot to be respectful. "Shut up, you fool! You
won't be master anywhere very long if you go abustin' in on a
shindy like this! Cock's life and body, man, that's the shay-
shay!"

The steward apologized later, after he had got Parris safely back
into the house.

"You don't know Negurs like I do, Mr. Parris, sir. Maybe
that wan't a very nice dance—but it ain't just a dance. It's con-
jure stuff, voodoo, black magic, I dunno what! It's the very

devil, sir, an' woe be unto any white man that breaks in on it! You don't like it an' I don't like it either: not so much because it ain't polite (I kinda like a good show, an' it ain't much dirtier'n some I've seen in Drury Lane) but there be danger in it. They get crazy drunk with it, an' that's bad. It's like that wake they had when your father died. It means somethin' to them Negurs that you an' me can't understand. No white man can. It's black sorcery, sir.

"I've seen men die of it—when nothin' ailed 'em. An' I've seen 'em get well—when they was as good as dead. But the worst thing I ever see—" his voice sank to almost a whisper—"the worst thing I ever see—was a dead man—walkin'. 'Twarn't a ghost, Mr. Parris—but a dead man come back!"

Parris questioned him but he would add nothing further. "I've said too much a'ready. Talk o' the Old Boy an' you'll see his cloven hoof. As to what to do about it—let it alone, sez I.

"I've worked for your father nigh five years, and I've learned somethin' about Negurs, though there's plenty I don't know. But we've had less trouble at Cotton Hall than most, an' Mr. Parris thought, an' I think, 'twas because we don't hold 'em down too hard. If you build a dam without a sluicegate, it's goin' to bust in floodtime. An' Negurs is liable to bus' out too. It don't do to forget they be heathens right fresh from the bush. These big Korumantis was cannibals, they say; an' so was the Caribs, a few generations back. An' at Cotton Hall there be just seven white men an' sixty-four blacks—an' eighteen-inch cane knives make damn good swords."

A fresh burst of hilarity came from the village. Compton stood up. "You'd best go to bed, Mr. Sam. They'll keep this up till cocklight. I'll go out an' take a look around."

If Parris had not been too busy to think about it, he would have been surprised at himself for finding the secular problems of plantation life so absorbingly interesting. In the sheltered life of his childhood and youth he had been altogether his mother's son: now the spirit of his father and of all the long line of merchant forebears woke in his blood. Money sufficient for things needful to him always had come like the air he breathed. Now every pound, every shilling, must be wrung out of the soil by his own endeavors.

It challenged his inner resources as nothing in his life before had done. With a zeal that was almost eagerness, he laid aside the Puritan preacher part of him as if it were a hampering cloak and girded himself for battle. If instead of preaching Christ he must plant cane he would be a successful planter. His jaw set in a hard line and his mouth was stern.

The whole plantation cried out for improvements. They were handicapped at every turn, losing money every year, because of old-fashioned and worn-out equipment.

The native 'Bajans were a hospitable people, and most of the neighboring planters had dropped in informally to extend friendly greetings to their new neighbor. It was a matter of some surprise to Samuel to observe the genuine respect and liking for Thomas Parris apparent in the attitude of these men, some of whom had lived neighbor to him for many years. Clearly it was for the father's sake that they were ready to extend welcome and courtesies to the son. Yet these men must have known that his father was living in sin.

"If you're as good a man as your father was—" they told him. And Samuel, who had always regarded his father as of commoner clay than his mother and himself, was a little at a loss to find an answer.

Some of the older men had never forgiven Samuel's uncle John for letting out a part of Cotton Hall plantation for a Quaker settlement in 1656. Most of the planters were Cavaliers and Royalists, and all the eleven parish churches were Episcopal (named for the saints of the Christian calendar) though the religious issue seemed of less importance than in either England or Massachusetts. But the Quakers, of whom there were many, were obnoxious to everybody. This was due principally to their awkward insistence that the black was a child of God as well as the white, and that he should be given the privilege of attending divine worship. This heresy was regarded as a peculiarly dangerous error, which must be firmly and promptly dealt with.

"We don't blame you for what your uncle did," they told Parris, "but feeling ran pretty high against him for quite a while. He was just stubborn and pigheaded, and carried the idea of toleration too far.

"Your father was a broad-minded gentleman, willing to join

forces with the majority. He could see that too much personal liberty was as hurtful as too little—specially in a slave-owning colony where white men ought to stand together and not let the Negurs get any fool notions. And those blasted Quakers, preaching to the blacks that they got souls and rights and privileges just the same as white folks—they're like to get us all murdered in our beds!"

The younger planters, too, were disposed to be friendly, but Samuel had some misgivings about them. As a rule, their conversation was more colorful than would have been tolerated in the best Bostonian society, and Parris suspected most of them of what he would have termed loose living. Yet they were good neighbors, kindly and agreeable, and apparently well regarded in the community.

One of the first visitors was George Webb, who owned the plantation of Hilltop, several miles up the coast. He dropped in one morning for a neighborly call.

Webb was about thirty years old, English born, but had been long enough in the island to show the effects of tropical life and the excesses associated with it. He was a big fellow, handsome as were many of his type; a little fat, a little dissipated, but tanned and hard from the outdoor life.

Parris was just waiting for his mare to be brought around to start on his morning ride over the estate.

"Don't let me keep you," Webb said after the greetings were over. "I'd like nothing better than to ride with you."

So the two set out across the fields to where the slaves were already at work in the cane. The cutting was just beginning and the workers swung the long knives to the rhythm of a favorite song:

> Hard time, hard time,
> Hard time a carry a day.
> Hard time, hard time,
> Fo' dey won't put cramouchin' away.

The black bodies bent and rose, bent and rose, with the slow and lazy motion that so exasperated the New Englander.

As their horses reached the nearest gang, a tall young woman straightened herself and faced them, her white teeth shining in a friendly greeting. It was Sheba. The months of toil in the hot cane fields had left her slimmer and harder than when she came. Standing bare and straight in the morning sun, she looked like a statue of burnished bronze—savage and beautiful.

Hastily Samuel turned away, but not before he had caught the challenge in her eyes. Once more the Song of Songs came back to him:

I am black, but comely, O ye daughters of Jerusalem . . . my mother's children were angry with me; they made me the keeper of the vineyards. . . . Look not upon me, because I am black.

Webb pulled in his horse. "By Gad, Parris, that wench is a beauty; too good by far for field work. Why don't you have her in the house instead of that crone, Tituba? Cock's life, man, where are your eyes?"

The overseer's sharp command made Sheba bend to her work again, but Webb's eyes still followed her as she swung the long knife.

Parris answered a trifle shortly: "I want no Korumanti to cook for me. Tituba uses me well enough."

"Cook! My eye!" Webb laughed, still watching the slave. "Who said she should cook? Is a wench good for nothing else, Parris? Your Roundhead ways will not last long under this sun, I wager!"

Parris turned on him sharply—a little too sharply. "The wench is nothing to me except for the work she can do."

"Well, every man to his taste," returned Webb, "but 'tis a crime for such charms to be wasted. I'll give you twenty pounds for her."

"No! We're shorthanded already. We can't spare her."

"Well, then, I'll trade you a well-seasoned slave. Or two of my older ones, as you like."

"Enough, Webb!" Parris snapped. "The girl is not for sale." And he felt his face flush at Webb's bantering laugh.

The days were burning hot and the nights were stifling, for the life-giving breeze of evening could not be allowed to enter. So night after night, Parris and Compton sweltered in the spacious dining hall, and by the light of one candle, which served only to bring the darkness into relief, discussed the past and future of the island. They talked of agriculture and sugar-making, politics and shipping; while a lonely owl voiced its weird cry in the branches of the silk-cotton tree; and small green lizards crawled among the rafters overhead, or now and then dropped on the great mahogany table. And the eyes of John Parris, still young in his gilt frame, followed them, turning at their slightest move.

When Compton had gone to his cabin, Parris retired to his hot bedroom and lay alone in the great bed that had been his father's, tossing for countless hours. When he finally slept, he did so fitfully, tormented by frightful nightmares.

Tituba's grateful efforts to please him were useless. With the help of her husband, John Indian, and four half-grown black boys who were too young to cut cane, she had cleaned and scrubbed the Great House and everything in it until it suited her ideas of what a "genelum's house" ought to be. All the housewifely lore that she had learned from her house-proud Spanish mistress she now put to use for her young Massa Sam. The wainscot and floors and furniture had been cleaned with a wash of orange juice and polished with brushes made from the soft brown husks of coconuts until they shone in the restored beauty of their proud young days. The same soft husks had been used to make springy mattresses for the beds, and the skeeter curtains were white and starchy with cassava. But for the most part, Parris paid little attention to what she did, unless she called attention to it.

Tituba watched him with anxious eyes. "Young massa need good magic," she told him once; but he answered her angrily and she said no more.

She had marked an X on each doorstep and nailed horseshoes above the doors and burned rosemary in a pan at bedtime to drive away the duppies. But Tituba could not drive away from her young massa the nightmares and erotic dreams which swarmed with the things his senses craved and his strict young soul abhorred. She could not rid him of these any more than she could rid the house of crickets and cockroaches and little green lizards.

Night after night he was hagridden. Morning after morning he woke with no memory of his dreams but only a confused sense of weariness and dread.

With the morning came the sunshine and fresh air that the closed shutters denied him, and a busy and active day in the fields. But the nights wore his nerves.

The tropic night is both a glorious and a fearful thing. When the sun has set and the blue-gray haze of twilight has deepened into the purple blackness of night, when the Southern Cross hangs low and the tall palmetto-royal stands a-tiptoe to touch its lowest star, and the breath of evening is sweet with tropic scents, then the waking night wind blows heavy with the scent of the sea, cool and life-giving after the heat of the day. But there is a menace in the darkness—a primeval fear. And there is the dread of the night wind, which the wise ones say brings sickness; so the heavy doors must be closed and barred; the windows shuttered and the great bolts drawn. To keep out the evil night wind? Perhaps. Perhaps to guard against that other and more imminent peril—the terror that walketh in darkness—the sons of Ham, bending under the ancient curse.

The human mind becomes accustomed to dangers, so that it all but forgets them. But the terror that Samuel Parris felt could not be forgotten. It was too real and frightening. There had been nothing in his life to prepare him for it. The blacks had been sulky of late. The cane was thick and heavy and the days were long and hot.

Parris tossed in his bed. He heard the sounds from the village, laughter and moans and shouts in an alien tongue—and worst of all the sudden silences—the fearsome hush that now and then settled on the village. He heard whispers in the passing breeze, and the cautious tread of naked feet outside his window, and the rattle of the shutters. Was it the wind? Or were there dark naked bodies slithering by, one after one, two after two?

And the girl Sheba haunted him: her savage grace and rhythm; the ripple of her firm muscles under the sleek brown skin; her untamed pride, standing naked and unashamed; and the great brown eyes like the eyes of the dog Protector that he had loved as a boy. The eyes of a dog? Yes. But also the eyes of a woman, proud and confident, even under the whip of slavery.

"I am black, but comely, O ye daughters of Jerusalem!"

Not even in the darkness of his shuttered room would he admit to himself that the slave girl excited him. To his Puritan soul unlawful desire in any form was shameful, but to look on a woman to lust after her, and that woman a heathen savage, would have been the ultimate disgrace. It was only in the dark chambers of Samuel's soul that the slave girl's image hid itself, unchallenged because unknown.

Yet he had a guilty feeling whenever he caught Tituba looking at him. Tituba knew something—something about him that even he himself did not know. If Tituba was a witch, perhaps she could see into a man's soul and read the past and the future.

He was a little afraid of Tituba, yet he was comforted by her. She was loyal and kindly, and grateful for his favor, and if she bewitched anybody it would be his enemies and not himself. He was afraid she was a witch, for one morning he found a charm under his pillow (he must have slept on it all night)—two needles bound together, point to eye, between two smoothly whittled pieces of ceiba wood. And when he scolded and asked her what it meant, she smiled her inscrutable smile and said:

"Him doan mean nothin', massa. Doan mean nothin'—dess bring good luck, das all—dess li'l good luck!"

Samuel woke suddenly one night a few weeks later. It was pitch-dark in the shuttered bedroom, but he had the feeling that he had not slept long and that some unusual sound had roused him. He lay stiff and still, the ever-present fear gripping him.

There was no sound of wind or storm. Was it the blacks, or the even more terrifying probability of a pirate raid? Lying thus, his quick ears caught a faint whisper of hushed voices outside his window—the soft pad-pad of naked feet—then stillness. Minutes passed, tense and fearful.

Then a new sound, soft and low, yet clear and unmistakable, just outside his window—the musical clear crooning sound of a woman's voice, singing, chanting, rising and falling in a sort of weird incantation. There were words to the melody—words in an unknown tongue—but even the Puritan ear of Samuel Parris needed no words to understand the meaning of the Korumanti love-call.

The sudden relaxing of his tense nerves left him weak and shaking. Sheba—it must be Sheba—it *was* Sheba—serenading him outside his window! The relief passed and left in its wake an anger, fierce and unreasonable, out of all proportion to the offense. The devil take the slut for her impudence! He would teach her manners, the damned strumpet! He sprang out of bed and jerked open the shutter, cursing her mightily.

Sheba was crouching, kneeling on the broad window ledge, and as the shutter swung back two slim strong arms embraced his knees. She clung to him with all her strength, her head pressed against his thighs, kissing him, crooning to him with a savage half-animal purr of pleading and triumph.

"God, help!" It was a despairing cry.

But God was far away in His high heaven, and Barbados was only a pin point on the map.

The sun was high in the heavens when Samuel awoke. He must have slept the clock around. He felt completely relaxed, and for the first moment utterly happy and at peace with the world. Then memory came and with it unthinkable shame and guilt.

"What have I done! O God, what have I done!"

He set to wondering—could such a thing have happened, really happened, or was it just another kind of nightmare? He was alone in the middle of the massive mahogany bed, with its starchy mosquito curtains hemming him round and rustling in the fresh sea breeze. He raised his head. The shutter was unlatched and swinging—the noontime sun beat into the room!

He dressed quickly and went out on the veranda. Tituba brought him his breakfast, smiling the same secret smile—was it the same?

"Massa sleep berry well—duppies all gone now," she said casually. She served him as usual. (Was there anything strange in her manner?) He ate what she set before him, saying nothing, his eyes on his plate. He finished hastily and ordered his mare. It was high noon and blistering hot, but the set of the master's mouth warned her to make no protest. Young massa would do what he would do.

So he set out grimly for the long ride to the Webb plantation, and arrived there an hour later, his mare covered with foam and about to drop.

Seeing him in such a state, Webb met him at the door with fear in his eyes.

"Parris! By all the gods, what's happened?"

Parris seemed not to hear him. He leaned from the saddle.

"Are you still of the same mind about the wench Sheba?"

Webb's mouth dropped open.

"Well—by—God!"

"Do you still want the Negur?"

Webb recovered himself. He grinned.

"You bet I want her!"

21

Harvest

No more—no more—Oh! never more on me
The freshness of the heart can fall like dew.
            —BYRON, *Don Juan.*

IT WAS cane-cutting time in Barbados: the happy harvest-time, toward which all the year's labor tended. For though the products of the island were luscious and varied, commercially it was a one-product land. Many appetizing foods enriched the planter's table, but only one crop brought him money. Sugar, molasses, rum; molasses, rum, sugar; rum, sugar, molasses: such was his cycle of prosperity.

At sugar harvest there was hard work for everybody, but there was delicious sweetness in the reward. The slaves coming home at night sucked the juice from long pipes of cane; the planter sweetened his tea with fresh juice; the oxen, hauling heavily laden carts from the fields, gorged themselves as they waited for the loading; the tired sugar horses snatched a nip as they wearily turned the old-fashioned crusher round and round, while black boys thrust bundles of cane between the upright, creaking rolls. The calves and pigs and goats feasted on scattered baegasse, the refuse cane, strewn about to dry for fuel under the boiling kettles, around which were gathered sticky little black babies, holding up their gourd dippers as they begged for the frothy dunder skimmed off the syrup. Everybody was tired, everybody was happy, everybody was getting fat at sugar harvest.

Day after day strings of patient donkeys toiled down the rocky road to the storehouse at Reid's Bay, laden with musko sugar in heavy bags hung pannierlike on each side and protected from the weather by tarred cloths. Each sturdy little beast would carry two hundred pounds up and down the tangled and slippery paths, picking out little ways in the woods as horses have not the wit to do. If by ill chance an assinego fell two Negroes were able to help him up, under the direction of the "Christian" in charge.

Day after day in the storehouse more "Christians" were busy overseeing the slaves who packed the sugar—coarse and brown and unpleasantly strong in smell and flavor—into weatherproof and ratproof hogsheads for shipment to England. Long years ago, in the earliest days of sugar, the enterprising pioneer planters had imported camels to solve the transportation problem; for a good camel will carry sixteen hundred pounds and go the surest of any beast. The camels did not long survive, but the cumbersome 110-gallon hogsheads of the camel days were still used for shipping sugar and molasses.

Day after day the carpenters worked, binding barrel staves from Boston with iron hoops from Taunton, making giant casks in which to ship musko sugar from the cane fields of Barbados to the refineries in England. From there it would be reshipped to the Indies and at last, in its crystalline whiteness, would achieve its proud destiny on the tables of those planters who could afford the luxury of "imported" sugar.

At every step of the process there was a tax. First was the four and a half per cent export duty; then the law which required English colonies to ship only to English markets in English ships sailing from an English port, commanded by an English captain and manned by a crew at least three-quarters English. There was the law requiring all sugar to be sent to England for refining; and as the last exaction came the import duty into England, and a freight rate of nine pounds per ton.

The day of the empire builders had dawned in the West Indies. It was Cromwell who first got the idea of beating the Dutch as Mistress of the Seas. It was Charles II who promoted it, having no objection to a good idea just because his opponent thought of it first. It was Charles's brother James, Duke of York, who added the important corollary that an officer in the British navy should first of all be a seaman, rather than a politician. It was the coffers of England that furnished the money to build the ships. And to make the circle complete, it was the Navigation Acts that forced colonial commerce into British vessels and colonial gold into the coffers of England.

The constant trade winds still blew from east to west across the rippling canebrakes of Barbados, but the winds of trade veered fitfully and blew the Indies no good.

The 'Bajans were a provincial lot. They didn't know much about empire building. They knew only that the storehouses at every port were crammed with sugar; and desperate appeals to England for more ships brought word that English merchants held that the decline in sugar prices so lowered their profits it was scarcely worth their while to run the hazard of the long voyage to Barbados.

Day after day the planters watched the rim of the sea. But only blue waves rose and fell under the glorious blue sky, with never a sail breaking the horizon's lonesome line. Three months dragged by and never a freighter entered Carlisle Bay!

Samuel Parris had put forth his best efforts for the sugar crop. Every day he had worked and planned for it. Every night he had knelt beside his bed and craved God's blessing on his endeavors. God had sent the sun and rain and wind as they were needed and the cane had grown tall and lush—the best crop in seven years, Compton said.

Parris had strained all his resources when harvesttime came; had worked the slaves from dawn till dark at the cutting and the grinding and the boiling, at the sugaring off and sacking and packing, until the storehouse at Reid's Bay could hold no more. In the evenings he and Compton had figured tonnage and freightage and the prices they ought to get and the profit they would make and what they would do with the money.

But the days and the weeks crawled by and only little fishing boats dotted the dancing waters of the bay which not so many years before had had the proud record of a hundred sail a year.

The unhappy planters met in the taverns at the Bridge, Master John Jobson's and Mistress Joan Fuller's, and talked and argued and hoped and despaired. As week after week passed, they ordered more often than was good for them the kill-devil rum of the grogshop crews, instead of the good Madeira which was a gentleman's drink. Nobody knew what the trouble was, except for some roundabout stories by way of the neighboring colonies, all different and probably all wrong.

In Samuel's guilty consciousness the thought of his night of sin loomed blacker and blacker. In the lonesome nights he knelt beside his bed, or lay face down on the floor in self-reproach, crying to God for pardon; repenting the lust of his flesh which had betrayed him. But God turned away His face. He heard not nor did he answer. In the darkness the devil leered at him and cackled with evil laughter.

Worst of all there came times, even in his prayers, when his flesh would burn with a madness of desire and his arms would reach out in the sultry darkness for the woman he had put away from him.

("Look not upon me, because I am black!") What a fool he was—what a fool! Who would be the worse if he lay with his slave? Who would know or care?

("I am black, but comely, O ye daughters!") And now she lay in Webb's arms. Doubtless her kisses were as warm for Webb as they had been for him! Damn the wanton baggage! Damn her! Damn Webb! Devil take both of 'em!

But when the morning came his conscience would subjugate his rebel body, and the agony of self-condemnation would begin again. Now and then he was beset with the idea that it was this sin of his that had brought calamity. For God had blessed the harvest but withheld the ships; a lack which never before had threatened the island. He remembered Jonah, but with the strange inconsistency of the religious mind he forgot that perhaps half the planters in the island were satisfying themselves with black mistresses. In the sincerity of his contrite spirit he had no thought for any sin but his own. He, Samuel Parris, who had been trained from his youth in the way of righteousness; he who from boyhood had dedicated his soul to God and his life to the ministry of Jesus Christ had become the vilest of sinners.

He thought of a high cliff in the rugged north end of the island where long ago a slave had hurled himself into the waves below and been beaten to death on the rocks. Perhaps in this way he might redeem the land from the curse his wickedness had brought. But he was afraid. He dared not go to meet his God with fornication on his soul.

His tortured imagination haunted him with the dread of impending calamities. From the cheerful, active man of a few weeks ago he became despondent, picturing just ahead of him illness and

death and damnation. Except for the damnation he would be glad
to die, he told himself, for life had nothing left.

He dared not to think of Elizabeth. His vileness had put her
forever beyond his reach. His very thought would contaminate
her purity, her loyalty to her vows, her high ideals. Sometimes
he woke with a confused memory of having dreamed of her—
dreadful, torturing dreams of his lost love: Elizabeth weeping
her heart out at his unfaithfulness—Elizabeth looking down on
him from high heaven as he burned in everlasting fire—Elizabeth in peril, screaming to him for help, and he struggling dreadfully to reach her but held down by a mighty weight—Elizabeth,
her gentle face hard and stern, turning away from him, shuddering with horror and fear of him, for the vile creature that he was!

Tituba watched him furtively, hardly venturing to speak, for
he regarded her with an unfriendly suspicion which he took scant
pains to hide. He mistrusted her of having had some part in
Sheba's visit, but from mixed feelings of pride and shame he
shrank from putting his accusation into words.

There was that queer charm he had found under his pillow,
put there by Tituba. Perhaps there was magic in that. Like as
not she and Sheba between them had bewitched him with their
juggles so that he was powerless to resist. But he was too honest
to get much comfort out of this theory. It was the lust of his
flesh and the desire of his eyes that had betrayed him.

He had seen Sheba only once since that night. A planters'
meeting was called at Hilltop to discuss the economic crisis; and
because his raw nerves feared that his absence might be marked,
Parris went, though he had as soon been pilloried. Sheba was not
in the room, but just as the planters were taking their leave she
peacocked down the stairs. And such a Sheba! Parris gasped and
turned away his eyes, but not too soon to see the insolent toss of
the head with which she greeted him.

She was clothed in a London gown of gorgeous yellow satin
and lace, the bodice low-cut and worn off the shoulders, revealing
her generous bosom; and the puffed elbow sleeves were slit open
to show the arm beneath. Her Nell Gwynne petticoats permitted
a view of high red-heeled shoes, many sizes too small for her
ample feet, so that she balanced herself precariously. Her black
wool had been laboriously trained over her forehead in stringy

little curls, like inverted question marks, made slick and shining with pomade. Around her neck was a string of gleaming stones.

Yet with all these bedizenments, Parris thought she looked more naked and more savage than he had ever seen her. Her statuesque, symmetrical body had become heavy and lumpish and her bare neck was fat under her jewels. A loathing like physical nausea swept Parris.

The guests, most of whom had partaken generously of their host's home-made rumbullion, greeted Sheba's entrance with cheers and booed at Webb when he tried to send her back up-stairs. Two young blades, a little tipsy, ran up the stairs and escorted her down between them, and with fulsome laughter and jests, drank a health "to our host and the missie!"

Parris, sick with disgust but not daring to refuse, drank the toast—his throat burning with the hot liquor, his face flaming with hotter shame. Then he hastily made his escape.

It was not until he lay in his bed that night that the meaning of some of the salty gibes came to him.

Sheba would have a child. Would it be Webb's—or his?

The blacks were sulky and sullen and at night the drums were drumming—far off somewhere in the hills. Soft and deep they were, muffled by distance and the forests—drums of Africa, waking race memories in Africa's exiled children: memories of mystic rites; of Papa Legba and Damballa the wise and the thunder-voiced Oguon; of blood-drenched altars where the goat without horns had lain.

Compton's matter-of-fact English head knew nothing of such mysteries, but through experience he sensed danger and devil-ment in the drums. And Cudjo, the big buck, had run off to the devil knew where. The bloodhounds had traced him to the edge of a mangrove swamp up near the Fair Maid Cave at the north end of the island, and would go no farther. They slunk back with their tails between their legs. And Cudjo was a drummer.

Compton had moved his few belongings to the Great House at Samuel's request.

"I like your company," Samuel told him, "and there's plenty of room for you here. Uncle John built this house when he was married and hoped to fill it with sons and daughters, but Aunt Susanna never bore him any children. If she had, I wouldn't be here now, I suppose. But here I am, a solitary bachelor in a lonesome house. Bring your things and take this room next to mine."

He could not admit to his steward that the lonesomeness was driving him crazy; that the evenings were endless and the nights were worse; that the shadows creeping in upon him were full of unknown terrors, and a bat flitting among the rafters or swooping close to his head would leave him weak and wet with clammy sweat.

He could trust Compton in any crisis, he thought with reluctant admiration. It puzzled him, for Compton was not a gentleman nor pious; he had neither breeding nor faith to sustain him, yet he believed the man was afraid of nothing in earth or heaven or hell.

"And, Compton," the master went on, "there's another thing. I come from Massachusetts where we don't care much about a man's rank or family, and we meet each other on equal terms. You and I are working together trying to make a success of planting; and you know a great deal more about it than I do. Your term of service is almost up, but I want you to stay on with me in some sort of arrangement which will profit us both. Let's forget this master and servant foolishness and be partners, and friends."

Compton's lips trembled a little, but his voice was just as usual: "Yes, sir, just as you say, sir. It's very good of you, sir."

Parris held out his hand. "It's a bargain, then. And, Compton, my name isn't 'Yes, sir.' It's Parris."

Compton had made no comment when he learned that Parris had traded Sheba for two middle-aged Congo wenches. It was not a bad trade. The Congoes were good workers, slow and stupid but steady and too dumb to make trouble. Compton himself preferred the high-tempered breeds, just as he preferred a thoroughbred to a broken-spirited work horse. He was proud of Sheba, just as he was proud of Cudjo, who, barring his limp, was as fine a buck as you could find on the island. But he admitted that Sheba was a bold-faced, lazy tom-rig and that her sassy ways had nettled the master. He thought nothing of it at first, but later he began to wonder if there was more to the story. Anyway, it was no business of his.

But he couldn't help noticing the change in young Mr. Sam,

and he didn't like it. It worried him more and more as time went on. It wasn't right for a youth just come of age to go into a decline, even if the business outlook was bad and the ships slow in coming. Mr. Tom had been through plenty of hard times, and his son ought to have some of the Parris pluck.

At first Compton had Tituba under suspicion. He hadn't liked that arrangement from the beginning. He didn't like Tituba's Carib blood, nor her shifty black eyes nor her catfooted ways. If he caught her at any sleighty tricks—!

But it didn't take him long to make up his mind that Tituba was as troubled and puzzled as himself. And at last it was Tituba who came to him with the problem, one day when Parris was in Bridgetown.

"Massa Compum," she questioned, "yuh know wha's mattuh Mas' Sam?"

Compton was not English for nothing. "What should be the matter with him? He's all right as far as I can see."

Tituba wagged her head. "Yuh needn' lie tuh Tituba. No 'ndeed! Yuh knows him soah 'flickded. Someb'dy set duppy on he an' dey keep on aplaguin' he. Him droopin' an' ailin' jes' like a fatul sperrit snatched holt o' he. Suah gwine be nuthuh funeyel less'n someb'dy pull duppy off'n he damqueek."

Because Compton was worried he scoffed: "Your head's stuffed with maggots!"

Tituba had already tried all the ordinary charms without success. She had sprinkled the blood of a sensay fowl on the fire to the accompaniment of powerful incantations. She had squeezed lime juice on ashes (ashes made from a piece of the sacred ceiba tree in the graveyard) and the mixture had bubbled and fizzed just as it should—but with no beneficial results that she could see.

Now she had appealed to Compton, and being rebuffed was forced to extreme measures, which involved doing certain mysterious things to a white gamecock. Since the rite involved serious unpleasantness to the cock, and the loss one at a time of most of his insides, he was sure to protest with loud and strident squawks as long as he was able. So Tituba had to wait for a time when Compton had gone to town and Massa Sam was watching the plowing far over the hill. Even at that, there might be trouble later on, for Massa Compton was mighty proud of his pet rooster, which he would back to whip any bird in St. Peter's parish.

But the compulsion of the zealot was upon her. Whatever the consequences, she must save young massa's soul alive. (She knew just how to scatter bloody feathers at the mouth of Brer Fox's den so that they would look all right to a white man.)

Having thus offered up her sacrifice, Tituba made ready a tasty dinner for her young massa and at bedtime brought him an ambrosial drink made of fruit juices and clear, cool water, drawn by means of a well sweep from one of the immense caverns which underlie the island. Into this draught went a magical powder, compounded under the light of the moon.

Tituba watched him as he drained the cup.

"Massa Sam, yuh got some'dy yonduh in shadduh lan' love yuh vehy much?"

Samuel was startled. "What do you mean by shadow land? Heaven?"

Tituba shook her head doubtfully: "No, suh, Mas' Sam. Des shadduh lan'. Yuh see, Mas' Sam, w'en yuh daid yuh cawpse go in graveyahd—sperrit go heaven—eithuh Chrishtun hell. Well, den—well den, w'ere shadduh gonetuh?"

Samuel was puzzled. "What shadow do you mean, Tituba?"

"Why, de daid man's shadduh, Mas' Sam. W'en man walk, he shadduh go befoah, behime, byside 'im. W'en man 'ceasded, w'ere den shadduh gonetuh?" Before Samuel could speak, she went on: "Shadduh stay behime—by grave—by house. Watch um chillun he love. Yuh see, Mas' Sam?"

Samuel's theological training fell a little short. There had been no course in shadows at Harvard.

"Some shadduh love you, Mas' Sam?" Her voice was low but vibrant with emotion.

Parris was strangely shaken. He forgot he was talking to a slave—a heathen. "My mother!" The words were a whisper. "She loved me—and went away to heaven—long ago—when I was a little lonely boy."

Tituba came close to him. She spoke slowly, with mysterious emphasis: "Huh not go 'way, massa! Huh shadduh close byside alltime! Yuh not see, massa. Yuh not hab seein' eye. Tituba see shadduh 'cause Tituba bohn wid a veil. Tituba see long tall angel all shinin' white leanin' ovuh Mas' Sam w'en he sleep. Maybe some night yuh lyin' all still as still—waitin'—watchin'—longin'—maybe bimeby yuh see huh too!"

Her bare brown feet went away silently. The owl in the ceiba tree wailed. The lizards croaked sleepily in the rafters. Parris felt strangely drowsy, strangely comforted, strangely at peace. He lay down on his bed without even saying his prayers, and slept.

Far into the night Tituba knelt in the cookhouse, burning incense before a grotesque little god who had once been a stone.

Samuel slept: and in his dream a tall angel, all shining white, leaned over him—an angel with his mother's face—loving him—comforting him—forgiving him—as she used to do when he was a wayward little boy.

He woke with only a confused memory of the dream. But the feeling of forgiveness and consolation remained. It seemed, somehow, that his mother was not dead, nor even in some far blue heaven, but rather a living presence, "her shadduh close byside alltime" as Tituba had said.

He flung himself on his knees beside the bed and stretched out his arms, invoking the comforting figure of his dream: "Oh, mother, my mother in heaven, go to God for me and crave forgiveness for the sin of my body; that He will not leave my soul in hell, nor be angry with me forever!"

For a long time he knelt there, his head resting on his arms, the comforting sense of his mother's presence reviving him like wine, bringing him back to sanity and peace. Strangely enough, it did not occur to him that he was dangerously close to that false papist doctrine of the intercession of the saints.

Samuel was just finishing his breakfast when Compton rode in. He had left the Bridge at sunup. It was the colt's first long trip under saddle and he was in a sweat. Compton threw himself out of the saddle and flung the lines to a black boy at the stable door.

"Brush him and give him a good rub down, but don't feed him till he cools off."

Compton came up the veranda steps and stretched out in a hammock. He seemed very tired.

A word from Parris sent the wielder of the orange branch scurrying to the cookhouse with an order for more breakfast.

Compton sat up. "Everything all right?"

"Of course," Parris replied. "We got the north field plowed yesterday. Got along fine. Only old Longhorn lost her calf in the woods. She bellowed for it all night."

Compton left the hammock and pulled a chair up to the table. His voice was low but sharp. "What do you mean, lost her calf? What happened to it?"

"Why, that we couldn't make out, exactly. I sent two of the boys to hunt for it, but they couldn't find it. They thought it must have wandered off and fallen into the big gutt."

Compton snorted. "Ol' Longhorn never lost a calf that way. Over at Hilltop a heifer broke a leg and had to be killed. But it didn't fool Webb. He weighted the carcass with rock and throwed it into the whirlpool. It's death to any Negur that's caught with fresh meat—but catchin' 'em is like catchin' fleas, hell burn 'em! I knowed they was up to some devilment. There's been too many drums abeatin' out in the hills." He broke off suddenly and talked of other things while Tituba brought him his breakfast. Then he went on:

"It's the same all over the island. All the planters are worried. The blacks are sulky and sly. They're like children—allus show when they're up to mischief. The main grievance is they're sick o' greens an' bread-kind an' crave meat. An' there's none to be had. A snow come in from Jamaica with a ton o' salt pork aboard her, but it was all gobbled up before I even heard of it. That's the devil of livin' on a little crag-in-the-sea like this. It's too small for cattle pens or ranches, and as soon as ships stop comin' there's nothin' to eat but greens an' sugar.

"And rum! God-a-mighty, Mr. Parris! The grogshops at the Bridge are pourin' so much kill-devil you can smell it halfway to the Hole. That's bad. Every Christian has need for all his wits, if the blacks begin to swarm."

He had bolted his breakfast and was on his feet again. "Whatever's happened to the ships, it ain't only in England. There's nothin' from Salem or Boston neither. Looks like somethin' big might o' busted loose—a new war, most like."

Every night there were goomba drums in the hills.

To Parris the long, low call of distant drums meant only another dance, in which the slaves expressed their passions by swaying bodies and lascivious abandonment. His puritanical disgust had softened under Barbadian skies to indifference. A slave's morality was not much more important than an animal's. The distant drums had become a part of the tropical scene—part of its lure and mystery, its bewildering beauty and charm, like the yellow moonlight and the rustle of the wind in the tall palms.

But Compton was uneasy, more and more as the nights went by. "It ain't right—that drummin'. There ain't no swing to it. Listen! 'Boom, bum bum—bomb, boomba, bomb—bum-bum-bomb.' Nobody can't dance to that. An' damme ef I can find out where it is. I been out every night for a week, rangin' the hills. Sometimes it's close by—then a mile off—over the next rise—down yonder gutt. It's like bein' pixy-led,—scary as Ol' Dowl! But I think 'tis a flesh-an-blood Negur doin' it. An' I got a good guess who. There's no news o' Cudjo yet, and the dogs jest run in circles—an' that devil's tattoo in the wilds sounds mighty like that black rascal's drum.

"We're in fer trouble, sir, just as sure as the devil's in London. That there drum's a signal!"

But there were white men as well as black abroad in the hills. Creoles "bawn 'n' raised" in the 'Bajan isle; boys who had hunted iguanas and stoned monkeys over the ledges and down the ravines since they were knee-high. Boys grown tall, who now wore his Majesty's uniform proudly as soldiers of the Colonial Guards and patrolled the hills at night, slid stealthily as shadows from tree to tree and rock to rock—hunting men.

One night the drums were silent and excited couriers spread the news that a plot to murder all the white men and abduct the women had been betrayed by a black mammy whose love for her golden-haired nursling was stronger than her blood loyalty.

Forty or fifty blacks were rounded up as leaders and their punishment was swift and terrible. Seven were burned alive. Eleven were beheaded and their bodies dragged through the streets and then burned. Twenty-five or more were hung in cages and left to starve—a frightful object lesson to all rebellious blacks.

Parris's Cudjo was recognized as the chief agitator and was the first of the seven to be burned. The crowd surged and scrambled in their eagerness to add kindling to the huge bonfire. A torch was put to the pile of wood and tar. The flames leaped and yapped like hungry hounds, driving the crowd back from their scorching heat. When the fire died, in the little drift of glowing ashes that remained there was no difference between the fuel and its victim.

The story spread among the blacks that Cudjo escaped in the smoke by turning himself into a fly.

"Fiah nevuh touch Cudjo. He outsmahted 'em all. Some night w'en de moon am full, we heah he drum 'Boom-ba—goom-ba—bum-bum-bomb' down in de Faiah Maid Cave."

Compton made only one comment: "The damned ongrateful runagate! After all I done for that foot o' his. I'd oughta let him rot!"

Parris indulged a sarcastic impulse: "I think you said you weren't afraid of that blackhearted son of Satan, because he was smart—eh, Compton! As for me, I think I'd rather have a dullhead."

To which Compton retorted: "Every man for himself. But I'd not trust your Tituba outa eye-shot. Though I will say I admire her cookin'." He smoked reflectively. "I'd damn well like to know what happened to that prize fightin' cock o' mine!"

22

Hurricane

This is no time to boast the rule of earth;
Things are abroad tonight we cannot see.
There is no comfort in the pagan mirth
That whistles through the boughs of every tree.
Something out there behind the wind is grinning,
Watching the lights blink out, the shutters close;
Planning his battles for a new beginning,
A final drive to crush his human foes.
The genius of the beaches lifts his hand
Blots out the sky and sea to vent his spite,
Then, howling evilly, stalks the cowering land
While twisted cedars writhe against the night.
                                    —JOHN R. SWAIN.

*I*N OCTOBER a ship came from England bringing news—bad news. Sir Jonathan Atkins, a courtier of King Charles, had been appointed governor of Barbados: to uphold the royal prerogative.

Although Atkins was unwelcome, the governor was the governor and ships were ships. Freighters were what they needed, but any ship was better than none.

In the excitement of preparing a proper welcome, the planters worked off some of their resentment and, though they still grumbled, began to look forward to the first real party at Government House in many years.

There was a grand ball at the Governor's Mansion for the gentlefolks; and for the rest, a barbecue and dance that lasted the night out. Though there were few fireworks except what the governor's ship had brought, there were bonfires on every hilltop, and at many of the Great Houses even the slaves were allowed a shoat or a kid or perhaps a sheep for their barbecue.

Parris was one of the committee of planters who met the governor and was cheered by his active interest in their problems and his straightforward friendliness.

To everybody's surprise, "the king's minion" turned out to be a champion of Barbadian rights. But his plea for relief from the hated four and a half per cent tax only brought the reply that "King Charles had his necessities as well as his subjects, and who could expect such a gift when the Exchequer was under the scandal of bankruptcy?"

Politics was in a ferment, but the sugar market improved. The increasing demand for refined sugar in England and the European market sent prices up again.

The merchants once more catered to the planters; ships once more crowded the bay; freight rates were lowered to compete with the smugglers; and the sugar in the warehouses was finally sold at a good price.

Some of the planters had been so discouraged that they neglected their planting, but those who had planted (Parris among them) sold the second crop at a good profit.

The common difficulties of the planters drew them together; and in the frequent planters' meetings, Parris found to his surprise that he liked politics and business and the excitement of pitting his strength against difficulties and opposition. Once again the merchant side of him rose to meet the emergency. And when one night he proposed a plan for chartering a ship for themselves and thus getting cheaper transportation, his neighbors clapped him on the back and said: "Ain't that his father for all the world!" He was absurdly pleased and flattered by their approval.

But the worst trouble was the slave labor. The Royal Adventurers, operating on the African coasts under the king's charter, were attempting to create a monopoly of the slave trade and making it hard for the smugglers to obtain slaves of good quality. The horrors of the dreadful Middle Passage from Africa to the Indies left the surviving Negroes in bad condition when the voyage ended.

Gangs of kidnapers roamed the streets of London, seizing men, women, and children whom they sold to captains in the Thames for shipment to the islands. Somehow, by whatever means, the broad fields of cane and corn and cotton in the colonies must be supplied with laborers, and the supply was never enough to meet the demand.

The primitive methods of cultivation took a lot of man power. The single-stick plow drawn by one yoke of oxen; the cultivation of broad acres by hand hoes; the cutting by hand with a knife, first lopping off the tops for fodder, then cutting the luscious canes for the hand-fed crusher; the boiling in copper kettles, watched by a black boy who strummed a calabash banjo as he lay beside the fire—and so on throughout the whole complicated process: all this wasted time, wasted labor, and wasted human life.

Parris, used to the bustling ways of New England, at first had scant patience; but as the months and years went by he, too, fell into leisurely way. He dawdled through his breakfast, slept in the heat of the day, and visited or entertained his neighbors in the cool of the evening. It was a pleasant life, and after he became accustomed to it he liked being waited on.

Nobody had any respect for a white man who did anything for himself. There was a theory that nobody but a Negro could labor under the tropic sun. It was only a theory, for there is no evidence that a white man ever tried it. Even the poor-white servants called "Redshanks," whom everybody both white and black despised, did nothing except to try to keep the Negurs moving. Even the speech of the 'Bajans was slow and drawling.

As Parris knew them better he liked their generous and hospitable ways; their inordinate and amusing vanity about their little island, which they boasted could protect England if a crisis should come. Notwithstanding their never-ending struggle against the king's oppression, he admired their continuing loyalty to the motherland.

Parris, with two seasons' profits in the bank, felt justified in making some badly needed improvements and repairs. He set about immediately to build a new roof for Cotton Hall, a fine breeze mill with a stone tower, and enclosed boiling house with big swinging kettles which made for ease and safety in handling the hot syrup.

The gardens at Cotton Hall, which had been a jungle, were given order and beauty by John Indian's care; while letters to Charles Morton and Andrew Marvell, after long months of waiting, brought precious seeds and plants from the gardens at Highgate Hill and Newington Green.

The weather had been favorable and the sugar making was well under way. It was the last day of August. The danger of hurricanes was about over, according to the Negro adage:

> June, too soon,
> July, stand by,
> August, come it must,
> September, remember.

Parris awoke early that morning and watched the dawn come up clear and cloudless. But before he had finished his breakfast the sky was overcast and the day turned blustery, with sudden squalls of wind and rain.

Along toward evening the wind dropped and there settled over the island a breathless stillness, sultry and threatening.

"Hurricane weather, if ever I saw any!" Compton said. "See them hounds, acrouchin' in their kennels. They know, damn 'em! We'd best round up the cattle, Mr. Parris, and get 'em into the pens."

The cattle felt the storm's approach. They smelled the coming tempest and pointed their noses at the sky with terrifying snorts, and efforts to herd them sent them scattering and bellowing.

From the village came a weird wailing chant, like a dirge. Tituba in the privacy of her closet made oblation to the little stone god.

The leaves of the great ceiba hushed their rustling, and the cabbages high aloft on the royal palms were still. All nature waited in an eerie hush for the wrath of the gods to break. The sun went down in a red haze; the moon and stars came out looking overgrown and near. The sky darkened suddenly, and though only a capful of wind was stirring, a hollow, mountainous sea broke over the reef, reflecting ink-black clouds which came from nowhere and rolled along, crossing and breaking, in dense masses edged at the horizon with fiery red. In the altered refraction it was impossible to estimate distance or size; familiar objects looked weird and distorted, and even the outline and color of the land itself was grotesque and fantastic like scenes in a nightmare.

Parris and Compton rode to the village and with the help of the white overseers tried to herd the slaves into safer shelters than their flimsy thatch-and-wattle huts provided; but the terrified blacks rushed about, clutching their treasures and magical talismans, crying aloud in a confusion of tribal dialects to their separate deities.

Suddenly the churning clouds loosed their volley of wind-lashed rain. The moon and stars were gone and the night was Stygian save for the lightning's flash. The wind veered to the north and then to northwest and blew so vehemently hard that in its fatal track little could withstand its fury. Land birds were swept like feathers into the ocean and seafowl were carried ashore or took refuge in ships, losing all fear of man. The air was full of flying thatch and broken branches torn from trees. Cattle were driven before the storm.

The outhouses were gone, or going piece by piece and rocking like a cradle so that they were worse than no shelter at all. As a last resort Parris and Compton drove the slaves out into the night again and as many of them as they could keep together in the dark were herded across the devastated cane fields to Cotton Hall.

Parris was the last to reach the shelter, lying close to the neck of his mare, clasping a half-drowned pickaninny in his free arm and shouting encouragement to its mammy, who clung to his stirrup, sobbing and praying as she stumbled along. The heavy door swung back at his call, and master, mount, and slaves came in together with a gust of rain. A dozen brawny shoulders forced the door shut, the iron bars fell into place and the refugees shivered and sobbed and thanked their gods for this respite.

All through the night the storm raged and the morning looked upon a scene of desolation. The proud new fan was wrenched from the breeze mill, its blades crumpled and broken and driven into the rain-soaked earth, leaving only the stone tower standing forlorn. The new sugarworks, where syrup was boiling when the storm began, was flat with the ground, the stone wall overturned and the timbers scattered. The field of Virginia cotton, which promised so well, was beaten into the ground, and the garden in its new beauty was laid waste.

The great stone house which John Parris had built upon a rock set its firm shoulders to the wind and bravely held its ground. But when after the night of battle the wind again shifted, this time into the southeast, and the storm began afresh, the fine new roof was lifted off neatly and completely, and lay beating itself to pieces on the coral reef, its ragged timbers drifting out to sea.

Yet Cotton Hall fared better than most, for it was one of the few left standing along the leeward coast. At Hilltop, the house which had been the pride of the Webbs for three generations, built of the cedars and mahoganies of the virgin forest, was a ruin, its timbers and carved wainscot strewn over a forty-acre tract of uprooted orchard trees. Webb and Sheba and her little son were driven into the storm and lay through the night in the lee of a low stone wall. When the wind died, they struggled across the torn and sodden fields and set up housekeeping in the stone mill tower, the only shelter left standing on the plantation. Parris, hearing of their plight, felt obliged much against his inclination to offer his hospitality, as he had done to some other unfortunate neighbors. He was both relieved and angry when Webb sent back a hateful refusal: "Tell him I said to go to hell, to go to hell, to go to hell!"

Nicholas Abbey, the great Elizabethan pile on the crest of the hills, whose owner had been the laughingstock of the whole island for building a house with fireplaces, withstood the storm with little damage and opened its hospitable doors to as many of the planters as could be sheltered within its massive stone walls and warmed at its derided hearths.

The Codrington mansion, the finest in the island, also was spared, as were several of its neighbors along the windward coast, but the damage at Bridgetown and along the bay was pitiable. The smaller shops and dwellings were a mass of torn and tangled wreckage.

The calamity was so general that few were able to help their neighbors. The governor and his aides took charge of the work at Bridgetown; setting armed guards to prevent thieving and gangs of laborers to clear the cluttered streets and speed the rebuilding. Ships carried the news to the neighboring islands and in course of time to England and America, and brought back cargoes of goods, which was sold at exorbitant prices. But in the country districts each isolated planter had to work out his own salvation as best he could with his own tools, his own supplies, his own slaves.

At Cotton Hall, Parris gave thanks that the wind had ceased. But the day continued wet and rainy, and with no dry clothes or shelter or fire or food, the refugees shivered and moaned. There was much to do under pressure of haste, for hungry men are dangerous. Compton showed his customary energy in dividing the blacks into gangs in charge of their overseers. Some were detailed to gather firewood, others to dig provisions from the miry ground, still others to salvage as much scattered timber as they could and rig up a temporary shelter in the demolished village, and get a makeshift roof over the Great House.

But here they met with serious difficulty. The big ceiba had been riven almost in half and part of it had fallen across the corner of the mansion house. The damage to the house was not serious, but no roofing could be done until the tangle of heavy boughs and leaves was cut clear and dragged away. With no machinery it meant heavy work for a gang of men. And not a Negro on the place would touch their "worship tree"—the sacred ceiba.

Compton came to Parris with the problem. "It's got me stumbled," he admitted. "I can't do nothin' with 'em. I've talked with old Quaco and Cuffee and goozoo Benaba and I can't budge 'em. They be scared purty nigh to death anyhow, and they just go wild."

"But only last month they cut a big cotton tree and made a canoe of it," Parris was puzzled. "What's the trouble?"

"Near's I kin make out, 'tain't the *cotton tree* but this here one's a worship tree, 'count of your uncle's grave—and his ghost is aharborin' in the branches. They ain't pertendin', Mr. Parris. They be skairt plum white!"

"I'll talk to Tituba," Samuel said, and went to find her.

"Yassir, Mas' Sam, ah knows whut dey talkin'—dose fool Wes'

Coas' Negurs wid dey wide-open Affiky eyes! Des open up one dem rum kags in de cellah an' day'll rare rightup an' spit in de debbil's eye!"

"But, Tituba, if they get drunk they go wild. They might murder us all!"

"Dey's ways o' doin' an' dey's uthuh ways o' doin' Mas' Sam. Yuh jes' pull de stopple outa de bunghole an' put in des li'l hahm-less magicum powduh—an' dey gwine feel pow'ful good foh spell an' den lay right down 'thout ev'n sayin' dey prayuhs an' sleep like a babe unbohn."

Samuel made a quick decision. "Go get your magical powder," he said. "If it doesn't work, God help you—and all the rest of us."

Parris told Compton, "I'm going to give them rum." He didn't mention the magical powder.

Compton said: *"Gawd!"* He stood silent for a minute, then: "Have all your pistols ready, Mr. Parris. And save one shot—in case you need it! Don't let the devils get their hands on you!"

The cask of rum, judiciously distributed among the chilled and hungry gangs, gave surprising warmth and cheer and Parris won for himself a rousing shout of "Tanky, Mas' Sam" when he prom-ised that if they worked hard and fast, to get food and shelter before nightfall, they should have a barbacued sheep and all the yams and greens they could eat. With the liquor warming their blood, they soon lost their fear of the "worship tree" and whooped and sang as they attacked the big boughs and sawed through the shattered trunk which had fallen against the house. But though they were very drunk and very boisterous, they were not unruly, and allowed themselves to be herded back to their village where the women were busy with the barbacue and yams, and fell asleep before they had finished their feast, sprawled out on the sodden ground.

As long as the pressure of the emergency lasted, Parris was brave and uncomplaining. In the completeness of the disaster, life and food and shelter and a fire to dry his clothes were all a man could ask for. But after those necessaries of existence were provided and life settled back into its everyday round, he began to count his losses and bewail the hardness of his lot. Would God never blot out his transgression? Must it always be that whatever undertaking he put his hand to would come to naught?

The years that followed the hurricane were the most difficult that the planters had ever known. For months many of them lived in flimsy huts little better than those of the slaves. The terror of the tempest struck deep into their hearts and its destruction was so complete as to exhaust their resources and sap their courage. Many were so disheartened that they were ready to abandon their plantations and return home or start again elsewhere. But without money they could not go, and if they tried to sell their lands, none would buy. Of necessity they were forced to stay and try to restore their ravished fields and orchards and buildings as soon as they could. Not only were their crops ruined for that year, but the young cane for next year's harvest was uprooted. The lofty trees had been torn up by the roots or their tall trunks snapped off. The orchards would take years to bring to bearing.

The Great Houses that crowned the hilltops with dignity and grace did not rise again. Their brave and hospitable amplitude gave place to craven cottages, crouching back against the low terraced hills like timid children hiding in their mother's skirts.

Parris would have sold Cotton Hall for half its worth had it been possible; not being able to find a buyer, he did as the rest did, made the best of a bad situation and stayed on. He had sufficient means and laborers to make the most necessary repairs on the house and the sugarworks; and he had fared so much better than some of his neighbors that he was ashamed to complain. His livestock had suffered considerably and a few pickaninnies were drowned or missing, but these were minor matters. He soon had a roof over his head again, and the store rooms and stables in the basement had suffered little damage.

His mercantile training was quick to see the possibilities for trade which the aftermath of the storm would open. At the first opportunity he sent letters to Mr. Felkin in London and Mr. Hull in Boston, ordering a supply of chairs, hammocks, and benches, household utensils, plain clothing, and bolts of coarse linen and woolen cloth—the cheap and plain necessities of living which the hurricane had destroyed.

Long before these goods arrived, he had the storehouse at the

Bridge ready for them and had moved to Bridgetown, leaving Compton in charge of the plantation.

He counted on the new enterprise to help in supplementing the meager income from the plantation during the lean years before canes and orchards would come to bearing.

Life on the island gradually settled back into its accustomed ways. The common misfortune made for a more friendly and comradely relation among the neighbors, who shared their belongings good-naturedly and laughed at their poverty. The increasing problems and need for action did not leave much time for introspection. More and more as time went on, Samuel lost the tense habit of mind which the Harvard atmosphere had stressed.

Once again, as had been his habit from childhood, the intolerable was put away from him. In the busy common sense of everyday problems he found forgetfulness, and in the laxity of the life around him he found extenuation. He was no worse than his neighbors, many of whom, like Webb, were living openly with black paramours, even as his father had done. It was only when he saw Webb or Sheba or the child that his heart beat faster and his humiliation returned.

Since the night he had seen Sheba at Webb's house she had lost all attraction for him. He could not understand how he had ever been tempted by her. But her little son drew him with a strange fascination. He saw the child only at long intervals, and always by accident, but at each opportunity he found himself studying the little fellow, watching for some sign which would determine his parentage; hoping, praying, that he might detect a resemblance to Webb. But from the first he had felt a terrible conviction that the child was his. (It was asking too much of God to spare him this.) As the boy grew in stature, his slim, tall body, his quickness of intelligence, his grace of movement and little tricks of gesture and expression, all pointed to Parris. There was nothing of Webb's square-built, deep-chested ruggedness about the boy; nothing of Webb's abrupt and jovial manner of speech.

The change in Webb's manner had long ago published his suspicions. His dislike of the child increased to harshness as the boy grew older. There were other children of his by Sheba: another boy and two girls, all chubby and rugged, and one with blue eyes like Webb himself, thus emphasizing the difference in their parentage.

Strange is the heart of man. As the thing that Samuel most dreaded became a certainty, there came with the shame, although he would never have admitted it, a sort of embarrassed elation and pride, an elemental joy in his fatherhood and in the beauty of this slender brown lad who was the fruit of his body.

23

Squire's Castle

Ghostly palms and a ghostly moon,
Half-risen, a blood-red dome,
Tropical odors, sickening sweet,
A sea as flat as an asphalt street,
And a thousand leagues from home.
　　　　　　　—NORA E. HUFFMAN.

SAMUEL'S mercantile venture at the Bridge did not turn out so well as he had hoped, but with the experience of his prentice days, he managed to draw a fairly brisk trade.

For a while he enjoyed the novelty of it, but it soon grew monotonous and the confinement irked him. He was homesick for the free outdoor life of the plantation and the feeling of independence and mastery that went with it.

The servile deference expected of a shopkeeper was distasteful to him, but having set his hand to it he would not turn back. As his trade increased he felt justified in hiring an assistant, a bright boy who could soon be trained to relieve him of the necessity of constant attendance, and not add greatly to the expense. He had received an offer for the letting of the storehouse and a purchase of the stock, to be paid for out of the proceeds of future sales, but it did not seem advantageous. Yet it would have left him free to go back to New England.

If he had to turn to his father's career of merchant, he had better be in Boston among his friends. Sewall had written him after the hurricane and urged him to return:

"With your knowledge of England and the Indies you should do well," he said, "and the merchants here are becoming more important every year. Almost as highly regarded as ministers and magistrates."

Aunt Susanna would be sure to welcome him. She was a widow again, and alone, now that Theodora was married to Peter Thacher and gone to Barnstable to live. It was five years since Uncle John Oxenbridge died, stricken in his pulpit after a Thursday lecture.

"He went as he wanted to go," Susanna had written. "He always said he hoped he'd die in the harness."

And there was Elizabeth. He was hungry for the sight of Elizabeth, but he wanted so much more than that. He thought of Tantalus, his lips forever at the water's edge, yet perishing of thirst.

Except for the dullness of shopkeeping, life at the Bridge was interesting. Here was the heart of the political and social and economic life of the little colony. Every incoming ship brought news—news from many ports: English and Dutch and French and Spanish. From the long line of settlements that was vaguely designated as New England and Virginia came news important or trivial, garbled by passing from ship to ship in transit, so that the first report of an earthquake in Jamaica might come by way of a Dutch man-of-war who had it from an English merchantman encountered at the Bermudas or off the Virginia coast—but nevertheless news.

Then, too, there were always social gatherings at Bridgetown: from grand affairs at Government House down to the genial chats of a little group at Master John Jobson's, gossiping over their Madeira.

Just now a rare bit of tittle-tattle was on every tongue. Sallie Squire—seventeen and just graduated from a select school in France, where young ladies were perfected in all the social graces —was at home again.

Big Dan Squire, Sallie's father, was reputed to be the richest man in Barbados, and to prove it he had built on the wild southeast coast of the island a castle the like of which had never been seen in the colony. Forty slaves and ten white overseers, and the best designers, carpenters, masons, mechanics, and landscape gardeners obtainable in the English labor market had toiled under the lash of Dan Squire's ambition; drawing on the resources of the mother country and the neighboring islands to provide a fit setting for young Mistress Sallie—the only creature in the world that Big Dan had ever loved in all his sixty years of hard-bitten, devil-may-care existence.

At last the castle was done and invitations were out for the home-coming and house-warming (if such a word may be fitly applied to a West Indian party) and the favors had been broadcast by the same lavish hand that had built the castle and laid out the grounds. Every planter in the island had been honored: the invitations printed in good clear type by Bowen & Son of Bridgetown, Stationers to his Excellency, the Governor.

Squire's Castle and his daughter's home-coming had been the talk of the island for several months, but Samuel was a little surprised to find himself included in the guest list, inasmuch as he had never met either host or hostess. The stories he had heard about Big Dan had not tempted him to an acquaintance, and his New England conscience led him to place the man definitely in the ranks of the ungodly. But seven years in the Indies had been a bit hard on Samuel's conscience. It had become soft and limp in the tropic air: but Parris had to draw the line somewhere, even in Barbados.

There were lurid tales about Big Dan. He had lived in the island some thirty years, during which time nobody had ever found out where he hailed from. He had brought with him, as his only introduction, several great casks and chests which tradition said were filled with jewels and gold and pieces of eight. There were some who had seen—or knew somebody who had seen—sacred vessels of gold and silver which could have come from no other source than a cathedral altar, and which had been desecrated and defaced by initials rudely scratched on their consecrated sides: "D.S."—just like that! He also brought with him, and used on occasion, as colorful a vocabulary as had ever been heard in tavern or grogshop.

With a chest of gold he had bought a large tract of rough woodland on a rocky bit of coast near Cobbler's Reef; hedged it about with a thicket of brambles; and built him a square stone house in the middle of it. An ugly house, with a tower to watch the sea and narrow slits for windows, like a fort. There he lived with some villainous-looking menservants he had brought with him and a half dozen husky blacks; keeping strictly to himself except for occasional convivial evenings at the grogshops.

From time to time more than a few vessels ran aground in the darkness and were beaten to pieces on Squire's Rocks, and grisly rumors went about that most of Big Dan's wealth was derived from their cargoes. Now and then a sailor who escaped with his life told a weird tale of flashing lights on the shore which the unhappy steersman mistook for the lights of Bridgetown—and the busybodies whispered that Dan Squire's half-wild Indian cattle wore lanterns on their horns on dark and windy nights.

Some years after his arrival, Squire bought and married a little Irish housemaid, kidnaped on the streets of London and sold to a ship captain bound for the Indies. She was a shy, pretty young thing, who bore him a daughter when he wanted a son. She struggled along a half dozen years more and died, leaving behind her the redheaded little vixen whom she had christened Cecilia, but who insisted on being called Sallie.

The child had her mother's beauty and her father's daring. She was as pert as a parakeet and as willful as a pig. Big Dan was her slave from the very first time she stamped her tiny foot and stuck out her tongue at him and declared her independence:

"Sallie won't! Sallie won't! By Sam Doshie, Sallie won't!"

After Sallie's mother died, the priest of St. Patrick's sent for Dan Squire. Nobody knew what passed between them, but the will-o'-the-wisp lights no longer flashed among the trees; the most villainous of the servants left the island; and a grandmotherly Irishwoman, whose incredible ugliness proclaimed her virtue, came to take care of little Sallie.

It was when Sallie was twelve years old that the priest again sent for Dan Squire and, by what means nobody but the saints ever knew, persuaded him to send his daughter away to school. Somebody who saw Big Dan coming from the church said he was pale as a ghost and went straight to his home like a sleepwalker, seeing nobody. Sallie sailed for France on the next ship and stayed five years and had come home a fine lady instead of the she-hoyden she used to be. So that even the strictest High Churchmen admitted that there might be some good in the papists after all.

Now that the invitations were out, the tittle-tattle grew from day to day. Wherever two or three were gathered together, the all-absorbing topic was Sallie Squire's home-coming and the party at Squire's Castle. Gossip had it that Squire had imported half a shipload of fine furnishings and striped curtains and valances and cushions and a Smyrna carpet; and would have none of the common stuffs offered by the local merchants.

Samuel was too proud to bid for a wrecker's trade—and said so. But he profited indirectly by selling some white serges and printed stuffs and gay velvets which had gone begging with the discouraged planters in the slack times. When his invitation had come, delivered by a black boy in uniform, he had tossed it carelessly to one side; but as the interest and curiosity grew, he sent a somewhat dilatory acceptance and even ordered a new hat, a cloth-colored serge suit, and shoes for the occasion (assuring himself that he had to have them anyway).

But when the time came, although he was among those present, he felt awkward and ill at ease. The castle was thronged with people, most of them the gay young Cavaliers who were the aristocracy of the island. His cloth-colored suit, which his tailor had talked him into against his conscience, looked sad and plain among the gay velvets of the younger set. The new fashion of coat and vest, cut from patterns just received from London, was not designed for tropical weather, and the square-toed, high-heeled shoes were stiff and tight.

The Negro musicians kept up an interminable din; the dancing was constant, the beaux almost fighting for the favors of their hostess and the small minority of ladies who had condescended to attend Dan Squire's party. Samuel couldn't tell whether his feet or his conscience hurt him the worst.

After a while he found himself in a smaller room with a group of the older men. There were tables and chairs here and there, and games of dice and cards, and slim, sleek Negro boys in uniform passing among the guests, carrying trays of glasses. Samuel drank sparingly, as was his habit, but it was considered an affront to refuse the hospitality of one's host, and the Madeira and brandy were of the choicest. By and by both his feet and his conscience felt better. He was friendly and tolerant toward the world, happy, and even a little gay. And when, at the end of the evening, glasses were raised to the host, Samuel's deep voice boomed out as heartily as any: "For he's a jolly good fellow."

In Barbados a party was a party. Guests came from long distances and even an informal call might mean a stay overnight or for several days. Parris was pleased and flattered to find himself in the score of young folks who were asked to stay on at the castle after the guests of the evening departed.

The week that followed was the gayest that Parris had ever spent. There were races on foot and horseback, and various feats of skill with prizes. There was dancing, wrestling, cockfighting, fencing; and exhibitions by the Negroes: greased poles and slippery pigs and clowning. Many of these were too sporting for Puritan taste, but Samuel could not resist racing horses for the prize of a silky-eared fox hound, which he and his bay colt lost by a neck to Webb and his big gelding.

But he won the "Quire of Ballads to be sung for by a number of songsters, all of them to have liquor sufficient to clear their wind-pipes." Perhaps his victory was due in part to his canny choice of a theme which found echo in the hearts of the 'Bajans: Drayton's *Virginia Voyage:*

> Britons, you stay too long,
>   Quickly aboard bestow you,
>   And with a merry gale
>   Swell your stretched sail
>   With vows as strong
>   As the winds that blow you.

The lilt of the song suited his voice; Mistress Sallie at her spinet was a delightful accompanist; and when he finished with the ringing challenge

> And in regions far,
>   Such heroes bring ye forth
>   As those from whom we came;
>   And plant our name
>   Under that star
>   Not known unto our North

he was greeted with a rousing cheer and calls for an encore. With Sallie waiting, her eyes flattering him, he bethought him of Andrew Marvell's old favorite, "Drink to Me only with Thine Eyes."

He was not thinking of his hostess. He was back in the long

ago in the little thatched cottage at Islington. When Mistress Sallie reproved his boldness with blushing cheeks and drooping lashes and the prettiest pout he ever saw, he was amused and immensely pleased with himself. He no longer grudged Webb his horse race. Little Sallie was a charming child, playing at being grown up. It did no harm to join in the pretty game with her.

But oftener, as the week passed, he smoked and chatted with her father. It surprised him to find Big Dan Squire an interesting and fascinating man: a wonderful spinner of yarns of adventure on sea and land, who in all his stories never let slip a word about himself.

That many of Squire's tales were out of his own lurid past, Parris did not doubt, but the puzzle was to sift the fact from the romance with which it was interwoven. Of one thing Parris became more and more sure. This man, for all his rough talk and weather-beaten appearance, this man who had made a fortune by dark and devious ways which probably involved piracy and murder and shipwrecking, had surely been to the manner born, and somewhere in his safely hidden past had known the ways of gentlemen.

Such a story was not unusual in those days. He was a younger son, perhaps, forced out in the troubled latter days of the first Charles, crowded out of England into a seafaring life, with the danger and devilment that went with it. Parris had heard and read of such things, but to come into personal contact with such a man intrigued his imagination.

Squire told him stories of Uncle John Parris, whom he had known in the wild days when Squire first came to Barbados. John was a stanch Roundhead, he said, his name posted in the list of delinquents to be banished from Barbados when the first Lord Willoughby came to enforce loyalty to the boy king, Charles II; and the hotheaded 'Bajans had a little war of their own, one side fighting for God and the Cause and the other for God and the King. Squire made a blasphemous comment: "Ever notice how God straddles in a fight, so He never gets licked?" and laughed uproariously at Samuel's shocked protest.

But the puzzling fascination of Dan Squire was intensified in his daughter. The more Samuel saw of Sallie the less he knew about her. Sallie Squire—five feet two of delectable feminine curves and undisciplined whimseys, from her curly red hair to her dancing toes. She had eyes of deep dark brown, fringed with wonderful curling black lashes, eyes which were by turns gentle or passionate, gay or melancholy, mischievous or devout, as the mood swayed her. Lips like Herrick's Julia:

> Cherry-ripe, ripe, ripe, I cry,
> Full and fair ones, come and buy,

and a temper like the devil's own, honestly come by from Big Dan himself and inflamed by seventeen years of coddling and spoiling.

Samuel was very certain that he disapproved of her and agreed with a young captain of the Guards who commented: "There steps as pretty a little giglet flirt as ever I did see." Yet he found himself condoning her inconstancies to an unbelievable extent. As his mood varied, he called her in his thoughts a little bud, little addlepate, little baggage, little toad—but always, no matter how stern and angry he was with her, there was that softening diminutive in his invective.

She was ten years younger than he and her minikin stature and elfin mischief made her seem more child than woman. His ministerial training tended to regard her as a frisky and bothersome lamb of his flock, in need of watchcare and guidance. Once he tried to speak with her about her soul's salvation, but she made a face at him and told him she paid the priest to take care of that! After all her schooling, she was still a brat!

Before his visit ended, he talked with her father in his best pastoral manner. Dan Squire listened in grave silence. Then he reached his hand across the table and clasped Samuel's.

"You're a good boy, son. But you'll be a damn sight better when you forget your Roundhead sanctimoniousness and learn more about life." In his serious mood the rough coarseness dropped from his speech. "You can't beat life and time for teachers.

"About Sallie, she needs the same teachin'—and bein' a woman she needs one thing more: a good man to care for her. I can't do for her, except just to love her. I ain't fit to touch her butterfly wings with my clumsy fingers. I've lived sixty years an' lived 'em hard an' fast. The devil's got a mortgage on my soul and my body, and he's about to foreclose and take over his property, which is his due. But before I go to hell, I want to see my Sallie married to some good man who loves her, and makes her love him.

"I can't choose her a man, but I can help to give her a stock to choose from, and that was why I gave this party. 'Twas the best I could do to give her the pick o' the island. Those we asked to stop with us a spell are all hand-picked, as ye might say. I've watched 'em all grow up, boy and man—except you; and I'll trust the Parris stock to fetch you out all right, when you outgrow the pious stage. (Your uncle John had a spell o' that too an' he come out all right—I don't think Tom was much bothered with it.)

"But what I set out to say was, if any of you young colts courts my Sallie and wins her promise, he has my blessing as long as he's good to my she-darling; but if the villain mistreats her, I'll haunt him from here to hell!"

His big fist banged down on the table and Parris shrank from the malevolence in his eyes.

Back under his own roof in Bridgetown that night Parris lay long awake thinking of Dan Squire's talk and Dan Squire's daughter. Somehow he had never considered Sallie as a wife. She seemed a creature of another world—a dryad, a pixy—far removed from the serious-minded young women he had met in Boston. In his seven years in Barbados he had met few women. He had been too busy with his own affairs to think much about them. And he had always thought of himself as irrevocably bound to Elizabeth. That she was married to another meant long and weary waiting, but someday the waiting would be over and she would be his, for their love was no fleeting thing—it was for all eternity.

Now for the first time he wondered if the waiting was worth while. In Aunt Susanna's last letter she had said:

Dr. Fairgrave is as spry as ever. The old coot sez he's goin to live to be a hundred an looks like he might make it.

Suppose he did, and the waiting stretched itself out for thirty years, one after another, until Samuel and Elizabeth were old? He started up in bed. Why, he would be fifty-seven and Elizabeth sixty-three—an old woman with tired eyes and gray hair: too old for passion, too old for children.

He tried to picture Elizabeth as he had last seen her, but the likeness was dim and faded, like a painting dulled by time.

And Sallie danced before his eyes: vivid and vibrant with life, youth and color—with butterfly wings, as Big Dan had said.

His mind ran back over his talk with Squire. Surely it indicated that Sallie's father favored him among her suitors—if indeed he could be called a suitor. He had not courted Sallie; yet her father of his own accord had expressed approval of him, and had made it quite clear that his daughter's dower would be generous and that at his death all his possessions would be hers: the new castle, the landscaped park and gardens and coconut groves, and immense wealth would be the portion of the fortunate man who married Sallie Squire.

There would be no more worries about money; no more laboring under the handicap of insufficient capital to make his plantations pay, no more shopkeeping which he detested. Instead, his would be the leisurely life of a gentleman planter, with a grand new castle for a home; with time and money for books, travel, and the higher life of the spirit: a man of influence in the little colony—and with all that a charming and lovely wife, and if God saw fit to bless their union, plenty of means to support and educate a family.

He dallied with the thought of Sallie as a wife, her papist folly forgotten (as, of course, it would have to be if they were wed), her bright curls tucked up under a demure Puritan cap, her brown eyes looking love at him as she sat at his table or ran out to welcome him when he rode in from the fields at evening. Then all unbidden came a thought of the night—Sallie Parris in a long white rail with her glorious hair rippling over her shoulders, her breasts, and down below her waist. Perhaps she would let him tangle his fingers in its little curls and bury his hot face in its glory—and at last find her lips. He forced his sinful thoughts away sternly and knelt beside his bed, praying that he might know God's will.

He dreamed all night of Sallie. It was a sign! In the morning he again visited his tailor and ordered two new suits: one of fine wool in the new shade known as French green, with a vest of damask, pewter buttons, and buttonholes embroidered in silver thread; the other of unbleached linen with pink silk hose and silver knee buckles. For the first time he discarded the wide Puritan collar, and instead wore a modish neckcloth, a scarf of fine sheer white linen over two yards long, passed twice around the neck and lopped in front.

The tailor tried to tempt him to adopt the very fashionable wig, but he had heard too many sermons against the black bushes of vanity. Besides, he had sense enough to see that his own thick and lustrous mass of curling black hair was far handsomer and more seemly than any wig. Wigs were well enough to cover up bald pates, but at their best they were filthy, louse-breeding inventions. The latest fad of the young gallants to stand around and comb their heads in public, he thought detestable.

Leaving his young assistant in charge of the shop, he set out for Squire's Castle, riding his mare. In his saddlebags he carried his Bible and the volume of Anne Bradstreet's poems which Aunt Susanna had sent him: the first to win Sallie Squire's soul from Antichrist to the true faith; the second to win her heart to himself.

When he paid his respects to Dan Squire and formally asked permission to address his daughter, Big Dan grinned:

"Good luck to you, lad! You'll need it to catch this hummingbird! But," his face darkened, "see to it you don't bruise her wings!"

Samuel laid his plans carefully. But with three or four enamored swains forever at her heels, it was hard to approach her with the seriousness which he considered fitting for a proper proposal of marriage.

Besides himself and George Webb, there were two younger men who had outdistanced the field: a dashing captain of the Guards and an ambitious and ardent undersecretary at Government House. Which of the four the charming Sallie would choose was any man's guess. Dan Squire umpired the game fairly enough, though Samuel felt that he had a leaning toward the two planters, because they were more certain to remain permanently on the island.

That there was bad blood between Parris and Webb, neither of them took any trouble to hide, but the nature of their ill will was such that both their tongues were tied. Parris was sure that Squire must know that Webb was living with a black mistress; but he knew enough of the leniency with which such irregularities were regarded in the island to be sure that such a matter would make little difference to Squire. If Webb should marry Sallie, he would sell Sheba and her children to a captain bound for Virginia or Jamaica or Surinam. That would be all. That Webb and he should be rivals was bitterness to Parris, but he felt that it was only another proof of the justice of the Most High, which bound a man's sins forever on his back.

Though Sallie's flippancy distressed him, he was patient and persistent in his wooing. There were times when he ached to spank her, and other times when he was minded to ride away and never see her again, but the thought of abandoning the field to Webb goaded him, and he held himself resolutely to the course he had determined upon.

One thing he had decided at the beginning: he would never wed a papist. Waiting a suitable opportunity, when he had Sallie to himself, he broached the point. He put the matter impersonally, stating his opinion that a woman should embrace her husband's religion, for the husband should be the head of the wife, even as Christ was the head of the church. He read her the story of Ruth: "Thy people shall be my people, and thy God my God."

Sallie raised dewy eyes to him. "If I loved a man"—her voice was dreamy—"I should want to go with him to his church. I should want to go with him everywhere. I would lie at his feet as Ruth did with Boaz—I would follow him to the end of the world—because I loved him!"

Samuel, having prepared for a siege, was a little nonplused by so easy a surrender. Should he make his avowal without further delay? The time seemed fit. But before he could arrange his words, Sallie went on:

"Besides—I think St. Michael's Cathedral is much more lovelier than St. Patrick's. And the new curate is a perfect he-darling! Have you seen him? Tall, and fair, with heavenly blue eyes and yellow curls all over his head—just like St. Michael in the stained-glass window. And he feels just as you do about wedlock. A husband must decide for his wife in all matters of the intellect —for a man's intellects are stronger than a woman's; and the Bible says, 'Wives, submit yourselves unto your husbands in the Lord, for this is right.'"

Parris choked on something that sounded very much like "Damn the curate!"

Sallie giggled. "Don't worry, silly! I'm not going to wed St. Michael." She hesitated, and looked down shyly. "Can't you guess why?"

For a bewildering instant her eyes looked full into his. Samuel started for her, but she ducked under his outstretched arms and sped up the stairs, calling back over her shoulder:

"I'd much rather be Mistress Webb! That's why!" Samuel rushed up the stairs in a black rage and Sallie, with a frightened shriek, darted into her room and bolted the door behind her.

For a long minute Samuel stood at the stairhead, looking at the closed door. Then he turned and slowly marched down the long staircase.

Dan Squire was standing at the foot. Samuel paused. His face flamed darkly under its tan and his hands were clenched so that the knuckles stood out white, but his voice was well under control.

"Your daughter and I have had a slight misunderstanding, sir. I am leaving your house. I thank you for your hospitality."

Squire held out his hand, but Parris made no move. The older man spoke, his eyes half-smiling, his mouth grave:

> A woman, a dog and a walnut tree,
> The more you beat 'em, the better they be.

Parris looked him in the eyes: "I never yet have beaten a dog, sir! Good-bye!"

It was late evening when Samuel reached the Bridge. His head ached with anger and weariness. He went directly to his bedroom. A letter lay beside his candle—from Aunt Susanna. He pushed it to one side. It could wait till morning. Then, thinking better of it, he broke the seal and glanced through the closely written pages. His eyes caught the words:

Dr. Fairgrave died early Lord's Day. He rid home fum Salem late Sat'dy an overdone himself. The funral was yestiddy. Few went. Lizbeth sez she'll go back to England. We're tryin to keep her but she seems firm set.

Samuel read the words over again and then again. He went into the shop and shook the boy awake.

"When did this letter come?"

"Two days ago."

Two days! Good God!! And Elizabeth firm set to go back to England! His Elizabeth! And he dallying with Dan Squire's addlepate daughter!

He ran bareheaded all the way to Master John Jobson's and got there just as they were ready to close the door.

"When am I like to get a ship for Boston?"

Jobson shifted his tobacco to the other side. "Wal, now, I dunno. The *Good Fortune* jest finished loadin' cargo an' weighs anchor at cocklight. But her an't makin' Boston this trip—her's bound fer Providence. An' her an't takin' nobody but jest rum an' surrup . . ."

But Parris was already on his way.

"That's my ship!" he whooped as he ran. "*Good Fortune* bound for Providence! *Laus Deo!* That's my ship!"

Jobson stood in his tavern door, looking after him, and shaking his grizzled head. "Now I wonder what's up. When thet young dizzard gits as old as *I* be (ef he lives that long, which he doubtless won't lessen he cams down some) he'll find they ain't nothin' kin happen as calls fer no sech haste as all that. . . . These young sprouts an't whut their fathers wuz. 'Tis the fust time I ever see a Parris roarin' drunk—an' I've knowed three of 'em."

It was only after the *Good Fortune* was well out of the bay and headed north with Samuel Parris aboard her that he found time to thank God properly for his narrow escape. But for the loving watchcare and merciful protection of his Heavenly Father, the news of Elizabeth's freedom would have found him bespoke to Sallie Squire. Never again would he doubt that the Lord is mindful of His own! Down in the glory hole, which reeked with the smell of Barbados rum, he prayed as he never had prayed before. A prayer of thanksgiving rather than petition. Only one thing more he asked of the Almighty; that He keep Elizabeth in Boston until he could get there.

The hours between midnight and dawn had been short and few. Parris had spent most of the time racing about waking people up and making them do things that they said couldn't be done.

Before the *Good Fortune* put out to sea he had rented his shop to the merchant who wanted it, and written a hasty letter to Compton giving directions about affairs at Cotton Hall and instructing that Tituba and John Indian be sent to Boston by the next ship and provided with decent clothing warm enough for the voyage and the New England winds. He had got himself aboard with sufficient provender to last as long as the voyage might. That he paid double the usual rate for abominable accommodations for once bothered him not at all.

At the end of the voyage he would find Elizabeth! "O dear God, don't let her sail for England! O Lizbeth, beloved, wait while this leaky little tub wallows through the waves to Providence! Wait while I ride forty miles through the woods to Boston! Wait for me, love! Dear God, make her wait!"

Book Five

Boston Town   *1680 to 1689*

24

The Way of a Man

*Falling in love is the beginning of all
wisdom, all sympathy, all compassion,
all art, all religion; and in its larger
sense is the one thing in life worth
doing.*

—ELBERT HUBBARD.

I T WAS late evening when Samuel Parris rode into Boston. The streets were deserted, the houses were dark, save now and then a dimly lighted window where some heavyhearted watcher sat beside a sickbed waiting for death or a woman labored to bring forth new life. Far up the High Way the night watch called, "Eleven o'clock—and all's well," and a little farther on the watchman challenged the lone rider and flashed his lantern in his face. Samuel greeted him, peering at him in the lanternlight, but it was not old Praise-God Moffett, it was a stranger. Somehow it gave Samuel a lonely feeling.

Thornhedge was dark—no tiniest light anywhere. Was it the peace of sleep or the desolation of emptiness? He could not tell. He turned the corner and entered the Oxenbridge gate. Here also it was dark; but his halloo was answered by an opening window, and a nightcapped head, dimly white against the black interior.

"Aunt Susanna," he called soft, "it's Sam Parris."

An indistinguishable cry of welcome answered him and in less than no time he heard the bolts drawn. The door swung open and he saw Aunt Susanna, her hand cupping a flaring candle.

"Man alive! How in the name o' sense come you here at midnight and ahorseback? Didja walk on the water like Peter 'cause you couldn't wait fer a ship? My patience, what a man you've

grown! Put up yer horse while I get you some food. You must
be plumb wore out."

But Parris must ask one question. He choked on the words.

"Elizabeth—is she still here?"

Susanna chuckled. "Yes, darlin', she's here an' well—all safe
an' sound an' snug abed—as decent folk should be! . . . Wait'll
I get a lantern. You'll find fodder an' blankets jest where they
used to be, an' a bucket by the well sweep."

Sitting by the fireplace with Aunt Susanna, still in her night
rail and cap, he wolfed down thick slices of cold corned beef and
journeycake, with a big wooden tankard of fresh apple cider. An
hour later, too weary to undress, he lay sprawled on his old bed
in the west chamber, fast asleep.

At daybreak he was awake again, rubbing himself with a damp
towel and putting on the least rumpled of the clothing in his
saddlebags; watching from his window until Elizabeth's door
should open. He could wait no longer. He stole downstairs with
his shoes in his hand so as not to wake Aunt Susanna; then went
out through the laden orchard to the break in the hedge and along
the neat shale path through Elizabeth's kitchen garden. The
saucy black-eyed Susans nodded and laughed knowingly, and
caught at his stockings as he walked. The purpling clusters of
wild grapes hung above his head as he passed under the arbor
and paused on the worn doorstone.

Elizabeth stood before the fireplace, her back to the open door,
making hasty pudding for her breakfast. A steaming black kettle
hung from the crane, and Elizabeth, with a big wooden spoon in
one hand and a handful of meal in the other, was stirring and
sifting rapidly, so that the mixture might be smooth and even.

Samuel strode silently across the sanded floor. "Elizabeth!"
He choked on the word.

The handful of meal and the spoon dropped together into the
boiling kettle as Elizabeth turned. Before she could wipe her
hand on her apron, Samuel had her in his arms. She had not
known a lover's arms could be so strong; nor his mouth so hot
with longing.

Some time later, sitting together at the table, they ate the
ruined pudding. Elizabeth wanted to make it afresh, but Samuel
begrudged the time. And notwithstanding the vigorous beating

Elizabeth gave the mush, the lumps would not be made smooth. Samuel manfully devoured mouthful after mouthful of half-raw corn meal and vowed it was the best pudding he ever ate.

Breakfast over, he took her in his arms again. "Elizabeth, my own darling, marry me at once—today—just as soon as we can go before a magistrate. Let us not have any wedding party—just you and me and Aunt Sue and Dora for witnesses at Mr. Hull's house; and then come home—" his voice broke—"come home—my wife and I."

Elizabeth drew back. "Oh, but I can't, Samel! Not just like that, right offhand. Why, you are such a stranger; I must know you better. You were a boy when you left—now you have come back to me a man."

Samuel had a rare flash of humor. "Well, darling, don't you want to marry a man? Most women *do* marry men, you know."

But Elizabeth did not smile at the jest.

"Yes, I suppose I do," she answered soberly. "But not a strange man. It has been seven years, Samel—seven long, long years. And you are so different." Her eyes searched his face as if she would read there the story of the seven lost years.

"I've kept remembering you just as you used to be—just as you used to look: so boyish and eager and ardent, like Sir Galahad in the old tale: a knight in armor, seeking the Holy Grail.

"It isn't only that you are older. You are somehow not the same person—harder—more arrogant—I know not how to say it. Perhaps it is not good for a man to be the master of slaves."

Samuel was hurt. "The years have changed you too, Elizabeth. The girl I loved has ripened into a woman, but the years have not changed my loving you. I have served seven years for you, even as Jacob did for Rachel. Now don't say that I, like Jacob, must serve seven years more. Every day of all the years I've thought of you. Every night of all the years I've dreamed of you —longed for you—held you in my heart. There has never been anyone but you. There never could be anyone but you—not if I lived a hundred years."

His voice throbbed with passion; his eyes glowed with sincerity. Under the spell of his own eloquence he believed every word he spoke.

Elizabeth, too, believed; but still she shook her head. "After all the years, a few more weeks will not be long. I love you,

Samel, but I must be sure—sure. It is so dreadful to marry and then find you have made a mistake."

Aunt Susanna was waiting for him when he came in. "Well, I see ye ben courtin' afore breakfast! Did she say yes?"

He shook his head. "She said she must wait till she's sure."

"Humph! Serves ye right—abustin' in on her thataway. No woman wants to be kissed on an empty stomach!" She patted his shoulder. "Don't be downhearted, Sammy boy. Any woman wuth her salt takes a bit o' wooin'. 'Tain't hardly decent to say yes fust-off."

With that Samuel had to be content. Indeed, Elizabeth's hesitation only added zest to his courtship. The apple one has to reach for has more flavor than a windfall; and he rather fancied himself in the role of a masterful man. Besides, it was doubtless more seemly to avoid any appearance of haste in their marriage.

It was only a few weeks later, as they stood under the locust tree with the autumn breeze showering them with yellowing leaves, that she gave him her promise.

"This day month we shall be wed."

Then she ran into the house and slammed the door before her lover could catch her, and Samuel walked back through the break in the hedge on a carpet of tiny golden locust leaves. It seemed a happy forecast of golden days ahead.

But Elizabeth was beset with whimseys.

"I wish we could live in a little house of our own," she said, "a house that would be just yours and mine—with no ghosts in it."

"Why, dearest, what do you mean?" Samuel was disturbed. "You never told me that Thornhedge was haunted."

"There are many things I haven't told you, love," she parried. "But I don't mean a real ghost exactly. Not one that you can see or hear; no moans or shrieks or crashing of falling things. It's just a feeling—and it wouldn't be a ghost for you, I suppose—not for anybody but me. But I'd like to live in a new house and forget the things that have happened here." She sighed.

Samuel, feeling relieved and superior and masculine, comforted her and assured her that his love would shield her night and day, so that she would never remember any more the sadness and unhappiness and disappointment of the past, but live only in the happy present and the ever-brightening future; and that she must not let herself give way to foolish fears and morbid fancies.

"But the house .s so big," she argued. "Couldn't we get us a little house, just right for us two?"

He answered by holding her close in his arms, his lips against her hair. "If God sees fit to bless our union, we may need a big house, my sweet. Surely it would be most unwise to give up your house without good reason just now when the dull times would make a sale disadvantageous. Our house—your house—is convenient and desirable. And with the slaves, John and Tituba, who should be coming any day now, you will have plenty of help."

Elizabeth looked anxious. "I fear me I shall not know what to do with slaves. Black folks are so strange. I think I am a little afraid of them."

It was only a week before the marriage day that the slaves arrived. Samuel had been keeping a close lookout for them, having no means of knowing when a ship might come; but the ship was in and her passengers come ashore before he heard of it. Hastily getting a horse and cart, he hurried to the wharf, searching the crowd which always gathered when a ship arrived, his eyes alert for dark faces among the white.

There they were, standing out of the way of the hurly-burly of unloading, waiting for their master as the seamen had ordered them to do: Tituba, alert and eager, looking this way and that; John Indian, stolid and dumb as he always was; and between them a small, nondescript figure that Samuel could not at first identify; a child, dressed in what apparently had been a sailor's shirt, with long sleeves dangling and tails flapping around slim, shivering brown legs, whipped by a raw wind off the harbor. As Samuel came nearer he suddenly stopped dead in his tracks, then went on again uncertainly. He had recognized the child's face. It was Sheba's little son. In almost the same instant he was conscious of a man he knew (he never afterward could remember who it was) regarding him curiously.

Getting a grip on himself he strode forward and greeted the slaves as calmly as he could. Tituba seemed to be trying to make some explanation, but he cut her short and hustled the three of them and the bundles at their feet up the wharf and into the rear of the cart. Mounting the driver's seat, he drove as rapidly as might be out of the crowd and into a quieter street. Here he stopped, and under pretense of rearranging the luggage, turned sternly to Tituba.

"Who is this boy and why did you bring him?"

Tituba had worried about this moment for five weeks. She told her story glibly, but the look on her master's face frightened her.

"Foah Gawd, Massa Sam, Ah nevuh went fo' to brung 'im. Heah us wuz all on boahd an' jes' foah de ship staht, all of a suddent, heahcum Massa Webb like Ol' Scratch wuz affuh him an' sez, 'Tek disyeah l'il alligatuh to dat—' Oh, Massa Sam, Ah feahed yuh whup me effen Al tells yuh an' foah Gawd Ah cou'n't hep it."

Samuel spoke quickly. "Tell me just what he said, word for word, and tell it fast. If you tell the truth I won't whip you, but if you lie to me I swear to God I'll strike you dead! Now out with it—and talk fast."

Tituba gulped. "He say, 'Take dis yeah l'il alligatuh to dat gawddam snivelin' Pu'tan preachuh o' youhs an' tell 'im dis settles ouah 'count an' tuh hell wiv 'im.' Oh-h, Mas' Sam, wat Ah'm tallin yuh's Gawd's dyin' trufe fum yeah tuh heavem!"

Parris stopped fumbling with the bundles. He turned and drove on slowly toward Susanna's house, his mind working fast. Tituba moaned and sniffled, and the brown midget whose presence had caused all the excitement began to cry, muffling his sobs in his voluminous sleeves. Parris turned in his seat: Webb had shown him the way out! He spoke soothingly:

"You need not be afraid, Tituba. You have told me the truth and everything is all right now. You did perfectly right to bring the boy. Mr. Webb owed me some money and could not pay his account, so he sent me the boy in payment, instead of money. He was angry with me because I demanded that he pay his debt; so when he brought the boy to you he cursed me and used wicked and profane language. You did right to tell me, but you must never repeat his vile language to anyone else. Do you understand?"

For a moment Tituba's eyes rolled as if she were going to have a fit. Then she nodded and smiled her cryptic smile:

"Yassuh, Mas' Sam! Yassuh! Ah suah sees now prezackly whah-fo' an' whah-in an' Ah'm proud to hol' mah reppatashun. Yassuh, Mas' Sam, Ah suah is!"

Parris stopped her: "Never mind your reputation! See that you hold your tongue!"

A few minutes later Samuel was repeating his explanation to Aunt Susanna, prefacing it with what he tried to make a genial introduction.

"I have a surprise, Aunt Susanna. A neighbor of mine sent me this black boy in payment of a debt he owed me. I suppose he thinks slaves are a current medium of exchange in Boston the same as in Barbados. I am glad to have this evidence of his good intentions, of course, but just what use I can make of an extra pickaninny I'm sure I don't know. I remember hearing of Negur babies being given away like puppies, when I was at Harvard—" His tongue, having started running, seemed quite unable to come to a stop.

Susanna mercifully interrupted him.

"Looks like first thing to do is to find him some clothes and get him warmed an' fed, instead o' talkin' about him. Poor little tyke, he's half froze! Seems like anybody oughta have more sense 'n to send a pick-nie to Boston stark naked. Run up to the store closet, Sammy, an' fetch a woolen blanket—an' see't ye don't get one o' my spick-an'-span new ones. The old 'uns is on the topmost shelf."

Samuel ran. It took him a long time to find the blanket.

Elizabeth did not see the slaves until the next day. They had been warmed and fed and scrubbed and combed. Susanna had rolled the shivering pickaninny in the blanket and dosed him with hop tea and rubbed him with goose grease and put him to bed, so that by morning he was as well as ever. She had fashioned him a little shirt and breeches and stockings out of an old knitted petticoat and had taught him how to dress himself, to his great puzzlement. In all his six years in Barbados he had never worn clothes and he felt queer and itchy and self-conscious. He hid behind Tituba's skirts and stuck his woolly head out like a chipmunk, appraising his strange surroundings. When Samuel came in with Elizabeth, he ducked out of sight completely, crawling far back under the settle.

Tituba reached for him. "Heah, yuh no-count nigguh-baby, wheah yuh mannuhs? Come outa dere turreckly an' mek yuh bow tuh youah new missie."

Elizabeth spoke quickly. "No, no, Tituba, let him be! No wonder he is frightened among so many strangers."

She dropped on a footstool beside the fire and held out her hands: her voice was a low and gentle crooning: "Come, little elf-child—"

With a sudden rush the child ran to her and burrowed his head in her lap. She patted his shoulders gently while she talked to the others. By and by he lifted his head and his brown eyes searched her face. He smiled shyly.

"What is your name, child?"

He straightened himself and spoke with pride.

"Name o' Corythus."

Elizabeth repeated it softly. "Corythus! What a pretty name! Where did you get it, I wonder. It sounds like a fairy tale."

Like a flash there came to Samuel the significance of that name: Corythus, in the old Greek story, son of Paris by the nymph Oenone, whom he deserted for the beautiful red-haired Helen. It was the last drop of wormwood in Webb's revenge!

Samuel spoke sharply: "'Tis near the lecture hour, Elizabeth? Shall we go?"

Elizabeth rose and put on her bonnet and cloak. "Come, Aunt Sue. Will you go with us? The first bell has only just begun to ring, but Samel is in hasty mood today, it seems."

She smiled up at Samuel, but sobered at the annoyance in his face. "Did I do anything wrong, dear? You and Aunt Sue must teach me how to deal with colored folks, you know. They are so strange. Like people from another world, almost."

Samuel forced a smile. "You never do anything wrong, my sweet! Only you must learn to keep servants in their place and not let them be familiar with you, or they will be a nuisance."

Elizabeth was puzzled. "Oh! You mean the baby, Samel? I couldn't help petting him a wee bit. He was so cunning, peeping out at me like an elf under a pixy stool. But I will take care not to spoil him. As for the others, I'll try to play the mistress and not let them find out that I'm afraid of them—but I am. 'Specially Tituba—there's something uncanny about her eyes—as if she could read one's thoughts, almost."

"She's a very good house servant and an excellent cook," Samuel assured her, glad to be on safe ground once more. "She did for me very well in Barbados."

"Then I owe her a debt of gratitude for that." Elizabeth laughed. "And I'll try not to think any secret thoughts when she is around."

Samuel gave her a startled glance. If she in the purity of her inward thoughts feared Tituba, what cause had he! Only three people in the world, he believed, knew or guessed the secret of his night of sin—and Tituba was one of them. Yet because she made him comfortable and he was used to her ways, he had brought her with him to New England. What a fool he was—what a cursed fool!

And Tituba, by Webb's coercion, had brought the boy. He recalled a ghastly old ballad of someone somewhere who had committed a crime and was sentenced to bear the body of his victim bound about his neck. Perhaps, for aught he knew, it was not coercion but collusion between Webb and Tituba. But in his soul he knew that it was neither. It was the just and awful sentence of a righteous God. For what said the Scripture? If I sin, then thou markest me, and thou wilt not acquit me from mine iniquity. They shall not escape (or as it was in the Hebrew) flight shall perish from them, and their hope shall be as a puff of breath. He might ship the boy to Virginia and Tituba to Surinam —but he could not outrun God.

There was only one way to forgiveness: to stand in the meetinghouse, as Captain Underhill had done, and confess before God in the assembly of His saints—and see the love in Elizabeth's eyes turn to grief and horror and loathing.

His firm jaw set defiantly. Never! Not if he died in torment and burned eternally! God knew he had repented bitterly enough, in nights as dark and lonely as that which had hidden his sin. More than that he could not do.

Preparations for the wedding went forward. Elizabeth decided to be married at Thornhedge with only a few of her closest friends and some of Samuel's college mates to give dignity to the occasion. Samuel Sewall had married Hannah Hull, the mint-master's plump daughter (gossip said she brought him a dower of her weight in pine-tree shillings). And Theodora Oxenbridge had married Peter Thacher and lived at Milton. It would be pleasant to have these four, and Aunt Susanna, of course; with Mr. Hull, who was now a magistrate, to pronounce the ceremony.

The house at Thornhedge was swept and garnished. The doors and windows were swung wide to welcome the crisp autumn breezes, which during Dr. Fairgrave's lifetime had been shut out for fear they would give him a crick in his neck. Fresh curtains were at the windows, and the store closet was bulging with lavender-scented sheets, pillowberes, blankets, and coverlids.

But the door at the top of the winding stair remained locked. Elizabeth broached the matter hesitantly to Samuel.

"I never told you just how Dr. Fairgrave died; I never told anybody—not even Aunt Sue."

"Why, I thought he rode to Salem and the trip was too much for him. That is what Aunt Susanna wrote me."

Elizabeth nodded. "That is true. But it is not all. He came home from Salem. (I never knew whom he went to see there, but I think 'twas about his experiments.) 'Twas the Seventh Day and he rode hard to get home before sundown. He scarce took time to eat supper. He seemed excited and eager to get up garret. I minded him 'twas Sabbath Eve but he went straight on. I sat late for him, but when he did not come I went to bed and slept. 'Twas past midnight when he came. He shouted at me: 'Eureka! Eureka!'

"I woke startled and saw him standing by the bed, his candle in one hand and a wineglass in the other. His eyes were wild and staring and his hands shook so that the liquor in the glass was spilling and the candle flared.

"'See! At last I have found it: The elixir! The elixir vitae!' He held the glass betwixt me and the candle flame and the liquor was red and sparkling like wine. He raised the glass and tossed off the liquor, his head thrown back. He choked and both hands clutched his throat. The glass shattered. The candle went out. By the time I could light another—his heart had stopped. I could not bring him to."

Her breath caught in a sob. "And then—I know not whether I did wrong—I swept up the broken glass before I ran for help. I told Dr. Alcock his fall waked me—and I told no more."

Samuel stared at her: he could not find his tongue.

"His elaboratory is locked and I have hid the key. What should we do about—his things up there?"

Samuel's voice shook a little, but he spoke with decision. "Give me the key and stay you here."

But she would not. "I dared not go alone, but I will go with you," she said.

There was not much to find up there. The sun shone pitilessly on dusty floor and cobwebbed rafters; on shelves set thick with oddities and rarities: a malformed skull which must have belonged to the two-headed calf of Roxbury; an enormous black bat, stuffed and mounted with wings spread; a petrified toad; a rattlesnake's skin; vials and bottles containing powders and liquids, carefully labeled in Latin. The odor of brimstone still hung about the place, and in the brazier pan there remained a few drops of red liquor. On a low shelf beside the window were several well-worn books, moldy with age and bound in rich leather. He picked one of them up gingerly: a priceless parchment folio, hand lettered in colors and gold: the title page illuminated with the symbol of the Rosy Cross.

Samuel turned to Elizabeth, shivering in the doorway.

"Bring me an old sheet!"

Spreading it out on the dusty floor, he dumped the contents of the room upon it and gathered up the four corners. (It was not so large a bundle to be the accumulation of a lifetime of research into the Mysteries.)

Down at the far end of the horse pasture, where the rowan tree grew, he dug a shallow pit wherein he placed the bundle; pouring on oil and tar, he burned it to ashes. (By rights such books should be burned in the square by the public hangman— but this way would do as well and make no talk.) Nothing was left but a few charred and broken fragments, and the clasp of beaten brass which had bound the secret folio of the Order of the Rosy Cross. He turned it over with his rowan-wood stick. It was a rarely beautiful design, centuries old perhaps—he put away the temptation. Such beauty was of the devil!

He shoveled the earth back into the pit and carefully replaced the sod. Next spring no one would find any scar in the smooth turf.

On a fragrant autumn evening, standing before the hearth at Thornhedge, Samuel and Elizabeth spoke their marriage vows.

The gay good wishes and banter were over and the guests had gone. Samuel held out his arms.

"My wife! After all the waiting, my wife!" he said. "I can't carry you over the threshold as I rightly ought, sweetheart. Will this do instead?"

He picked her up in spite of her laughing protests and carried her up the stairs and over the threshold into the dark bedroom. She was so little and frail and sweet!

"We forgot the candle!" Elizabeth laughed with a little catch in her breath.

He did not answer. She could hear his heavy breathing and his arm around her trembled as he led her to the window—the window he had watched so many lonesome nights from his little west chamber. Close outside stood the sentinel cedars and, beyond, the militant thorns, guarding their fastness.

For a little they stood together, looking out at the beauty of the autumn night: the stars, diamonds on dark-blue velvet; the moon, a pale-gold scimitar low in the west.

In the near-by cedar tree a sleepy bird twittered to his mate. Suddenly the stars blinked out and the moon was no more and there was nothing in all the universe but the two of them, man and woman, and the mystery that made them one.

25

Sailing Ships

> My soul is sailing through the sea
> But the Past is heavy and hindereth me,
> The Past hath crusted cumbrous shells
> That hold the flesh of cold sea-mells
>   About my soul.
> The huge waves wash, the high waves roll,
> Each barnacle clingeth and worketh dole,
>   And hindereth me from sailing.
>   —SIDNEY LANIER.

THE FIRST Sabbath after Parris came back to Boston, young Cotton Mather preached in the old First Church. He was just out of college, a handsome, upstanding youth of seventeen. In his veins was mingled the blood of two famous lines of ministers: the Mathers and the Cottons. Two weeks earlier, on his first Sabbath at home, he had stood in the pulpit of his father's father, Richard Mather of Dorchester; the next Sabbath he had preached for his own father, Increase Mather of the North Church; now he spoke to the flock of his mother's father, John Cotton.

By the grace of God and the Mather spirit and the careful training of his good schoolmaster, Ezekiel Cheever, he had almost overcome the devil's handicap of a stammering tongue. He spoke with the authentic Mather voice, and if his enunciation was slow and painstaking, his message was made only the more impressive thereby.

Samuel Parris, from his seat in the young men's place, watched him closely and critically, with mingled emotions, as he recalled his first meeting with the little lad trudging the dusty road from school, tear-stained and stuttering, but arrogant and boastful by right of birth and training. Aunt Susanna's prophecy had not come true: the Mather pride had not been humbled; the Mather name was in everyone's mouth.

Why had God chosen this frail and stammering child to be His mouthpiece in Zion; while he, Samuel Parris, had been rejected and turned aside? Surely he could speak better than this callow youngster with his grandiloquent style and florid metaphors: "sweet-scented hands of Christ," indeed! There was no meat in his discourse; naught but a plethora of words. Yet the people (especially the women) listened as if to an angel's voice.

Parris wondered if the lack was in himself. He had heard few sermons during his years of exile, yet he could still thrill to the memory of Bishop Ken amid the candles and incense of St. Paul's and Mr. Vincent in his great bare tabernacle—there was real fire there.

But it was not for him to question the ways of the Almighty, nor was there room in his heart for bitterness. God had given him his heart's desire: the dearest woman in all the world to be his wife, and the joyous task of making a home for her and perhaps for sons and daughters who might be given them.

He was almost glad that there was little of Dr. Fairgrave's fortune left—his losses had been heavy in the recent Boston fires. After his estate was settled there would pass to his widow less than a hundred pounds and the home at Thornhedge—a fine, comfortable old place but not elegant. It could not be said that he had feathered his nest by marrying a rich widow.

Now that the all-important matter of wooing and wedding was over, Samuel turned his attention to the prosaic matter of earning a living. He had brought with him most of his ready cash and trusted Compton to provide him with a small income from the plantation. But that would not be sufficient to maintain a proper standing in Boston society, even though Thornhedge provided shelter and much of their food. And his own ambitious temperament would not be satisfied with the quiet life of a gentleman of leisure even if he had the means. The Parris side of him was alert and eager, looking over the situation, finding his place in the little world of Boston.

It was a bigger Boston than he had left seven years before. There had been two bad fires, which cleared out all the old warehouses and the shabby district along the waterside. The burned section had been quickly rebuilt, with slate roofs after the London fashion, and the new city made a fine appearance.

Nor had the conflagrations been without their spiritual benefit, for by the instigation of Increase Mather and the order of the General Court, a synod had been called to discuss: "What Evils Provoked the Lord and What is to be Done so that these Evils May Be Reformed."

The first part of the question was easy to answer, for most of the godly agreed about the evils; but the remedy was not so quickly found, for the wicked refused to forsake his way and the unrighteous man still thought his unrighteousness thoughts pretty much the same as he did before the synod.

Each year the unregenerates were more insistent in their demand for an extension of the vote to nonchurch members having a sufficient property qualification. The Mammon of Worldliness was undermining the walls of the Wilderness Zion.

It was the beginning of the rise to power of the well-to-do merchant class. The colonists built ships with the cod's head and mackerel's tail for a pattern. Down the draws between the hills thirty-ox teams hauled out the mighty pines for mainmasts.

From Salem and Boston and the Rhode Island ports and New Haven, American-made ships were setting sail: carrying American cargoes to Bermuda and the Canaries and the Gold Coast; bringing back wine and slaves to the Indies; then running home again laden with molasses and sticky brown sugar. It was a gambler's trade, for added to the perils of the high seas was the chance of confiscation by British men-of-war on the watch for smugglers or the chance of pillage and murder by pirate crews.

Parris had lived long enough in Barbados not to be squeamish. He knew something about West Indian trade from both ends of the line; he talked with merchants and shipmasters and common sailors, and with some picturesquely attired gentlemen-of-the-sea whom he strongly suspected of being pirates. Having digested his findings and counted the cost (in advance), he decided that the game was worth playing. He had not enough money to buy a ship but he could hire one, picking out a master who seemed to know his business and to be not too great a scoundrel. Such a man he found in David Johnston, late of Nantucket, a sturdy and weather-beaten Scotchman with a small but seaworthy craft manned by a two-fisted crew which looked villainous enough to cope with all the dangers of the deep.

He talked the matter over with Samuel Sewall, who was a near neighbor now, sharing the ample home of his father-in-law John Hull just around the corner from Thornhedge.

From him Parris got an honest and intelligent opinion of prospects in trade, politics, and reliable business connections.

But Peter Thacher expressed his disappointment that Parris had given up his plans for the ministry.

"You know your own heart," he said, "but I feel that your place is in the pulpit. You have the gift to speak the Word with power, which is vouchsafed to only a few."

However, the years in Barbados had dulled Samuel's spiritual aspirations. As for entering the ministry, he felt, as the saying was, that his day of grace was out.

Elizabeth had wanted to delay their marriage a year until he could complete his course at Harvard and take his Master's degree. When he would not hear to it, she suggested that they lease Thornhedge to one of the new families that were crowding into the town, and she would go with him to Cambridge, so that he might live at home and continue his course. But he would not.

"You can't turn back the shadow on the dial, dear heart. I could not go to school again with a parcel of children. 'Twould make me a laughingstock throughout the colony." His mouth hardened. "I made my offering, and the Lord saw fit to reject it, as He did Cain's. Now it is too late. That dream is over."

Elizabeth did not urge him. She saw the truth of what he said. But she saw, too, the bitter disappointment that still tormented him when the preacher part of him was uppermost.

Theodora and Peter Thacher had come to Boston for the wedding and stayed a few days. Elizabeth had seen Samuel's face when Theodora proudly told of Peter's success at Barnstable, his first pastorate; and of his call to Milton, which was by way of being a promotion.

"The Barnstable folks wanted him to stay with them always," she said, "and when he rode away, fifty-seven horsemen went with him as an escort of honor."

Elizabeth, watching Samuel lovingly, knew that the old urge was strong within him. Though she said nothing, she knew that he saw himself in Peter's place, riding up the road with a retinue of fifty-seven horsemen—like a prince, conquering and to conquer.

After the excitement of the wedding was over and the winter days came on, the household at Thornhedge settled into a serene and well-ordered life such as Samuel had never known since his childhood days at Islington. In Elizabeth he found satisfaction for his ardent body, his restless mind, and his troubled soul. She was the mother he had lost; the sister he never had; the sweetheart of his youthful dreams; the wife of his bosom.

There were times when he was so happy that it frightened him. For always there was lurking in some dark corner of his consciousness a hovering shadow of evil, a threat of a day of reckoning to come—a day when his sin would find him out.

The presence of the slave child irked him like a hair shirt. He could hardly force himself to speak the name of Corythus, yet he feared to call attention to the name by changing it. His common sense told him that only his own guilty conscience interpreted its significance.

With a child's unerring intuition, little Corythus felt his master's dislike, and was shy and silent in his presence. But he adored his new mistress. Samuel was much annoyed when he found that Elizabeth was teaching the child to read. He reproved her sharply.

"But, Samel, he must learn to read God's Word," she argued.

"What nonsense, Elizabeth! He is a Negur, a slave; with no more need to read than an animal. That is what he is: a clever, useful little animal. 'Tis against Holy Writ to try to make a Christian out of a slave."

Elizabeth looked at her husband gravely.

"You mean, a Negro has no soul?"

Parris laughed. "Only the Quakers think a Negur has a soul!"

Elizabeth was still serious.

"But, Samuel—he is so beautiful and so intelligent. His skin is not black and his features are not grotesque. Aunt Susanna says mixed blood is very common in the Indies and he is probably half white. If he is, Samuel, the white half of him must have a soul."

Parris could not trust himself to reply. He turned abruptly and went out of the house.

The first rays of the morning sun shining in Samuel's face awakened him. He had been dreaming all the night of Elizabeth —passionate dreams of youth. He raised himself on his elbow and looked at her as she lay beside him. The sunbeams flickered on her face, but she slept soundly, like a child, her red lips half parted in a smile.

To her husband, his blood hot with memories of his dream, she was the loveliest and sweetest thing the Lord God ever made.

"With tresses discomposed and glowing cheek, unwakened Eve, was not more fair." And she was his wife—his—his—to have and to hold, to love, honor, and cherish "until death us do part." In the sunshine of a perfect morning there was no death—only years after years of life stretching endlessly before them.

Like an epicure tasting the wine cup, he delayed the moment when she should wake and look into his eyes and hide her flushed face in his breast. Then suddenly he remembered. 'Twas the dawn of the Lord's Day, which must be kept holy. Even to kiss his wife on the Sabbath was unlawful—the lusts of the flesh— and the desire of the eyes—and the pride of life. He lifted his head and gazed steadily out the window: through the ragged branches of the ancient cedars, across the scarlet berries of the thorn, to the rosy clouds of morning over the bay with the sun breaking through. If ever an hour was made for love 'twas this.

His eyes turned back to his wife, lying so sweet and still beside him in their marriage bed, one rounded arm thrown back across the pillow; her night rail fallen open at the throat revealing the gentle rise and fall of her breathing and a hint of the full curve of her breast. All the passion and rebellion of his lonely years of waiting surged into mad desire so that he trembled from head to foot. Yet his lips were gentle as he laid them against hers and kissed her awake, so that she welcomed him with a little cry of gladness, marveling at the adoration in his eyes. She gave herself to him in the pure abandon of a perfect love. As they lay drowsy in a blissful world, there came upon the morning air, breaking in upon their paradise, the sound of the church bell calling to the house of prayer.

It was like the voice of God speaking in the Garden in the first morning of the world. With a feminine impulse as old as Eden, Elizabeth clutched her night rail together at the throat. Her eyes were frightened and her voice tearful:

"Samuel! 'Tis the Lord's Day. And we have sinned. Oh, how could we have forgot?"

Samuel held her hands tight in his own. "Look at me, Elizabeth, my wife!" And when her eyes lifted to his, he smiled and spoke very gently. "Look at me, my love, my own, and tell me you are glad—that we—forgot."

As she hesitated, he went on: "Let the sin of us both be upon my head, for I am glad. Though it be sin, yet am I glad!"

Elizabeth sighed. " 'Tis passing strange. It does not seem like sin. Oh, my husband, by own beloved, though it sound like blasphemy, I will speak true. 'Twas like a sacrament—like the holy of holies. 'Tis what the Lord meant when he said, They twain shall be one flesh."

But this mood of exaltation died with the passion that gave it birth. Later, when Elizabeth knew there was to be a child, her heart was heavy with repentance and dread. For a child conceived on Sabbath Day would be born on Sabbath Day; and the sin of the parents, thus exposed, would be visited upon the child by denying it the saving rite of baptism.

For weeks Elizabeth kept her fears a secret, but she grew worried and wan and when Samuel questioned her, she told him. Both of them had been eager for a child, but now the best they could hope, the only way of escape they could see, was that the child might die unborn. Better so than that they should be disgraced and their child forever lost.

It was hard enough for Elizabeth, who had forgot, but for Samuel, who had sinned with premeditation, there was no extenuation. The look in his wife's eyes was torture to him. Though they repented and prayed for pardon it was with little faith. Repentance might bring forgiveness, but it could not be counted on to avert the consequences of sin.

Samuel had loved his wife before, but his earlier passion was as nothing to the tender consideration which was all he could give her to show his devotion and self-reproach. When her time was almost come, he could bear the strain no longer. He appealed to Tituba.

"Tituba, is there anything that one can do to bring a child to birth on a certain day?"

Tituba chuckled. Her Massa Sam was very wise about many things but he didn't know much about babies!

"La, now, Mas' Sam! Yuh needn't tuh do nuffin 'tall 'bout dat! Dat li'l baby-chile know 'bout dat hissef 'thout nobuddy doin' nuffin'. W'en de time come fo' him tuh come, he des come he own se'f. Das all! Now doan yuh plague yusse'f no moah 'bout dat, Mas' Sam!"

"But you don't understand, Tituba," he explained patiently. "Your mistress is fearful lest the child be born on Sabbath Day, when it is unlawful to labor or do any work. Is there anything that you can do, any medicine or . . . anything at all, that would bring the baby on a weekday?"

Tituba, not being a Puritan or a theologian, knew nothing of the law of retribution. But she had lived long enough in a Christian land to learn that the Lord's Day must be strictly kept. She regarded her master doubtfully. Christians had such queer notions; you never knew how to take them.

"Yuh wants Ah wukka chahm, Mas' Sam?"

Parris hesitated. He was in sorry straits.

"I don't want you to do anything wrong, Tituba; nothing that would hurt anyone. But if it *could* come a day sooner or a day later—"

"Yassuh, Mas' Sam, Ah sees how 'twould look tuh membahs an' sinnuh-folks an' de neighbahs an' all, effen dat l'il baby-chile broke de Lawd's Day fust off—an' we doan't want Mis' Lizbet 'sposed foah de 'sembly ob de cong-gashion. Ah'll see whut Ah kin do, Mas' Sam. But seem lak all de powah done gone outa muh sench Ah 'rive in dis yeah Chrishtun lan' o' Bossem." She sighed regretfully. "Effen Ah jes' had mah scahlet jumbee beads now—wid de brack spots on 'em—play-gone dat sailohman dat tooken mah beads right offen mah neck—yassen deed—an' mah gold yearring too, dat Ah woah tuh shahpen mah sight.

"But doan yuh fret yussef no moah, Mas' Sam, 'twell Ah sees whut-all Ah kin 'complish. Effen Mis' Lizbet want me tonight, des tellah Ah's goad pambulatin' in de moonshine an' Ah'll be back long foah de 'crackin' o' day."

After Elizabeth had gone to bed, Samuel sat late by the dying hearth-fire. He could not sleep; he could not read or write or pray; he could only wait—tormented between hope and dread.

In the witching hours of the night he opened the great door softly and stood on the doorstone looking out at the night. The moon was near its setting and the beacon on the hill cast its shadow—like a giant gallows tree. There was a brisk wind and here and there light clouds went scudding across the sky. From somewhere far above him came shrill cries, broken by the cedar branches lashing in the wind.

Was it waterfowl flying south—or cackling laughter?

The child was born on a Tuesday. A lusty boy with a thatch of black hair like his father's. Before the midwife laid him beside his mother, Elizabeth slept, her lips curved with a smile of happiness and peace. But before she slept she had whispered, as her husband bent to kiss her:

"God heard our prayers and forgave us our sin."

Samuel, prone on the floor of the spare chamber, poured out his heart in thankfulness and consecration.

In the meetinghouse next Lord's Day, with Elizabeth watching from her pew and Tituba smiling broadly from the black women's bench in the gallery, Samuel Parris offered up to God in baptism his little son, in the solemn assembly of God's saints.

His name was Thomas—for his two grandfathers.

26

Thornhedge

Of all the seed that in my youth was sowne
Was nought but brakes and brambles to be mowne?
                    —The Shepheardes Calender.

THE WINTER before Samuel Parris came back from Barbados, the king had ordered Edward Randolph to New England to enforce the Navigation Acts. Randolph was peremptory and highhanded. The colonies were resentful and cocky. The quarrel grew hot and for four years the struggle went on, but in 1684 the old charter was vacated. And the next spring brought even worse news: King Charles, with his easygoing colonial policy, was dead, and his brother James, a dour fellow and an avowed papist, now sat on the English throne. What he would do to New England depended on his personal whim, now that the charter had fallen.

Under such conditions of uncertainty and stress Samuel Parris sought to establish himself as a merchant in the West Indian trade. He pitted his youthful mettle against the difficulties of political upheaval, inadequate capital, uncertain markets, and pirate raids. He vowed himself to win.

All up and down the coast, at Salem and Scituate and Portsmouth and New Haven, men were piling up fortunes. There were thirty merchants in Massachusetts worth ten to twenty thousand pounds apiece, and many others who had considerable estates and great trades.

There could be no such actual free trade as that of a cheaply built ship, carrying goods escaped from customs, runing against an expensive vessel laden with a taxed cargo. So America dared the Navigation Acts and defied the revenue collector.

Parris, lacking capital for long voyages across the Atlantic, chose the smaller ventures and quicker returns of the West Indian trade. Yet it seemed that Skipper Johnston had more than his

share of bad luck. He always had a good story to excuse his losses
—storms or pirates or the king's men—but Parris had his doubts.
Yet if he broke with Johnston and hired another master, he might
only go farther and fare worse. The other alternative, of making
the voyage himself and looking after matters personally, he steadfastly refused to consider. Never again would he put the rolling
brine between his Elizabeth and himself.

For in his home and family he found a deep and growing
happiness, and the simple life at Thornhedge brought out the
best that was in him.

" 'Tis strange," he told Elizabeth. "I used to hate this thorn
hedge and long to cut it down, but now—'tis so different seen
from the inside—you and I together and all the world shut out."

This was the mother part of him speaking. But there were
other times when the merchant blood in him was impatient for
the success that was so long in coming. Here he was, entering his
thirties, with no fortune more than a comfortable living. Indeed,
there were times when, had it not been for the home at Thornhedge, which furnished a good part of their food from its orchard
and garden, they might have felt the pinch of poverty. It galled
him to remember that they were in any way dependent on Dr.
Fairgrave for their comfort. It was a matter of pride with him
that Elizabeth's small inheritance be kept intact. Not a penny
of it had been touched. There was also a small and more or less
uncertain income from Cotton Hall plantation under Compton's
management; and the payments on the Quaker settlement lease
came as regularly as the post from Barbados arrived. All in all,
he was not so badly off.

But his desire for power and position was not satisfied. The
Old World barriers of class and birth had been to a certain extent
forgotten in the colony; but in their place was growing up a
new aristocracy of ministers, magistrates, and men of property.
Parris, as a church member, property owner, and taxpayer, was
on the fringe of this ruling class. He had a voice in church and
town meetings. He could wear the garb of gentlemen with gold
and silver lace and buttons if he chose; or buy his wife an alluring silk or tiffany hood—such luxuries as were denied to men
and women of mean condition, education and callings. But his
seat in the meeting had not the dignity to which he felt he was
entitled, and though he was sometimes asked to serve on com-

mittees, he was never put up for office nor was he consulted about important matters in church or colony, as Sewall and Thacher were.

There was John Wise, also, who, although he was settled in the remote parish of Ipswich Village, was being spoken of as a coming man. The four men had been in college together and were about the same age. But while he had been driving Negroes his old college friends had become solid citizens and leading men in their communities.

Both Sewall and Thacher had married daughters of wealthy and prominent men, who had brought their husbands goodly dowers and social standing. Parris must make his own way, unaided. He was proud and independent enough to be glad that it was so, and he wouldn't have traded his Elizabeth for any woman in the colony, yet he was a little jealous of his mates who were leaving him behind in the race for money and power.

And there was the future to consider. A growing family meant rapidly increasing demands if the children were to have their chance. There were two children now, for Baby Elizabeth had followed her brother with only a year's interval. She was a fairylike creature, with wondering blue eyes like her mother's and adorably shy ways. Her name was the biggest part of her, as Aunt Susanna said, so she was always called Bettie.

Samuel loved them both, but his hopes and ambitions centered in his son, a sturdy and venturesome youngster with his father's dark beauty and intense passions. "De ve'y spit an' likeness ob he pappy," as Tituba put it. Samuel was fatuously happy in the resemblance. In little Tom he saw himself reborn, and in the child's future he saw his own youthful dreams fulfilled.

Yet there was in the child a unique something which was not his father's gift nor yet his mother's, so that at times he seemed a stranger. In the depths of the brown eyes that were so like his father's there was a secret wisdom brought from that mysterious source from which he had come. Now and then his face would light up with an eager smile at some fleeting memory— but before he could put the mystery into words, a cloud would veil the glory and leave only the dull gray world of everyday.

"What is it, Tommie darling? What did you see?" his mother would ask.

But he would only shake his head shyly, as if fearful that his secret would escape. Yet there was no unfriendliness in his withdrawal—the vision was lost and he could only look at her with puzzled brown eyes and a tender, grave little smile. As suddenly as it came, the spell would pass. As if released from an evil enchantment, he would come back to the humdrum world of everyday living: running away and quarreling and teasing and hairpulling and pouting and sneaking off to bed with dirty feet— the safe and normal world of little boy affairs.

And his mother would kiss and cuddle him and his father would say proudly:

"He's a real Parris. He's up to all my old tricks!"

Yet always there lurked in their unspoken thoughts the knowledge, vague and frightening, that from the beginning little Tom was different from other boys.

Only Aunt Susanna refused to admit it. But Aunt Susanna didn't know that he was conceived in sin!

Sometimes his father thought of that Sabbath dawn so long ago and wondered if this eerie quality was a gift from God or the devil.

Susanna warned Samuel sharply: "Don't make an idol of that boy, Samuel. Remember the first commandment. The Lord gave him to you to be trained up in His service, and you never so much as lay your finger on him no matter what he does."

Samuel followed the child with adoring eyes. "My mother never laid a finger on me, Aunt Sue."

Susanna sniffed. "Humph! Mebbe 'twould 'a' ben better for you if she had, now and again!"

But she patted Samuel's shoulder and smiled at him to take the sting out of her words. She was very fond of her big nephew, and his faults somehow made her love him all the more.

As little Tom outgrew his babyhood, more and more his father's pride in him was overcast by a creeping shadow of shame. For in the child's dark face and slender, graceful body he saw—or fancied he saw—a likeness not only to himself but to another: the slave child, Corythus.

They came down the path to meet him one evening—Corythus holding Tom's hand and steadying his wobbling steps—and Parris for the first time saw the likeness. His heart almost stopped beating and a suffocating horror of shame swept him from head to foot. Yet the next instant the shame gave place to a flood of primitive joy and pride in his virile body that had put the stamp of his paternity on these two sons: different in race and color; one slave and one free; one the fruit of that dark Barbadian night of lust, the other conceived in holy wedlock in the glory of a Sabbath morning—but both undeniably his own. The Puritan in him castigated his shrinking soul with shame and horror for his sin, but the pagan exulted.

So far as he knew, no one else noticed the resemblance which his own guilty knowledge made so apparent. If it had been in the Indies, where such a situation was an everyday matter, it would have been taken for granted; but in New England, where Negro slaves were few and black mistresses almost unknown, even the gossips were not looking for such a relationship. There was Aunt Susanna who might guess. But whatever she suspected she would never speak of it. There were times when he wondered about Elizabeth. Was there, now and then, a brooding look in her eyes as she watched the two little lads?

Though the matter had never been referred to again, he knew that the forbidden lessons in hornbook and Scripture had been continued (Elizabeth could be very froward when she chose), and once he had come upon Corythus in the barn, preaching to some of the neighbor children with an eloquent fervor unmistakably borrowed from Parris himself as he expounded the lesson at the family altar.

Although he promptly broke up the meeting, he was less angry than amused. Perhaps he had sired a Negro preacher!

Little Tom jumped up and came running to take his father's hand.

"Mother's been having a visitor from London: a mighty fine gentleman all dressed in velvet and lace. I think it was the king! He's coming back to supper. Mother's in her best bonnet and gown and Tituba's flaxin' round getting ready. She shooed us out of the kitchen."

Elizabeth met them at the door. "We're having a guest, dear, just lately come from England, and full of news," she said. "Mr. John Dunton, the London publisher, with a letter from your old schoolfellow, Daniel Hawley. And just think, Samuel, he's married to Dr. Annesley's daughter Elizabeth. I used to know her and her older sisters when we were girls and lived neighbors in London."

"There must have been a flock of Annesley girls," Samuel said. "Hawley married one of them, I think. But what is Dunton doing here? And what does he want of me? Introductions all around, I suppose."

Elizabeth was a little crestfallen. "No, I think he was just friendly. He said Mr. Francis Burrows had gone surety for him in the town and helped him find a warehouse to display his books."

"Good! I'm glad that's taken care of, and I hope he's not late for supper. I'm hungry."

"I'm sure he won't be late, he was so happy to come," Elizabeth said. "He doesn't like Boston taverns. Oh, there he is now." She ran to let him in.

Samuel was not well impressed with Dunton's gay dress and easy manners, but when he found that the bookseller had been invited to a feast in the Townhouse to meet the Governor and Magistrates, he warmed up considerably and seconded Elizabeth's cordial invitation to run in any time for a chat or a meal.

"He's the most alive person I ever saw," Elizabeth said after their guest had gone, "and he knows so many interesting things and tells them so well."

And Samuel, feeling some obligation to the man because of Hawley, soon surrendered to his charm and his stories of London folks and their doings.

"I was doing a thriving business in London," Dunton said, "until Monmouth's insurrection ruined trade, and sent me across the ocean to retrieve my damaged fortunes. Daniel Hawley told me to look you up as soon as I got to Boston. I believe you were together at Morton's."

"Yes," Parris replied. "But I haven't heard much from him since. What is he doing?"

"Well, he is one of our London group of young intellectuals," Dunton said. "He's made quite a reputation for himself as a pamphleteer, and after the king's death, he raised a regiment and joined in Monmouth's Rebellion. But his men were yokels mounted on plowhorses, which at the first sound of guns, fled madly across the fields. It's a sore subject with Hawley, who has been unmercifully teased about his incontinent retreat."

Dunton had brought a book of poems by Andrew Marvell, published after his death, which he wished to present to Parris.

Samuel seized upon it eagerly, and was surprised to find an introduction attesting the authenticity of the poems, signed by "Mary Marvell, Widow of the Author."

"What does this mean, Dunton? I did not know Mr. Marvell ever married."

Dunton grinned. "Nobody else did, I guess. The thing made quite a flurry when the book came out and it's still a mystery. Nobody could find any record of his marriage. Some say that this Mary Marvell was the woman he lodged with."

Parris was mystified and troubled. "His housekeeper at Highgate Hill was named Mary," he said. "But she was a common person, kindly and all that, but—surely not his wife."

"The talk was that she got what little estate he left," Dunton said. "Though he had no relatives to contest it, I think, and strict proof might not have been required." He spread out his hands and grinned again: "Some say 'Mary Marvell' was a fiction of the publisher to help sales. It might be. *I* didn't publish it, you know."

"It doesn't matter much, I suppose," Parris said slowly. But it did matter to him more than he cared to say. Marvell was still his hero. And yet—some of his poems were a little—well, indecorous according to Puritan standards.

"I suppose you know he died under peculiar circumstances," Dunton said.

"No, that was when I was in Barbados and seldom saw a London newspaper. I didn't even hear that he was dead till long after."

"It was almost eight years ago," Dunton said. "About Christmas he published his *Account of the Growth of Popery and Arbitrary Government in England*—a bold and vigorous discussion of the constitution and the limits of the royal prerogatives. The government offered a reward for the discovery of the author of this 'libel.' Marvell took the matter coolly and laughed about it—and continued to publish his political pamphlets unmasking the corruption and political degradation of the court.

"I saw him only a few days before he died, and he was ruddy and vigorous—apparently in perfect health. There was strong suspicion that he was poisoned. But nothing was done."

He shrugged his shoulders. "Oh, there's been a motley of scandal and scares about the papists. 'Twas bad enough that

Charles should have a Catholic queen, but when he went to France and came home with a French Catholic mistress, Louise de Querouaille, the fat was in the fire. The people had always loved Nelly Gwynne, you know, and they resented this new rival. When Titus Oates started his papist panic, feeling ran pretty high against Louise. One day Nelly was driving in the royal coach when it was set upon by a mob who thought Louise was in it. They began to hoot and pelt her, but they couldn't scare Nell. She stuck her impudent gamin face out of the coach window and cried:

"'Pray, good people, be civil; I am the Protestant whore!'

"And the crowd laughed and cheered her and made a lane for her to pass. It's hard to get ahead of pretty, witty Nell!"

By November, Dunton had disposed of most of his stock and was starting back home.

"I can't stay away from my little Iris any longer," he said. "We're always Philaret and Iris to each other and our life's just one love song. When I'm away I always write her everything I do (even about the occasion when I kissed my landlord's thorn-back daughter and she nearly blushed to death). I wrote her, too, about a woman whose name I won't tell you, who does things I think can't be done without the devil's help. She'll take nine sticks and lay 'em across, and by mumbling a few words make 'em all stand up on end like ninepins!

"She'd best have a care, else from using the devil's help to make sport, she may quickly come to do mischief."

He rose from his chair. "Well, friends, good-bye! The hour is late, and my ship sails in the morning."

He shook hands with Samuel, and then raised Elizabeth's palm to his lips, his eloquent eyes on hers.

"I'll never forget you—both!"

With a sudden dramatic gesture of farewell, he turned and went down the path without looking back.

Samuel slammed the bolt into place. "His manners are too foppish to please my taste. He's play-acting every minute!"

"He's like a sparkling wine." Elizabeth smiled and sighed. "Now we'll go back to our New England ale. I suppose it's more wholesome."

She turned and went quickly up the stairs.

Samuel was glad to see the last of Dunton. He didn't like his flirtatious manner toward Elizabeth nor her easy acceptance of his gallantries. But what worried him most of all was his certainty that Dunton's sharp eyes had not missed the resemblance between the two boys, Tom and Corythus.

It would make a capital story to take home to his friends!

Soon after Dunton's departure Parris received a letter from Charles Morton. Recently (Morton wrote) he had received repeated invitations to come to Massachusetts as president of Harvard College. As Mr. Increase Mather, the acting president, had now added his personal urging, he had decided to come to Boston and look into the matter.

Parris was absurdly flattered by the complimentary closing: "Your affectionate Brother and Servant in Our Lord." Charles Morton, the ideal of his adolescent hero worship, had recognized him as an equal in the kingdom of the Most High.

The following July Mr. Morton landed at Charlestown. But the months between his invitation and his acceptance of the presidency had made a vast difference in colonial affairs. For Massachusetts had become a royal province and Sir Edmund Andros, the first English governor, had arrived and taken his oath of office four days before Christmas.

The town boiled with indignation, and to show their independence, the shops were open as usual and people going about their occasions on Christmas Day. Sir Edmund might as well understand from the start that Puritan Boston was not minded to change its ways or violate its conscience for him, nor for that surpliced priest he had brought with him!

A few months later, without so much as a by-your-leave, the Church of England was established in the South Church, and the governor announced that mass would be observed each Sunday morning—after which the Puritans (who owned the building) might hold their meeting.

The Puritan dream—a state governed by Scripture—was over. Zion-in-the-Wilderness was desolate.

A year later, John Wise, the minister at Ipswich Village, was in Boston Prison, and the town was buzzing with the story.

Andros and his Council had imposed a tax of a penny a pound, but when the order came to Ipswich to collect the tax, the minister spoke right out in town meeting.

"Let us not pay the tax because it has not been imposed by our representatives," said he.

The square in front of Boston Townhouse was packed with people, so that the constables had to push through the crowd in bringing the prisoner from the jail. Parris had come early and stood close by the Townhouse door. He found himself very anxious to see and hear all that went on at the trial.

He had seen nothing of Wise since their Harvard days, though he had heard some mention of him. (More than he was worth, Parris thought enviously.) But now the wheel of fortune had turned and there might be serious trouble.

The waiting crowd in the square buzzed with comment.

"Dunno what'll we do up to Ipswich Village ef they send our parson to prison." A farmer shook his gray head. "He's the only preacher we ever had up there. When the village parish was fust set off from Old Ipswich seven year ago, the General Court wanted to settle Jeremiah Shepard on us, but we wouldn't have him. We knowed a'ready who we wanted fur menister an' we told 'em so—Mr. John Wise!"

"Aye, John Wise!" a shock-headed blacksmith broke in. "He doant seem like a parson a-tall. Jest as common as anybody an' easy as an old shoe. But smart? By cracky, there ain't nobody kin outtalk him."

A sorry-looking fellow in a shoemaker's apron spoke sadly: "Yea, but now the minister's in trouble, and what may come of it, there's none can say. 'Stirrin' up ye townsfolk to resist ye law' the charge read; and that's a bad business—a bad business for him and all of us."

A murmur from the Prison Lane announced that the prisoner was coming. Boston Prison was not a comfortable or clean place in which to await trial, and Wise was dirty and unkempt. His unruly thatch of hair had no better comb than his fingers and his face was streaked with dirt and sweat; but his head was high and his shoulders square as he pushed through the crowd. His keen blue eyes missed nothing, giving unspoken recognition to his friends and fellow townsmen.

Parris avoided the eyes. He had never liked the fellow, and this was no time to renew acquaintance. Yet he was conscious of

a glance, half amused, half contemptuous, and wholly understanding, from those blue eyes as the prisoner passed him.

The trial was a farce. Parris forgot his dislike of Wise in his
indignation at the summary proceedings. The packed jury, the
partisanship of Judge Dudley, and worst of all the final instructions to the jury: "We expect a good verdict from you, seeing
the matter hath been so sufficiently proved against the criminals."

Wise, as the leader, was fined £50 and costs, and put under
£1,000 bond to keep the peace. When he pleaded the rights of
an English citizen under Magna Charta, Dudley told him
viciously:

"You shall have no more privileges left you than not to be sold
for slaves!"

"Do not think," another judge put in, "the laws of England
follow you to the ends of the earth!"

After he had lain three weeks in jail, Wise was released on
bond, his fine and costs were paid by his indignant fellow townsmen. He became a popular hero, still maintaining that "true
government must honor three elements in men: Reason, Liberty,
and Equality."

The next autumn, Charles Morton was arrested for a sermon
said to contain seditious expressions, and bound over to the Superior Court under bonds of £500. Though he was cleared in
the end, the trial was perplexing and expensive.

Without a doubt, the action was intended to intimidate the
ministers as a class, rather than Morton alone, for Randolph,
writing to England, charged that the clergy were the chief pro-
moters of the rebellion.

"All things," he wrote, "are carried on by a factious rabble
animated and encouraged by the crafty ministers."

As for Parris, the attack on his idolized master roused all his
fighting blood. For once in his life, his mother's idealism and his
father's business sense pulled together.

The future of the colony depended upon freedom of speech
and of the pulpit. More than ever, it was necessary to maintain
these rights now that a papist sat on the throne of England.

October, 1687, brought the governor's lady, and by the same
ship, the word that Captain Phips was knighted: so there were to
be two ladies in Boston Town. Sewall hastened to congratulate
Lady Phips and to offer her his house by Mr. Moody's, but she

had already bought Sam Wakefield's house for £350, much to Sewall's disappointment.

The quiet Puritan town had become gay and worldly to a degree that offended the godly. With the English officers and their ladies came English fashions and English manners which corrupted the manners and morals of the Puritan maidens to a shocking degree. Hooped petticoats, gold-laced coats, pointed shoes, and elaborate and immodest cutting and curling and laying out of hair became distressingly prevalent, especially among the younger sort.

As always, the women loved the pomp and pageantry of war. With redcoats marching up and down the streets and eight companies training on the Common, reviewed by the governor, the president, and other notables, training days were festive occasions. They lasted from early reveille to bonfires and fireworks on Fort Hill in the evening.

Even on the Sabbath Day people strolled about the Common or along the water front, and even skated on the pond. Coming home from meeting one chilly day in January, Samuel fell in with Sewall and stopped to talk about Mr. Increase Mather's going to London. The two of them had just walked down to Scarlett's Wharf to see if the ship in which Mr. Mather's passage was engaged had been righted. She had been loaded too heavy with molasses between decks, and lay on her larboard side shipping water.

So Samuel was late for dinner and came in rubbing his hands and holding them out before the fire.

Tituba was putting his dinner on the board: corncake and roasted leg of mutton and boiled lentils.

"All steamin' hot, Mas' Sam," she told him. "It's so frigidy cole outa-doahs Ah din't think de Lawd'd kyeah effen yuh did have hot pot-vittels on a Sunday. Miss Lizbet an' de chillun, dey dun finished."

Samuel's nostrils quivered hungrily and he laughed: "I don't believe 'tis a mortal sin—the Good Book says we may show mercy on the Sabbath Day." He sat down at the board. "Where's your mistress?"

"Huh go out jes' foah yuh comed in, Mas' Sam. Huh went tuh set wid a sick-a-bed lady."

"Who was it? Not Aunt Susanna?"

"Nossuh, Ah doan' know who—des some lady dun tuk sick-a-bed an' dey sont foh Mis' Lizbet tuh comfoaht huh jes' lak huh allus do. Teks 'em comfoahts fum de sickroom shelf an' reads de Good Book an' prays wid 'em an' all—twell dey jes' riz up on dey footses an' walk."

Little Tom got up from his stool by the fireside and leaned against his father's shoulder.

"The lady isn't sick any more—she's in a coffin with long tall candles at her head and feet."

Samuel was startled. "How do you know, Tom?"

"I saw her," the boy said. But the dreamy look was fading from his eyes, and he could tell no more.

When Samuel came home from afternoon exercises, his wife was sitting by the fire.

"Have you heard the news?" He asked her. "Lady Andros is dead."

Elizabeth raised tearful blue eyes. "Yes, I know." She hesitated a moment, then: "That was where I went this afternoon. I was with her when she died."

Samuel stared at her. "You—were with—Lady Andros? The governor's wife?"

Elizabeth nodded. "We were friends," she said. "And this last week, since she has been so ill, she wanted me with her. She was so alone, poor dear. I have been there every day."

"But why didn't you tell me? And how did you come to know her in the first place?"

"Why, you see, we were very near neighbors, and when I went by her house, she was sometimes walking in the garden. She looked so forlorn and lonely—and I nodded to her—and once she asked me about a certain tree (it was a red maple) and some shrubs and plants, if they would winterkill. Just things like that, as one woman to another.

"When she was taken ill—she knew from the first she couldn't get well—she sent for me.

"'I am so alone, so terribly alone,' she said. 'Nobody but the officers' wives—gay silly young flyabouts—afraid of me because I'm going to die. Will you come as often as you can? It won't be very long, you know.'

"So when she sent for me this afternoon, I went. I held her hand until she died."

"But why didn't you tell me?"

Elizabeth smiled, and a mischievous little dimple played in her cheek. "I thought you might forbid me, because you hate the governor. I didn't want to disobey."

Lady Andros was buried with great ceremony from the South Church, and there were long tall candles at her head and feet.

27

Pompocitticut

A ship that beares much saile, and little or no ballast, is easily overset; and that man, whose head hath great abilities, and his heart little or no grace, is in danger of foundering.
—ANNE BRADSTREET, *Meditations*.

THE WINTER after little Tom was seven he was taken seriously ill. Dr. Alcock came and looked grave.

But Samuel would not give up hope. He hardly left the boy, day or night. Yet when the end came, Elizabeth was alone.

Tommie had seemed better and was sleeping with his mother watching beside him. Slowly his eyes opened and he smiled at her.

"Mother, I've had a nice dream. The beautifulest garden I ever did see. And an angel opened the gate and said: 'Come in, Tommie Parris, Jesus is here.'

"You'll come too, mother. Don't be long!"

His face clouded over with a troubled frown.

"Poor Father! He has to go the long way round." He cried out in terror. "No, no, father! Follow the straight path! Oh, mother! Tell Father not to go over the hill!"

Before Elizabeth could call for help, little Tom had gone through the gate.

Elizabeth comforted Samuel, who was almost out of his mind with grief. For days he lay in delirium.

He seemed to be sinking down and down and down to infinite depths; down into a phantasmagoria of horrid slimy Things with claws and teeth and smothering batlike wings.

He struggled and tried to pray and words echoed in his mind: From the depths of hell I cried unto Him.

The claws tore his inwards and the batwings closed about him —he screamed in terror.

The doctor came and poured something down his throat. But the Things still dragged him down—to the depths of hell.

Susanna's words came back to him and would not let him rest: "Don't make an idol of that boy, Samuel. Remember the first commandment!"

Over and over he moaned: "God hath brake my idol. He hath slain my first-born because of my sin!"

After the fever was gone the obsession still persisted, and with it the terror that his two Elizabeths might also be taken. He called Mr. Allen and in agony of soul acknowledged his sins of the flesh and of the spirit. As soon as he was able to be carried to the meetinghouse in a sedan he made his public confession.

"God hath humbled my pride," he said. "He hath laid His hand upon me heavily because of my sin. I made me an idol of the fruit of my loins, and He hath brake my idol and left my house desolate."

He confessed also his worldly ambition and love of gain; his froward spirit and prideful heart; the sins of his youth and the temptations of his flesh. But only his God knew the particular sin to which he referred—the black night of sin which could never be bared to the curious eyes of his neighbors though his soul's salvation depended on it.

Standing in the old First Church, gaunt and hollow-eyed and trembling with weakness and emotion, his eloquent penitence and self-reproach moved his hearers to tears and sympathy when he pledged himself to forsake his vanities and transgressions and dedicate the poor remnant of his life to God's service, in whatever capacity might be opened to him.

A few months later, when the spring freshets were over and the roads were passable, the call came. The people of Stow wanted a preacher. Young Edward Bulkeley, minister of the neighboring town of Concord, brought their request to Boston, and Mr. Allen promptly referred him to Samuel Parris, who had talent and Harvard training and was ready to work in the vineyard of the Lord.

There was not enough money in the small and scattered settlement to pay a regular pastor, but they begged for a supply minister who would come from week to week without settling. The twenty-five miles through the woods would be no hardship to Samuel, with his English love of the saddle. Perhaps nowhere could a man better find peace for a troubled soul and strength for a fever-wasted body than in a long and solitary ride through the wildwood. And old Judy, his Rhode Island pacing mare, had the broad back and ambling gait which carried a rider easily.

So Parris rode back with Parson Bulkeley, and where they could ride abreast they talked of the Lord's work. Years before, when the first settlers came, three towns, Concord, Sudbury, and Lancaster, were laid out on land of their own choosing, leaving a triangle, hilly and rough, called by the Indians Pompocitticut and encirled by the Brook Assabet, which the white men called Elizabeth.

It was a barren wilderness, with only cattle trails straggling through woods of oak and pine. There were no fertile valleys like those of Sudbury, no elm-shaded dooryards like those of Concord; only a remnant of mean land of little use to the white man, but valued by the Indian for hunting and fishing and for the high lookout on Pompocitticut Hill which was used as a watchtower. During the war with King Philip, the red men made this hill their rendezvous, sallying out in midnight raids on the surrounding towns, though they spared Concord.

"That was because of my father, Peter Bulkeley," the young minister said. "When they were planning their raid, one of the chiefs said: 'We no prosper if we go to Concord: Great Spirit love that people: great man pray there.'

"That is something to live up to," the young man said, his eyes shining.

Now that the war was over, the Indians, a forlorn and scattered remnant, still hung about the hill, living in a big common dwelling, a hundred feet long and thirty feet wide, and making their poor living by game and fish and their native crafts.

There was a tavern on the road from Marlborough to Concord

at the old Rice place. There was a blacksmith shop; and scattered houses clinging to the hillsides here and there—rough-hewn structures of logs or stone—many with only one room and a chamber above it, tucked in under the low roof. There was a common and a burying ground down by the brookside. But there was no meetinghouse and no ministry house and no schoolhouse: those three essentials of a New England town. Back in the hills in the big tepee, the devil still held visible sway, with naked savages squatting around a fire, or carrying on their heathen orgies.

Here, by God's leading, Samuel Parris began his ministry. He felt like John the Baptist, preaching in the wilderness. On a sudden impulse, on his first Sabbath in Stow, he laid aside his prepared sermon and preached from St. Luke's text:

The voice of one crying in the wilderness, Prepare ye the way of the Lord, make his paths straight. Every valley shall be filled, and every mountain and hill shall be brought low; and the crooked shall be made straight, and the rough ways shall be made smooth; and all flesh shall see the salvation of God.

The spirit of prophecy was upon him. His eyes no longer saw the mean and ramshackle shanties of a little frontier town: they saw a vision of the centuries ahead, when the wilderness should blossom as the rose; and in all God's holy mountain there should be nothing that troubleth nor maketh man afraid. He saw churches on the hilltops and schoolhouses at the crossroads; and young men who saw visions and old men who dreamed dreams: a land filled with the beauty of the Lord—the New Canaan of our inheritance, where the Lord our God hath established His Zion.

There were so many people at the afternoon meeting that the little house would not hold them and they gathered in the yard, with the preacher using the doorstone for a pulpit. After the service, Rice, the tavernkeeper, shook the preacher's hand and offered the great room of his hostelry if next Sabbath should be rainy.

When Parris thanked him, Rice disclaimed any credit: "Nay, nay, parson, 'tis t'other way round. Ef ye preach like that there'll be folk from all the countryside comin' to hear ye, an' they'll buy their vittels an' drink from me. Ha, ha! Fortune tellers an' preachers an' puppetmasters—I allus speak 'em fair. Them fellers draws a crowd an' puts gold in my moneybag."

Sabbath after Sabbath the fame of the preacher spread. With the power of the true evangelist, Parris won not their hearts only, but their purses as well.

"Bring ye all the tithes into the storehouse," he admonished, "and see if the Lord will not pour you out a blessing that there will not be room to receive it."

Not only must the pittance to the preacher be paid. The community must be made respectable by a meetinghouse and a ministry house close by, where a settled minister could dwell, so that there might be preaching in foul weather as well as fair— though the roads to Boston should be blocked.

Later in the summer when the roads were settled and the building well under way, Elizabeth rode with him, watching with covetous eyes the progress of the little cottage with its two fireplaces below and a hearth in the chamber above and a leanto at the north to keep out the winter winds. And best of all to her housewifely soul, it had a cellar.

She joined her pleas to those of the people that Samuel become the settled minister.

"I love it," she said. The people are so hungry for the Word and so friendly. And the little house is just what I've dreamed about. Just right for you and Bettie and me. We could sell Tituba and John, and keep only Corythus to do chores. He is a big boy now, and I have taught him my ways. But I have never learned to like the Caribs—I am still afraid of them—especially Tituba."

But Samuel would not hear of it. His first glow of enthusiasm had faded with the wild roses, and he longed for a wider field and larger opportunity.

"Do you want me to bury myself alive in this miserable place, remote from the world? To have no part nor power in conferences and synods? No influence in the affairs of the colony? To be a poverty-stricken country parson with one cloak to my back, writing sermons for a few score of bumpkins and lousy Indians, while in the cities Cotton Mather and Sam Sewall and Peter Thacher are running the colony?

"I tell you, Mrs. Elizabeth Parris, this place is only a stepping-stone. When I take a settled pastorate, 'twill not be in the backwoods! Someday my chance will come. I'll wait for it. You'll see, Mistress Elizabeth, your husband is not such a poor stick as you think."

His petulant mood changed suddenly and he caught his wife in his arms and danced her gaily around the little room.

"You'll see, sweetheart, you'll see! There's a wider field ahead of us than the village of Stow. You will be proud of your husband yet!" He nuzzled her in the little hollow of her neck where she was ticklish.

Elizabeth broke away, laughing and smoothing her hair. "Fie on you, Samel, to act so. What would folks think of us, to act so shameless?" Then she added, serious again: "I am proud of you now, Samel. There is no higher calling than to be the Lord's mouthpiece. The people of Stow are as precious in God's sight as the people of Boston or Salem, and they are so eager for your message. They need you so.

"But you must follow the call, Samel, wherever it leads. I am proud of you, my dear, and I think you are a wonderful preacher. I am very proud—and very humble—to be your wife."

When the autumn rains made travel difficult and uncertain, Samuel missed the week-end trips to Stow more than he would admit. The workaday problems of trade seemed sordid and un-worthy. The wharves with their filth and slime and smell of fish and rum; the drunken sailors and bedraggled sluts; the stray dogs and rats and cats and beggars and cheaters; the foul air of the smugglers' passages running back underground into the town; the business necessity which forced a merchant into unlawful and distasteful subterfuges—all these seemed to submerge his soul in a choking fog.

The laying aside of his parson's cloak seemed to strip him of dignity and power. He was Galahad without his shining armor; Samson shorn of his strength. Life had lost its meaning, and God, who seemed so close and glorious on Sabbath morning, withdrew to His far heaven and left the bustling, cheating, smuggling, quarreling world of Boston commerce to its wretched devices.

With that rare gift of understanding which God sometimes gives a loving woman, Elizabeth knew as well as if Samuel had told her the cause of her husband's discontent.

Three years before, young Cotton Mather had been ordained by his father as assistant pastor of the North Church and Boston fairly purred with admiration for the young man's talents, his handsome countenance, and his enthusiastic devotion to the cause of God and his father. Everything that money and family and coddling and pushing could do had been done to advance him.

The elder Mather, in his ordination sermon, had spoken of Aaron's garments being put on Eleazer, intimating that he knew not but God might now call him out of the world. Samuel, who had been present at the service, was much impressed. But with a shrewdness that the matter-of-fact Sewall lacked, he sensed that the call which Increase Mather anticipated would be to London as a diplomat rather than to heaven as an angel, leaving his son to carry on the Mather tradition in the Mather way in Boston.

Now the call had come, and Cotton Mather, at twenty-five, was left in charge of the leading church of Boston, the busiest man in Boston and perhaps the most popular.

Once again Samuel was picturing himself in another's place and his heart was bitter with jealousy.

It was during this troubled time that Samuel's nephew, the eldest son of his brother John, came to Boston to live. Several years before, John had written Samuel (his first letter in many years) to say:

My son Thomas hath lately removed to Long Island, wch I believe is in your Neighborhood. With him is his widowed Sister, Ann Williams, who goes to keepe his house, and her young childe.

Wee of the Puritan persuasion be harde prest in England & Thos. hopes for Better Things in ye New Lande.

He is a yong Lad to goe soe long a Journey & I trust that you will keepe a Watchfull Eye upon him that hee goe not astraye from ye Lord's Goode Waye & that hee come nott to Wante.

Samuel had smiled a wry smile. "John never troubled himself much about me when I was left orphaned," he had told Elizabeth. "For all his 'watchful eye' I might have died of want. But now it seems he feels the tie of blood. 'Tis very like him. And he thinks Long Island is in Boston Harbor, evidently. Fortunately for us—it isn't."

He had tossed the letter into the fire.

But now nephew Thomas was in Boston, and lost no time in looking up his father's brother. He came to Thornhedge one morning when Samuel was not at home, and enlisted Elizabeth's ready sympathy.

Since coming to Long Island, he said, he had married and his sister had died, leaving her female child to his care. His wife was ailing, and had two babies of her own, and they had small means. They could hardly provide for their own. 'Twas his wife's thought that his uncle Sam, with his fine house and servants, might help them out by taking Abigail, at least for the winter.

"Of course, we will take her, Samuel," Elizabeth told her indignant husband. "Poor little motherless thing! Suppose 'twas our Bettie in like place. She is such a pretty child, with your dark eyes and lovely black curls, Samuel. I'm sure we shall all love her."

So little Abigail Williams became one of the family.

28

Then Cometh the Devil

From his brimstone bed at break of day
A-walking the Devil is gone,
To visit his snug little farm of the earth
And see how his stock goes on.
Over the hills and over the dale
He walked, and over the plain,
And backward and forward he swished his long tail
As a gentleman swishes his cane.
                    —*Variously attributed to*
          PORSON, SOUTHEY, *and* COLERIDGE.

BY THE spring of 1688 the bitterness against Governor Andros had become acute. The use of the little cedar meetinghouse was no more satisfactory to the governor and his Episcopalians than it was to the ousted Puritans; and every effort was made to find a site for a new chapel. But for once Yankee avarice was conquered by Puritan obduracy, and not a landholder in Boston would sell a foot of ground for such a purpose.

The deadlock continued till at last the governor, at the end of his patience, took possession of a piece of land belonging to the town—the Old Burying Ground, in which plot the sacred dust of the founders awaited the last trump. A small wooden chapel was built on the southwest corner of the tract. The sagging gravestones were neatly straightened and reset. Rightly or wrongly, it was charged that the new graveyard was more orderly than exact; and that the stones had been moved so that the inscriptions were now untrue.

As things turned out, however, Sir Edmund was never to worship in the King's Chapel. On April 4, 1689, young John Winslow brought news from Nevis that William of Orange had landed on the English coast. Sir Edmund tried to suppress the story, but there was no stopping such good news. Though nobody knew whether Prince William or King James would prevail in England, everybody knew that if William lost it would cost them their heads. Boston rose in arms, besieged Andros in the castle, and took over the government in the name of his Highness Prince William and the English Parliament.

A few days earlier Increase Mather had slipped away to England to plead for the restoration of the old charter. His mother's ambition that he should stand before kings was being realized in full measure.

But though William of Orange was willing to say civil and friendly things to Massachusetts, he was not at all disposed to let go of a valuable colony. Somehow Mather succeeded in continuing the provisional government based on the old charter, which had been set up after the downfall of Andros.

The theocracy took heart again and dreamed wild dreams of a new charter even better than the old. On the strength of these dreams, Increase Mather became the hero of New England.

But for the present there was no charter and it was contended by the Andros government that with the fall of the charter the land titles given under that charter fell also. Parris, stopping at Sewall's on an errand one day, found his friend more disturbed than he had ever seen him.

For the first time, Parris thought of him as middle-aged. Yet he was only a year older than Parris himself, a deputy to the General Court, and already accounted a leading citizen. In reply to Samuel's anxious questions he let loose the vials of his wrath.

"Their pre-emption of our meetinghouse is only the beginning. There are writs out against me and other landholders as being 'violent intruders into the King's Possession.' Intruders! In lands which we and our fathers have held for half a century!

"I do not want it noised abroad at present, Parris, but I shall go to England as soon as I can arrange my affairs here. God willing, I may be of some help to Mr. Mather there."

A few months later, fortified by a day of prayer at his house, though his ship was loaded too much by the head and would sail badly, Samuel Sewall set out of Boston harbor an hour after sunup with a very fair wind, bearing with him the hopes of the Massachusetts Bay Colony for its land titles.

It all looked very dark to Parris. With the government in upheaval, there was no security anywhere. Trade was a perilous adventure. Merchant vessels were overhauled and their cargoes ransacked or even dumped into the sea. It made little difference whether pirates or tax collectors did the damage. There was talk of all manner of wild possibilities: the port of Boston might be blockaded; there might be revolution; there was already frequent rioting and lawlessness.

Parris had sustained heavy losses. His money was almost gone and what little he had was so depreciated that it would not buy much. About all he had left was the home at Thornhedge. Even that, in these troubled times, would not bring the half of its actual worth; though it was a fine old place and the town was filling up with officers, civil and military, who had good English sovereigns to pay for what suited them. Thornhedge belonged to Elizabeth and Samuel would not touch it save as a last resort.

But here again he might lose all by holding on, in case the government could enforce their writs and evict him and his as violent intruders into the king's possession.

One spring Sabbath Samuel and his family had just begun their frugal Lord's Day dinner, when Aunt Susanna walked in.

"Why, Aunt Sue!" Samuel sprang up to welcome her. "Where were you this morning?"

"Yes," Elizabeth chimed in as she untied Susanna's bonnet strings, "we were uneasy about you. We missed you at morning worship and stopped at your house. Mary said you went to meeting and hadn't come back. We didn't know what to think." She kissed her aunt's soft cheek. "Tituba, set another trencher on the board for Mistress Oxenbridge, right next to me. Slide along, Bettie, and make room."

"Well, now, it's kinda nice to have somebody worry about me —but I've lived in Boston long enough to know my way round. I'd just as lief Mr. Allen didn't know where I was, but I s'pose he'll find out. Boston's a dreadful town for tittle-tattle. Not that I meant any slight to Mr. Allen, but he might take it thataway, bein' I've set under him so long I'm reg'lar as the pews. If you want to know—I've been to North Church to hear young Cotton Mather. 'Twas buzzed about he was goin' to talk about the Goodwin children bein' bewitched by Old Glover and I had a mind to hear it fusthand. I saw her hung, an' such foul cursing I never did hear. She even cursed the devil himself because he'd gone an' left her with none to stand by her."

"I missed the hanging," Samuel said, "being in Charlestown that day, but I was at her trial. She was pert as you please: boasted of torturing the children and plainly said that the devil was her prince. Then on a sudden she looked up and said: 'No, he's gone!'"

"Poor thing, she must have been crazed," said Elizabeth pityingly.

"No," Samuel answered. "To make that clear the court appointed five or six physicians to examine her very strictly. In the upshot, after much time spent with her, the doctors returned her *compos mentis*, and sentence of death was passed upon her."

Susanna assented. "Yes, and on the scaffold she said the children would not be relieved by her death, for others had a hand in their affliction. And Cotton Mather told this day how 'twas proved so.

"But just the same, Glover or no Glover, bedeviled or not, that Goodwin young'un is a minx. Mr. Cotton Mather's too young and handsome for the task he's undertook.

"He told how she'd ride the devil's hobbyhorse up and down stairs—but when she come to his study door she'd cry out:

"'They are gone! They are gone! God won't let them come in here!' And she'd be as devout as any plaster saint—but as soon as he turned to his sermon the devils 'ud seize her again.

" 'So,' says he, ' 'twas plain they managed her with a special design to disturb me.' " Susanna chuckled with enjoyment. "I tell ye the jade's a minx—and young Cotton Mather is no match for her."

Samuel protested: "Yet she was healed, Aunt Sue—healed by his prayers and ministrations."

Susanna sobered and spoke slowly and thoughtfully: "Yes, I suppose she was. Three days on end of prayer and fastin' 'ud take the devil outa many a saucy baggage, witch or no witch. . . . You're right, Sam Parris, though you didn't mean it quite that way, I guess . . . I'm jest a nasty-minded old woman—an' when that fool girl telled about throwin' an' kickin' at the man that prayed—an' couldn't hit him . . . 'twas true. A man who's got his affections firm set on things above is safe. Why, Cotton Mather . . . he don't even know he's ben tempted!"

Parris laughed unpleasantly. "I won't quarrel with you about what C. M. knows or doesn't know, Aunt Sue. But as for this witchcraft, the evidence at the trial was not only convincing, it was overwhelming. That wicked old harridan tortured those children within an inch of their lives. Their bones would be put out of joint; they would be drawn together like those that are tied neck and heels; and at the first mention of God or Christ, or any of the things which are not seen and are eternal, they would be cast into intolerable anguish. It was dreadful to see."

Elizabeth interrupted sharply: "Samuel, do hush! Nabbie's eyes are as big as moons and Bettie is white as a sheet. Don't frighten them with witch tales or they won't sleep tonight."

Samuel turned on his wife indignantly: "Why in God's Name shouldn't they be frightened? Any Christian child must be taught to fear and shun the devil and those foul hags who do his bidding. Would you hide from them that there are wild beasts and savage men in the woods? Would you risk their lives rather than frighten them?"

"I would guard them, while they are so little. I would fear for them and keep them safe from harm." Elizabeth's lips trembled a little. "I would keep them from the evil—by my love."

"For a minister's daughter," Samuel commented, "you have some very strange ideas. Unbelief in the devil soon leads to unbelief in God, my dear. 'Tis dangerously near to heresy. We will say no more about it now, but you had best talk with Mr.

Allen about the duty of parents in the instruction of their children."

Susanna cut in: "Tut, tut, Sammy! Such an ado about nothing! We all believe in witches and devils and everything else we're s'posed to! To hear you go on anybody'd think we was heathens!

"Come, Lizbeth. If we set any longer we'll be late for afternoon preachin' an' Mr. Allen will sure think I've backslid. Get your hood and cloak, dearie, and we'll start on ahead. Sammy's legs are so long he'll catch up before we get there."

29

Flits a Dream

> Youth now flees on feathered foot,
> Faint and fainter sounds the flute,
> Rarer songs of gods; and still
> Somewhere on the sunny hill,
> Or along the winding stream,
> Through the willows, flits a dream:
> Flits, but shows a smiling face,
> Flees, but with so quaint a grace,
> Nor can choose to stay at home,—
> All must follow, all must roam.
>   —R. L. STEVENSON.

SAMUEL PARRIS had not given up his dream of the ministry. Now and then, after his summer at Stow, he had calls to supply neighboring churches between pastorates, and occasionally he filled the pulpit of a minister who was ill or absent. The pulpit at Salem Village had been vacant for two years, and some of the elders had approached him from time to time about a settlement there. They had not treated their former ministers very well, according to all accounts, and he had not taken the matter seriously until recently. But, as things were, it might not be a bad idea if he could get a suitable contract. One thing was sure;

he would not settle among them without a satisfactory agreement in black and white.

He decided to encourage them a little and see what came of it. Salem was the mother church in the colony where the Lord had established His Zion-in-the-Wilderness—and though Salem Village was not Salem Town, it was next door to it.

And in Salem Andros had met unexpected opposition to the theory that with the fall of the charter the land reverted to the king. Major Stephen Sewall (Samuel's brother), with the Reverend John Higginson to back him up, argued that the charter concerned the government only, and the land titles derived from the Indians who were the original owners. To uphold this ingenious doctrine, they had hunted up some Indians who were (or might be) heirs of the original landed gentry and procured from them a unique document known as the Indian deed, conveying the Salem to the selectmen as trustees for the town or other proprietors or purchasers. Whether such a theory would hold in court, Parris had his doubts, but it seemed to be a case of any port in a storm.

He mentioned the matter to Mr. Morton one day.

"I am more than half minded to get out of trade and take a pastorate for a time—at least till matters settle down," Samuel said.

His old master looked at him with a quizzical and kindly smile. He made no answer but to open the Bible on his desk and put his finger on the text while Samuel read:

No man can serve two masters: for either he will hate the one, and love the other; or else he will hold to the one, and despise the other. Ye cannot serve God and mammon.

Morton spoke gently: "A parson's cloak cannot be donned and doffed with every change of weather, my son. Commit thy way unto the Lord and lean not on thine own understanding; trust also in Him and He shall bring it to pass. 'Tis the only way to peace, Parris. You are like Saul of Tarsus: it took a bolt from heaven to bring him to his Lord—but what a preacher he was!"

"I've had enough experience to make me wary," Parris returned a bit sharply, "and you must consider that I have a family to provide for. The church at Salem Village has made me an offer and invited me to the Sixtieth Anniversary celebration of the founding of the First Church in Salem Town—the mother church of the colony. I think I shall go and see what comes of it."

"Do that," Morton approved. "And be sure to take your wife with you."

So Parris, with Elizabeth behind him, rode through the woods on the sweet July morning. And as they had started at daybreak, perhaps he might be excused later for feeling drowsy in the hot and stuffy meetinghouse.

He was never a good listener, for he caught, now and then, some thought which sent his mind adventuring on a quest of its own, more interesting to him than the words of the speaker.

Now, as his thoughts went straying, the dramatic instinct which from his childhood had brought events before him as vivid pictures re-created the past of the little town into a pageant of history.

It was July 20, 1629, and Samuel pictured himself in Governor Endicott's "faire house newly built." In his nostrils was the incense of new boards fresh from the saw-pit and of useful herbs in the garden just outside.

The newly ordained minister, Francis Higginson, lifted his thin white hands and the congregation stood with heads bowed:

We covenant with the Lord and one with another; and doe bynde ourselves in the Presence of God, to walk together in all His waies, according as He is pleased to reveale Himself unto us in His Blessed Word of Truth.

Solemnly, phrase by phrase, the words fell from the minister's lips and were as solemnly repeated by the congregation.

It was Francis Higginson's hand that had written the convenant —so simple a covenant—so easy to write—and so impossible to keep.

It was Francis Higginson who, by the simple laying on of hands (hands consecrated only by toil and sacrifice), had been dedicated to the sacred office of minister of the First Church of Salem, the New Jerusalem in the Wilderness.

The newly ordained pastor raised his hands and pronounced the benediction.

The handful of people passed out into the dooryard, little

Governor Endicott hospitably greeting them at the door. Groups formed here and there along the path, talking of the crops and the fishing. The women exchanged gossip, and new ways of making tasty the inevitable diet of punkin and fish and Injun corn. The sun hastened to its early setting behind the forest-crowned hills in the west. The herbs of the garden gave out a good smell.

God had established His Zion-in-the-Wilderness.

The pageant faded: 1629 gave place to 1689. John Higginson (son of the first Francis) bowed his bald head and lifted his thin white hands in benediction, and the congregation slowly left the church.

Samuel Parris came out of his daydream as Nicholas Noyes, rotund and ruddy, grasped his hand in a plump and cordial grip.

"Glad to see you, Brother Parris! They tell me you may hear our Macedonian call and come over and help us."

Mr. Noyes was the new minister at Salem Town who had come seven years before to assist the beloved John Higginson, who was too old to carry on the work of so large a parish. Parris had not seen Noyes since the Harvard Commencement eighteen years before. Apparently the years had been good to him. He kept the same boyish and genial manner, though he was now florid and fat and forty-two. Parris thought he looked more like a host at a tavern than a minister.

Mr. Noyes was beaming up at him. "You're stopping with us over the Lord's Day, of course? Aye, that's good! I shall be busy every minute over the Sabbath playing host, but on Monday, after the visitors go, come and see me. Want to talk things over with you. Come to dinner Monday noon. My housekeeper will have the company dishes done by then, I trust. We're keeping ten visitors at the parsonage—not so bad for Bachelor's Hall, eh?"

Parris jumped at the invitation: "Just what I should like, Mr. Noyes. Many thanks."

Noyes shrugged his shoulders. His tone was comically apologetic. "You know, Parris, for the moment I plumb forgot the missis—but you're a benedict, aren't you?"

Parris laughed. "I've the best wife in the world—and the most discreet—but Monday I shall come alone."

"No offense, I trust," Noyes gave back. "But I never talk quite so free before the ladies—God bless 'em!"

Mr. Noyes lived well and his dinner was bountiful and well chosen.

"While we eat we can talk," he said. "It is not the least of my housekeeper's good points that she is somewhat deaf. We may as well get to the point at once. What is your feeling about the village pulpit?"

Parris hesitated. "I hardly know what to say—From all I can learn, it is a hard post. The former ministers have apparently worked against considerable difficulties: there are rumors of quarrels, backbitings, jealousies—I know not what—which have reached me from different sources and which I fear would make a minister's life miserable."

Noyes gave him hearty reassurance. "Don't let that worry you, my friend. They've never found the right man to handle 'em. That's all. When they do, he'll have 'em eating out of his hand.

"Look 'em over. The first one was James Bayley, a young sprig only two years out of Harvard and barely turned twenty-one. Somehow he didn't seem to suit the farmers. He was a quiet, scholarly chap and liked to putter around his garden. They thought he didn't work hard enough at his preaching; and it got around that he didn't perform family prayers any too regular. And some thought his wife was high-toned and uppity. There were plenty for him and only a few against, but they were bitter and noisy.

"Bayley built him a house over Putnam Hill way; and in the course of time his wife's young sister, Ann Carr, married Sergeant Tom Putnam. This marriage put her into the center of the Putnam clan, and her sister, Mistress Bayley, being the minister's wife, they maybe set themselves up some and held their heads too high to please the common folks. Then Mistress Bayley died, and Bayley retired from his ministry and lived like a quiet country gentleman, which suited his taste better than battling for the Lord as we preachers have to do.

"The next one was George Burroughs: a little black man from the wilds of Maine, where he barely escaped with his life in an Indian attack—was really quite a hero—"

Parris interrupted: "Didn't I meet him at Harvard Commencement the first year I came to Massachusetts? He won the wrestling match from Wise by some trick or other, and then did some unseemly vaunting and boasting."

"Aye! the same man and the same brash talking. Swore his wife not to give up his secrets, and such foolery. He left soon after I came and (betwixt you and me) there's no doubt he was ill-treated by the parish. No less a man than old John Putnam was caught in the lie and made to eat his words. But after all that's been said, Mr. Burroughs were a strange man for a preacher, and did strange things.

"(He was only a lay preacher, you know, never took his degree at Harvard and was never ordained.)

"His first wife died in September just after they moved into the new ministry house, and he married again forthwith (too soon, some thought at the time) but as it turned out 'twas hardly soon enough to make the new wife's child respectable—'twas born next June—and for some reason best known to himself, Mr. Burroughs din't baptize the infant. Of course, there was gibble-gabble about that—you know how the old hens cackle when like enough there's no egg in the nest.

"Being a celibate—" he waved his pudgy hand to dismiss the subject— " 'tis not for me to sit in judgment. I leave such matters to the midwives and mothers in Israel.

"I hope I'm not boring you with all this history. There's just one more—Deodat Lawson: an able scholar and a brilliant preacher; but no talent for getting along with people. Always rubbed 'em the wrong way, with the best of intentions. You know, Parris, a minister must be all things to all men, as Paul says, if haply he may win some. A minister—" he leaned across the table and lowered his rich voice to a confidential undertone— "a minister, if I may say it without irreverence, must have a certain notion of business as well as piety; he must be all courtesy and good manners, not easily provoked by the bad usage of others, whether it be by accident or design. As the Good Book says, you know, he that humbleth himself shall be exalted."

Parris nodded thoughtfully. Across the years he heard the echo of Mr. Felkin's precept: "a tradesman must take it." Was the ministry, then, only a genteel business of selling oneself to one's parishioners?

He hesitated: "If I were sure I could make a success of it

. . . but I am no longer in my youth, Mr. Noyes. I am weary of wandering and change. I have been by turns merchant, planter, shopkeeper, preacher, and back to merchant again. My mother's people were ministers and scholars. It was her plan for me. Deep down in my soul it has always been my desire also. But I cannot be a mendicant, having no continuing city. I will not be pushed from pillar to post.

"A man of God should also be a leader of men. He must have a place in the community—not change every year or so—and he must have peace and security for himself and his household. Can I have these in Salem? Living in a house not my own; getting my pay in shillings and pence wrapped in papers so that they shall not be mistaken for strangers' money; or in corn and beans and pumpkins figured at the market price and in cordwood at the woodcutter's convenience."

Noyes shook with laughter. "Oh, come, come now, Parris, being a preacher ain't the worst in the world. Don't you merchants get your pay for pipe-staves in molasses and rum, and pay your taxes in the same kind? Look at me." He patted his rotund stomach. "I've been a preacher in Salem for seven lean years, and I've never seen the righteous forsaken nor his seed begging bread. The Lord is mindful of His own, my brother. A minister, like any other man, gets his reward pretty much as he values himself. They want you at the village, man. 'Tis a rich land—hills and valleys and orchards—make 'em give as the Lord hath prospered 'em. They need tact and leadership—a strong man to rule 'em like a prince; a parson to be proud of."

(Like a prince—the words brought back to Samuel's mind the story of Peter Thacher, escorted by fifty-seven horsemen on his triumphal progress from Barnstable to Milton.)

Noyes was still talking: "Look at our successful men: the Mathers, Willard, Wise, Thacher, Higginson—they're as much fixtures in their churches as the cornerstones. That's the way it ought to be. The relation of pastor and people is as sacred as marriage. All this bickering is of the devil.

"They want you, Parris. You've got the support of both clans, which nobody else ever had. For the first time in the life of the village, Landlord Putnam and Goodman Nurse are dipping out of the same dish. Price your services at what they are worth and make 'em pay it. They'll like you all the better for it.

"And there's another thing (mayhap I shouldn't speak of it but I know 'twill go no farther): Mr. Higginson is nearing his allotted span. When the Lord calls him to a higher station, there is no one I should rather have for my assistant than you, my friend."

(Parris thought of John Wise at Ipswich Village, the idol of his parish and a leader in the affairs of the colony,—and the son of a bondservant!)

"Thank you, Mr. Noyes! I'll not forget your friendship nor your good counsel, however things come out." He held out his hand.

The dusk was coming down as Samuel and Elizabeth rode to the village to put up for the night at Deacon Ingersoll's. It seemed a little farther from Salem Town than Samuel had been told: "Just out the road to Andover ten crooked miles north-westerly across the wooden bridge beyond the cow sheds and keep agoin' till you come to the meetinghouse on Watch-House Hill— an' there ye be!"

There were six or eight of them in the party, laughing and talking companionably as they followed the winding road down the hill, across the log bridge, and up the western slope. To the south lay the wasteland, with scraggly cedars keeping their precarious foothold on the rocky moor, guarding the narrow glens which crept down to nowhere between moss-covered hills. Somewhere among the sedges along the river a bittern boomed. Ahead of them on the left the highest hill of all thrust jagged rocks through the scanty soil. From its crest surprisingly rose a magnificent locust tree; its topmost bough reaching to the darkening sky where the lady moon hung her slim crescent.

Suddenly Elizabeth clutched Samuel. "Look, Samel! A body hanging from the locust tree! 'Tis not yet dead—it twists and writhes!"

Samuel laughed at her. "Hush, foolish little one," he reassured her, " 'tis only a broken branch swaying in the wind."

Parris talked the matter over with the church fathers.

"In Boston I have my own home and a comfortable living from my business," he told them. "I cannot give up a certainty for an uncertainty. Perhaps in a year you would tire of me, as you have tired of others, and I and my family should be left without a roof over our heads or a shilling in our purse.

"Since I left Harvard, I have eaten at my own board and sat by my own hearth. Even a humble servant of the Lord must protect his wife and children against want. I can't persuade myself to accept your offer, brethren," he told the committee; and rode back to Thornhedge in the morning. Elizabeth, riding behind, rested her head against her husband's shoulder.

"I know not whether I should be sorry or glad," she said. "The women were so sweet to me. All the Mistress Putnams (I fear I could never keep them straight in my mind) and Mistress Walcott (she is a Putnam, too, I think they said) and some of the younger sort whose names I don't recall.

"But there was something strange and unhappy about the place: those tall palisades to keep out the Indians; and the thick, dark woods crowding up betwixt the hills; and the black cat crossing my path as I entered the parsonage door. And that fearsome thing hanging on the locust tree—are you sure 'twas naught but a dead branch, Samel?"

Samuel was half annoyed, half amused. "What foolish fancies, dear one! You were not frighted by woods nor Indians at Stow, which was much deeper in the wilderness."

"No. . . . The woods and the Indians were friendly at Stow. But they have killed two Salem men this very year. And though this parsonage is larger and finer, the little house at Stow promised welcome and shelter.

"Of course, you wouldn't understand, Samel. And I can't explain it. But it was all very different at Stow."

Samuel would not admit it but he, too, had been startled by the black cat. Deacon Ingersoll had no more sooner opened the door of the ministry house than the creature rushed out—an enormous black tom that spat at the intruders venomously as he dashed past and vanished in the shrubbery. It was quite the biggest cat Samuel had ever seen.

Deacon Ingersoll said it was Mr. Burroughs's cat, and had hung around the place ever since.

"Though since Mr. Lawson left, the house has stood vacant three years, and how the critter gets in and out beats me. I nailed the cathole shut with a brace across it, and the foundation stuns is all in place, but he must have found a secret way somewheres."

It was an evil omen—perhaps a warning—yet had other conditions of the offer been to his liking, Parris would have chanced it. For the outlook in Boston was not so bright as his brave talk indicated. With the government in chaos and the future darkened by uncertainty and the threat of property confiscation, the life of a merchant was a chancy trade. He was half sorry he had not taken what he could get, but pride would not let him concede anything now.

But the matter was not yet settled. A few weeks later, a delegation of the young men of the village rode to Boston.

"We want you for our minister, Mr. Parris; to dwell among us as long as God wills. We have voted you sixty-six pounds a year to be a tax on our inhabitants; and we bring you this deed of warranty, conveying the ministry house to you and your heirs forever. We will read you our vote:

That we will give to Mr. Parris our ministry house and farm, and two acres of land next adjoining to the house, and that Mr. Parris take office upon him amongst us and live and die in the work of the ministry amongst us.

"You won't say no to that, Mr. Parris?"

Samuel tried not to seem too eager. His eyes ran swiftly over the parchment. It was a better offer than he had hoped for: better than Wise had at Ipswich Village; almost as good as Thacher's at Milton; in fact, one of the best in the colony. And there was the future prospect that Noyes had suggested. That would mean eighty pounds a year!

He opened the study door: "Elizabeth!"

He held out the indenture; but she read the news in his shining eyes. Her hand went to her heart.

"We are going to Salem Village!" she said.

His voice was jubilant.

"It seems to be God's will, my sweet!"

"Then . . . God's will be done!"

He caught her hands. They were like ice in his grasp but he was too excited to notice. He drew her into the study.

"Brethren," he cried gaily, "will you join me in a toast? . . . To Mistress Elizabeth Parris, wife of the new minister of Salem Village!"

Book Six

Salem Village   1689 to 1691

30

The Bishop Farm

'Twas but a village then: the goodman ploughed
His ample acres under sun and cloud;
The good wife at her doorstep sat and spun
And gossiped with her neighbors in the sun.

           —LONGFELLOW.

WHEN FRANCIS NURSE bought the Bishop Farm from the Reverend James Allen, he didn't know that he was taking hold of the hot end of the poker. Like enough it wouldn't have made much difference if he had known, for the Nurses weren't given to knuckling down to anybody, and they coveted to possess the Bishop Farm.

It was a generous and sightly homestead, lying northwest and adjoining the Endicott land, and the house was known as Bishop's Mansion, built with a cellar and foundation walls of stone, and every timber of solid oak, hand hewn by the broad ax.

But Townsend Bishop had not lived in it ten years before he was disciplined for his Anabaptist heresy. He sold his estate to John Endicott and left the colony. A few years later, when young John Endicott brought home his bride, the governor gave him the Bishop Farm as a marriage portion.

Young John did not long survive his father and the farm went to his widow; who promptly married Mr. Allen of Boston. When she died five years later, the farm went to her husband. And he, being no farmer but minister of the First Church of Boston, sold the Bishop Farm to Francis Nurse for £400.

Now, everybody in Salem knew Francis Nurse: he was an early settler and for some forty years had lived near Skerry's on the North River up Beverly way. He was a very respectable person, who earned a meager living for his large family by his trade

of traymaker. Everybody knew Francis Nurse—and the better
they knew him the more struck of a heap they were by the news.
The Nurses were thrifty and 'twas likely enough that Rebecca
might have something stowed in her stocking—but £400! But
there was the deed, duly signed and sealed and witnessed and put
of record in Salem Courthouse. And more than that, the Nurses
had moved in bag and baggage . . . though all they had would
spread pretty thin in that big house, if it wasn't for the things Mr.
Allen's Endicott wife had left there, that Mr. Allen didn't take
the trouble to move.

Then it came out that Francis Nurse had given back a bond
to Mr. Allen, which was put of record in Boston, and which was
to be paid back year by year out of the proceeds of the farm.

When the neighbors found out about the bond, they turned up
their noses at the Nurses more than ever. Long after the debt
was paid in full, they still spoke of the place as "the farm that
Mr. Allen leases to the Nurses."

Mr. Allen had plenty of money and more land than he could
well look after. He was also a shrewd Yankee and not in the
habit of giving anything away. But the Bishop Farm brought him
no favor with the Endicotts, and the Endicotts were a powerful
family, whose ill will would cost more than even Mr. Allen could
afford. He must get it off his hands without delay.

Mr. Allen had known the Nurses a long time: an industrious
and thrifty family with four sons and four daughters, all grown
up and some of them married; who found themselves cramped
in the town, but had no money to buy land which a half century
of colonizing had made valuable. What could be better?

Mr. Allen dropped in at Nurse's to order some new woodenware for his kitchen. He admired the newest grandchild.

"The Lord hath blessed you, Goodman Nurse. As fine a family
as any in the colony. But this little one looks spindling. You
should get some color in her cheeks."

"Aye!" said Rebecca. "But wi' all the rough-talkin' sailors an'
fishermen raisin' Cain in the town, I daren't let the chit outa eye-
shot. Salem do get worse year by year, till 'tis like as roisterly
as Old Yarmouth."

"You should move out to the village," Mr. Allen replied. "My
farm would be just the place for you, with room for all the chil-

dren and grandchildren that the good Lord may send you. What say you, Goodman Nurse?"

"Aye! A fine plan, Mr. Allen!" Francis Nurse scoffed. He broke out singing:

> If I had but a thousand a year, Gaffer Green!
>> If I had but a thousand a year!
> What a man I would be an' what sights I would see,
>> If I had but a thousand a year, Gaffer Green!
>> If I had but a thousand a year.

Mr. Allen threw back his head with a hearty laugh.

"Good! We should have you set the tune in meeting, with a voice like that! But as to the farm—I'm not jesting. Perhaps it might not be so preposterous as you think. Suppose you and the goodwife come over and have a look at the place; and then, if you like it, we may be able to figure out a way."

"W-e-l-l," drawled Nurse, "lookin' ain't buyin'."

Rebecca riding pillion, tightened her arms around her husband.

"Oh, Francis! 'If we like it!' said he? 'Tis the most beautiful place I ever saw. Even Mr. Nathaniel Putnam and that rich widow he married that brought him Hilliard Verin's fortune have not so fine a mansion. And three hundred acres! We'll give each o' the young'uns a farmstead an' have enough left for all the grandchilder! Oh, Francis! I've been prayin' the Lord to open a way out of our puzzlements—an' disbelievin' whilst I was aprayin'—an' all the time the good Lord had this in store for us! Francis Nurse, I'll never mistrust Him again in all my days!"

So the Nurses came to dwell in Salem Village.

It was pretty hard on Zerubbabel Endicott, young John's older brother, with his father's will saying plain "the longest liver of them shall enjoy the whole" and all signed and sealed and dated —but thrown out of court just because it wasn't witnessed.

Zerubbabel could look out his upper windows at Orchard Farm and see strangers enjoying his inheritance—cutting a great piece right out of a choice corner of his farm. It was a rank injustice, and Zerubbabel had too much of his father in him to "take it settin' down." He said he would fight the case till his dying day, if it took his last penny, before he would submit to such an outrage.

Besides this there was the boundary question. Endicott on one side, Nathaniel Putnam on the other, and Francis Nurse between, were all entitled to so many acres each: but there were not enough acres.

In the beginning there was no government survey. The boundaries were marked by blazed trees, or ran "southeasterly from the big oak to the boulder by Beaver Dam." In the beginning nobody cared. There was enough land and more than enough.

Nathaniel Ingersoll said he could remember that when he was a little lad his father leased a parcel of land from Townsend Bishop, down by the wolfpits and fenced it in. Old Governor Endicott told him he had his fence set too far east, beyond his boundary.

"So?" said Ingersoll. "Then I'll move the fence."

"Nay, nay!" said the governor. "Let it stand. When you set up a new fence you can make it right." It was an easy going and friendly agreement between the fathers—but the children's teeth were set on edge.

With Zerubbabel Endicott on the east and Nathaniel Putnam on the north, each claiming his full quota of acres, Francis Nurse in the middle was left short.

It was none of his quarrel and had he been of a milder nature he might have yielded to the demands of his neighbors and sought redress from Allen. But with four strapping big sons and three husky sons-in-law, it was a little too much to expect of human nature.

And there were other grounds for bad blood. The Putnam clan did not forget that Rebecca Nurse was a Towne; and that her sister married an Easty. So when Francis Nurse bought the Bishop Farm and his sons and daughters built homes of their own on marriage portions given them from the ancestral acres, behind them were forty years of quarrels over boundaries with the Endicotts and the Putnams: for the Nurses were not given to knuckling down to anybody, and neither were the Putnams nor Endicotts.

Zerubbabel Endicott went into court, trying to push the Bishop grant northwest over the land of Nathaniel Putnam. A jury of his neighbors decided for Endicott in the local court; but the highest court in the colony decided against him on appeal. With his failing fortunes, his mind failed also, and he gave himself over to a blind rage. He sent his hired men to cut timber on the disputed tract; and for several days they cut and felled and hewed: making beams and joists for a house.

One morning when they came back to work, logs and frame and all were gone. Putnam had sent teams in the night and neatly cleaned out the whole. The timbers were found a mile away, piled beside Putnam's dwelling.

The General Court consented to a rehearing of the case: strictly forbidding Endicott to strip the land meanwhile. But with the fervor which had prompted Governor John to cut out the cross from the British ensign and hew down Morton's Maypole, Zerubbabel sent crews to cut his winter firewood under his personal direction.

The sound of the ax brought Francis Nurse, demanding: "Whose men are you?"

Endicott answered: "My men!"

At that Nurse's two sons-in-law came in a violent manner and hauled the wood out of the sleds. For two days the Battle of the Wilderness raged: the Endicott forces cutting and loading; the Nurses pitching it off; the Putnams guarding the western boundary and everybody boiling mad.

The court confirmed its decision against Endicott. Under this final blow, the doughty Zerubbabel broke down, took to his bed, and died a few months later. But the Endicott spirit survived the frailty of its flesh: his will recited:

Whereas, my late father, by his last will, bequeathed to me his farm called Bishop's or Chickering's farm, I do give the said farm to my five sons, to be divided equally among them.

It was an empty gesture of defiance. But in the minds of the jury of farmers who upheld him in the local court, and in the hearts of the neighbors who remembered the governor's will and the accident that had made it invalid, there was a burning sense of injustice. The Endicotts, first family in the village in priority and in importance, had been robbed of their inheritance.

Francis Nurse, who had benefited by that injustice, was an interloper.

31

Ordination

We work in three dimensions, but we dream and love and worship in the fourth.

—CORA JARRETT.

THE REVEREND SAMUEL PARRIS stood in his pulpit on his ordination morning. The village meetinghouse, a barn-like structure thirty-four by twenty-eight feet with a gallery at each end, was filled to capacity with men, women, and children, come to start the new minister on his way.

The minister had noted when he first awakened that the morning was by favor of the Lord an auspicious omen: clear and crisp as a mid-November day should be, with never a cloud overhead. The night before had brought a light snowfall, blanketing fields and roads with white, marred only by the tracks of cart wheels and horses and the feet of the worshipers, all converging toward the meetinghouse—the center of life and interest in a New England village.

Most of the men were belted and sworded and many carried firelocks on their shoulders, for the Indian plantation at Will's Hill was uncomfortably close and the temper of the red men was unfriendly. Even the meetinghouse itself bore witness to the peril, for it was still blocked up with rocks which had been set during King Philip's War. And the men as they entered stacked their arms inside the door by the end of the soldiers' seat to be instantly ready in case of need. The heavy boots stamped noisily on the puncheon floors and the loose planks which formed the seats clattered as the members of the congregation took their places.

A lively interest brightened the stern faces, for the ordination day was a gala day and the new minister was all the more welcome because he had to be coaxed to come. The women were in their Sabbath best and some of the younger and more frivolous wore ruffles and ribands in honor of the occasion.

The covenant embodying the new church was read by the Reverend Nicholas Noyes of Salem Town, and solemnly assented to by the people, phrase by phrase. The ceremony of ordination was also pronounced by Mr. Noyes, who with Mr. Sam Phillips and the Reverened John Hale of Beverly, consecrated the new minister by the laying on of hands.

At last the time came for the sermon, and the congregation took advantage of their last chance to shuffle their chilly feet and adjust their cramped bodies to the rude plank benches on which they sat.

Six years before, in honor of Mr. Lawson's coming, the meetinghouse walls had been lathed and plastered and daubed and a canopy put over the pulpit. The village prided itself on the canopy, a funnel-shaped sounding board, bearing the motto in ornate letters: "Holiness is the Lord's." It was suspended from the high-pitched roof by a precariously slim iron rod, and as Samuel was a tall man, the funnel hung all too close and threatening, giving him the look of a light under a bushel, which at any moment might come down and put him out. High above, in the dim, dark region of the rafters, the dusty spiderwebs swayed and swung as the wind whistled in through crevices where the daubing had fallen out.

The minister opened his little sermon book. He had written many sermons; he had preached more than a few: but today for the first time he spoke as one having authority: as a duly ordained minister and settled pastor in Zion. He leaned forward:

"Beloved Brethren and Sisters: my text is from Joshua 5:9: And the Lord said unto Joshua, this day have I rolled away the reproach of Egypt from off you."

The preacher forgot himself and the drafty meetinghouse and saw only the host of Israel passing over Jordan River to the Promised Land. He talked of the priests who bore the Ark of the Lord, the Lord of all the earth, standing still in the midst of the river; while the waters which came down from above stood and rose up upon a heap; and those that came down toward the sea of the plain failed and were cut off, until all the people passed clean over Jordan.

And when the kings of the Amorites and the Canaanites heard

what the Lord had done, their heart melted, neither was there spirit in them any more, because of the children of Israel.

And Joshua circumcised the children of Israel: and the Lord said unto him: This day have I rolled away the reproach of Egypt from off you.

The hourglass was empty. The minister laid his little sermon-book down, and as his hand touched the smooth surface of the pulpit there came back to him across the years the memory of Hugh Peter.

His voice trembled as he spoke: "Brethren and Sisters, the ways of the Lord are past finding out. I have been told that this old pulpit where I stand was given to you, the farmers of Salem Village, when the First Church in Salem built their new meeting-house. From this very pulpit, then, half a century ago Hugh Peter preached before he went back to England to serve as chaplain in the army of the Great Protector, and die a martyr for the Puritan cause.

"As a little child, I remember a day when Mr. Peter dined at my father's house in London and told us tales of Salem-in-the-Wilderness in his sweet New England. Then he laid his hand on my head (I can hear his voice speaking): 'This little lad may live to see the New Canaan and to stand in a pulpit where he may proclaim the word of the Lord without fear or favor.'

"Brethren, it was a prophecy' The Lord God in His own way hath brought to pass this miracle: that I, though all unworthy, should by God's grace be brought to stand in Hugh Peter's pulpit in the Zion he loved." There were tears in his eyes and tears in his voice as he prayed for grace and guidance to carry on the work that his martyr predecessor had begun.

Yet while the preacher part of him was absorbed in his devotions, the merchant part of him was alert and eager, appraising the effect of his words on his new flock. That most of them were pleased he could not doubt—approving nods and neighborly nudges proved that—and some were much moved.

Little Mrs. Ann Putnam was perched on the edge of her seat in the east gallery, her head cocked to one side, gazing down at the preacher. She was a small woman, and thin, in an age of plump and generous figures. In an effort to seem as tall as her neighbors she unconsciously carried herself very straight and stretched her skinny neck to its utmost in order to hold her head high. She gave herself importance by her quick and decisive movements and her alert observation of everything that went on around her. Her face, small and thin and tapering to an insignificant chin, was bisected by a very prominent nose, from either side of which her shortsighted gray eyes peered sharply at the world. She gave an absurd suggestion of an anxious hen scanning the ground for a choice morsel, but keeping a wary eye out for possible hawks or weasels.

Parris sternly checked a smile at his foolish fancies and turned his attention to the foreseat on the women's side, adjoining Elizabeth's pew. There in a dignified row sat five more Putnam women: wives of Edward, Jonathan, John, James, and Benjamin. That did not count Lieutenant Thomas's widow, Mistress Mary Verin Putnam, who sat in lonely luxury in a specially built pew, with a back and a cushion. The minister skipped a line in his closely written sermon and never missed it—he had never noticed before how many Putnams there were in the village church.

Farther back in the middle section was a sweet-faced little woman whom he recognized as Martha Corey—a regular attendant but not a member, he had been told. She smiled at him in a motherly way, and every now and then looked across at her tall husband on the men's side, nodding her head to emphasize some point in the sermon. But her gestures brought no response other than an occasional shrug or a noisy shuffling of boots; and almost before the benediction was pronounced Goodman Corey was out the door, ignoring his wife who called after him:

"Giles, come back! Ain't we goin' to stay to the ordination dinner? I fetched a roasted mutton leg."

Giles paid no heed. He made off toward the horse house with long strides. From the meetinghouse door Parris watched him with disapprobation:

Uncivil lout! he thought.

A hand touched the minister's arm, and he looked down into the eyes of a thin-faced, long-legged girl of fourteen or so. She spoke rapidly:

"I saw him!"

"Saw whom, Corey?" Parris asked, still nettled by the fellow's boorishness.

"I saw Joshua! Leading the host of Israel through the river."

Her voice was low and throaty, yet there was a passion in it that woke an echo in the minister.

"You saw Joshua?" he repeated curiously.

The girl's thin body quivered and her eyes shone with excitement. "The waters rolled back—and we all went across the river on the dry sand—marching and singing—following after Joshua . . . 'Twas a long time ago in a far country—but I remember!"

Samuel felt a tingling up and down his spine.

"Who are you, child?" he asked sternly. "What mean you by such a story?"

The glow faded, leaving her eyes dull and lusterless, and as the minister repeated his question, she whirled and was off, running cross-lots toward Ingersoll's where the ordination dinner was to be held, her prim Puritan skirts lifted scandalously high as she cleared the hummocks.

The Salem Villagers had done well by their pastor when they built their ministry house, which was large and comfortable, having two stories and a cluster of four great chimneys in the center. It was practically new, according to local standards, having been built only eight years before for the accommodation of Mr. Burroughs. The stormy days of the early pastorates, however, had not been favorable to homemaking, and after three years of supply preaching and disuse it was only a vacant house which had never really been a home.

To Elizabeth, the big bare rooms seemed as forlorn as an empty bird's nest; and with the touch of the natural homemaker, she set about giving the place a lived-in look. Great fires in the four big chimneys drove back the autumn chill. House plants brought from the garden at Thornhedge brightened the windows. The closet beside the fireplace gleamed with well-polished pewter and copper. A calico carpet covered the oak table and gay patchwork cushions welcomed the weary to the straight-backed chairs. Yet the new mistress was not satisfied.

"I don't know what's the matter with it," she told herself. "It looks all right, but it doesn't feel right."

She sent Corythus to the woods for rowan branches. Their gay red berries gave the room a cheerful look, and though she did not say so, even to herself, she remembered the old song:

That wicked witches have no power
Where there is rowan tree wood.

The best room had windows to the west and south: small swinging windows with lozenge-shaped panes of greenish-blue glass which let in little enough light even on sunny days. As this was to be the minister's study, Elizabeth sent to Widow Smylie in Boston for some of her bayberry candles for the minister's desk, and spread a bright Turkey-worked carpet over the table. The walls were wainscoted in oak, which Tituba rubbed with candle wax until they glowed in the flickering light of the fireplace; but she, too, complained:

"Dis' yeah no'thern timbah doant take de shine lak de 'hogany wood in de Inges. 'Taint nohow fitten fo' a genle'um's house. 'Hogany wood shined up wid orange juice—das sumpin fine."

But to the master of the house the place was perfect, for it was his own—not his by gift or inheritance, like Cotton Hall; nor by marriage, like Thornhedge; but the fruit of his own effort, his own talent, his own determined bargaining. His half of the indenture, with its wavy irregular edge which would fit nothing in the world but its counterpart, was safely hidden in the secret drawer of his escritoire, and not even his wife knew how to press the hidden spring that would bring it to light.

He had not come to Salem Village with his eyes shut. From one and another he had learned the whole disgraceful history of the quarrels and difficulties of his predecessors. The parish had borne a bad repute from the beginning; as if the devil was determined to oppose this outpost of the Lord which encroached upon the unbroken forest which was his stronghold, and had set one against another even as Christ had said, till a man's foes were those of his own household. But God had given to him, Samuel Parris, this charge to keep; this fortress of Zion to hold against the hosts of evil until Christ set up His visible kingdom in this New Canaan. "They need a strong man to rule 'em like a prince," Noyes had said. Parris threw back his head and began to sing, marching up and down the study with a martial tread:

The Lord descended from above
    And bowed the heavens hye
And underneath His feet He cast
    the darkness of the skye.

> On cherubs and on cherubimes
>   full royally He road
> And on the winges of all the windes
>   came flying all abroad.

In the "keeping room" at the east side of the house Elizabeth heard the psalm and smiled tenderly as she spun gray wool into blankets for the coming winter. Three steps forward, three steps back; keeping time to her spinning song:

> Some good men left
> Their homes and friends
> And wandered far away—

Her song hushed to a soft humming, listening to Samuel.

> They went o'er many and many a mile
> For many and many a day . . .
> There came one day—

There! The thread was broken! "Tush!" said Elizabeth. "See what comes of letting thoughts go woolgathering!" But her lips still curved happily as she mended the thread. Samuel was happy, she thought. Happier than she had ever seen him . . . doing the work he wanted to do . . . God's work . . . the greatest work in the world! And she was happy too. Of course, she was happy—why shouldn't she be? What was there to worry about? A dead branch on a tree? A black cat crossing her path? 'Twas nothing strange that Mr. Burroughs's cat should hang about the place! Cats always stayed in places; 'twas only dogs that followed people—anybody knew that. If Mr. Burroughs's cat wanted to lie on her chimney shelf and blink his yellow eyes—what was that to her?

The break was mended and the psalm was ended. The black cat spat and backed against the chimney with arching back and tail like a brush. Corythus burst into the room with a bedraggled puppy in his arms.

"He fell off a woodsled on the road to Andover an' the men went on an' left him," he gasped. "Can I keep him, Mis' Lizbet? Please! He's a wunnerful puppy-dog! His ears are jes' like black velvet. An' I never had anything alive that b'longed to me. An' he'd be so furry an' warm to sleep with on cold nights. Please,

Mis' Lizbet! You know"—he swallowed hard—"everybody in our fam'ly sleeps with somebody—'cept me."

Elizabeth considered. "Yes, I think you may keep him, if you train him to be neat and obedient," she said. "Only I fear there will be trouble if he and the cat get together."

Corythus lighted up in a wide grin: "I'll sure be mighty careful to keep him an' Lucifer apart—anyway till he gets bigger. And I've thought of a name for him: Moreover."

"Moreover?" Elizabeth repeated. "That is a strange name for a dog."

"It's a Scriptuah name," Corythus maintained. "Massa Sam read it in last Sabbath's lesson 'bout Lazarus. 'Moreover the dog came and licked his sores.' "

Samuel looked up from his book with an unpleasant laugh. "Now, Mistress Parris, I hope you are satisfied with the advantages of education for the Ethiopian! What did I tell you? 'Moreover the dog,' indeed!"

Elizabeth flushed and bit her lip. "That is unworthy of you, Samuel," she said. "You know well that any child might have made the same mistake, and you would only have smiled at it. Sometimes I wonder . . ."

Samuel saw that he had gone too far.

"Forgive me, my love, I was only jesting."

Then turning to Corythus, he welcomed the newcomer. "He is a fine puppy, Corythus—an English setter. You can hunt pigeons with him when he is trained. I had a dog when I was a lad. His name was Protector after the great Cromwell."

The recollection brought sad memories. The king's men had killed Protector when the plague came to Islington.

32

Corythus

*He that walks among briars and thorns will
be very careful where he sets his foot.
And he that passes through the wilderness
of this world, had need ponder all his steps.*
—ANNE BRADSTREET, *Meditations.*

JUST A week after Samuel's ordination the weather, which had been mild for the season, suddenly turned cold, with a northeaster driving the snow across the hills and heaping it in the valleys. Corythus came in from his evening chores and huddled on the rug before the fireplace with his puppy in his arms and went to sleep. At bedtime Elizabeth tried to rouse him, but he protested.

"Please, Mis' Lizbet, let me stay here. Ah'm so cold. Cayn't I jes' lay by the fire till mornin' come?"

Elizabeth left him there, though Samuel warned her: "You are too easy with the boy, my dear. A Negur is a lazy beast and won't bear spoiling."

She only smiled: "Indeed, he's not lazy, Samuel. He has worked hard all day, stacking firewood under the kitchen porch. He's tired and cold and 'twill do no harm for him to lie by the fire if he likes."

At the first gray of dawn, the puppy began to howl and whimper. Samuel, snug in his bed, refused to stir, until the little beast began to claw at the stair door and wail. Then he went down, muttering imprecations, to see what the fuss was about.

Corythus lay still before the fire, his body strangely inert. His forehead was cold under Samuel's hand. The puppy licked the set face, shivering and whining. The black cat sat on the hob, purring loudly, his yellow eyes gleaming in the murky dawn.

Samuel ran back upstairs to tell Elizabeth. Then he sent John Indian for the doctor—though he knew it was too late. It needed only one touch on the clammy brow to tell him that.

Dr. Swinnerton came in haste, and pronounced the one word: "Dead."

"What was it, doctor?" Samuel asked. "He was not ill, save for chilling a little last night."

The doctor hesitated. "It is not easy to say, offhand, knowing naught of his history. These colored boys are not too hardy in our severe climate. The sudden cold may have congested the lungs or put too much strain on his heart. It is not easy to say—"

Elizabeth came back from the kitchen with a glass and the doctor drank the cordial eagerly.

"Thank you, Mistress Parris. This goes right to the spot on a cold morning." His voice was loud with professional good cheer. "Your own making, I'll be bound. You can't trust servants to make a proper drink."

Elizabeth disregarded the flattery: "What took the lad, so on a sudden?"

The doctor cleared his throat and began a lengthy discussion freely sprinkled with Latin words, and explanations which did not explain. In the end he suggested hopefully that he might "make an anatomy" but both Samuel and Elizabeth shuddered and the doctor said no more.

"Never mind," Elizabeth said. "Words matter little now. They cannot bring back the dead. If wou will tell us, doctor, what needs to be done . . ."

The news of the death in the ministry house spread through the village and the people responded according to their kind, making a beaten path to the parsonage door. Some were moved by curiosity, some by morbid desires, some by fear, but most of them by kindness. Their hearts went out to their new minister, whose door had so soon been darkened by death.

Though Dr. Swinnerton might be reticent, there were plenty who would talk. No matter how you looked at it, it was an evil omen. Whether it was the Lord's hand or the devil's, there were too many deaths in the ministry house.

The house had been built for Mr. Burroughs in the summer of 1681 and in September his wife died. There was a great scandal about that, because he had no money to bury her. But for all that, he had married again soon—he needed someone to care for his little daughter Hannah, and the old wives gabbled when he had Mercy Lewis, one of the neighbor girls, as help. But the second wife also died—three doctors were called in, but not one of them could name the cause of it. As if this were not enough, there was talk that Mr. Burroughs was hard and cruel and that both his wives had feared his bad temper and abuse. Even when he was away from home, as he frequently was on some pretext or other, he seemed to have a way of knowing what was going on, and if it was not to his liking, he made them smart for it when he came home.

Oh, yes, he were a strange man, was Mr. Burroughs, a very strange man for a parson, and 'twas a good day for the village when they got rid of him.

Mr. Lawson took Mr. Burroughs's place. He was a good man and, though he heard tales about the place, he came. ('Twas he who put in the witch doors and the Holy Lord hinges to keep the witches out.) But in a year or so his wife died also, and her small daughter soon followed her. The double loss took the heart out of Mr. Lawson.

"The devil is in the place," he said, and he took ship for England without delay.

That was almost three years ago, and since then the village had had no permanent pastor, only supply preachers, and the ministry house had stood empty.

Samuel was angry. "Why in God's Name didn't you tell me the house was haunted?" he cried.

Deacon Ingersoll reproved him gently: "Now, now, Brother Parris! That's goin' a bit far. People will talk, you know, but you can't say a house is hanted because somebody's died in it. Folks die in most all houses, soon or late. I've lived here—right cater-corner acrost the road—ever sence that house was built, and I've never seen hide nor hair of a hant. Nobody ever thought of such a thing (unless it mought be some silly females lookin' for excitement).

"Mr. Lawson maybe spoke a bit hasty, but you have to make allowances for him. He was a very loving husband and father and his chastisement was sore. But he never even hinted that he ever saw or heard anything amiss about the house. 'Twas only the memories of sad afflictions and loneliness that he couldn't bear. So he went back to England for a spell. He's back now, preaching at Scituate."

Samuel was sadly troubled by the death of Corythus. He had
been fond of the boy in a way: proud of his straight supple body
and eager mind which he fancied were his gift to the child. Yet
each year added to the danger that someone would notice the
resemblance. Also Corythus at fourteen was becoming interested
in himself as an individual.

Once he asked Parris: "Did you know my mammy, Massa
Sam? Tituba says she was a princess in her homeland far 'cross
the big water before the white men stole her for a slave."

Parris tiptoed over thin ice. "I have seen her. She was a
comely wench and a servant in Mr. Webb's house. But I never
heard she was a princess. That is Tituba's nonsense. You had
best ask Tituba no questions and she'll tell you no lies. She
imagines many things and likes to hear herself talk."

There was a growing peril in this sort of thing. Parris wished
himself rid of the boy, but he had a fatalistic feeling that nothing
he could do would help matters. Was it not written in the Scripture: Be sure your sin will find you out? All in all, perhaps it
was safer to keep the boy under his eye and leave the future to
God.

Now God had removed his thorn in the flesh.

Parris took his record book down from its place and turned to
the page headed:

DEATHS IN SALEM VILLAGE

It was not the first entry he had made, for during the pastorless
years he had several times been called on to labor with a dying
sinner or comfort a departing saint. He mused over the entries.

Persons departed by death in Salem Village

1688		Age
Nov. 30	Nathaniel Sheldon, son of Wm. Sheldon, well on monday, sick tuesday, distracted on thursday, and so continued till friday he died . . .	10
Dec. 20	Saml Wilkins a very naughty man died very hope-fully	52
1689		
Jan. 1	Saml Fuller at meeting ye Sabbath well, before tuesday speechless and died this day ½ hour be-fore I came	27

Nov. 11   Tabitha, daughter of James Smith, well and dead
           in four days   15

He dipped his quill and wrote:

Nov. 25   My Negro Lad   .   .   .   .   .

His hand stopped, poised above the page. Somehow he could not
bring himself to write the name. To put it in black and white
for his successors to read, and perhaps to wonder about as their
classically trained minds recalled the legend of Corythus, son of
Paris and the nymph Oenone. He had rarely called the child
by any name at all: Bub, perhaps, or Kinky, or in moments of
tenderness, Lad. He dipped his quill again and set down in the
column to the right, his age: 14. It had been his custom to add
to the bare fact a brief obituary comment, giving the cause of
death, but here again he considered, and let the record stand as
it was.

Corythus was gone, buried under six feet of frozen earth, but
the manner of his taking off was better left unwritten.

Five deaths in a house only eight years old—and not one of
them by a proper complaint! No wonder Mr. Lawson had fled
the place! Parris was tempted to do likewise.

But he had ventured his all on this pastorate. His mercantile
ventures had gone so badly that he had turned his business over
to his creditors in settlement of his debts. Thornhedge had been
sold for half its worth to a customhouse officer from England.
Business in the Bay Colony was facing ruin. Even Sewall, with
all his money, was scrambling around, trying to dispose of his
holdings at whatever they would bring.

The ministry house and his salary were all he had, except for
the undependable profits from Cotton Hall plantation—and the
pittance from the Quaker settlement lease, which never failed.

If he left the village it would be to face poverty—perhaps
want. Yet if he stayed . . . would his wife, or his darling little
Bettie, be the next? He could not risk that. He would go at
once.

But Elizabeth would not hear to such a thing. Her eyes re-
proached him.

"Samel, what are you saying? If Mr. Burroughs trafficked with the powers of the air as some think, and Mr. Lawson was like a bird that flies before the storm, will you also desert your post at the first onset of the Evil One?

"Doubtless 'tis as Mr. Cotton Mather says: 'that we of New England are settled in those which were once the devil's territories to accomplish the promise of old made unto our Blessed Jesus, that He should have the uttermost parts of the earth for His possession. Wherefore the devil is calling his legions to make an attack upon us, because he knows that the last days have come and his time is short.'

"Oh, Samuel," Elizabeth went on, "I feared to come to this place, but the Lord called you to guard this outpost of Zion-in-the-Wilderness after other men had failed of their trust; and God will give us strength to do His will."

Samuel put his hands on his wife's shoulders: "Dear heart, your courage puts me to shame. The Lord will indeed strengthen our hearts. You have given me a text for next Lecture Day:

Be not afraid of sudden fear, neither of the desolation of the wicked, when it cometh. For the Lord shall be thy confidence, and shall keep thy foot from being taken.

But despite his determination to stand his ground, Parris could not shake off his uneasiness. His nerves were on edge and he started at the falling of a log in the fireplace or the cracking of the timbers in the cold. He began to have fancies too.

It seemed that the puppy shared his master's uneasiness. He no longer lay on the mat before the fire as he used—the mat where Corythus had died. He would circle it carefully, his sensitive nose aquiver, whining softly.

"Poor doggy," Elizabeth would say, "he misses his young master."

Was that all, Parris wondered, or did the setter sense what human beings could not see, that he should circle and sniff and choose a place at the far side of the hearth?

On the pretext of a congested feeling in his lungs, Samuel consulted Dr. Swinnerton, and being assured that he was in the best of health save for a slight cold, he put some guarded inquiries about the death of Corythus and the bad repute of the parsonage.

The doctor pooh-poohed any idea of witchcraft or haunting.

"These countryfolks scare themselves with silly folk tales," he said, "but persons of learning, like you and me, should know better than that, Mr. Parris. The Royal Society is leaning more and more to the view that most supernatural occurrences are to be explained by natural laws, and that these stories of witches and apparitions are mere old wives' fables. But to these country people the woods are as beset with devils as a dog with fleas, and every untoward happening is charged to sorcery."

Parris put his next question earnestly: "What am I to understand by that statement, Dr. Swinnerton? Do you set up the Proceedings of the Royal Society against the Bible? Will you despise the words of our Lord Jesus Christ Himself, who bade His disciples cast out devils in His Name?

"I knew a man in Boston (he called himself a doctor) who dabbled in this science. He died a victim of his own wretched experiments. But truly, this is strange talk for a professing Christian!

"You, with your learning, know well that the giving up of a belief in witchcraft is in effect giving up the Bible."

Dr. Swinnerton smiled ruefully.

"*Et tu, Brute?*" he murmured. "Somehow, I hoped for a more modern view from you, Mr. Parris, with your London background and liberal education. But the world moves slowly at best."

Parris rebuked him. "I trust I shall not move so swiftly as to outrun my Master! A man who has lived in the Indies as long as I cannot be unmindful of the wonders of the invisible world which crowds so close upon the world of sense and sight. And in this little strip of Christian earth between the sea and the primeval forest we have pushed the outposts of God's Kingdom into the very fastness and fortress of Satan. I pray you, Dr. Swinnerton, and I pray God for you, that your study of the new science shall not rob you of the old faith in the things of the spirit."

33

Puritan Priest

His speech is a burning fire;
With his lips he travaileth;
In his heart is a blind desire;
* In his eyes foreknowledge of death;*
He weaves, and is clothed with derision;
* Sows, and he shall not reap;*
His life is a watch or a vision
* Between a sleep and a sleep.*

—SWINBURNE.

THE MYSTERIOUS death of the slave boy, Corythus, occurring so soon after the arrival of the Parris family, revived the superstitions about the ministry house. The village came flocking to the funeral, all agog and awe-struck, gazing at the calm young face in the coffin and whispering comments behind their hands.

To Samuel, the occasion was an ordeal hardly to be borne. Death had aged and hardened the clear-cut features till to his guilty consciousness it seemed impossible that anyone could fail to see the likeness which was so plain to him. In every glance and whisper he read suspicion or accusation. The lad's death, which he had fatuously thought might end his chastisement, was to be instead God's way of branding him in the assembly of all the people!

The brief and simple rites seemed an interminable ordeal, and as he stood at the open grave while the clods of frozen earth thudded upon the coffin, in a sort of waking nightmare he saw himself disgraced, ostracized, dismissed from his pastorate, driven from the village. God in His justice had permitted him to look across Jordan at the Promised Land of his heart's desire—the land which because of the sin of his youth he could not enter.

There came back to his memory the horror of those nightmare dreams in Barbados, when he saw Elizabeth turning away from him, shuddering with horror and fear of him, for the vileness of his sin. Suppose some woman should bring the tale to Elizabeth! His hands clenched till the knuckles stood out white as he vowed vengeance upon such a mischiefmaker. To do him justice, he was more concerned for Elizabeth's suffering than for his own. After all his years with her, she was still his St. Elizabeth, too pure to bear the touch of contamination. He was sure she could never understand, she could never forgive, and the shock of the knowledge would kill her. He stared into the grave like one in a trance.

He looked up—and met the eyes of the girl who had followed Joshua: strange, heavy-lidded eyes with a gleam in their amber depths, watching him curiously. He pulled himself together and met the eyes. The gleam dulled to a sullen heaviness as the girl turned away. She was still sulking under his reproof.

He knew now who she was: Jonathan Walcott's daughter Mary, their next neighbor. She had come often to the ministry house with some neighborly gift from her mother, and had stayed to make friends with Abigail and Bettie and show them how to make poppets out of cornhusks with round black beans for eyes.

The winter days went by serenely. The snow whitened the new mound in the burying ground. Sabbath sermon and Tuesday lecture came in their turn. Nathaniel Ingersoll shouted neighborly greetings across the snow and Captain Putnam stopped by on his way home from Salem Town to warm his hands at the minister's hearth while he told the latest news: an expedition of French and Indians from Montreal had fallen on the little village of Schenectady at midnight, and burned it and massacred most of the inhabitants. One attack would lead to more. He was calling out his men for daily practice at the training field.

After a week or two, Parris began to breathe again. But his feeling of safety and assurance was gone, and with it much of his faith in himself. He felt, or imagined, an obscure change in the spirit of the parish: something undefined, but vaguely unfriendly. It was like the hush that precedes the coming of darkness; like the quiver of birch leaves before a summer shower. As yet it held no menace. But the time might come—he sensed it uneasily— when it would be as ominous as the dread stillness of that breathless night in the Indies before the hurricane unleashed its fury.

The minister knew well enough what the trouble was. He saw himself as God must see him: a fornicator, a liar in word and deed, a despicable hypocrite—unspeakably vile. Yet he steadfastly shut himself outside God's mercy. The Scripture said, God will abundantly pardon, but the condition of that pardon was confession of sin in the assembly of the saints, and that he would not, could not do.

In his necessity he tried to bargain with the Almighty. Though he would not stand in the market place and beat upon his breast, he would repent in secret, and let his light so shine before men that they should see his good works and glorify his Father which is in heaven.

There was nothing of the devotee in his nature. The practice of meditation and contemplation which were Cotton Mather's daily habit was alien to his manner of life, and his healthy body rebelled against the fasting and prayer which were the accepted way of buying divine favor or forgiveness. But his uneasy conscience goaded him to feverish activity which he mistook for zeal in the Lord's work.

He called frequent meetings of the brethren; sometimes at the ministry house, sometimes at the home of one or another of the members, where they could sit around the hearth and consider the questions of Baptism and the Lord's Supper and the Means of Grace and other essential matters, with an informality and physical comfort which were impossible in the icy meetinghouse.

He would tell them of the days at Harvard, and the meetings of the synods, where knotty questions were discussed and decided and became the rule of the churches of New England. He would expound for them the inner meaning of puzzling Scripture texts and encourage them to consult with him in his study about their doubts and fears.

Elizabeth started the pleasant fashion of bringing in a pitcher of cider and a big trencher of caraway cakes, and the evenings would end with cordial good feeling and a growing respect and admiration for the erudition of their minister. The brethren, after a while, became his devoted bodyguard, and the church a fortress of defense and assault in the evil days that were to come.

But outside this inner circle were the unregenerates: the unchurched inhabitants, taxed to maintain a church they didn't belong to, and a preacher they never went to hear; but having no say-so in either church or village. When Samuel was at Harvard, he recalled, he had heard it discussed that out of 25,000 population, only 1,100 had the right to vote; but since those 1,100 were the Lord's elect, it seemed a good arrangement. If the unregenerates were let to run the government, the efforts of the Founders were in vain.

But with all his labor in the vineyard of the Lord, the minister found no assurance of God's forgiveness or favor. Sometimes in the night watches, the devil seemed to jeer at him, as if biding his time.

Yet for a while things went smoothly. The brethren were proud of their new minister. He was no ordinary country parson, they felt. He cut a handsome figure as he rode about the village on his headstrong black-and-white gelding (whose spotted coat betrayed old Judy's indiscretions with some roving Indian pony). He was no less impressive in his pulpit.

He didn't pay much attention to the sisters, unless he was sent for to pray with the sick or afflicted. No woman he had ever seen could hold a candle to his Elizabeth.

He didn't know much about women's ways. He even thought that Mistress Ann Putnam's quivering lips and Mary Walcott's glowing eyes evidenced the power of the Holy Spirit invoked by the preached word.

Mary came to play with his little girls, and it amused and flattered him one day when he was rehearsing a sermon, to see Mary peeping through the crack of his study door, spellbound by his eloquence.

Elizabeth had spoken to him about the child once. "I don't know what to do about Mary," she said. "She's underfoot most of the time. I think she is unhappy at home, poor dear; she has a stepmother, you know. But she worries me a little. She's too big to play with our children."

Samuel looked up from the *Exposition of Habbakuk*, his finger marking the place. "Well, what of it? They get along together, don't they? I haven't heard any quarreling."

"Oh, no! 'Tisn't that. But it isn't quite—wholesome, I'm afraid. Mary's always whispering behind her hand. She may put notions into their heads—about the lads and suchlike things, you know."

"She's only a child."

"She is going on sixteen, Samuel, and taller than I. She should be at home learning to mind the house."

Samuel was impatient. "Well, you can't send her home. Her father is Captain Jonathan Walcott and her stepmother was Deliverance Putnam, Thomas Putnam's daughter: leading members of our church and a wealthy and respected family. We can't afford to offend people like that."

"No," Elizabeth agreed. "Of course, I didn't mean anything like that. I don't want to hurt the captain nor his wife nor Mary. 'Tis only that I'm puzzled what to do."

Samuel pulled her down into his lap and kissed the two little wrinkles between her brows.

"Don't do anything, my love. There's nothing to worry about, I'm sure. I remember when I was a lad at Morton's we used to have secret signs. But they were nothing but schoolboy foolishness. There was no harm in them."

He considered a moment: "Perhaps I should have a talk with Mary about her soul. She has given very close attention to my sermons of late, I've noticed."

He didn't say she peeped at him through the crack in his study door. Elizabeth might not like it. Women were queer—even Elizabeth was a little queer sometimes.

Now that the matter had been brought to his attention he wondered if he had not been remiss in shepherding his flock.

It was a pleasure to write sermons and a delight to preach, but pastoral visitations were an irksome duty. He himself always felt resentful if people came prying into his affairs and giving him unwanted advice. (He turned regretful eyes on Habbakuk and marked his place.)

Well, if it must be done it must. And he wouldn't cozen his conscience by visiting his neighbors the Walcotts.

He flung the saddle on Punch and galloped along the winding road toward Seven Men's Bounds and turned in at the Corey farm.

The black sheep of the village was old Giles Corey. He had come to Salem from his native England in the early years of the settlement and for some time lived in the town. But ten years before Parris came to the village, Corey had bought a sightly farm of an hundred acres about a mile south of Bald Hill, where he lived in comfortable independence with his wife, Martha.

When his two daughters married, he had given them homesteads out of the paternal acres, and he and his sons-in-law farmed the tract together.

Corey was rough and uncouth in appearance: a tall, raw-boned, hard-favored son of the West Riding of Yorkshire, a mining district where men lived like beasts and children starved or snatched and fought to keep their miserable bodies and souls together. Being stronger than most, Giles won his fights. He ran away from the filthy hovel he was born in; shipped as a stowaway; and after years of cuffing and kicking and misadventures on land and sea rolled off a freighter at Salem. He found a woman who made for him the first home he had ever had; liked it; and stayed. He was a hard worker and a hard fighter and three meals a day and a bed at night meant luxury to him. Whatever was left over went into the sock, so that in the course of time he acquired a house and lot in Salem Town and meadows near Ipswich River. Salem was filling up by that time, and Giles wanted room to stretch his legs, so he sold his Salem property and moved ten miles west where there were no neighbors to pester him.

He had no interest in the Lord's Zion and his ways were not Puritan ways. The habits of cursing and fighting and helping himself to what he wanted without a by-your-leave were born and bred in him. He had a good many rough passages. More than once he was up before the court on some charge or other; but in most cases the charge was proved to be without foundation or a mountain made out of a molehill. But as time went on the railing took on a bitter and angry tone. It came to be the fashion to charge all sorts of minor crimes to Corey; and if anything was lost or mislaid, "Corey took it."

Then, in 1676, a man named Goodell, who had been working on Corey's farm, was carried home by Corey's wife in a serious condition, and died soon after. The talk was that he had come to his death at the hands of Corey, who had violently beaten him. Corey was arrested and tried and feeling ran high against him, but the evidence was conflicting, and notwithstanding the prejudice against Corey, he was acquitted.

Not long after, John Procter's house burned in the night, and again Corey was accused, because Procter had been an arbitrator in a case which had gone against Corey. But again he was cleared.

But Corey by his own admission was a man of scandalous life and a challenge to the ministers of the community, who coveted to bring him to the mercy seat, a brand plucked from the burning. So far, however, the preachers had come off second best in every encounter.

It was with considerable satisfaction that Samuel Parris had recognized this redoubtable sinner in meeting on his ordination morning; and he was correspondingly chagrined by Corey's hasty and uncivil departure as soon as the sermon ended.

Therefore it was inevitable that the minister of Salem Village, setting out to warn and charge against vices, should aim at Giles Corey. If, after others had failed, he could bring old Giles down on his prayer-bones, it would be beating the devil at dice.

It was disappointing to find that Goodman Corey was not at home; but the goodwife received the minister cordially, ushered him into the neat kitchen, and seated him in her husband's barrel chair beside the clean-swept hearth.

"I am so sorry that Giles ain't to home," she said, "but he hauled a load of wood to Salem Town an' likely'll not be back till near dark.

"Maybe 'tis the Lord's plannin' thet Giles ain't home," she added thoughtfully. "Seems like it must be, or 'twouldn't 'a' come about thataway. The dear Lord allus has His reasons—don't you think, Mr. Parris?—even ef we don't know right off-hand what they be. Won't you read a lesson from the Good Book an' then go to prayer with me? And like enough, while we be yet speakin' God will show us His will."

The minister was a little at a loss. In a state midway between amusement and dismay, he began to wonder if Goodwife Corey was going to make a convert of his reverend self. He caught at his slipping prestige and began to question her solemnly about the state of her soul.

"Your words are the words of faith," he said, "yet you attend worship only when you choose and your name is not in my church book."

Goodwife Corey looked puzzled and distressed.

"Why, parson, I've never felt fitten to number myself with the saints of God for fear of eatin' damnation. But ef you say 'tis my duty, it must be, an' twill be the happiest day of my life when I set down to the Lord's table."

Parris had somewhat the feeling of a hunter who went out after a grizzly and brought home a tame rabbit—even though he knew that in God's pure sight every soul is precious.

A few days later the minister rode down to the farm again. Corey was there, but in cantankerous mood. Though Parris held his temper and used his most persuasive manner, Corey refused to talk religion at all, and made some frank and unflattering comments on preachers and their nosy ways.

He flatly refused to be prayed for, though Martha added her tearful pleas to the parson's; and finally strode off to the barn, after telling the preacher to his face:

"When I want to sin, I want to sin; an' I doan't want any non-sinners tellin' me when I can an' when I can't!"

This was bad enough, but the final affront came later, when Parris learned that Corey had gone straight off to Mr. Noyes in Salem Town and, professing himself a seeker after salvation, had been received into the fold of the First Church.

He indignantly told Noyes the story of Corey's impudence, and it did not soothe him when Noyes took it as a rare joke, holding his fat sides and rocking with laughter.

" 'Tis a preacher's business to be ill-used and resent nothing, Parris. Didn't I tell you? A parson must have no flesh and blood about him. Don't hold it against me that I laughed. A merry heart doeth good like a medicine, the Good Book says, and tomorrow the laugh will be on me, like enough. 'Tis the ups and downs of a preacher's life.

"Corey's an unruly sheep—an old black ram—born for trouble as the sparks to fly upward. Before we get through with the old cuss, you may be thanking your lucky stars you didn't get him."

But old Giles Corey was not the only malcontent. There were many of the Salem Villagers who did not cotton to Samuel Parris. He was not common enough. He was high in the instep and strait-laced; and worst of all, he was unpleasantly insistent when his salary was not paid according to contract.

More and more, throughout the colony, the minister's pay was becoming a sore subject. The New Englander did not like to pay taxes, and he particularly disliked paying the minister's rate if he did not like the minister. But the heart of the trouble was the growing opposition to the theocracy.

The ungodly were demanding religious liberty—not only freedom to worship God, but freedom to worship or not as their hearts desired. Only a few rugged souls dared put the matter in plain words. Perhaps they themselves did not quite understand what the meat of the controversy was. Old Giles Corey had the very kernel of it when he defied Parris:

"When I want to sin I want to sin: and I doan't want any non-sinners tellin' me when I can and when I can't!"

It was the challenge of the heretic. Democracy was bubbling and the lid of the kettle would not stay down.

As the cold increased, it appeared that there was a misunderstanding about the minister's wood, which was a part of his salary. The big parsonage, with its four fireplaces, took a lot of wood in a New England winter if the minister was to live like a gentleman: and Parris made it very clear that he had no intention of living otherwise.

The contributions in money and country pay fell off also; though after each service, as was the custom, the deacon would say:

"Brethren, there is now time left for contributing, wherefore, as God hath prospered you, so freely offer."

Perhaps, now and then, the merchant side of Parris got the better of the minister, as he looked down at the stingy contributions.

He had spent too many years as a merchant to be tolerant of the easygoing, unbusinesslike habits of the farmers. To him a bargain was a bargain. He spoke in no uncertain terms when his salary was in arrears and dribbled in from week to week, or when the country pay glutted him with knurly apples and cow pumpkins, with scarcely enough side-pork to grease the pot and a side of goat-mutton was given him instead of the steer's hindquarter that had been promised him.

Nor did it help Samuel much to know that his plight was no worse (in fact, much better) than that of many of his brother ministers. The gospel said the laborer was worthy of his hire, and he for one intended to live in comfort or know the reason why.

The constant shortage of firewood irked him more than anything else. There had been bickering about that from the first. The parish had offered him £6 extra salary if he would furnish his own wood, and he had reluctantly consented to try it for a year. But as it turned out, he didn't get even his regular salary, to say nothing about extras, and he didn't get the firewood either. He had lived too long in the tropics to tolerate the chill of the New England countryside swept by the raw east wind.

But there came a time when all these minor complaints were blotted out by something far more serious.

At a parish meeting almost two years after his ordination, the parish sought to repudiate their conveyance of the parsonage to Samuel Parris, though the matter was duly recorded in the parish record book.

It was a beautiful basis for a quarrel. Originally, the land had been donated to the parish for a ministry house and the parish had no right to convey it away. But when the time came that the parish wanted to offer special inducements to the minister of their choice, they calmly voted to make void and of no effect the entailment. They were farmers with no knowledge of the law. They knew what they wanted to do and doubtless never questioned their right to make the conveyance.

Parris, relying on their action, came to the village and moved into the parsonage, and it was not until much later that the question of his ownership came up. When it did it set the village on fire.

Parris had no mind to give up what he felt was rightfully his. The village tried to bind him to an earlier vote (which he had refused to accept) by which he was to find himself firewood and keep the ministry house in repair. His high temper flared and he said in his wrath that he neither heard nor knew anything of it, neither could nor would he take up with it or any part of it. For good measure he added that they were knaves and cheaters that entered it, and stalked out of the meetinghouse declaring:

"I am free from the people and the people free from me!"

This was no proper way for a minister to talk, of course, and made matters worse than ever. For Parris would not budge an inch on his claim to the parsonage. The brethren who had executed the coup rallied around the minister, if only in self-defense. The old factions took up arms again; the old quarrels and grievances took on a sharper edge. Once more the church was split by the devil's wedge of contention.

34

Hobgoblins

Who would believe what strange bugbears
Mankind creates itself, of fears, . . .
For fear does things so like a witch,
'Tis hard t' unriddle which is which.
—BUTLER, *Hudibras,* 1678.

HINGS were going very badly in the ministry house in the winter of 1691. The shortage of firewood had driven the minister out of the sacred quiet of his study into the living room, where the various activities of the household were carried on and Bettie and Nabbie whispered and giggled under Elizabeth's admonitions to be good and quiet.

Samuel's patience was worn thin, and as soon as supper was well out of the way he would pack the girls off to bed to be rid of them. There they would be out of the way and safe, he told himself, and their foolish chatter would not drive him distracted.

At bedtime Elizabeth would tiptoe in to see that they were asleep and warmly tucked in. Then the household would settle down to darkness and dreams. But little maids with enterprising minds cannot sleep all evening and all night, too. And all unbeknown, after their elders were asleep, the children's adventure began.

It was Mary Walcott who thought of it. She had hung around and watched while the ministry house was building, and she knew a *secret* that nobody else but the carpenter and Mr. Burroughs knew. There was a secret staircase and a secret room, snug and warm, in the heart of the great chimney cluster. There they could sit as late as they pleased, with Tituba telling ghost tales and old Goody Good calling up "sperrits"—nobody would know.

There were many houses in New England which had such hiding places to afford protection from Indian attacks when a house might almost any day have to be a fortress. People knew about some of them; but the ministry house had kept its secret well. Mr. Burroughs, who planned the chamber, had left the village in bad temper; the carpenter had moved away; and Mary had almost forgotten about the place until the Circle meetings began—then she remembered. Sometimes they met at Good's, but her poor shack was too cold. Sometimes they went to Mistress Putnam's, but there was always the danger of neighbors dropping in. So, in the nick of time, Mary remembered; and with finger on her lips, she extorted solemn promises never to tell a living soul, and revealed her secret to Nabbie and Bettie—and Tituba.

The way to the secret chamber was an adventure in itself. One first went into the black room back of the chimney: a big windowless closet with doors opening into each of the upstairs chambers and a cubbyhole into the lean-to storeroom where the slaves slept. There were broken chairs and trundle beds in it, and quilting frames hobnobbed with garlands of dried apples and corn hung by the husks to dry. The thrill of feeling around for the secret spring which let one into the holy of holies was an ecstatic one to the girls. It was like a bottomless black hole with a winding stair leading down down down into depths of darkness and finally landed one in the cellar in a snug warm chamber in the center of the chimney stack, with stone walls and a tiny fireplace in one corner.

Here on many a winter night, the Circle met, huddling about a tiny blaze of charcoal or faggots while Tituba told the eight girls weird tales of the Caribbees. Elizabeth complained of the noise and said that there must be bats in the chimney, but John Indian could never find any. Samuel was too wrapped up in his own troubles to pay heed to trifles.

The Circle meetings were more and more exciting. Tituba could read your palm and tell what kind of girl you were and when you would be wed. Old Good could hold her hands tight against your forehead and mumble an outlandish lingo and put you to sleep—and when you woke up everybody would laugh and tell you the funny things you did while you were asleep. Old Good was a poor woman who often came during the day to beg food from Elizabeth. Elizabeth was kind, but Bettie and Nabbie knew that most of the neighbors were suspicious and disdainful of her. So when she came to the ministry house for food, they never by word or expression let on what went on in the secret chamber by nights. Mary Walcott could see pictures in the water in a black kettle—sometimes pictures of things that had happened and sometimes things that were going to happen. And after the meetings were over, the girls would go to bed and dream the strangest things—and sometimes the dreams would come true.

It was very mysterious and sometimes very frightening. Most of the girls were almost grown up and said: Pooh, they weren't scared! But Nabbie and Bettie would scurry up the crooked little stairs and through the black room and jump into bed with the covers pulled up over their heads and hug each other tight—tight—tight—so that the black man wouldn't get them. Tituba had known of folkses (even big folkses) that were carried off to nobody knew where by goblins—and never seen again. She would shake her turbaned head and say solemnly:

"An effen yuh evah tells yuh pappies er yo' mammies any of de secret signs—wo-be-yuntuh-yuh!"

The time came when Nabbie couldn't stand the excitement any longer; and in the middle of a dark January night she began to scream and scream. Samuel and Elizabeth came running in, in their long white nightgowns. At the sight of them Bettie began to shriek too: and both of them kicked the covers off and hid themselves under the bed babbling strange words that Samuel said were neither Latin nor Greek nor Hebrew nor any other tongue he ever heard of.

Elizabeth tried to soothe them, but they were out of their heads completely and screeched when she came near them, not knowing who she was. Tituba heated water in big kettles to bathe them and put hot stones at their feet, but nothing did any good.

Then Samuel sent John Indian posthaste through the snow for Dr. Griggs, the new doctor who had come occasionally to Salem Village after Dr. Swinnerton had died in December. Dr. Griggs was a grandfatherly old man with big wooden-rimmed spectacles and a long white beard. He made the children drink a medicine made of powdered peony seeds dissolved in wine which restored their wits and comforted their senses and made them forget the nightmare. He left a tiny package of root of the male peony to be given them with all their drinks and broths. He was very kind and told them of the ancient physician who first took knowledge of the herb which took its name from that good old man: Paeon. The medicine seemed to help the children at first. They became still and quiet before the good doctor had finished his story about Paeon and his herbs. But almost as soon as the doctor was gone they began to have fits again; and Elizabeth had to lie with them in their bed till morning patting and comforting them.

When daylight came, their fears left them, but a night or two later the fits came on again. That time Dr. Griggs was sorely troubled and said he feared the children were under an evil hand.

Only then did Samuel mention the tales which had been told about the former occupants of the ministry house: the two wives of Mr. Burroughs, Mrs. Lawson and her child, the slave boy, Corythus. At that Dr. Griggs looked very grave indeed. Being newly come to the village, he had heard naught of the trouble, he said, but the matter looked bad. It might be as in the time of our Lord: This kind goeth not out but by prayer and fasting.

Parris, badly frightened, and having kept a fast by himself without success, sent for Mr. Hale and Mr. Noyes and Mr. Lawson to join him in a day of fasting and prayer; requesting that they come privately and make no mention to anyone of the curse that had once more fallen on the ministry house.

He had thought of sending to Mr. Cotton Mather for aid, but Dr. Griggs advised against it, pursing up his lips and puffing out his cheeks in his best professional manner.

"Mr. Cotton Mather is a busy man and his zeal is not always according to knowledge," he said. "Not that I am in any way belittling Mr. Cotton Mather, you understand, but confidentially I may say that I think him too young a man to handle a case of this kind with discretion."

"But the Goodwin girl was healed and restored," Samuel protested, his jealousy of Mather put aside in his emergency.

The doctor puffed his cheeks again. "Aye! And so also, if my memory serves me, were her brother and sisters who were not under Mr. Mather's care.

"But there is a man in Boston, Deacon Sanderson, who is so fortunate as to possess a copy of Perkins's *Discourse of the Damned Art of Witchcraft*. That book is the best authority in England. I believe the deacon would be willing to lend it to you in your necessity. Meanwhile we will continue constant in prayer, putting our faith in the Great Physician."

The news of the trouble at the parsonage spread and the villagers hastened to offer consolation and help. Everybody had a different remedy which had given relief to someone similarly afflicted.

Samuel shut himself up in his study to fast and pray, and between the visitors and the children Elizabeth was almost distracted.

In one way, however, the affliction brought a blessing. Parishioners whose rates were long overdue brought in contributions in country pay: a bushel of turnips; a sack of ground corn; a side of hog meat; a steer's hindquarter; and countless wild pigeons and rabbits and a turkey or two. The most welcome of all was a huge sledload of oak wood from an unexpected source: Giles Corey.

He saved his face by explaining to Elizabeth that the wood was to pay his wife's obligations; but it was plain to be seen that he was fairly eaten up by curiosity in regard to the bewitchment. He told of cases he had known in his native Yorkshire long ago. His gaunt frame was tense with emotion and his pale-blue eyes were fierce as a hawk's as he denounced the devil and his agents. His wonder tales frightened Elizabeth almost to death, so that she cried after he was gone.

Later the same day Goodwife Corey came. "Giles telled me he'd ben to see you," she said, "an' I jest had to ride over an' tell you not to take to heart anything he said. Giles is an old fool about bewitchments. He sees Old Horny in every bush, seems like." She patted Elizabeth's shoulder. "Jest put your trust in the Lord Jesus, dearie. He healed the sick and cast out demons when He was on earth, and His power is just the same today. Satan has no power beyond what the Blessed Lord gives him, dearie, and the Lord never telled him he could torment His little ones. Suffer the little ones to come unto me, he says, dearie. An' He'll guard 'em, never you fear.

"I don't hold with them as sees witches in ev'ry untoward hap'nin'. I'm past threescore an' I never yet did see a witch, an' never expect to—not in a Christian land. Mebbe they have 'em in heathendom—but not in the Lord's own Zion. Never fear, dearie. The Lord is mindful of His own."

Elizabeth, being a minister's daughter and a minister's wife, knew well enough that such a philosophy was heresy, for if one disbelieved in witches 'twas only a step to disbelieving in the devil, and the next thing one knew one wouldn't put faith in God either. But she found comfort in it. And she could not but feel that Martha was a woman of faith, for before she left she dropped on her knees before the hearth and went to prayer, with a simple assurance that seemed to bring the Lord Jesus right into the room, with His hand outstretched to heal and save.

35

Rebecca Nurse

I never knew her harm a fly,
And witch or not, God knows,—not I.
I know who swore her life away;
And as God lives, I'd not condemn
An Indian dog on word of them.
—WHITTIER, *Mabel Martin.*

IN THE prime of her youth when Rebecca Nurse had come to Salem, she was very tall, and carried herself proudfully as if she were better than her neighbors. But half a century of pioneer life and the bearing of nine children and bending over washtubs and ovens and cradles and trundle beds and pitifully small mounds in the burying ground had bowed the proud shoulders, so that now she had to hold her head well back, that she might still look the world in the face.

Time had blurred the sharp features. The brow had deep furrows. The sagging cheeks had lost their firm contour and the mouth dropped a little at the corners when she was tired or sad. The keen black eyes had faded and retreated into their sockets from which they peered out sharply at the dimming world, with a startling expression of alertness and interest in the affairs of herself and her neighbors.

Some years earlier she had worn the clumsy spectacles of the period, but recently her sight had improved surprisingly, so that she could see better than some of her daughters, and was always ready to thread the needles at the quilting bees. The women gossiped about it over their work and some said that she had second sight and could see better than she ever could. Sometimes there was a queer, far-off look in her faded eyes as if she could see things hidden or long past or even yet to come, which God-fearing folks were not supposed to see.

And when that stripling grandson of hers strayed away into the darks woods and down the ravines, it was always she who went to seek him, with that eerie call of hers—"Ei-ei-oe-aye"—and the two of them would come wandering home with their arms full of flowers and plants and laughing together as happy as fools.

When the village church was organized with Samuel Parris as its pastor, Francis Nurse and his sons put down their names. But not so Rebecca, who said:

"I've set under Mr. Higginson more 'n thirty years an' seems like I wouldn't feel to home settin' somewheres else. An' I don't much cotton to Mr. Parris his way o' preachin' for one thing. An' for another, 'tis hard to look up to a preacher that's young enough to be my son.

"John Higginson's a plain man that's lived amongst us all his life an' knows what we've ben through. When he prays, I kin jest shut my eyes an' see the heavenly gates openin'. An' then too, I've set in that same pew ever sence the new meetin'house were built twenty year agone, an' the corner jest fits the lame spot in my back. Them backless benches in the village—there ain't no comfort in 'em."

Though Rebecca kept her membership in the First Church in Salem, fate decreed that she should sit more often in the village meetinghouse. Her husband and children were stanch supporters of Mr. Parris and with all the family going to the village, it was inconvenient to convey Mother several miles in the other direction on a Sabbath morning.

Besides, as the menfolks thriftily urged, why pay a rate in the village and in Salem Town too? So Rebecca worshiped in the village, and the Committee did her the honor of seating her on the same bench with Mistress Mary Verin Putnam, widow of Thomas Putnam, who until his death three years before had been the head of the Putnam clan. Out of respect for the age and dignity of the two women, the bench was provided with a back and a cushion.

Rebecca Nurse was a good neighbor, and when the news of the trouble at the ministry house reached her, she lost no time in going to the aid of the parson's wife. Nor did she go empty-handed. Though her husband's rate had been paid in full, she tucked about her in the sled a cheese, a roll of freshly churned butter, a crock of quince preserves, and a goodly assortment of dried and powdered herbs, which might be useful in illness.

After Elizabeth had described the symptoms of the afflicted children, Goodwife Nurse nodded in an I-told-you-so way.

"Hm, hm, I ain't one bit surprised. 'Tis them Circle meetin's they ben havin', Mis' Parris. Sech things is of the devil an' best let be. I don't blame the children, poor innocents, but it's no time to mince words, an' the minister should've known 'twas playin' with the deil's fire. But I s'pose he hated to speak out—her bein' sech a prominent member. An' you and him bein' newcomers didn't know what I know."

She pulled her chair a little closer.

"Mis' Parris, I hate to speak agin a neighbor, but Ann Putnam ain't all she'd oughta be someways. She means well enough, I guess mebbe, but the Carrs was all a bit weak in the upper story. She was sister to Mis' Bayley, the wife o' the first minister at the village, you know, an' they was both flighty and always follerin' after first one whimsey an' then another. She was jest a young maid when Mis' Bayley brought her here to live with her. Mr. Bayley built a house over Putnam Hill way; an' Ann Carr (she was then) set her cap fer young Tom Putnam and made a good match—someways. Tom's smart and quick to turn a penny, an' I s'pose he's the richest man in the village since his father died. Fer a Putnam, Tom ain't so bad. He's allus spoiled Ann—had to to keep the peace, I reckon.

"Well, this winter she's got that fortunetellin' befoolment in her head. (They tell me the malady's bein' spread through the colony by travelin' quacks an' tricksters, I dunno.)"

Elizabeth sighed wearily: "Goodwife Nurse, I haven't slept for three nights, and I can't think very well; but I haven't the faintest idea in the world what you are talking about. Won't you please begin at the beginning and tell me what the minister and I ought to know?"

Rebecca Nurse peered at her with her keen old eyes. Finally she spoke: "Mis' Parris, I don't know how in the world you can be tellin' the truth—but I believe you be. I'll tell you all I know.

"The first was when John Procter stopped by one night, madder 'n a wet hen. He was out of all patience with these Circle meetin's he sez, an' 'was agoing to the village to bring Mary Warren, the jade, home; for, if let alone, these girls would make us all devils and witches together quickly. They should rather be had to the whipping post.' But he would fetch his jade home, and thrash the devil out of her. He said there was some young wenches practicin' palm readin' and conjurin' tricks an' scarin' themselves into fits.

"Well, then one night a week or so later, mebbe, I was comin' home past midnight from settin' up with Goodwife Peabody, who was havin' her fourth, an' I met three-four young females traipsin' down the road from Tom Putnam's. An' old Osburn was with 'em. You know how none of us cotton to her after the way she behaved when her proper husband died—going an' marryin' that Irish redemptioner she bought to work her farm. I know she's seen a heap o' trouble in her time, but that don't lessen her carryin's-on none.

"Well, when they see me they was that scared they begin to screech and thought I were a hant. I stopped 'em an' ast 'em what they was adoin' gaddin' about that time o' night when decent folks was abed an' rogues ajoggin'. An' when I see Mary Walcott among 'em and Dr. Griggs's niece I said I'd tell the minister. And then your Nabbie sung out at me:

"'Yi, yi, Old Granny Nurse, the minister knows all about it and some o' the time we meet at our house. So now, Old Meddle-fingers!! Tell him if you want!'"

Elizabeth gasped: "Why, they never met here. Surely you are mistaken, Goodwife Nurse. It couldn't have been Nabbie. She and Bettie are always in bed betimes."

Rebecca Nurse snorted: "Then they git up agin! My eyes ain't so far gone yit thet I don't know your two little maids, Mistress Parris. There was a wanin' moon, an' snowlight. And Abigail had on her new white Sabbath hood—though 'twere on a Thursday. An' ef that wan't enough, that Injun wench o' yourn wuz with 'em."

Her voice softened at the bewilderment on Elizabeth's face. "There, now, Mis' Parris, don't take it so to heart! 'Tis plain to be seen you never knowed a thing about it. But when you've raised as many young'uns as I have, you'll learn you have to keep your eyes open day an' night. Young'uns that age—jest goin' over Fool's Hill—are the very Old Harry fer tricks. You gotta watch 'em every minute an' you can't take nothin' fer granted.

"But the Lord is good. He forgives our sins and most of our foolishness too."

From upstairs there came the thumping sound of a fall and a childish shriek of terror.

Elizabeth sprang up as Samuel came running down the stairs, calling: "Come, Elizabeth! Nabbie is having her fits again." Then, as he saw Rebecca Nurse: "Oh, Goodwife Nurse, we are sorely stricken. Will you come up and see the children? 'Tis said you are a great hand at sickness—perhaps you could tell us what to do."

But Goodwife Nurse was edging toward the door as fast as her stiff old legs would carry her. She looked frightened and her voice cracked.

"Nay, nay, Mr. Parris, don't ask me that! I couldn't bear to see 'em, poor young'uns. Hearin' 'em is bad enough and folks say 'tis awful to behold. I pity 'em with all my heart and go to God for 'em. But I had fits myself once when I had the greensickness an' I don't want to have 'em agin."

Parris shut the door after the departing guest. He shut it hard, and ran upstairs after Elizabeth to do something—anything—he had no idea what—to relieve the afflicted children.

He felt outraged and indignant at Rebecca Nurse. The affliction was bad enough, God knew, without a person's acting as if 'twere leprosy or the black death! He had never heard that fits were catching!

But a few days later he was not so sure. Little Ann Putnam and Mary Walcott were having fits too!

When Samuel Parris heard Goodwife Nurse's account of the Circle meetings, he went into action. Palmistry and conjuring tricks and Tituba's heathen lore! The whole fantastic tale bore out the doctor's diagnosis of witchcraft.

Questioning little Bettie proved worse than useless. She only stared at him with terror-stricken eyes, like a frightened baby rabbit, and sobbed and shivered and finally fainted.

Leaving her to her mother's ministrations, he started on Abigail. At first she was pert and saucy and defied him, her black eyes (so like his own) snapping fire.

"I won't tell, Uncle Samuel. It's a *secret* and you can't ever make me tell! Not if you torture me and shut me in a dungeon for a thousand years till my bones rot! I won't! I won't!! I won't!!! I won't!!!!"

Samuel took her by the shoulders and shook her till her teeth chattered. His face was white with anger and his voice so hard and stern it sounded like a stranger's.

"Now, you saucy little baggage! Out with it and talk fast! Tell me who 'tis that afflicts you. Quick! Before the cat gets your tongue!"

At this dreadful threat Abigail shrieked and clapped her hand over her mouth to avert such a dire calamity. In a muffled voice she wailed:

" 'Twas Tituba!"

"Who else?" Parris pursued his inquisition. Between sobs she mumbled, "Old Good—and Osburn."

Parris stamped down the stairs. He found Tituba in the kitchen.

"Come with me!" he ordered.

Grimly he led the way to the barn, Tituba following in frightened silence. Once inside, he shut the door and fastened it. Still without a word, he took his riding crop from its peg by the door.

"So!" he barked. "It is you who have been raising the devil and bewitching my children. At your old tricks again after all I've done for you! You . . . snake!"

Tituba dropped on her knees and groveled before him.

"Oh, Mas' Sam! Oh, Mas' Sam! Oh, Mas' Sam! Ah nevuh done 'witched nobody!

> By Sain' Petuh, by Sain' Paul,
> By de livin' Gawd of all,
> Ah nevah put 'em so!"

Parris did not speak. He raised the whip and brought it down on her cowering shoulders—once—twice—thrice. He held his hand. In the nineteen years he had owned the wench it was the first time he had struck her, he never even struck a dog.

He waited. She spoke again, shivering:

"Ah nevah put duppy on 'em foh true, Mas' Sam! Ah nevah goed foh to hurt 'em. Ah woun't hurt Li'l Bettie—Ah love

Bettie . . . Ah jes' lookt in dey han's an' telled 'em whut de lines
said—an' mebbe sometimes numerated li'l tales to 'stonish 'em
. . . das all . . . Mas' Sam. Hones-ta-Gawd, das all!"

"What kind of tales?" Parris snapped. "Devil tales?"

No answer. Tituba rocked and wailed and shivered with cold
and fright.

The whip came down again—once—twice—thrice—with a
deadly rhythm.

"Oh, Mas' Sam! Foh true Ah din't go foh to hurt 'em. Des
li'l spook tales . . . an' mebbe 'bout witches an' hants an' sech
. . . an' whut Ol' Satum does to folks effen he cotch 'em unnah
wares . . . Des ord'nry li'l tales . . . Hones-ta-Gawd, Mas'
Sam, das all! By Sain' Petuh—"

Parris cut her short. "Just little harmless tales that scared
them into fits!" he snarled.

But Tituba cried out in protest.

"No, no, Mas' Sam! Ah nevah did nuffin' bout does fits, so
he'p me! 'Twas ol' Good put 'em so by some sleighty trickses Ah
doan know nuffin' bout. Huh putted huh han's on dey haids some
curus way an' stroket 'em to sleep . . . an' tol 'em whut to do
w'en dey woked up—an' foh Gawd dey done it." Her eyes
glowed with admiration. " 'Twas wunnerful, Mas' Sam, hit suah
was. But Ah neveh coun't figuah out how-all huh done it."

Parris resorted to a trick question.

"How do you know they were bewitched, if you had no hand
in it?"

Tituba hesitated, her eyes rolling. The whip fell again. She
screamed.

"Wait, Mas' Sam! Ah'll tell. Ah's jes' gittin' ready foh tuh
tell yuh! We-all wuz awonderin' effen dey wuz 'witched, an'
Mis' Sibley—you know Mis' Sibley youah chu'ch membah, huh's
a mighty good ooman—an' Mis' Sibley telled John Injun tuh
mek a li'l cake of oaten meal mixed wiv de chillun's watah an'
bake it in de ashes an' feed it tuh de dawg, an' effen de dawg got
sick de chillun wuz bewitched foh suah. An' Ah made de cake
des lak she say an' gived it to Moreover. And dat dawg Moreover
he was awful sick all ovah mah kitchin floah when Ah'd jes'
sanded it."

Parris caught her up quickly: "How did Mistress Sibley hear

of it? I told you not to talk of it, and you set the village afire with your foolish gabble."

Tituba wagged her head solemnly. "La, Mas' Sam, doan 'buke me! Effen Ol' Debbil stahts awukkin' he doan need Tituba to 'nounce it. He des snap he fingahs an' all he li'l imp-de-dumps fly up lak spahks in de chimley an' it's evvyone foh hissef an' de Lawd foh us all!"

Parris dared not keep the matter in the shade any longer. Why the Lord had visited this humiliation upon him and his house he did not know. It was a sore rebuke and very humbling providence. But since the course had come upon him, it was no time to palter or blink. The time for secrecy and dawdling was past. His only course in such an extremity was to drive matters to a crisis.

He rode to Salem and after a conference with the ministers there it was decided to lay the thing before the magistrates. Sickness and sin were the province of the medical and clerical professions, but witchcraft had centuries before been declared a crime and put under the jurisdiction of the courts. It seemed beyond doubt that this must be witchcraft. But whatever it was, Parris felt relieved that it was out of his hands.

Four of the brethren, Joseph Hutchinson, Thomas Putnam, Edward Putnam, and Thomas Preston, yeomen of Salem Village, signed a complaint against Sarah Good, Sarah Osburn, and Tituba Indian for "injury done to the bodys of Elizabeth Parris, Abigail Williams and Ann Putnam, sundry times within two months."

The warrants read: "Charged with High Suspicion of Sundry Acts of Witchcraft and Wicked Arts . . . against the peace of Our Sovereign Lord and Lady, the King and Queen."

The minister of Salem Village was no longer responsible for the outcome. His heart was lighter than it had been for six weeks.

The constable did his duty. On the 29th of February, the three women, Good, Osburn, and Tituba, were arrested in the midst of a terrific out-of-season storm of thunder and lightning and rain. Along the village road people peered out from doors and windows, cowering in terror and awe. If any had questioned the guilt of the hags, they could no longer doubt this sign.

Somewhere up there, in the wild sky above them, God and the devil were battling for the souls of men!

Book Seven

Endor   1692

36

Three Hags of Darkness

> *Round about the cauldron go,*
> *In the poisoned entrails throw.*
> —SHAKESPEARE, *Macbeth.*

*M*ARCH came in like a lion. The tempest of the night before had ceased; but the morning dawned gusty and raw, with gray fog whipping inland from the sea. Cutting the murk with its strident call, a trumpet blared its summons to the meetinghouse.

From east, west, north, and south the people came flocking. From Rial Side to Andover, from Topsfield to Lynn, the pilgrims converged toward the meetinghouse where three hags of hell awaited judgment. In the crowd mind there was no doubt of the guilt of Old Good, Sarah Osburn, and Tituba Indian.

The meetinghouse was dim and damp with the fog. At the foot of the pulpit a rude platform had been set up where the magistrates sat in their robes of office. At their left was a chair for the prisoner. The Lord's table, stripped of its white linen cloth, was doing duty as a reporter's table.

Old Good was brought in first. Her hands were grimy and her hair, a tow-colored fuzz like the stuffing of a mattress, bushed out around her sallow face. Her eyes were bright and brown and glanced alertly from side to side like a chipmunk's. She spread out her draggled skirts and smoothed her apron. (She had made the constable wait while she rummaged for a clean one.)

A row of tall tallow candles threw their flickering light into the faces of the prisoners, the magistrates, and the clerk who sat at the denuded Lord's table, busily sharpening his quill.

Beyond the reach of the candles, in the outer darkness, the crowded seats and galleries were only a darker blur, with rows and rows of faces: ghastly gray phantoms in the murk. Up above among the beams and rafters a bat fluttered and now and then swooped downward into the regions of light.

Huddled together on the foreseat were three awe-struck little girls, clinging to each other's hands, their teeth chattering: the afflicted children—Ann Putnam, twelve; Abigail Williams, eleven; Elizabeth Parris, six years old.

The clerk stepped forward and read the charge:

. . . for injury done to the bodies of Elizabeth Parris, Abigail Williams, Ann Putnam, sundry times within two months, by Wicked Arts of Witchcraft.

The worshipful esquire John Hathorne, magistrate, leaned forward, his hands clutching the table. He was a spare man of sixty, with a stern Puritan face and black hair and eyes. As he moved, the row of candles cast his gigantic shadow on the walls— multiple shadows, grimacing and gesturing in a goblin panto- mime. When he put a question he looked hard at the prisoner, and his eyes jumped forward in their sockets, showing the white rim.

"Sarah Good, what evil spirit have you familiarity with?"

"None."

"Have you made no contracts with the devil?"

"No."

"Sarah Good, why do you hurt these children?"

"I do not hurt 'em. I scorn it!" (Her answers were in a wicked, spiteful manner.)

The children on the foreseat clung to each other, whimpering. Magistrate Hathorne turned his staring eyes on them. They clutched each other, crying and sobbing. Behind them was a confused sound of scraping feet and grumbling voices. Ann Put- nam fell on the floor and the other two fell on top of her, scream- ing and kicking.

Hathorne's voice rose stern above the clamor: "Sarah Good, do you not see what you have done? Why do you torment these poor children?"

"I do not! I scorn it! What do I know? You brought in two more!"

"What is it you say when you go muttering away from persons' houses?"

"If I must tell, I will tell."

"Do tell us then."

"If I must tell, I will tell. It is the Commandments." She sniggered. "I may say my Commandments, I hope!"

"What Commandment is it?"

"If I must tell, I will tell." She leaned toward the judge, a cunning glitter in her eyes. "It is a psalm!"

Sarah Osburn was next brought in. Feeble in body and mind, her answers were driveling nonsense. But she had not been to meeting for a long time and such iniquity counted heavily against her. The scandal about her marriage also had turned the good-wives against her: she had disgraced not only herself but her sex by buying herself a husband. A woman who would do that would do anything.

Last of all came Tituba. Her dress of necessity was plain homespun, but she wore the gay new turban that Susanna Oxen-bridge had sent her from Boston, and around her neck (as a sub-stitute for the long-mourned jumbie beads) a double string of red holly berries. Where had they come from, at the end of a New England winter? Only Tituba knew.

After the third degree that Parris had given her, she was keenly aware of her danger. Her eyes were alert and her hands twisted nervously in her lap. Judge Hathorne began by assuming her guilt.

"Why do you hurt these poor children?"

But Tituba denied and evaded, parrying his thrusts like a skilled fencer, until she forced him back into generalities.

Who hurt them? It might be the devil, for aught she knew.

What was he like? (The room held its breath.) Tituba's eyes were deep wells of mystery as she sought for words to describe the occult.

"Like a man—Ah think. Yestiddy Ah ben in de lean-to cham-bah—Ah saw a thing—like a man—dat tol' me serve him, an' Ah tol' him No! Ah woun't doe soe!"

The room shuddered and caught its breath. Hathorne's eyes were like doorknobs. Now they were cutting the knot. His questions came hard and fast. "What about Good and Osburn? And were there others?" The magistrate's quill almost burnt the paper in his haste to set down the answers.

"What other likenesses besides a man hath appeared to you?"

"Sometimes like a great black dog—four times . . . They told me serve him . . . that was the Black Dog."

Samuel Parris turned pale. It was the Black Dog which appeared to the witch of Edmonton. Tituba had never heard of the Witch of Edmonton—and yet—the tale ran true to form!

Hathorne was a glutton for evidence and Tituba gave him all he wanted.

Yes, there was night-riding: "Ah ride upon a stick or pole, and Good and Osburn behind me; we ride takin' hold of each othah. Ah din't see no trees—no path—but suddenly was theah, when we wuz up."

There was a Thing that had wings and two legs and a head like a woman and "a Thing all ovah hairy; all de face hairy, an' a long nose. Ah doan know how tuh tell how he face looks. Wiv two legs it goes upright an' it's two-three foot high. An' las' night it stood in Mas' Parris his hall."

There was "a man wiv black cloaths, an' a tall man wiv white hair."

Tituba bent forward toward the magistrate, and all the drama of her race was in her deep tones:

"Las' night dey tell me Ah mus' kill Mas' Putnam's chile wiv a knife. Ah mus' cut off she haid!"

Little Ann Putnam let out a screech and grabbed her little noodle with frantic hands.

Samuel Parris rose from his seat. He thought he knew his Tituba.

"Judge, may I put a question?"

Hathorne consented. Parris fixed his eyes on the witness.

"Tituba, look at me! Why did you not tell me these things when I asked you? None of your lies now!"

The slave tossed her head insolently. She was drunk with the heady liquor of fame. The big judge admired her story; and the big judge said if she confessed he wouldn't hang her for a witch.

The stripes of her master's whip still smarted—but Mas' Sam dassent touch her now. She looked at him, big-eyed.

"Fo' Gawd, Mas' Sam, Ah was agwine foh tuh tell yuh—but dey won't let me. Dey say effen Ah tells, mah haid will be cut off!" She illustrated in pantomime.

"De man an' Good an' Osburn's wife, dat's whut dey all say!

An' Goody Good she come tuh me at prayuh time an' stopt mah years an' won't let me heah when mah massa wuz at prayuh."

Parris sank back in his seat. As well try to stop a mad Atlantic gale! The hand of God lay heavy upon him; Satan was let loose in his own household. He would do what he could to see justice done, but the outcome was in the hands of a higher power.

He wasted no pity on the three hags who had brought such affliction upon his children: they were guilty as hell!

Before he slept he wrote a letter to Mr. Deodat Lawson, minister at Scituate:

Dear Bro. in Christ: God in His wisdom hath again let loose Satan in this Parish. Witch Craft hath broke out in ye Ministrye-House by ye Affliction of my Little Daughter & Niece. Likewise ye dau. of Thos. Putnam & others.

'Tis hinted by some, ye Ministrye-House hath an ill Repute from ye beginning: by ye Death of Mr. Burroughs his two wives & your wife & Child, by some enigmatical cause.

Seeing you have ye repute of a Larned Scolar in these matters, wee Pray You come to Oure Aide. Bringe alle you maye have by *Waye* of *Authorities* & Bee Prepared to Preach to Us.

Yrs Most Respectfully,
SAM. PARRIS.

On the same day Parris received from Deacon Sanderson of Boston Mr. Perkins's *Discourse on ye Damned Art of Witchcraft*, which Dr. Griggs had recommended.

37

Scattered Firebrands

Fire burn and cauldron bubble,
Trouble, trouble, trouble, trouble.
                          —SHAKESPEARE.

IT WAS ten o'clock on a dour March morning. Elizabeth Parris stood in the middle of the big hall, trying to bring her mind back to ordinary living after three hectic days. Little Bettie was in bed, heavy-eyed and feverish from excitement and the chill of the dank meetinghouse. Nabbie had run off—to Deacon Ingersoll's or the Walcott's most likely. Elizabeth hoped she was in good hands but she was too weary to search for her.

She'd only be underfoot if she was here, she thought, or having fits and getting Bettie all stirred up again. I ought to go seek her—but I just can't.

This room's a disgrace. But with Tituba in jail and John Indian having fits all over the place and rolling around like a hog, I don't see how the good Lord can blame me if I have to let things slide. I surely hope nobody comes till I get the dishes done.

She caught up a wooden bucket and ran out through the shed to the well. The sweep was heavy and the full bucket was heavy and as she tried to hurry the water slopped, making untidy little puddles on the sanded floor. She filled the big kettle, stirred the logs till they blazed briskly, and started scraping yesterday's greasy leavings off the wooden trenchers.

The knocker sounded a gentle tap-tap and the door was pushed open before Elizabeth could wipe her hands. A tall, thin woman came in—Mistress Stephen Sewall, wife of the clerk of the court at Salem Town. Elizabeth knew her casually, but they were not close friends.

If people would only stay at home and leave me alone, she thought resentfully. She tried to be mannerly in greeting this unwelcome guest, hoping her voice would not betray her.

Mistress Sewall took both her hands. Her brown eyes looked deep into Elizabeth's. The friendliest eyes I ever saw, Elizabeth thought. Her voice was like her eyes, friendly and calm. She was taking off her hood and cloak.

"I'm glad I got here in time to do dishes." She smiled. "Your kettle's bilin', Elizabeth—my name is Margaret."

Elizabeth began to laugh foolishly. It seemed to her it had been a long time—days and days—since she had laughed. Now she was started she couldn't stop. Mistress Sewall doing dishes in her messy kitchen seemed the funniest thing in the world. Margaret didn't take notice. She hung her cloak and hood on a peg behind the door and began dipping hot water from the big kettle into a greasy pan.

"It beats all how things do stack up, don't it? These look like Francis Nurse's trenchers, they be so smooth. He's a right good workman, ain't he?"

The visitor must have brought good luck, for the dishes were all done, the room tidied, and dinner in the pot before Bettie woke.

"Let me go up," Margaret said.

"No, no! She's timid with strangers,—she's seen so many lately, poor child!"

"If she's afraid of me, she'll be the first young'un I ever see that were. You just sit down a bit and let me try."

She went up the stairs and opened the bedroom door. Bettie was sitting up in bed, her face flushed and frightened. She stared at the stranger.

Margaret Sewall stepped inside, smiling. She left the door open. "Mother says dinner is most ready. Do you smell it?"

Bettie's nose twitched like a bunny's. But she was still staring. "Are you a witch?" she asked.

"Do I look like a witch?"

The child considered. "No-o, you look like a horse."

Margaret Sewall's lips quirked humorously: "That's what I've always thought myself, but nobody else ever told me so. Do you like horses?"

"I don't like Punch but I like old Judy."

"Do I look like Punch or Judy?"

"You look like Judy. Your big brown eyes and your long

nose. Punch rolls his eyes and pops 'em out at me—like Judge Hathorne."

Margaret Sewall choked and changed the subject.

"Can you guess what's for dinner?"

Bettie sniffed. "Mutton stew—and carrots—"

"And dumplin's," Mrs. Sewall added. "Shall I help you dress?"

"I can do all but the apron that ties behind," Bettie boasted, hopping out of bed. "Is Father come yet?"

"He rode to Beverly to see Mr. Hale, and won't be back till late evening, likely."

Bettie looked frightened again. "Will he be gone after dark? Will the witches get him?"

"Mercy no, child! Witches dare not hurt a minister. They'd run like Old Splitfoot for fear of him."

Before the afternoon was over, Mrs. Sewall had persuaded Elizabeth to let Bettie come to stay with her until the excitement was over.

"I watched her yesterday at the trials," she said, "and the poor moppet was scared out of her wits. She is not like Ann and Abigail. Some young'uns thrive on thrills, but 'twill well-nigh kill Bettie—or drive her quite distracted."

Elizabeth knew she was right. Bettie was a sensitive child and the terrors of the past few days had made her really ill. Yet to send her away would doubtless look strange and bring Samuel under censure. He would not approve, she felt sure, and he might be angry. At last she begged the question by leaving the decision to Bettie herself. God would judge between them by the choice of the innocent child.

"If she will go with you of her own desire, take her. However it turns out, I shall never forget your help and kindness this day. I have felt so terribly alone. Samuel—any man, I suppose —cannot understand. You came to me in my trouble, a stranger. We part firm friends. Just asking me to call you Margaret helps —I don't know why. I never had a sister, but no sister could have meant more to me than you have today, Margaret."

Mrs. Sewall went out into the yard where Bettie was playing with Moreover and put the question.

Bettie considered: "Do you have any little maids for me to play with?"

"Yes: there is a little maid (she would think you were a wonderful great girl) and a little lad who is learning to read his Absey Book, and a darling roly-poly baby named Susanna, with fuzzy red curls all over her head."

The baby decided it. "Could I hold her in my arms sometimes? Oh, goody! I want to go." Then the fear came back and she asked anxiously: "Are there any witches there?"

Margaret Sewall shook her head. "Witches in Salem Town? No, indeed!" Under her breath she added: "Not yet, thank God!"

Samuel came home tired and hungry. Elizabeth gave him what was left of the mutton stew and some hot corncake fresh from the oven.

"How are the children?" he asked between bites.

"Nabbie has been gone almost all day. She ran off without asking leave, and I couldn't find her, but Deliverance Walcott said she and Mary had gone out to Ann Putnam's. She came home just before sundown and was jumpy and fearful, but I gave her a supper of hot bread and milk and some of the gilliflower conserve Mistress Sewall brought, which she says is good for the falling sickness, and she soon went to sleep."

Samuel did not answer. He looked weary and troubled. Elizabeth doubted whether he had even heard. She went on determinedly.

"Mistress Sewall rode over from Salem and has been with me all the day. She has been wonderful helpful and kind."

Samuel roused himself. "Stephen Sewall's wife, you say? Her husband is one of the most important men in Salem and her father was the Reverend Jonathan Mitchell of Cambridge, a celebrated minister. I am very happy that she came, my dear. I trust you entertained her well." He glanced at her plain gown and rumpled apron.

"We got on very well together," she said demurely. "She is so simple and comfortable, and wondrous kind." She paused a moment, gathering her courage, but her voice was calm and matter-of-fact.

"She quite fell in love with our Bettie and Bettie with her. She took her home to stay with her until these dreadful trials are over. She says Bettie is too frail to bear up under all the excitement."

Samuel was all attention now.

"What's that? Took Bettie home with her? But that won't do, Elizabeth. You should have known better. Bettie is an important witness. She and Abigail and Ann must appear and testify against the accused. What will people say, if I, the minister, send my child away while others are afflicted? Two more were stricken today. My soul and body, Elizabeth, what were you thinking of?"

Elizabeth faced him. "I was thinking of Bettie, my child. She is too young, Samuel, to know her own mind or be a reliable witness. And she is a very sick little maid. (You don't realize, Samuel.) She was burning with fever all last night after the trials yesterday. I sat with her while you slept, bathing her little hot face with rosemary water to comfort her. Margaret Sewall offered to take her, wanted to take her; and Bettie wanted to go. 'Twas her own desire without a word from me. But I am so glad and thankful to have her safe away from the village."

Samuel held his temper. "I see, my dear. 'Tis a woman's way to let her heart run away with her head. I'm not blaming you; the Lord made women so. I can explain to Mr. Sewall how it came about and bring our Bettie back. No harm has been done."

Elizabeth flushed but her voice was low and gentle. "Bettie will stay with Margaret Sewall until I bring her home. I am her mother. If your witchcraft hangs on such frail shoulders, it may well fall."

Samuel's mind worked fast as it always did in a tight place. A father had complete control over his minor child and the mother had no rights. But what a laughingstock would the minister of Salem Village be if he invoked the law in a quarrel with his wife! Elizabeth could be very froward when she chose; and now she was firm set. There was still time to save his face if he spoke quickly.

"Why, my dear, I'd no idea you felt like that! You are tired and overwrought and unreasonable (little wonder with the heavy afflictions of the last few days) but if it means so much to you, we will say no more about it. It puts me in a very uncomfortable position, of course, but it's no use to argue with a woman."

He sprang up from the table without finishing his supper and went out into the night, too angry to stay under the same roof with his wife.

One word that she had spoken burned him to the quick. "My witchcraft, indeed!" he muttered as he strode down the road. "Does she think this frightful curse that has come upon us my doing? A raree-show got up for fools to marvel at?"

For the first time in his life with her, his Elizabeth had failed him. He was weary to the bone and longed for bed, but he tramped the half-frozen roads till long past midnight and then doubled himself up on the settle, still too angry to lie beside his wife.

Elizabeth, tossing restlessly in her lonely bed upstairs, had spoken the hateful pronoun without thought of malice and had no idea how she had hurt him.

"If he thinks I'll give in about Bettie because he champs the bit, he doesn't know me," she told herself stubbornly. "Bettie belongs to me—I don't care what the law says. Men make up laws to suit themselves, but God gives babies to the women because He knows they'll take care of 'em."

Deodat Lawson came Saturday, the 19th of March. Parris invited him to stay at the ministryhouse but he said he had already accepted Deacon Ingersoll's kind invitation to stay at his tavern. He did not wish to impose on Mistress Parris in such a time of trial. As a matter of fact, he had no wish to spend more time than necessary under the parsonage roof, after the stories he had heard. It did credit to his courage to come to the village at all, but his sturdy English temper did not shrink.

He found Salem Village in an uproar. Matha Corey had just been arrested and lodged in the village jail waiting till the Sabbath was past for a hearing. Before he had finished his early supper, Mary Walcott came to see him and was stricken with a fit, much to his amazement and discomfiture. John Indian, coming in a little later, rolled around on the floor, grunting and wallowing on his belly like a hog. Mr. Lawson left his supper half eaten and went to his room, where he barred the door and set a chair against it, while he knelt to implore God's mercy before keeping his appointment at the ministry house.

His prayers were interrupted by a knock: Deacon Ingersoll hoped he had made himself comfortable and Mr. Parris was below, awaiting his convenience.

When they arrived at the parsonage it was orderly and quiet. Elizabeth greeted him with polite concern as to his comfort: then she left him with Samuel in the study. (Since the witchcraft broke out there had been plenty of fire logs, if only John Indian could be made to bring them in.) The two men settled themselves before the hearth to discuss the subject in hand. Mr. Lawson's interest centered in the mysterious deaths in the parsonage. He recounted the symptoms of his wife and child; he recalled certain rumors about Mr. Burroughs and his family affairs. Parris in his turn told of his slave boy, stricken mysteriously within a week after they came to the village.

Suddenly Lawson, facing the entry and stairway, sprang to his feet with a cry: "Holy God!"

Parris whirled. A little figure in a long white robe was coming into the room. He spoke sharply:

"Abigail, go back to your bed!"

The child did not seem to hear. With eyes fixed and staring and limbs moving mechanically she approached the fire. Instinctively the men drew back out of her path. She passed between them, seemingly unconscious of their presence. On the hearth she paused, slim arms outstretched toward the flames; then slowly began to weave backward and forward, her limbs and body swayed by some inward rhythm like a pagan dance. Slowly at first, but faster and faster, she wove in and out in a mystic pattern. The leaping flames cast her shadow on the floor, the walls, and the ceiling. Her linen gown revealed in darker silhouette her slender, childish body in its gauzy draperies.

Even to Parris, who knew who she was, it was uncanny. To Lawson she seemed a disembodied spirit.

Samuel's mind went groping back through the years for a buried memory, which like the figure before his eyes danced just beyond his reach. At last he found it—the May-day morning on the hilltop where the fairest maiden danced beside the ancient stone.

And as in that earlier time, the movement of the dance quickened. Faster and faster the child whirled, snatching up firebrands and scattering them about the hearth; leaping high in a delirious whirl of frenzy as if she would vanish in the flames—till with a wild cry, "Wh-o-o-o-sh! Wh-o-o-o-sh!" she fell senseless.

Samuel knelt beside her, his hand on her heart. It seemed to have stopped.

"Water, quick!" he shouted.

Before the petrified Lawson could move, Elizabeth was kneeling on the hearth dashing water on the little white face and chafing the icy hands. The child moaned.

"Carry her upstairs, Samuel," Elizabeth said. Her voice was steady though her face was pale. "I thought she was asleep, so I came down to wash the dishes. She slipped through the entry and I didn't see her." She picked up the candle and led the way upstairs; Samuel followed.

The child he carried was limp as a rag doll.

As soon as the Sabbath was past, Martha Corey was brought up for hearing. Little Ann Putnam had complained against her. But old Giles really started the trouble by his angry bluster that time she hid his saddle so he couldn't go to the witch trials. He got there finally but too late to hear much: he was hopping mad at his woman and everybody within earshot knew it—little Ann Putnam among the rest.

By the next day Giles had got over his temper and felt terribly when the officers came and took Martha. He hadn't meant to hurt her. He didn't really think she was a witch; but he had never understood her very well and under cross-examination he let out several things that were used against her. There was an ox he thought was hipt—and a cat that had fits—and Martha spent more time prayin' than was needful—kneeling before the hearth after he had gone to bed. It bothered him and when he tried to pray he couldn't speak his desires. Another time he was "frighted in the cowhouse," and his wife found fault with him for saying, "Living to God and dying to sin," which apparently he cherished as an eminently proper and pious phrase.

Giles was honest but dumb, and once tangled in the mazes of the law and the prophets he hopelessly enmeshed his wife and himself also. But for the present he was let alone. There were bigger fish in the net than old Giles Corey.

There was a rumor that Rebecca Nurse was to be brought out. Elizabeth Procter heard it. (She was a sister of Judge Hathorne.)

"She must be warned," she told her husband. So the two of them went to Rebecca's house and found her in a weak and low condition in body, as she told them.

"I ha' been sick almost a week, but I bless God, I've had more of God's presence than sometime I have had, but not so much as I desire."

Then of her own accord she began to speak of the affliction that was among them, and in particular Mr. Parris his family.

"How I am grieved for them," she said, "though I ain't been to see 'em, by reason of fits I used to have, but I pity 'em with all my heart an' go to God for 'em."

She sat silent awhile, then went on again:

"I hear there be persons spoke of that are as innocent as I be, I do believe."

After much to this purpose, they told her she was spoken of also.

"Well," she sighed, "if it be so, the will of the Lord be done." She sat still awhile, being as it were amazed; and then she said: "Well, as to this thing I am as innocent as the child unborn; but surely what sin hath God found out in me unrepented of, that He should lay such an affliction upon me in my old age?"

Mr. Lawson preached in the village meetinghouse on the Lord's Day, March 20th. The people who heard him pronounced it a masterly sermon, a fearless attack on the prince of the power of the air.

But there was a shocking and disconcerting interruption just as he entered the pulpit. From a pew in the gallery where a row of little girls sat, Abigail Williams shrilled:

"Now stand up and name your text!"

The congregation gasped and Mr. Lawson looked up indignantly, almost dropping his sermon book. The child's eyes were shining with mischief and impudence—a saucy little girl thrown off her balance by too much spoiling and attention.

But even as the preacher's hands itched to spank her, he could not forget that scene on Sabbath Eve and the eerie dancing on the hearth. That was something very different from childish mischief! What it was he did not dare to think.

He caught at his dignity and announced his text:

And the Lord said unto Satan, The Lord rebuke thee, O Satan; even the Lord that hath chosen Jerusalem rebuke thee: is not this a brand plucked out of the fire?

His hands shook as he turned the pages. He was thinking of the scattered firebrands and that weird whistling "Wh-o-o-o-sh!" like the soughing of a ghostly wind.

Before the week ended Rebecca Nurse was arrested on complaint of Mistress Ann Putnam who was in great distress because of Goody Nurse's bewitching of her. The next day at the examination there was great disturbance, Mistress Putnam complaining much. The dreadful shrieking from her and others was very amazing.

The witches' brew was bubbling!

The next Sabbath Parris preached his first sermon on witchcraft. "The text," he said, "is from John's Gospel: 'Have I not chosen you twelve, and one of you is a devil?'"

Sarah Cloyse, sister of Rebecca Nurse, sat in her place, her mind harrowed by the events of the past week. She had come only by much persuasion, because it was Sacrament Day and her absence would be noticed. Her hands were locked together and an angry pulse throbbed in her throat.

The minister leaned forward over the pulpit, his eyes burning.

"Christ knows how many devils there are in His church, and who they are. Too often there are devils found among the saints.

"Terror to hypocrites who profess much love to Christ but are in league with their lusts. Oh, if there be any such among us today, forbear to come to the Lord's table, lest whilst the bread be between your teeth, the wrath of God come pouring down upon you!"

Sarah Cloyse could bear only so much. She sprang up and went out of the meeting, and slammed the meetinghouse door.

The congregation gasped and almost jumped out of their seats. But the minister only raised surprised eyes for a second and went on with his sermon.

38

In the Minister's Pasture

Charm break the rest
Of the Parson distrest.
From his eyes let the blessing of slumber depart;
Lucifer aid me
And Night overshade me,
Spirit of Beelzebub, lend me thine Art.
          —SWINBURNE, *The Sorceress.*

T HE LAST day of March was kept as a day of fasting and prayer in Old Salem Town. There were all-day services lasting till late evening in the big meetinghouse, which was far too small to hold the crowd, which overflowed into the church-yard and street. The King of Hell had stormed Zion's Fortress and the people of God must rally to the defense.

To judge by the crowd, everybody for a dozen miles around was on the Lord's side. Even those who weren't quite certain which way their sympathies lay hastened to declare themselves, for did not the Scripture say, He that is not for me is against me? If anybody didn't go to prayer in such a time as this, it might look queer, to say the least. And in such a time as this, nobody could afford to be thought *queer*. Even the Quakers in their little gray meetinghouse were keeping the fast.

It was late in the afternoon when Abigail Williams slipped out of the assembly of the saints and stole down among the willows by the South River for a moment's privacy. A minute later, she heard somebody coming. Mercy! It might be a man! She peered through the leaves and scrooched down among the tangled withes to keep out of sight. It was a man! It was two men! Their boots swished through the thicket. They talked in low tones as they walked. And then they stopped—close by her hiding place. She squatted like a scared rabbit and almost held her breath, waiting for a chance to get away unseen.

But they stayed right there, talking.

"Is everything in readiness?" It was the little man speaking. His voice was high-pitched and sharp, thought it was almost a whisper.

"So fur's I know," the big one rumbled. "I've warned 'em to be thar tonight at moonrise; an' to pass the word to others as be like-minded." He chuckled. "In the minister's pasture! Cock's body, you be a smart 'un. I ne'er couldna thunk o' that place for't."

"Shut up! E'en these bushes might have ears." There was a little stirring in the willows as they moved. The heavy voice spoke again in a low growl.

"Hev ye got all the trappin's ye need?"

"I have the wine and mummeries. Can you bring platters and bread? Good. That's all we need."

Again the willows rustled as the men pushed through. Abigail held her breath and crossed her fingers. Would they see her? No, the boots were going back the way they came.

When she was sure they were gone, Abigail hurried back to the meetinghouse yard. She was so excited she could hardly breathe. Something mysterious was going to happen in the minister's pasture tonight. Somehow she was going to see it, if she had to walk the whole ten miles. It was a long walk for eleven-year-old legs, and an empty stomach.

She wandered down toward the horse sheds with her fingers crossed for luck. Everybody was feeding the horses (it was not a fast day for them) and getting ready to stay the evening.

No, not everybody. Dr. Swinnerton's stepson, Bartholomew Brown, who was the new doctor in the village since his stepfather died, was putting the saddle on his horse. Uncle Samuel wouldn't have young Dr. Bartholomew in the house because he didn't take stock in witches. Now he was going to leave the meeting and go home and likely get his supper just as if it weren't a fast day. He was an infidel and a Sadducee and a menace to the community. (She had heard Uncle Samuel say so!) But he had a horse and he was probably going her way.

She stepped up to him boldly. "I'm Abigail Williams, Mr. Parris's niece—" Her courage was slipping.

"Yes, Miss Abigail," he said, and waited.

The child gulped and spoke fast. "I've got a awful bellyache—and I have to go home—and I cain't disturb the meeting—"

The young doctor's smile widened. "And I have a horse and am going right past your house. So far, so good; but what would Uncle Parris say?"

Abigail lied glibly. "Oh, that's all right. Aunt Elizabeth said I could be excused if I could get a ride." She looked down and twisted her kerchief. The doctor watched her, still smiling; but his eyebrows lifted a little. She felt that her case needed strengthening. "It looks like a special providence, don't it—your going right by my house?"

Dr. Bartholomew shouted with laughter. "I think it must be!" He mounted his horse and reached down to take her hand. "Put your foot on my stirrup and up you come. 'Twould be a fine chance for a gallop—if you didn't have a bellyache." He was still laughing.

She gathered courage. "Oh, that wouldn't hurt! I'd love to gallop!" she said. "I never rode in front before, right next the horse. It's much nicer than behind."

Across the wooden bridge, the horse slowed to an easy canter. Abigail, her hands on the pommel, leaned back comfortably, the doctor's arm around her flat little body. She was quiet for a while, studying something. At last she questioned:

"Dr. Bartholomew, what are mummeries?"

Behind her, the doctor raised his eyebrows. "Mummeries? They are tricks or disguises to fool simple folks. Like masks or juggling tricks, you know."

The child considered this. She shook her head. "The kind I mean are something to eat. They go with wine and bread."

The doctor's left arm tightened a little.

"Where did you hear about them?"

"Some men were talking. They had some wine and mummeries for supper and they were going to get some bread to eat with them."

The doctor's face twisted into a wry smile.

"That must be another kind," he said. "Why won't you ask your uncle about it? He ought to know about such things. He is a very learned man."

The ministry house was dark when they came up the meeting-house road. No sign of a candle anywhere. Dr. Bartholomew rode up to the barred gate.

"Isn't anybody home?" he asked.

Abigail didn't know. "John Indian's somewheres 'round, I guess. He was s'posed to mind the place and feed the critters. He didn't have to fast an' pray 'cause he's a heathen, you know. He might have gone huntin'."

"I had better go in and light your candle," Dr. Bartholomew said.

But Abigail spoke quickly. "Oh, no! I know just where to find the candles and I'm not scared—not a teeny bit." She was anxious to get rid of him before it happened—whatever it was that was going to happen in the minister's pasture. It was almost time for the moon to rise.

Dr. Bartholomew lifted her off the horse and dropped her gently over the bars. "You're a brave little maid," he said. "Good-bye!"

He wheeled his big horse and rode away.

"She's cute as a bug's ear and smart as a whip," he muttered. "But I'd hate to have my life depend on the word of a chit like that. God save us! 'Bread and wine and mummeries for supper,' eh? I wonder, now, just what's behind that. She's an awful little liar, but that was not made up."

As the doctor rode home in the deepening darkness he puzzled about it.

There was nobody at home, not even Moreover. He must have gone hunting with John.

Abigail did not light a candle. She crept up the dark stairs and through the big west chamber, past the ghostly canopied bed to the window. To the northwest behind the house was the orchard and beyond it the pasture. The late moon gave barely light enough to show the trees, smudgy patches against the gray background. She swung the casement open and leaned out. That was better, but still she couldn't see much of the pasture. There were no north windows; the lean-to chamber warded off the winter winds. She waited hopefully.

And then she heard a trumpet blast. The meetinghouse trumpet —but it shouldn't be blowing now—the meeting was in Salem Town ten miles away! She hurried to the south window, bumping into a chair and stumbling over a footstool, to look across Ingersoll's pasture at the meetinghouse. At the top of the peaked roof

where the weather vane stood she saw outlined against the dark
sky a shining trumpet! It swayed, circled, lifted and blew again—
a weird, pale, glowing thing showing plain against the night—
and no trumpeter to blow it! And then it sank into the murk and
vanished.

Abigail let out a wild shriek of terror and ducked under the
bed, dragging Elizabeth's best coverlid with her, and mumbling
between her chattering teeth a charm which Mary Walcott said
would keep away hants and witches:

> Matthew, Mark, Luke and John,
> Bless the bed that I lie on,
> If anything appear to me,
> Sweet Christ, arise and comfort me.

It worked, for in a few minutes curiosity overcame panic and
she crept to the window again. There was no trumpet. The
meetinghouse was a still black shadow. But something or somebody was coming across the churchyard: a man—hurrying up the
lane toward the pasture. Up the meetinghouse road from the
east two more were coming. And from the west a little group in
long dark cloaks—hurrying—hurrying—

It was what Abigail had come ten miles to see—but she hadn't
expected it would be as scary as this. She mumbled Mary's charm
again and for good measure knelt down beside the rumpled bed
and said the Lord's Prayer—out loud.

Then she put on an old black cloak of Elizabeth's and pulled
a hood far down over her face, and stealthily let herself out
into the night, following the little procession up the lane to the
pasture. It was awful scary: everybody hurrying—hurrying and
still as still—no laughing or chaffing.

There was a flare of candlewood under the wide-spreading
branches of a great basswood tree. The smooth-sawn top of a
mammoth oak stump had been spread with a black cloth to serve
as a table. There was a tankard and wooden platters with broken
bits of red bread. Beside the table stood a little black man in a
long black coat and a big man with a high-crowned white hat.

The little swarthy man was preaching and urging folks to come
up and write their names in a red book that lay open on the table.
It was a strange outlandish kind of preaching—everything topsy-
turvy and wicked—

"Pull down the Kingdom of God," he cried, "and set up the Kingdom of this World! What has God done for you? What has the church done but grind our faces in the dust? Why wait for some far-off shadowy Kingdom of Heaven after we are dead, when the Prince of the Power of the Air stands ready to give us Power and Glory and Dominion here and now? The Prince of This World is Our Leader: the Kingdom of This World is our Right. Eat the sweet bread of Conquest; and drink, yea, drink abundantly of the Wine of Power. 'All this Power will I give thee, and the glory of them; for that is delivered unto me; and to whomsoever I will I give it. If thou therefore wilt worship me, ALL SHALL BE THINE!'

"Who dares to eat? Who dares to drink this heady wine? Destroy the church! Destroy Salem Village and begin with the minister's house, and we shall be free—*free*—FREE!

"But heed ye. We must work by stealth—in silence and in secret—here a little, there a little—till we have strength to WIN!"

(Someone shouted: "We have an hundred fine young blades with rapiers. What wait we for?")

The preacher shrugged his shoulders. " 'Tis not enough—not yet! We must have more than rapiers. Our weapon is the Power of the Air—spreading terror and blight and plague and death!"

The tall man was passing through the crowd with the bread and wine. He offered some to Abigail.

"Take, eat!" (It was the voice she had heard in the willows.) She spit at the foul stuff and pushed it away.

"I will not eat, I will not drink; it is blood!" she screamed.

A woman near her wailed, rocking her body:

"Aye! There'll be blood afore this fearsome matter be done— blood in the sun and the moon!"

Abigail ran for home, stumbling and tripping over her long cloak.

When Samuel and Elizabeth came home after the long fast, they found Abigail asleep in the big canopy bed, its curtains drawn tight around her.

Wild-eyed and tear-strained, she sat up and told her story. Elizabeth soothed her, cuddling her close.

"There, darling, you're all safe at home; but you shouldn't

have run off with a stranger. You've been lonely and scared, dear child, and had a bad dream."

But Abigail would not be put off. "No, no! It was true! The pasture was full of wicked witches and the devil was their minister! There was bread red as raw flesh, and red drink."

Samuel took a lantern and strode out into the darkness. When he came back his face was very stern.

"Somebody was there. The new grass has been badly trampled. And the child's story is very like the old records—tales she never heard. There seems little doubt that she has seen the dreadful rite of the Witches' Sabbath, that obscene and scurrilous travesty of the Holy Sacrament—God pity us!"

He lowered his voice for his wife's ear alone. "Moreover went with me and he flushed two couples lying in the hazel thickets. They scuttled off with their hands over their faces to hide their shame. Such orgies are a part of the Sabbath, you know—defilement of every kind—unspeakable, some of it. I went to the churchyard, but the graves were not disturbed."

Elizabeth shuddered: "Oh, Samuel, they wouldn't!"

"Thank God, they didn't! There was no sign of ghoulish banquetings."

39

The Caldron Bubbles

April 11th, 1692. Went to Salem, where, in the Meeting-House, the persons accused of Witch-craft were examined; was a very great Assembly; 'twas awfull to see how the afflicted persons were agitated. Mr. Noyes pray'd at the beginning, and Mr. Higginson concluded.

—SAMUEL SEWALL, *Diary.*

EARLY in April, Sarah Cloyse (who had slammed the meeting-house door) and Elizabeth Procter were arrested. John Indian, Mary Walcott, and Abigail Williams were called as witnesses. The examination was before the Council of the Colony, the highest civil authority. It had passed out of the hands of the local magistrates.

Deputy Governor Danforth examined the witnesses.

"Abigail Williams, did you see a company at Mr. Parris's house eat and drink?"

"Yes, sir: that was in the sacrament."

"How many were there?"

"About forty, and Goody Cloyse and Goody Good were their deacons."

The story had grown a little, as stories are apt to do. The people gasped with horror: for Goody Good had been in prison more than a month!

"It must have been her specter!" the whisper ran.

By and by one of the afflicted girls screamed:

"There is Procter going to take up Mrs. Pope's feet!"

And her feet were immediately snatched up!

The examiner turned to Procter: "You see! The devil will deceive you! The children could see what you were going to do before the woman was hurt. I would advise you to repent, for the devil is bringing you out!"

Mary Warren, a servant in Procter's home and one of the Circle girls, was the chief witness against him. His bringing the jade home and thrashing the devil out of her had not been successful, after all.

Before the month of April was past, John Procter; Bridget Bishop, the tavernkeeper; Mary Easty, another sister of Rebecca Nurse; Giles Corey, and perhaps a score of others were in jail.

Among them was little Dorcas Good, the four-year-old child of Sarah Good, who had been wandering around the village like a stray kitten ever since her mother went to jail.

To Samuel Parris it seemed a very sore rebuke and humbling providence that the Lord ordered the horrid calamity to break out first in his family. Afterward he sadly acknowledged that he should have lain low under all this reproach, with his hand upon his mouth.

But meek inaction was neither his temperament nor his training. Satan had attacked his citadel, and instantly all his forces rallied to its defense. Like Cotton Mather he believed his own advancement was what God needed to restore His Kingdom and the opposition and bitterness he encountered were only further proofs of the devil's warfare against the saints. Cotton Mather had conquered the hosts of Apollyon in Boston. The minister of Salem Village would do no less. The Scripture was clear and plain: Thou shalt not suffer a witch to live!

Noyes of Salem Town, on his right, and Hale of Beverly, on his left, held up his hands: but it was his church which had been attacked and he did not shirk the responsibility.

From his childhood he had dramatized himself so that he was incapable of anything else. He saw himself a second Elijah, pursuing the prophets of Baal, that not one of them escape.

Yet far down in the secret places of his soul he had the guilty consciousness that he had known from the beginning that Tituba was a witch—Compton had warned him—the love-charm under his pillow on the night of his undoing had confirmed his suspicion—yet he had harbored her and brought her with him to New England because she served him well and he loved his comfort!

There had been a day soon after they settled in Salem Village, when Elizabeth had come to him, troubled and hesitant:

"Samel, have you ever wondered if Tituba might be a witch? In the lean-to chamber there is a queer little black figure made of stone—do you suppose it could be—an idol?"

"I'll see about that," he answered angrily, and stamped up the stairs and in Tituba's absence searched the chamber—and found the little black god. Wrathfully he raised the thing high above his head to smash it on the floor, just as Tituba, coming into the room behind him, cried out:

"Oh, don't Mas' Sam! Don't!"

The sheer terror in that cry stopped him. He turned on her fiercely, the image still held high. And then with a shock he could never forget he knew that her terror was not for the little black god—but for him!

She reached out shaking hands for the idol, sobbing: "Oh, Mas' Sam, Ah had sech a awful feelin' an Ah run up staihs! Bres de Lawd, O mah soul, Ah got heah jes' in time!"

Samuel's hands relaxed and Tituba clasped the little stone god against her breast, sobbing wildly.

Later, when he could trust himself to speak about the matter, he had told his wife:

"I have talked with Tituba about the little image, my dear.

It is a keepsake which she seems to value highly, and I think there is no harm in it. The West Indian people have many odd fancies. They are only children in understanding, you know, and 'tis best to humor them when we can."

Now the curse had come upon him because he had spared the abomination. For the Lord thy God is a jealous God! And the curse had fallen upon his children! After Tituba went to jail, he searched high and low for the image to destroy it—but it had disappeared.

The new charter, which had taken a masterly bit of engineering on Increase Mather's part, in the end satisfied nobody. Massachusetts was to have a royal governor, after all! But Mather had maneuvered the appointment of Sir William Phips, his own friend and colleague in the diplomatic mission, and a member of his own church in Boston. Phips would do whatever the Mathers wanted in religious matters.

As Cotton Mather confided to his diary: "The time for favour is now come; yea, the set time is come."

The first favor the Mathers wanted in the present emergency was the appointment of a special court for trying the witchcraft cases. The Court of Oyer and Terminer was the perfect flower of diplomacy. It was a civil court in name, but under the control of the clergy, who were the recognized authorities on the devil and his works.

There were seven justices, all of them prominent men and of good report. None of them was a minister, though several had been educated for the ministry.

There were to have been eight, but Saltonstall was not in sympathy with the witchcraft prosecutions and refused to serve. Stoughton, the chief justice, was witch-mad; Corwin was puzzled and bored; Samuel Sewall, as the chase grew hot, was afraid for his life.

Later, serious questions were raised as to the right of the governor to appoint the court and the right of the court to try the cases—but that was after the jails were full, and nineteen persons had been put to death by order of the said court!

By the middle of May more than forty persons were in jail awaiting trial, and the Grand Jury was in almost continuous session in the upper room of Justice Corwin's house in Salem

Town, which came to be known as the Witch House. Here (in the house which Roger Williams had built and from which he had fled when the order for his banishment was given) the afflicted children pointed shaking fingers at their tormenters. When they met the eyes of the accused, they shrieked with the pain of the pinchings and fell on the floor in dreadful fits. And here, perhaps in yonder corner where the light was dim, one gifted with second sight might have glimpsed a ghostly revenant, come back to the house which he forsook that wild night in 1635, with only his compass and his Bible to guide him.

As Parris had foreseen, there was much disapproval of the withdrawal of his daughter as a witness. He met the thing boldly, taking all the responsibility.

"I have sent my daughter Bettie to bide with the clerk of the court at Salem Town until the excitement at the ministry house is over. Mistress Sewall very kindly consented to care for her."

And in reply to the storm of indignant protests: "There are plenty of afflicted ones for witnesses—and more every day. My niece is at your service, and the older girls of the Circle, and Mistress Ann Putnam and her daughter. They know all that Bettie knows and more, and their testimony will carry more weight. Bettie is too young to be a competent witness. We want all to be regular and above blame in these matters of life and death."

The terror was spreading like a plague. The prisons in Salem Town, Ipswich, Boston, and Cambridge were crowded.

In Boston, Cotton Mather was preaching from Revelation:

Woe to the inhabitants of the earth and of the sea! for the devil is come down unto you, having great wrath, because he knoweth that he hath but a short time.

The minister of Salem Village was afraid. Afraid of God who withheld His hand in this time of crisis; afraid of the devil who went about like a roaring lion; afraid of his neighbors who avoided and shunned him; afraid of the witches he had helped to bring to justice and more afraid of those unknown hags who were still at large. But most of all he was afraid of himself— of what he had done and what he was doing and what, God pity him, he must still do before this dreadful work should end.

There were times when he longed for death. But he was afraid to die: to stand before the Judge of all the earth with his sins like a bundle bound upon his back.

The Black Night of Sin which had tormented him so many years sank into the limbo of forgotten things in the overwhelming guiltiness of the dreadful present. Yet as he traced the pathway which his errant feet had followed since he came to this accursed village he could hardly find the place where he had turned aside from the strait and narrow way of righteousness. There were plenty of mistakes: times when he had kept silence when he should have spoken; more times when he had spoken when he should not. But surely these were not enough to shut him away from God's presence forever.

The words of Rebecca Nurse troubled him: "What sin hath God found in me unrepented of, that He should lay such an affliction upon me?" He set his teeth: if repentance meant exposing his naked soul in public for fools to gloat at—he'd be damned first!

He prayed unceasingly because the habit of prayer was strong upon him, but it meant no more than telling beads. The words echoed emptily and rang in his ears. Sometimes toward the end of a sleepless night he would think he heard a chuckle beside his bed, and in the dark corner of the room where the moonlight never shone he fancied he saw shadows dim and ghostly—more frightful because veiled.

He could hardly bear the canopies of his bed hemming him in; and when he quarreled with his wife about sending Bettie to Salem Town, he made his displeasure an excuse for moving into the "naked bed" in east chamber and sending Abigail to sleep with Elizabeth. He repented his words before they were out of his mouth, and the lonely nights were a torment to his spirit and his flesh, but he would not recant.

As he strode about the village his face was like a mask. The faces he met were masks also: only their eyes were alive. And in the eyes there was none of the good will and jollity of the earlier days. The eyes haunted him: cold and hostile; fawning and treacherous; watchful and sly.

As the warm days came, the men got out their plows and planted their grain (where would they be when it was ripe for harvest?). The bulls and rams were turned into the common pasture (who would cherish the young lambs and calves till their wobbly legs were strong?). The housewives watched the fruit trees blowing white (would Mary bake fresh apple tarts for John this year?). Life must go on according to its pattern, though none dare think of tomorrow.

Samuel came home one night later than usual. Elizabeth had left a candle on the shelf for him as she always did. He dragged his feet up the steep stairs and entered the east chamber. The candle showed Elizabeth asleep in his bed, her lips parted a little, one arm thrown over the pillow. He drew a surprised breath and stood looking down at her. His hand shook and the flaring of the candle woke her. She smiled up at him sleepily.

"I must have gone to sleep in the wrong bed." She was half laughing.

He set the candle down and dropped on his knees, his arms around her, his lips on hers, mumbling incoherently: "No, no, my sweet! You have come home to me—you love me—and you know I love you, don't you?—don't you?—even if I am a damn fool."

She patted his shoulders comfortingly. "You're so weary you don't know what you are talking about, dear heart. It's a dreadful warm night for May. Open the south windows—I think there's a breeze coming up—and put out the candle so the moths won't come in."

He slept that night with his wife held close in his arms. Though his pride would not let him confess it, he was thankful to her for sending little Bettie away. He had visited the child at the Sewalls'. She had been playing with the Sewall baby and her eyes had been bright with the lighthearted sparkle of childhood. She had told him there were no witches in Salem Town.

"Once the Great Black Man came to me and told me if I would be ruled by him I should have whatever I wanted and go to a Golden City. But Aunt Margaret told me it was the devil, and he was a liar, and bid me tell him so if he came again, and so I did and he came no more.

"And Aunt Margaret says the witches can't hurt my mother 'cause she's one of God's precious saints; and they can't hurt you 'cause they'd run like Old Splitfoot if they saw a minister."

The minister buried his face in his daughter's sunny curls to hide his emotion; thanking God's mercy that he was not to be punished through the suffering of his darling.

Bettie squirmed and giggled: "Ouch, father! You tickle my neck when you whisper."

40

The King of Hell

Last night upon the stair
I met a man who wasn't there.
He wasn't there again today.
I wish to God he'd go away.
—UNKNOWN.

ONE evening in April, Little Ann Putnam had seen the apparition of a minister, at which she was grievously affrighted and cried out:

"Oh, dreadful, dreadful! Here is a minister come! What, are ministers witches too?"

Whereupon the specter tortured and choked her, and tempted her to write her name in his book, and when she would not, he told her that he was George Burroughs, and that he had had three wives and bewitched the first two of them to death; and that he had killed Mistress Lawson and her child, and a great many others.

He also told her that he was above a witch. He was a conjurer.

Ann's father and others of her family made oaths that they saw and heard all this, and beheld her tortures and hellish temptations by her loud outcries:

"I will not, I will not write, though you torment me all the days of my life."

The next day Thomas Putnam, Ann's father and a clerk of the court, wrote to the Honored John Hathorne and Jonathan Corwin of "matters high and dreadful—of a wheel within a wheel within a wheel, at which our ears do tingle."

A secret order was obtained for the arrest of George Burroughs, preacher at Wells, Maine, he being suspected of a confederacy with the devil.

The officers lost no time. They came upon their quarry eating his frugal supper with his family. His clairvoyance must have failed him to let himself be taken so easily; though he showed neither surprise nor fear. His bushy brows drew together, and the keen blue-gray eyes beneath them glinted like steel. But he did not even get up from the table.

"What do you want?" he snapped.

"We've got a warrant for ye, and we come armed." The officer pointed his pistol. "Ye might as well go peaceable."

Burroughs turned to his wife and the pistol jabbed him in the ribs.

"We got no time to waste palaverin', ye spawn o' Satan! Bestir yourself, fellow, we can't wait all night!"

Five days after the order was given the prisoner was in Salem Jail—and in another five days a private session of magistrates was held, in which Burroughs was called to account for absenting himself from communion and for bringing none of his children except the eldest for baptism.

After the secret inquisition was over he was taken to the place of public examination, and as he entered the room the afflicted children were so tortured that authority ordered them to be removed.

"What think ye of these things?" Burroughs was asked.

"It is an amazing and humbling providence," he said, "but I understand nothing of it."

Mr. Burroughs was a little man and "very puny but wonderful strong." Even in his college days he had been a famous gymnast, and his life in the wilds had hardened his muscles till they were like iron bands. Much of the testimony against him went to show his superhuman strength. It was averred that he could hold a gun seven foot long at arm's length by the barrel, and carry a hogshead of molasses from a canoe to the shore; but the record shows that he "denied the melasses."

He was a strange-looking man, like a gnome, Parris thought, watching him. His neck was so short that his head seemed to sit tight upon his brawny shoulders. The head was shaped like an egg, with a pointed chin, wide cheekbones, a hawk nose, and a forehead which rounded back in a smooth curve from his heavy eyebrows to the waving mop of coarse brown hair combed back to reveal a widower's mark extending high on each side. His hair was long and shaggy and bushed out under his hat at the back. His cup-shaped ears gave him a listening look. His eyes, deep-set under shaggy black brows, were like blue steel—startlingly bright and piercing as they shifted alertly from side to side with the watchfulness of a seasoned woodsman, sizing up his surroundings.

The eyes met fear and horror and a fascinated curiosity, but nowhere in the crowded room did they find pity or understanding or friendliness.

The man knew he was beaten. He did not need the return of the jury to voice his sentence. His insurrection against the Mather dynasty had come a generation too soon, and he had made the sorry mistake of fighting the devil with fire.

He stood in the prisoner's dock—a plain, dark, lonely little figure of tragedy. Behind him the magistrates sat in grave dignity; in front, the afflicted girls with their half-demoniac terror; beyond them the wildly excited crowd; and the child on the witness stand, telling her awful tale of ghosts in winding sheets, with napkins round their heads, pointing to their death wounds, and sobbing that their blood did cry for vengeance against their murderer.

There was evidence that Mr. Burroughs had a trumpet which he blew to summon the witches to their feasts near Mr. Parris his house. This trumpet had a blast that resounded over the countryside far and wide; so that the witches, hearing it, would bestride their besoms, and alight in a moment in Mr. Parris's pasture—but its sound could not be heard by any other ears!

It cost the court a deal of trouble to take the testimony against him, for whenever he turned his piercing steel-blue eyes upon the witnesses they were struck down and fell into long and tedious fits.

Mercy Lewis, who had not forgotten the beatings he had given her that time she was his servant at the ministry house, was the chief witness against him, though her terror of him was painful to behold.

But it was Little Ann Putnam with her lurid tales of ghosts in winding sheets who destroyed him.

Mr. Burroughs was sent to Boston Prison, where he was heavily chained and confined in the dungeon. There was so much testimony as to his supernatural strength that it was feared ordinary methods would not restrain him.

Every day brought new arrests, and among the things high and dreadful was the apprehension of some of the most prominent citizens of the community.

People were beginning to flee the place, as they had fled before the plague in London. Here, there, and everywhere doors were barred. There was no reputation so blameless, no station in life so secure as to be above suspicion. Fear haunted every street. Melancholy dwelt in silence in every place, after the sun went down, and the innocent suffered with the guilty.

Samuel Sewall, justice of the Special Court of Oyer and Terminer, was frightened. He didn't like his job. At the beginning his sense of civic duty and his appetite for strange occurrences pulled together and he had accepted the appointment with satisfaction. It was, perhaps, as high an honor as the colony could bestow—to speak the word of life or death for those accused of the most heinous crime in the Puritan code.

Sewall had full confidence in his ability and his integrity— at the beginning. Now he had sorry misgivings about both. Yet his dignity and sense of duty and a dreadful fascination would not let him resign. He was caught in a tangled skein, an impalpable web of mystery and deceit and lies which enmeshed both character and intelligence, and left him for the first time in his life struggling helplessly against the enemy of souls—with no sense of God's presence to help him.

He had no qualms about the first conviction: Bridget Bishop, the tavernkeeper, a shameless hussy whose gay dress and bold manners had long been an affront to the godly. She was convicted on the 2nd of June and hanged on the 10th, still wearing her black paragon bodice with its gay lacings as she swung from the locust tree. It had been hoped that this prompt and firm action would strike fear into the hearts of others and halt their wicked arts, but it seemed only to make things worse. Not a day went by without new complaints and new arrests, and the

Grand Jury was in continuous session (save for the respite of the Lord's Day).

Samuel Sewall was no Sadducee. The wonders of the invisible world were as real to him as they were to young Cotton Mather in Boston, writing them down in his Wonder-Book. They were as real as they were to Samuel Parris with the black mysteries of tropical nights still haunting him.

Sewall's days were torture and his nights were worse. When the court was in session he stopped at his brother Stephen's house, where his sister-in-law gave him the best chamber and all the comforts which a thoughtful hostess could provide. But the room might as well have been a cell, for the first thing the judge did when he entered it was to close and bar the windows; draw the heavy curtains; assure himself that nothing was hiding in the clothes press or under the bed; and then make fast the door. Yet these precautions gave him slim comfort, for the Thing he feared was not of this world.

Before the month ended Rebecca Nurse came up for trial. That trial (it lasted several days) was a horror that Sewall never forgot, for Goodwife Nurse was known as a godly woman and a mother in Israel. She was over seventy and almost too ill to stand. Sewall, who had a great reverence for age, could hardly bear the sight.

A few days before the trial a jury of women had searched the body of the prisoner for evidence of fornication with the devil and found the witch-mark on her (though one of them, whom some thought to be the most ancient, skillful, prudent person of them all as to any such concern, did express herself to be of a contrary opinion from the rest, and did then declare that she saw nothing but what might arise from a natural cause). A petition was presented for some other women to inquire into this great concern but the court gave no attention to it.

There was also a petition headed by Nathaniel Putnam, Sr., and signed by thirty-nine other respectable citizens, testifying that they had known her for many years, and according to their observation, her life and conversation were according to her profession.

Among the signers, strangely enough, was Jonathan Putnam, one of the two complainants who procured the warrant for her arrest. Parris thought he knew the reason for this change of front. Doubtless Jonathan had been visited by the same loyal sons and sons-in-law who had come to the ministry house with petitions and protests to induce him to intervene in behalf of their mother. Parris had told them plainly that it did not help their cause any to try to hinder justice by such underhand means. The place to determine the matter was in open court by due process of law. It was not for the minister to intervene.

The chief witness for the prosecution was Mistress Ann Putnam, who told a lurid tale of six children in winding sheets, who had spoken to her, saying that Goody Nurse and two other women had murdered them.

Again Judge Hathorne put the question to the prisoner at the bar: "Are you an innocent person in regard to witchcraft?"

Here Mistress Putnam shrieked: "Did you not bring the Black Man with you? Did you not bid me tempt God and die? How oft have you eat and drank your own damnation?"

Then there rose a wild clamor, everybody talking at once and women wailing and shrieking. The afflicted children fell in fits. The old woman at the bar swayed drunkenly, almost fainting with weakness and fear.

At the reporter's table, Samuel Parris, in the midst of the hubbub, was trying to hear and set down in shorthand with flying fingers the rapid give-and-take of question and answer which meant life or death for Rebecca Nurse.

That night Judge Sewall left his candle burning and covered the crack under his door with a mat (not wanting his sharp-eyed sister-in-law to know of his cowardice). But whether he lay wakeful or slept from sheer weariness, haunts and evil dreams tormented him—and six children in winding sheets stared at him with dead eyes.

Besides the spectral evidence, there was proof of a neighborhood quarrel of long standing. When Townsend Bishop built his mansion he had laid out a garden on the rough land just across the brook. In the years after Bishop left the colony the garden had been left to nature and had "snatched a grace beyond the reach of art." When Mr. Allen sold the place, Francis Nurse bought the farm, but his wife Rebecca took for her own domain the neglected garden. It was never a labor for her to prune and train, to weed and plant. Townsend Bishop, being a heretic, had not followed the Puritan rule to restrict his planting to those flowers which have a culinary or medicinal use. And Rebecca could not find it in her heart to destroy beauty.

"Seems like the good Lord wouldn't 'a' taken all that pains to make 'em pretty, if he hadn't cherished 'em," she justified herself—and let them grow.

But just on the other side of the fence lived Benjamin Houlton and his pigs. The fence was not so tight as it ought to have been (the Nurse boys had been too busy plowing and planting to get at it) and "pigs is pigs."

Sarah Houlton, relict of Benjamin Houlton deceased, told her story in open court.

"About this time three years, my husband was as well as ever I saw him till one Saturday morning that Rebecca Nurse came to our house and fell arailing at him because our pigs got into her field. All we could say to her could noways pacify her, but she went on railing and scolding, and calling to her son Benjy to go get a gun and kill our pigs, an' let none of 'em get out of the field—though my poor husband gave her never a misbeholding word.

"A few days after, my poor husband was taken with a strange fit in the entry. All summer after he was much pained at his stomach, and often struck blind. But about a fortnight before he died, he was taken with strange and violent fits, acting much like our poor bewitched persons; and the doctor could not find what his distemper was.

"The day before he died he was very cheerly, but about midnight he was again most violently seized upon by violent fits, and departed this life by a cruel death."

Mary Walcott supplemented this—and her testimony carried great weight with all who heard her.

There was something about Mary—something mysterious and otherworldly. Among the girls of the Circle she was like a rare flower in a garden of geraniums. She was not like the Walcotts (stocky English farmerfolk) nor yet like the Sibleys (spindlin' and droopy).

Mary was seventeen now, tall and slender, with the grace of a wind-swept reed, and her young body gave a hint of delectable curves under her prim Puritan dress. Her skin was white as the water lilies on the pond, and her hair was tawny like her brows and the curling lashes which curtained her amber eyes. Beneath a straight and proper nose, her lips were pouting and red-ripe.

Some folks who had known the Sibleys in England long ago recalled a story about an ancestress of Mary's—generations back —who lingered late on the beach one night with an amorous sailor. Ever since, now and then, there had come a madcap child—a Sandy Sibley who had the Gift.

Parris had never heard the foolish yarn, and had never noticed Mary much (except her eyes—strange eyes—almost hidden by their heavy lids and lashes). She was around the parsonage so much that he paid no heed to her. After Elizabeth had called his attention, he had intended to talk with the girl about her soul's salvation, but in the cares and puzzlements which beset him he forgot about her—until the witch fever broke out. Then he found that she was a wonderful witness, with the rare gift of second sight. She did not rave and screech and fall into spasms as some of the afflicted children did; but would lie in a trance like one dead, only her lips moving, as she told her visions. And the things she told came true. It was the Gift.

But Mary was not entranced today. In her own proper person and in open court she testified:

"On the 24th day of March the apparition of Rebecca Nurse did most grievously torment me . . . And on the evening of May 3d, she told me she had a hand in the death of Benjamin Houlton . . ."

The dreadful words were spoken in a low and clear monotone, in startling contrast to the hubbub around her. But her very calm made her words more damning, and the crowd went wild:

"Hang the witch!"

"Hang her!"

"She's guilty as hell!"

Yet in the face of all this uproar and the strong leaning of the court against the prisoner, the jury brought in a verdict of "Not Guilty."

At that the mob broke out in dreadful clamor, yelling like fiends:

"Pull down the house about the judges' ears!"

"Tear the jurors to pieces!"

In the rush toward justices and jurors benches were smashed and missiles thrown.

A few cracks on the heads of the leaders halted the rioting, but the crowd was still dangerous, and Justice Stoughton sent the jury back with the question:

"Have you not overlooked something?"

Again the jury went out, and in a few minutes the foreman begged leave to ask the prisoner's interpretation of some troublesome words: did she mean one of us witches or one of us prisoners when she spoke of Deliverance Hobbs (a confessed witch) as one of us?

But Goodwife Nurse, being somewhat hard of hearing and full of grief, made no answer.

"Whereupon," Foreman Fish said afterward, "these words were to me a principal evidence against her."

The amended verdict of "Guilty" was approved by the court, thus defying all the rules of law and precedent. The governor saw cause to grant a reprieve; but immediately the accusers renewed their dismal outcries against her. Insomuch that some Salem gentlemen prevailed with the governor to recall the reprieve—she was executed with the rest.

The Salem gentlemen who thus prevented the governor from carrying out his intended clemency were a committee of vigilance during the continuance of the trials, who had undertaken to ferret out all suspected persons. Like all such societies, their meetings and membership were a dark secret.

It was these same Salem gentlemen whom young Joseph Putnam defied, when all that dreadful summer he kept two of his best horses saddled and his pistols ready; and let it be publicly known that whoever came to get him wouldn't live to tell it.

There is no record that anybody came, though there is a story that his sister, drawn into the courtroom by curiosity, was cried out upon, and had to flee and hide in Middleton Woods.

41

Brethren

Like one that on a lonesome road
　Doth walk in fear and dread,
And having once turned round walks on,
　And turns no more his head,
Because he knows a frightful fiend
　Doth close behind him tread.
　　　　　　　　　　—COLERIDGE.

SINCE Rebecca Nurse's sister, Sarah Cloyse, had got up and left the meetinghouse and slammed the door behind her none of the Nurse's kin by blood or marriage had been to meeting.

In the orderly Puritan way, each member of the congregation had his own place, so that the empty places on the long benches were as conspicuous as missing pickets in a fence. Each bare spot was an affront to the minister. He could not overlook them, nor could he forget them. There were a lot of bare spots here and there, for Francis and Rebecca had eight children living, and four of them were married and had young ones of their own. Then there were the Cloyses and the Eastys and their offspring.

At first Parris thought best to disregard the matter; but as the months went by, he decided that something must be done about it, if the church and its minister were to maintain their dignity in the community. So he brought the matter up in meeting. A committee was chosen by vote of the brotherhood to discourse with the dissenters about their withdrawing from the Lord's table and public worship of God. The dissenters desired further time.

Parris showed his surprise: "You know, brethren, of your dissent and surely you cannot be to seek the reason for it."

The brethren squirmed and looked at each other. At last John Tarbell spoke:

"We got a right to set out our whys and wherefores orderly."

Parris yielded the point and set a later date. At the appointed time the three brethren appeared and Samuel Nurse read a long remonstrance, reciting that whereas the three offended brethren had gone a long time under great grievances by reason of some unwarrantable actings of Mr. Parris, they did not understand the regularity of the proceeding against them, because they esteemed themselves to be the parties offended, who were in an orderly way seeking satisfaction, according to the rule of the Lord Jesus Christ, laid down in Matthew:

If thy brother shall trespass against thee, go and tell him his fault between thee and him alone: if he shall hear thee, thou hast gained thy brother. But if he will not hear thee, then take with thee one or two more, that in the mouth of two or three witnesses every word may be established.

When at last the slow reading was finished, Parris reached for the paper, but Nurse snatched it back.

"No! We ain't agoin' to let this go out of our hands!" But on the minister's insistence, they consented that Deacon Putnam make a copy of it while they waited.

"Who wrote this thing for you?" Parris demanded. "None of you wrote it, 'tis certain."

They looked at each other. Tarbell spoke.

"We don't choose to say."

Parris knew well enough who wrote it. He would have known, even if Tom Putnam had not reported to him that the three dissenters had gone to Ipswich the day before.

It was not the first time that Wise had interfered. He had opposed Parris's methods from the beginning, and in the case of John Procter had tried to intervene: heading and circulating a petition with thirty-two signers for the man's pardon.

From their Harvard days, Parris had looked upon Wise as a dangerous radical; but his people at Ipswich Village stood by him no matter what he did. Now he had put in his oar again to encourage the rebellious brethren, and in the present ticklish situation he might be dangerous.

Parris held his temper. "You should have spoken to the pastor himself, before you went to consult neighboring elders."

"We didn't know," they said.

Tarbell was the main spokesman and he spoke to the point:

"You be guilty of idolatry, Mr. Parris, in askin' afflicted persons what they see on others. You be like old King Ahaziah in the

Scripture when he sent messengers to inquire to Beelzebub, the god of Ekron, whether he should recover of his disease. And the prophet Elijah met the messengers an' says to 'em, 'Ain't there a God in Israel, that ye go to inquire of Beelzebub the god of Ekron?'

"Your oath ain't safe in court, that folks is knocked down by other folks's looks an' raised up by their touches.

"And if it hadn't a been for you," he shook a threatening fist, "my Mother Nurse might still be livin'. 'Twas you that killed her, Mr. Parris, *you!* 'Tis you that's been the great persecutor!"

Parris stood his ground, though his face was gray.

"My opinion was confirmed by known and ancient experience in such cases. I do not yet see sufficient grounds to vary it. You must give me my opinion as I will not quarrel with you for yours."

His voice was as cold and hard as his face, but beneath this outward calm his soul was being torn asunder.

Meeting after meeting, month after month, the fight went on. Once Brother Nurse read a scroll of about fifteen articles. Seven of them were reasons for absenting themselves from worship and the other eight were causes of separation from Parris's ministry.

The most serious charges were the pastor's preaching dark and dismal mysteries, his not rendering to the world a faithful account of what he wrote on examination, his unsafe oath against the accused, and his zeal in seeking out the suspected.

The document was signed by forty-two names, all in the same hand. Parris asked for the original. They said they knew not where it was.

"Did these men write their own names?"

"Yes!"

"All in the same handwriting?"

"They wrote 'em or they was wrote by their order."

Then the minister asked: "Will you set your hands to this paper, testifying that no name is there but such as are consented to?"

But none would yield to this.

Parris told them, "We must know what to do. Have I to deal with displeased people or displeased brethren?"

They looked at each other. Samuel Nurse spoke.

"We come as brethren."

Throughout the quarrel, the church stood with the pastor and against the dissenters. It was voted that they had proceeded disorderly and that the church would hear these brethren if they would bring their charges in an orderly manner.

But the villagers, the great unchurched, were "agin the preacher." Some of them liked the Nurses and some of them didn't, but they stood together against a common danger—the charge of witchcraft. Fear kept them silent, but here and there were little knots of stern-faced people who fell suddenly silent or broke up and sauntered away with elaborate unconcern if the preacher drew near.

Parris had never thought himself a coward. As a lad he had been careless of safety in the Great Fire. In his prentice days he had trudged the London streets with no thought of fear. In the Indies he had gone through the hurricane with credit. But the present crisis tugged at his courage and wore him down, day after day. For it seemed that he wrestled not against flesh and blood, but against principalities, against powers, against the rulers of the darkness of this world, against spiritual wickedness in high places.

The fear and distrust which he read in the eyes of others, seemed only a reflection of his own soul. Try as he would he had no consciousness of God's presence, no sense of His help and guidance. Nor was the devil a personal reality, tempting or threatening. There was, rather, a dreadful miasma which penetrated to the very core of body and soul until he knew neither good nor evil, but went through the days like a sleepwalker, tormented by evil dreams.

The day Rebecca Nurse was hanged, he had found Elizabeth sobbing heartbrokenly.

"What is the matter?" he asked.

"I can't help thinking about poor Goody Nurse," she said. "Oh, Samuel, I can't believe she is a witch. I think she is a good Christian woman—and they're hanging her today."

He looked at her vaguely.

"Is this the day? I had forgot."

She stared at him.

"Forgot?"

He shook his head impatiently as if to clear his brain.

"Why, yes. This is the day. Stupid of me, very. The 19th of July. Of course, this is the day."

His wife was frightened.

"Samuel, you are ill! Oh, Samel! These awful trials are like a plague. You are the minister. Can't you do something to stop them before we all go mad?"

He did not answer. She doubted if he had heard. She brought him a mug of cordial and watched him anxiously as he gulped it. His face was haggard and his eyes dull.

She passed a hand over his forehead. It was cold and clammy —in mid-July.

"This cursed thing is killing you, Samel. It is killing us both."

He drew away impatiently.

"Don't fuss, Elizabeth! There's nothing wrong with me—save that I'm tired—so tired. I can't think what I've done to make me so tired."

42

Cotton Mather Sees It Through

> *Cotton Mather came galloping down*
> *All the way from Boston Town*
> *With his eyes agog and his ears set wide*
> *And his marvellous ink horn by his side.*
> *—Adapted from* WHITTIER.

HUMANLY speaking, the rule of the saints was ended in New England and the Wilderness Zion had lost its power and prestige. For the new charter, despite all that Increase Mather could do, gave the right of the vote to anybody with forty pounds to his name, no matter whether he be saint or sinner. Forty pounds made rascals like Hobbs and Burroughs and Procter the equals of Higginson and Parris and Noyes. Forty pounds! The price of a ballot on election day, though the man was a thief or a drunkard or an adulterer. Forty filthy pounds! Increase Mather, in a last desperate effort, had bargained for the right of the colonists to appoint the governor and other officers for a year—after that no one knew what might happen!

But in the terror of the attack of the powers of darkness, the people turned to the ministers to save them from the foul fiend, and the church took over the mechanism of civil power. It was the church that was in peril, and it was the church that denounced and punished.

Early in August the court met again and six more were condemned to death: among them George Burroughs and Martha Carrier, the king and queen of hell.

Martha Carrier was the woman of Andover, by whose wicked arts Mary Walcott was at divers times tortured, afflicted, pined, consumed, wasted, and tormented, as the indictment read. But tormenting Mary Walcott was the least of the said Carrier's crimes, for before her trial several of her own children confessed that their mother had made them witches also.

There was talk that Carrier's sons did not so testify until they were tied neck and heels till blood gushed out of their noses. Inasmuch as there was enough to proceed upon without it, it was thought best that this evidence be not produced against the prisoner.

This Carrier was a most wicked, spiteful creature, and when some witnesses had their necks twisted almost round by her shape coming to them during her trial, she said:

"It's no matter, though their necks had been twisted quite off!"

Elizabeth Procter's sentence was stayed because of her pregnancy, and the old wives chuckled and counted the days till they should know whether that which was conceived in her was the devil's get or John Procter's.

But worst of them all was George Burroughs, whom the testimony of the confessors and others showed to be a wolf in sheep's clothing: the leader in a plot to destroy Salem Village, body and soul—gradually—slyly—secretly—surely.

There were some three hundred witches in the land and the destruction was a systematic plot and plan: silence, darkness, mystery, diabolism, all brooded over it and lent their aid.

It was all the fulfillment of prophecy. Mr. Cotton Mather had studied the writings of the Prophet Daniel and the Revelation of St. John: the parable of the woman fleeing into the wilderness where she is nourished for a time, and times, and half a time, from the face of the Serpent. The dragon was wroth with the woman, and went to make war with the remnant of her seed, which keep the commandments of God, and had the testimony of Jesus Christ.

Cotton Mather had figured the time, and times, and half a time—and the war with the Lamb would begin with the turn of the century. The time was at hand!

Satan and his cohorts were taking counsel for the overthrow of the Puritan church and state and the setting up of the Kingdom of Satan. The revelation of the witchcraft plot confirmed the Scripture prophecy. And Salem, by her good record in the Christian calendar, had so much a worse one in the spectral books of the archenemy of mankind.

Salem was doomed: not for her sins, but for her righteousness.

It followed, therefore, that those who opposed the church were secretly allied with the devil—(had not Christ said, He who is not for me is against me?)—and involved in a conspiracy deep, satanic, and beyond pardon. Whatever of personal motive and malice there may have been, there was certainly this whirlwind of fanatic terror, and behind it all a pitifully childlike faith in the long-looked-for Second Coming.

New England under the leadership of her clergy was taking literally the command: Watch therefore, and pray, for ye know not the hour when the Son of man cometh. But before this glory must come the reign of the prince of the power of the air—brief but horrible.

Salem Village, in her dire trouble, was but the beginning of the end.

George Burroughs and Martha Carrier, because they were to be king and queen in the abominable kingdom, fell under the special vengeance of 1692.

Mr. Burroughs was the Great Heretic, the archrebel of the day. Some said he was a sorcerer and some said he was a saint, but nobody understood what was going on in that queer, active brain of his. His mother was a God-fearing woman of John Eliot's flock in Roxbury, which should have started him on the right path. He went through four years at Harvard, which should have turned him out a proper Puritan (but didn't).

Perhaps he delved too deeply in some of the curious volumes

which John Harvard had left to the library—volumes laboriously written on parchment long before Puritanism had purged away certain dark and dreadful mysteries of earlier times. John Harvard had a catholic taste in such matters, it would seem, and the censors of the press never thought of looking in the College Library for books to burn in the public square!

When Burroughs left Harvard he became a preacher, though he never was ordained, and apparently moved about a good deal from one frontier settlement to another, before he came to the Salem Village pastorate. After that unfortunate venture into Zion he went back to the border again. He had the frontier virtues of strength and courage and cunning. Perhaps the abuse he had suffered at Salem still smoldered when Zion-in-the-Wilderness started its heretic hunt, and drew him back to fight against the saints.

The church had given a hard name to such an uprising: witchcraft. It was a ready weapon to him who dared grasp it. George Burroughs had borne injustice meekly, but it still rankled—and he had waited a long time for God. He took up the two-edged sword!

There is a half-forgotten tale that Cromwell, on the eve of the Battle of Worcester, took Colonel Lindsay with him to a wood not far from the army. After they had gone a little way into the wood, Lindsay was seized with a chill of horror so that his teeth chattered.

"How now?" said Cromwell. "What, troubled with the vapors? Come forward, man!"

But Lindsay on a sudden stood still and durst not stir one step farther.

"Fainthearted fool!" Cromwell sneered at him. "Stand there then, and be witness!"

And Lindsay, watching, saw his general go deeper into the wood, where he met an ancient man in a robe of rusty black, who delivered to him a parchment, which, when Cromwell had read, he burst out angrily:

"This is but for seven years; it must be one and twenty!"

"Nay," said the old man, "it cannot be for any longer time; and if you will not take it so, there be others who will."

Then Cromwell took the parchment, and returning cried: "Now, Lindsay, the battle is ours!"

Colonel Lindsay was so beset with fear that he deserted after the first charge, and swore:

"If ever I strike a stroke for Cromwell again, may I perish eternally. For well I know he's made a league with the devil, and the devil will have him in due time."

And as everyone knows, Cromwell died that day seven years, in the midst of a wild storm of wind and rain and lightning, which tore up ancient oaks and cast great ships ashore.

God knows if the tale be true! But if it be, was one man's soul too high a price to pay for a nation's liberty?

George Burroughs roused from his uneasy sleep, and soothed his festering ankles as well as he could with his manacled hands. The dawn was just creeping into the dungeon—a thin lance of sunlight. Burroughs poked his neighbor with his elbow.

"Wake up, Giles, ye lazy lout, and bear me company! By good rights, ye should be going up the hill with me today; but you'll come soon enough. 'Tis the rope for both of us, for you're as deep in the mud as I am in the mire."

Corey hitched himself a little nearer.

"I ain't done fightin' yet, Mr. Burroughs." He was whispering close to Burroughs's ear. "I were askin' Mr. Wise about it when he come to see me. 'Doan't there be any way?' sez I. 'It ain't thet I mind dyin', but I bain't a felon though I be a rebel, and I doan't want to swing."

He paused, breathing hard, and Burroughs prompted.

"Well?"

"Well, Mr. Wise sez, 'There be a way, but it's unthinkable,' sez he. 'It won't bear speakin' of!' An' off he went. But I've sent him word by my son John Moulton. 'Ye gotta tell me the way,' sez I. An' Mr. Wise give John his promise he'd see me agin an' tell me the way."

On this 19th day of August the whole countryside was astir at dawn. For this was no ordinary hanging day.

This day, on the Hill, God and the devil would come to grips. If God won the battle New England would be saved; if the devil prevailed—but of that no one dare think. The morning was hot and sultry and the sun rose out of a moving mass of clouds that cast sudden shadows over the land and the silvery harbor. But close to the ground there was no breeze and the daisies along the roadside were dusty and still as if they, too, were waiting and listening.

On the hill a little knot of men were scooping out five shallow graves among the rocks of the crevasse. In the house of Mr. Noyes the neighboring ministers knelt in prayer, and drank more rum than was good for them, making the heat their excuse.

Not even in their prayers did they put into words the terror that haunted them—the dread that the devil would intervene— the dread that they could not hang George Burroughs, the king of hell!

"Cotton Mather came galloping down, all the way from Boston Town." His face was ruddy with the heat and his big white horse was stained with sweat. His arrival put heart into the ministers. Cotton Mather had not been present at any of the hangings, but this time reinforcements were needed. Even Samuel Parris had urged that Mather come. Although the devil might not appear in fire and flame and snatch his chosen away from the noose, the people were in an ugly and dangerous mood and there might be mob violence on the Hill.

The order of the executions was carefully planned. Burroughs was neither the first nor the last. When his turn came he mounted the ladder and made a speech declaring his innocence in a most solemn and serious manner. He prayed with such seeming fervency of spirit as drew tears from many of the spectators; and he repeated the Lord's Prayer—with never a slip or a stumble!

A murmur ran through the crowd: they surged closer:

"He bain't no wizard, to pray like that!"

"His blood be on us if we hang him!"

"Take him down!!"

The shouts rose above a confused muttering of angry voices, roaring like a storm as the mob surged forward.

Then young Cotton Mather proved his mettle. Boldly he spurred his horse through the crowd to the very foot of the ladder, and as Burroughs dropped and the noose tightened around his neck the Mather voice boomed out:

"My friends, be not deceived! The devil has often been transformed into an angel of light. This man was tried by a jury of twelve good men—your own friends and neighbors. He could not make any plea for himself that had any weight. He had the liberty of challenging the jurors, and used that liberty to challenge many, yet the jury that were sworn before God to tell the truth, brought him in guilty.

"Be not deceived, God is not mocked, for whatsoever a man soweth, that shall he reap."

The Thing that had been George Burroughs hung limp, the neck broken by the drop.

He was dragged by the halter to the hole between the rocks, his minister's garb stripped from him, and his half-clad body thrust underground. The earth was hastily thrown over him, and as it was tramped down, an arm poked through, one stiffening finger pointing to the sky!

The sheriff spoke sharply to the yokel with the spade:

"Finish your job, there! Tromp that arm down an' cover it!"

The man looked at the Thing and backed away, his fingers spread with loathing.

"No! No! I burried him oncet! I'm through, I tell ee and I doan't want no pieces of siller, neither!"

With a sob of terror he turned and ran down the Hill.

Still the arrests increased and the convictions swiftly followed. It became harder and harder to tell "which was witch" and who might be falsely accused. The crowd was drunk with blood, and demanded more—and more—and more.

Samuel Parris was sick of blood. Sick of the smell of sweating bodies crowded into the courtroom; sick of the same testimony repeated in case after case, while his nimble pen set it down in shorthand and in the evenings transcribed it into the king's English.

It seemed monstrous that so many should so abominably leap into the devil's lap at once. If only he could know for a certainty. If God would reveal to him where to strike his blows. But he was fighting in the dark. If he could look into the hearts of men and know the truth; if he could look into the future and see what was to be the end of all this turmoil.

It was the old, old story of King Saul, the perfect pattern of witchchaft:

And when Saul saw the host of the Philistines, he was afraid, and his heart greatly trembled. And when Saul enquired of the Lord, the Lord answered him not . . . Then said Saul unto his servants, Seek me a woman that hath a familiar spirit, that I may go to her, and enquire of her. And his servants said to him, Behold, there is a woman that hath a familiar spirit at En-dor. And Saul . . . went . . . and came to the woman by night. [*And when the woman had brought up Samuel, Saul said to him*] God is departed from me, and answereth me no more, neither by prophets, nor by dreams: therefore I have called thee, that thou mayest make known unto me what I shall do.

The minister forgot the Scriptural story and its tragic sequel. He remembered only his emergency and his need.

Mary Walcott could tell him the things he must know!

It would not be like going to a woman of bad repute, he reasoned. Mary was like one of his own family, almost. And Mary had the Gift.

His theological training warned him that it was evil—but surely it was doing evil that good might come of it. And like King Saul, he went down the tortuous path to Endor. It did not seem so evil: Mary looking into the water in a black kettle and seeing things present and to come. Her visions had helped mightily in bringing some of the worst wretches to justice (some who but for her might never have been apprehended, such base hypocrites they were). And Mary's testimony was supported by others also—Mistress Ann Putnam and her daughter and many more.

Earlier in the proceedings the question of spectral evidence (or the testimony of witnesses gifted with clairvoyance) had been put up to the council of ministers and approved by them—with the recommendation that great caution be used in the matter. Cotton Mather, the acknowledged authority on the wonders of the invisible world, had written the opinion. The other ministers, including Charles Morton, whose judgment had great weight with Parris, had endorsed Mather's findings.

It was indeed the only means of getting evidence on such mysteries, which everybody knew were beyond the reach of human ken.

Yet John Tarbell had accused Parris of idolatry in asking the afflicted what they saw on others. He held it was going to the

God of Ekron. But Tarbell surely was wrong; blinded by his personal feelings for his Mother Nurse.

Surely this was not what the Savior meant when he spoke of the unpardonable sin. Or was it? Was he trying by Satan to cast out Satan? He indignantly denied it.

There came a time when Mary's vision failed her. The black water was only black water with never a picture. There was desperate need for knowledge and for wisdom to meet what was to come. And there was no knowledge and no wisdom. Only black water in a black kettle, with his own distorted face staring back at him.

George Burroughs (whom some people still believed a saint though there had been evidence enough to hang a dozen men) had been executed only by the grace of God and Cotton Mather's timely eloquence.

But there was high excitement in the village. Parris going to and fro from the courthouse heard hostile murmurings—and sometimes as he approached the talk would cease and in a breathtaking stillness he would pass through the crowd and into the courthouse door.

What would happen when the next hanging day came?

It was a sorry time for Mary's sight to fail!

"Can't you see anything at all?" he pleaded, gazing hopelessly into the black water.

Mary shook her tawny hair.

"The kettle ain't potent enough for times like this," she sighed. "If I could go to the wishing well down by Grandther Walcott's —I might see. That is where I first saw the visions. On the night of the full moon the well comes to life. But you wouldn't want to go so far—through the woods at night."

Parris was in the mood to go through all hell to know what lay ahead of him.

"There's a full moon this day sennight," he said eagerly. "Will you meet me there?"

"I'd go from here to Kingdom Come—to help you, Mr. Parris." She raised her eyes to his. They were wide open now, and in their depths there was a glow of ardor which warmed the minister's heart. He was grateful for loyalty now; hungry for friendship.

" 'Twill help me mightily if you can see the way out of this trouble, my girl." He patted her shoulder.

Her eyes gleamed fiery amber as she looked at him.

"The best time to see," she said, "is the witching hour of two. Will that be too late for you?"

"No!" he said, and added under his breath, "Please God I hope not!"

The moon rose high in the heavens as Parris came to the well. Mary was waiting for him, standing still as a statue in the shadows. It came into his mind that he had never known a person who could stand as still as Mary. She did not speak as he joined her—only raised her eyes and laid a slim finger on her lips. Side by side they stood together, gazing at the dark mirror of the water. The well was almost full. There was a sheen of moonlight on its surface.

Mary whispered, "You must wake it with a bit of silver."

Parris produced a pine-tree shilling. The girl took his hand and moved it round and round, round and round in ever-narrowing circles, keeping time with the rhythm in a little singsong charm until the coin was over the center of the well.

"Now!"

The shilling dropped from his fingers; bubbles sprang to the surface; the ripples widened, quieted and were still. Eagerly Parris watched the water, but he could see nothing. Presently Mary sighed softly and her body began to sway slowly back and forth. Her eyelids drooped and closed. The wishing well was working its magic; the girl was entranced. Parris supported her with his arm or she would have fallen. Her lithe body was rigid; her closed eyelids were smooth white marble like the eyes of a statue.

Parris had seen her many times in a state of trance in the crowded courtroom; but this was different. The sordidness and excitement, the physical discomforts of heat and noise and tightly packed bodies were left behind. In the peace of midnight and the magic of moonlight Mary's message seemed like a saint's vision.

But it was a vision of doom. The girl began to speak in the mechanical utterance of the trance. The minister must bend his head and hold his breath to hear.

"I see the Hill—and crowds of people flocking. I see a cart
. . . with men and women riding . . . bound with chains.

"I see the bodies hanging—like empty garments swinging in
the wind."

All at once the low voice rose in a scream.

"Run! Run! They cry for vengeance! Someone has a rope
—they surge about the minister . . . the sheriff's arms are bound
. . . O God!! Let me not see any more!!! Let . . . me . . .
not . . . see!"

The voice faded away. The girl lay like one dead, her weight
against Parris's shoulder, her body rigid as a post as he supported
her with his arm. The silence was worse than any speech.

Then the low voice again, gentle and soothing:

"A bridle path winding through the forest to the sea . . .
a ship leaving Marblehead at daybreak . . . a tall man riding
through the forest . . . with one behind him on the pillion . . .
I cannot see her face . . . her hair is tawny as a panther's coat
. . . riding . . . to the Indies . . . and safety . . . and joy!"

The minister's befogged senses awoke. Was she in a trance?
Was she shamming? He bent his face close to hers, his eyes
hard and suspicious. The marble eyelids flickered just a little.
There was the faint shadow of a tremor about the full lips.

With one savage thrust of his body and arms Parris flung
the inert body to the ground. Without so much as a glance behind
him, he strode back up the path to the village. His whole being was consumed with murderous lust and as his long legs swung
along the path he cursed himself because he had not choked the
breath out of her devilish lying throat before he left her.

He struck out easterly through the ravine till he came to the
road leading north, and returned home by a roundabout route.
The rage had gone out of him, and the trembling that followed
it, before he reached home; but there was a look in his eyes that
was not good to see.

Elizabeth was waiting up for him. Since the witchcraft trouble
had started she would never go to bed until he came home. He
could see her through the open window as she sat sewing by
candlelight. He stood a moment looking in at her, and it came
to him with a kind of numb shock that Elizabeth had grown old
since she came to Salem Village.

Her shoulders bent wearily over her work, and under the

candle flame her hair looked faded and dull. There was a patient droop about her mouth that wrung his heart. The summer had been hard on Elizabeth.

Well, it had been hard on him too. He knew now that he had battled for a lost cause. Like the silly hero of that Spanish yarn he had been fighting windmills—made a fool of by a passel of maggoty-headed wenches performing their conjuring tricks. Yet even in the savage rage that gripped him he knew that it was not a mere matter of tricks and befoolments. Behind all this there was some terrible reality beyond the utmost borderland of trickery and fraud.

He opened the door and went in to Elizabeth. She smiled a welcome but said nothing. When the storm signals were out 'twas a good time to keep silence.

Samuel sat down at his desk and fiddled with his quills. Then he sprang to his feet and came swiftly across the room; dropped on his knees and kissed his wife with a long, passionate kiss.

"Elizabeth," his voice caught in a sob. "Elizabeth, whatever happens—whatever the future brings—don't forget that I love you—more than anything—more than my very life—and that in my thoughts and in my body I have always been true to you."

"Why, yes, Samel dear. Of course, I know. I've always known."

She raised surprised eyes to his face—and what she saw there brought her to her feet. For a long minute they stood apart, swept by emotion too deep for words.

Elizabeth broke the silence with a little sob.

"Samuel! You look so strange! As if you had just waked up!"

"Yes, I have waked up! Oh, Lizbeth, I'm such a fool—such a God-damned fool! Though thou shouldst bray a fool in a mortar among wheat with a pestle, yet will his foolishness not depart from him."

His wife crept into his arms and snuggled her head against his shoulder.

"The Heavenly Father forgives our foolishness as well as our sins, dear heart. He made us the way we be—and He doesn't expect us to be very good or very wise. Sit down while I fix you a cool drink, and then we'd better get to bed before the cocks begin to crow."

Samuel screwed up his courage.

"There's something I must tell you first, Lizbeth—before we go to bed." His face flushed and he paused miserably.

Lizbeth smiled up at him impishly.

"Suppose I tell you—'twill be quicker and easier. You've been led away on a wild-goose chase with Mary Walcott, and found out she's not such an innocent child as you thought she was. It had to happen sooner or later—and now it's happened.

"You've quarreled with her, 'tis plain—and that's dangerous. But now you know what the danger is and can be on guard. . . . Drink your nightcap and you'll feel better—I made it plenty strong."

Samuel stared at her. "How did you know?"

She laughed. "I might make a mystery of it, but I won't—there's too much wonder-working as it is. I haven't any gift or visions or second sight (thanks be!)—only the sharp eyes love gives a woman.

"Mary has been hanging around all afternoon, fairly bursting with some secret or other, watching me out of the tail of her eye and hinting this and that.

"Then you start off afoot in the middle of the night, making the excuse it was too hot to sleep and taking the same road I saw Mary take a half hour before. And now you come bursting in to tell me that you love me and that you are a fool and that there's something you must tell me before you go to bed, and you don't know how to begin!"

She threw her arms around him, laughing and crying at once.

"Oh, my dear, my dear! After all our years together, don't you think I know you love me? But you don't quite trust me, Samel. You don't let me share your worriments. 'Twould be better for us both if you would."

Almost Samuel was persuaded; but pride held him back. "There's nothing worth telling about Mary. She led me on a fool's errand; but no harm is done and she knows better than to do the like again. She's a silly child and too much excitement has gone to her head."

He picked up the candle. Elizabeth smothered a sigh as she answered him: "You will have to watch her, my dear, for she's not a child, and she's tricky as a pet snake. For pity's sake be careful—and don't worry about me!"

Parris well knew that he had made a dangerous enemy in flouting Mary Walcott. He had acted on impulse in the heat of rage, but if he had thought it over for a week, he told himself, he would have done just the same.

He had been a blind fool, perhaps. But he had never thought of seventeen-year-old Mary as a woman: only as his neighbor's daughter and the friend of his children; and since the trials began, as a wonderful witness because of her gift of clairvoyance. Now, he realized, that gift would make her a dangerous enemy.

He knew she was shamming that night at the wishing well. How many other times, he wondered, had she perverted her gift in her testimony against others? She had been a chief witness against many of the accused. Had she told the truth? Had she really seen the specters of Rebecca Nurse and of Burroughs's two wives? She ought to be denounced, exposed, pilloried before all the village! But it would take a braver man than he to do it. For the crowd, once roused, would not halt its vengeance with Mary Walcott. There was his Abigail, and the two Ann Putnams, and the other afflicted children. It would raise a scandal that would set the village afire—and it was too late to right whatever wrongs had already been done.

All he could do was to watch and pray (if it was not too late for prayer) and keep his guard up against the time when Mary would strike back at him. For she was sure to strike—he had no doubt of that.

He had not long to wait. It was only a few days later that Mary was testifying at a hearing.

Judge Hathorne leaned forward:

"Who is't afflicts you, girl?"

Mary Walcott's amber eyes shifted; the heavy lids narrowed to a slit; then she threw her head back with a sudden defiant motion and, looking straight at Parris, cried out:

" 'Tis the minister's wife!"

The crowded courtroom gasped with horror and amazement.

The minister at the table laid down his quill and slowly rose to his feet. His eyes burned black as he fixed his gaze on the witness. His black robe fell about him and his face was well-nigh as white as his Geneva band—-the scribe had become a priest. He stretched out his long arm toward the girl and spoke with the authority of a prophet of old.

"What is this thou sayest, Mary Walcott?

" 'Tis a dreadful thing indeed if the devil hath ventured thus far! The minister's wife, sayest thou? Our godly land is blessed with many ministers.

"Speak out, daughter, here in the assembly of the people of God! Speak out, I adjure thee—the truth as God bears thee witness. In all this colony of Christian folk, what minister doth consort with a witch?"

The girl before him cringed, and as his gaze held hers she shook from head to foot and wrung her hands.

"I cannot tell! She won't let me!"

The minister raised his right arm high, his finger pointing to heaven, his eyes still holding the eyes of the girl.

"The name! The minister's name! We will have the name!"

The witness shrieked: "I am blind! I cannot see!"

She fell on the floor in a swoon. The crowd surged forward. The officers held them back. The bailiff sprang upon a table.

Above the uproar Stoughton shouted:

"COURT IS ADJOURNED. CLEAR THE COURTROOM!"

43

The End of the Road

Still with gray hair we stumble on,
Till, at last, the vision gone!
Where hath fleeting beauty led?
To the doorway of the dead.
　　　　　　—R. L. STEVENSON.

OLD GILES COREY stood in the prisoner's dock while the charge against him was read, staring straight ahead.

"Guilty or not guilty?" the judge thundered.

The prisoner gave no sign that he had heard. His pale-blue

eyes, still keen and piercing after fourscore years, turned neither to right nor to left.

Judge Stoughton leaned forward.

"Is he stone-deaf?" he asked the constable.

"He can hear well enough if he wants to. He's a stubborn old cuss."

Stoughton's lean jaw set at this outrage to the dignity of the court. His voice was loud with official authority when he repeated his question.

"What dost thou plead, Giles Corey? Guilty or not guilty?"

There was no response. The prisoner stood still as stone, his eyes still fixed on something far away. There was no fear in his face—no hope—only a grave dignity which seemed beyond the reach of the sordid scene around him: the packed courtroom; the black-robed justices; the king's attorney with the Bible and Hale's Reports before him. It was as if he had already passed the boundary between life and death

John Wise had come to him again, as he had promised, and told him what to do.

The seven justices moved restlessly, looking at each other with silent questioning. Samuel Sewall's face was very red, as if he were like to have a stroke. Hathorne's eyes were popping. Even Corwin forgot his boredom and gave his full attention to the old man standing before them. They began to whisper behind their hands. Then they called the king's attorney into council.

"What shall we do, when this man refuses to plead? It is contempt of court, defiance of the laws of England. What shall we do?"

Thomas Newton, king's attorney, was well versed in the law.

"The case has its precedents and its remedy," he said, "though the ancient law has seldom been enforced this hundred years. The man may be sentenced to 'peine fort et dure'—he may be pressed to death."

The court shuddered. They adjourned to consider the matter further. They had it up and down, pro and con, for the rest of the day. And drank themselves to sleep.

The next morning, Corey still remaining obdurate, they had no choice but to pronounce sentence. Perhaps that would bring the stubborn wretch to his senses. But he still stood mute while the courtroom chilled with horror and anticipation.

After that they visited him in his dungeon, one or two together, and tried to reason with him. They sent a shallop to Nantucket, and Richard Gardner came as fast as a fair wind would blow him, to talk some sense into his old-time friend. But the more they talked the more firm-set was Giles.

He even chuckled about it, like a naughty schoolboy playing a trick on the master.

"John Wise told me 'twould put 'em in a bad spot," he bragged, "an', by cracky, he were right. I've done 'em, Dick. Them judges is so moppled they be floppin' round like chickens with their heads off! They dunno whut to do!"

"But, Giles," Gardner pleaded, "it's you who will be put to torture. You'll die by inches, man, in awful agony. And it's a mortal sin—self-murder!"

Old Giles looked at him straight. His faded eyes were shining with fanatic zeal.

"Thar bain't no way tuh die as pleasures a man much, an' I'm boun' tuh die. I've overlived threescore an' ten by 'leven year—an that's the Scripture span.

"I heared the Skriker screechin' last night—an' I heared the splashin' of its feet, like old shoon awalkin' in soft mud. 'Tis a warnin'. I'm boun' tuh die.

"I allus ben a fightin' man, but my fightin' days is purty nigh done. I figger I got jest one more good fight left in me, an' I'd liever fight them bastard judges 'an ennybody I know, an' I doan't count it no sin. When I tell St. Peter about the goin's-on down here, I bet he sez,

" 'Come on in, Giles, I doan't blame ye none fer whut ye done.' "

He was silent for a minute or two, then he spoke again: "Thar be another thing I wouldn't tell tuh ennybody but you, Richard Gardner.

" 'Twere my fool blunderin' tongue thet sent Marthy to her death by blabbin'. Marthy's a good woman, ef enny thar be, an' she's gonna swing on 'count o' me. It's no more'n fair I hev it tougher 'an her. See whatta mean, Dick? It's comin' tuh me fer bein' sech a blasted fool."

There was one thing more that might bring the stubborn wretch to his senses: the threat of eternal doom.

On the day before the time set for execution the old rebel was carried to the meetinghouse and, standing in the middle aisle with all the town crowded around, heard the dreadful sentence of excommunication pronounced upon him.

Mr. Nicholas Noyes stood in the pulpit, robed in all the dignity of his office, and with firm and dreadful emphasis read the fateful words: the same words with which Wilson had pronounced sentence on Anne Hutchinson before she was driven out into the wilds; the same by which Rebecca Nurse had been cast out:

Therefore in the name of the Lord Jesus Christ, and in the name of the church, I do not only pronounce you worthy to be cast out, but I do cast you out; and in the name of Christ I do deliver you up to Satan, that you may learn no more to blaspheme, to seduce, and to lie; and I do account you from this time forth to be a Heathen and a Publican, and so to be held of all the Brethren and Sisters of this congregation and of others: therefore I command you in the name of Jesus Christ and of this church as a Leper to withdraw yourself out of this congregation.

The audience was shuddering and sobbing; a woman fainted and a man fell in a fit, foaming and gibbering. But the prisoner stood unmoved, stock-still as he had in the courtroom: defying the law of God as he had defied the law of man; staring straight ahead of him, with a strange light in his old eyes—a light that was not of this world.

During the few hours that remained to him he kept the same silence—ominous—dramatic.

The jailer's hands shook as he offered food and drink to this man who looked like a dead man and would take nothing at his hands.

Only when they carried him out of the dark dungeon into the sunlight the eyes blinked and looked around the circle of faces till they found what they sought. John Wise stood close beside him as he had promised.

"Is there anything I can do for you, Giles?" Wise had asked, when he visited the prisoner for the last time.

And Giles had said, " 'Twould help ef ye wuz there—where I could see ye."

Wise took the old man's hand in his strong young grip. "I'll be there, Giles. Right beside you—till the end."

"No matter how long I be adyin'?"
"No matter how long, Giles."

A ballad in the old style tells the story.

> They got them then a *heavy Beam,*
>   They layde it on his Breast,
> They loaded it with heavy Stones,
>   And hard upon him prest.

> "More weight," now sayd this wretched Man,
>   "More weight," again he cryed,
> But he did no Confession make
>   But wickedlie he Dyed.

Three days later the death cart made its last trip to Witch's Hill. There were eight passengers this time—seven women and one man, Samuel Wardwell, the fortuneteller. The night before the hanging day, after the dark had come down and the streets were quiet, the seven had been quietly taken from the jail to an old deserted house at the far end of Broad Street: the last house before the crooked path wound through the common pastures up the stony road to the Hill.

It was an evil-looking old house, with an overhanging second story and little bare windows high up under wide eaves—like eyes peering out malevolently from under beetling brows. It had been vacant so long that nobody remembered whom it belonged to—like enough to one of the Anabaptists that Hugh Peter drove out half a hundred years before. There were a few old sticks of furniture left scattered about, as if the unknown tenants had fled hastily. All in all, a fitting place for a crew of witches to pass their last night on earth; and conveniently near the hanging place in the morning. The way from the jail was long and there had been overmuch excitement among the people of late. Everybody agreed that 'twas best to get the executions over with as quickly and quietly as might be.

In this cartload was Martha Corey, one of Parris's own flock—until a few days before when she had been cast out, the record duly made in the church book by the minister's own hand.

Late in the evening the equinoctial rain had begun with a slow drizzle, and by morning the stony ground on the hillside was sodden and slippery. But there were plenty of folks climbing the Hill. Not even the execution of Mr. Burroughs had drawn such a crowd, for the manner of Giles Corey's death had spread its horror like a miasma over the countryside.

Most of the colonists had never heard of such a punishment, and the cantankerous old man had by his death become a hero and a symbol of tyranny and the tortures of the land they had left in quest of liberty. Death by torture had been rare in the colony. Even the approved English methods of beheading, drawing and quartering, and burning a man's entrails before his eyes had been left behind. Even witchcraft, which in England was punishable by burning alive, was in the new land satisfied by the ordinary death at the rope's end.

So dismay and consternation drove them, and the slippery roads were thronged. From north and south and east and west they came: from Topsfield and Marblehead; from Andover and Rial Side; from Ipswich and Lynn; like flies they swarmed to the carcass.

The death cart was coming now. It was overloaded and the wheels creaked under the strain: seven witches and a wizard were more than any ox cart should bear.

Halfway up the hill the cart stopped. The oxen stood still, their bodies swaying from side to side. Their rain-wet sides heaved as they forced the breath from their nostrils. Their eyes rolled in their sockets, showing a rim of white. The driver cursed and prodded them with his goad. They snorted and tossed their heads stubbornly, but their feet did not stir in their tracks.

A murmur ran through the crowd—whispered words that would not bear loud speaking.

" 'Tis God's hand stopped the cart!"

"Nay, 'tis the devil's!"

"Aw, the Hill be steep an' slick—they've struck a stun."

"The beasts be like Balaam's ass—look't them eyes—they see the angel of the Lord standin' in the way awavin' of his sword!"

It was only a brief pause, then the driver got the beasts started again; but to the crowd already on the verge of hysteria it seemed a sign.

When they started on again, Fear stalked beside them and Frenzy nipped at their heels.

* * *

Martha Corey was praying on the scaffold: for her fellow witches, for her enemies, for the magistrates, for the ministers.

To Parris's tense nerves it seemed that the prayer went on endlessly. Would the woman never leave off praying? Now she was praying for him—that God would cleanse his soul of the guilt of innocent blood! His hands clenched till the nails cut into the flesh, and when he opened them the palms were stained with blood. Blood on his hands!

He thrust them inside his cloak and wiped them on his shirt—but the dark stains still showed when he looked at them slyly. Blood on his hands!

What was that line from Macbeth? Not all the perfumes of Araby can cleanse that hand!

A phrase of Martha Corey's prayer drummed in his ears like a dead march:

> May Christ forgive mine enemies
> When I have come to die.

Thank God, the prating old hypocrite had come to an end at last. The ladder was jerked from under her and her neck broke. Practice had made the hangman skillful.

Parris turned to go. He had forgotten his brother ministers. He had forgotten the crowd. He was all alone—with blood on his hands!

Noyes was pointing at the locust tree. His voice rang with triumph:

"THERE SWING EIGHT FIREBRANDS OF HELL!"

Epilogue

It was the last hanging. The witch frenzy had burned itself out. As in a fever there comes at last a morning when the sufferer wakes from his delirium and sees about him the familiar walls and furnishings of his sick-chamber: the chair by the bedside, the dawn-light brightening the window, the dresser with its tall candle-sticks, his mother's portrait smiling from the wall—dear accustomed things which only last night had been capering imps and grimacing hobgoblins—and with a sigh of relief and a shudder of remembrance comes back to sanity and everyday living. So New England woke to reason and repentance.

God's hand had stopped the death cart on the Hill; and they, the people of Salem, had wickedly disregarded this warning, and now stood before the Judge of all the earth, bloodguilty.

The yellowing eaves of the locust tree dropped softly on the accursed ground, whispering Martha Corey's prayer as a litany over the dishonored dead: a supplication for the living: Father, forgive them, for they know not what they do. The long seed pods turned sere and brown; they writhed and twisted on the branches in a devil's dance of mockery of the witches who had hung there, then tore themselves loose and rolled over the wind-swept Hill, their seeds rattling like dry bones.

The locust tree stretched its long shadow down the hill; beyond the dwelling of Caleb Buffum, maker of coffins; over the old tavern where the hanging-day crowds made merry; over the witch house; over the oldest burying ground where Martha Corey lay in an unmarked grave; over the empty prison; on to the corner of Howard Street—where on stormy nights Giles Corey's ghost cried for "More weight! More weight!"—over the meeting-house; down the bay; across rivers and moorlands to Boston Town; to Cotton Mather, writing of memorable providences; to the executive mansion, where the governor's lady had been cried out upon—on and on until in all the colony there was none but felt the chill of the shadow—lengthening—darkening.

When the winter came and the skeleton boughs lashed and groaned in the gales, the villagers scurrying home along the dark road saw (or thought they saw) eight glowing firebrands swaying in the wind, and as their footsteps sounded on the Old Town Bridge there came an echo—faint and fitful—of muffled oars passing down the stream.

The years passed by: spring, summer, autumn, winter, in their turn and "the Hand of the Lord was still stretched out against His people in manifold judgments; cutting short their harvests; blasting their most promising undertakings more ways than one; unsettling them, and by His more immediate hand snatching away many out of their embraces by sudden and violent deaths."

The afflicted children forgot their fears and went back to normal living.

Mary Walcott married and left the village.

Abigail Williams, at last accounts, still held to her story of the Witches' Sabbath, but lost her terror of the devil and claimed that she could talk with him as well as she could with a man.

Ann Putnam, bereaved by the death of her parents, lived a melancholy life, broken in health, feared and shunned by her neighbors. Her dreadful fits still tormented her, but she had lost faith in her visions: and in a public confession craved forgiveness for things that she could not understand and "would not do again, no, not for the whole world."

And the same pitiful puzzlement appeared in the confessions of others much older and saner than Ann.

Public opinion completely reversed itself. Yesterday every suspicious character or unpopular neighbor was a witch: today all the suspects were saints and martyrs—victims of the spite of their accusers.

The blacksmiths quit forging chains and fetters and went back to their horseshoeing and andirons.

The doors of the prisons were opened in such a jail delivery as had never been known in New England, as one hundred and fifty persons of all sorts, good and bad, guilty or innocent, were turned loose with a clean bill of health and no questions asked.

The slave Tituba, who had confessed to save her skin, and had been held in jail as a witness, was at last sold for her fees, which Parris refused to pay. She had cost him far too dear already, he said.

The judges and ministers became the scapegoats, bearing the sins of the people and driven out into the wilderness of public condemnation.

With the popular verdict against him and the hand of the Lord heavy upon him, Samuel Sewall stood in the Old South Church asking pardon of men and of God and desiring to take the blame and shame of it.

The jury confessed "that we ourselves were not capable to understand nor able to withstand the mysterious delusion of the Powers of Darkness and Prince of the Air and do justly fear that we were sadly deluded and mistaken; for which we are much disquieted and distressed in our minds."

Only Chief Justice Stoughton held firm, with his angry outburst when the court fell:

We were in a way to have cleared the land of these. Who is it
obstructs the course of justice I know not. The Lord be merciful to
the country!

And Samuel Parris, who in the days of repentance would not
repent, and in the midst of confessions had no confession to make
save only his *Meditations on Peace:*

. . . As to my writing; it was put upon me by authority, and therein
have I been very careful to avoid the wronging of any . . .
Professing, in the presence of the Almighty God, that what I have
done has been, as for substance, as I apprehended was duty, however
through weakness, ignorance, &c. I may have been mistaken.

Beyond this he would not go. Nor would he be driven from the
village until he had received his just dues. He had received
offers from other parishes, but first he must be justified.

In the midst of the strife, Elizabeth took to her bed and quietly
gave up the ghost, and was laid to rest in the Wadsworth Burying
Ground, awaiting the Resurrection Morning.

The ministry house was an empty bird's nest after that and the
village was a desert waste, yet Samuel would not give up the
fight, though all his world tumbled about his ears.

At last the long battle was over: the parish admitted his claims;
paid him his salary; and bought back the ministry house. He had
won his fight, but the victory tasted like defeat. The girls' chatter
drove him mad and he sent them to visit Aunt Susanna in Boston
to be rid of them for a while.

He was free now to leave the village—and he hated the village
with a perfect hatred. The people of Stow wanted him back.
Well, it might as well be Stow as otherwhere. It would be quiet
there, and peaceful and friendly. And he was tired—tired. Someday, perhaps, when his earthly pilgrimage was over, he could lay
his weary bones in the quiet graveyard, with the Brook Elizabeth
to lull him to sleep and the cypress trees sighing overhead.

With a promptitude that scandalized the villagers ("his good
wife hardly cold in her grave yet, an' him with his plans all
made") he settled his affairs, packed his household goods, and saw
them loaded in young Jonathan Walcott's big wagon and on their
way to Stow. Then he saddled his horse.

One last thing remained to do. The westering sun looked down on a broken man kneeling in the graveyard—carving an inscription on a gray slate stone.

ELIZABETH PARRIS
Died July 14, 1696.
ae. about 48 yrs.

Sleep precious dust, no stranger now to Rest.
Thou hast thy longed wish, in Abram's brest.
Farewell Best Wife, Choice Mother, Neighbor, Friend,
We'll wail the less, for hopes of thee in the end.

S. P.

With his customary care he set a precise period after each initial, rose from his knees, whistled to his horse, and without a backward look rode down the path toward the setting sun.

THE END